He stood before the squatted demon.
Its hideous face gave him the willies. The last time he had encountered this thing, it attacked him. While it showed no outward signs of an unnatural life, he was still cautious. He summoned up the courage and reached inside the mouth, hoping that the gem from his dream would fall into his hands. There was nothing here. Marty swallowed hard. If they had come all this way to find nothing, it would be a very long trip home.

He began to examine the figure more closely. He could feel goosebumps raise on his arms and crawl up the back of his neck. He stemmed the growing panic that threatened to overcome him. He cautiously approached the statue in the dim light. He couldn't see the figure's back in stark light, so he blindly ran his finger between the wings. He could feel a narrow crevice like a seam. He felt past the seam to the opposite side. The small ridge felt like a button. *Could it be that simple?* He pushed in the center of the ridge to hear a faint click and a small rattling sound. The mouth of the devil clicked, allowing the jaw to drop from hidden hinges. He eased his fingers into the cavity and touched something soft in the hole. Carefully, he removed the object wrapped in soft cloth. Marty looked up and around the small vestibule. The old man was nowhere to be seen. Softly, he said, "Guys, I found something."

In the Shadow of Men

by

Darren Swart

In the Shadow of Destiny Series

This is a work of fiction. Names, characters, places, and incidents are either the product of the author's imagination or are used fictitiously, and any resemblance to actual persons living or dead, business establishments, events, or locales, is entirely coincidental.

In the Shadow of Men

COPYRIGHT © 2017 by Willem Darren Swart

All rights reserved. No part of this book may be used or reproduced in any manner whatsoever without written permission of the author or The Wild Rose Press, Inc. except in the case of brief quotations embodied in critical articles or reviews.
Contact Information: info@thewildrosepress.com

Cover Art by *Debbie Taylor*

The Wild Rose Press, Inc.
PO Box 708
Adams Basin, NY 14410-0708
Visit us at www.thewildrosepress.com

Publishing History
First Fantasy Rose Edition, 2017
Print ISBN 978-1-5092-1823-3
Digital ISBN 978-1-5092-1824-0

In the Shadow of Destiny Series
Published in the United States of America

Dedication

I am humbled by all those who have rallied around me
through the process of writing this novel.
As with most journeys, I am amazed at
the lessons the process has taught me
and the patience of all those
who have helped move forward through the process.
I am honored by the ceaseless support
from my wife Cindy and daughter Brianna;
my niece and nephew Katie and David;
my sister Ann;
my friends, Michael Como, Caroline Morris
and Roger Blackburn.
While other pieces may follow,
this will always be the first.

"Nature shows us only the tail of the lion. But I do not doubt that the lion belongs to it even though he cannot at once reveal himself because of his enormous size."
~Albert Einstein

Prologue

The Holy Land, 1187 AD

His gaze darted in the dim light; time was short, his options limited. If he snapped the handle in his hand, he could use the sharp end. The walls and ceiling were sand, but he doubted if he could create a cave-in that would accomplish the task. His sword and weapons were carefully packed away in the armory, which was securely locked on the surface. There was no way to get to it without alerting the others. A knot in his stomach grew worse with each passing moment. He could feel time slipping through his fingers like the sand. He clung desperately to the distant hope that he would find a way to end his life.

His eyes burned with fatigue. He stared vacantly at the fresh dots of blood on the wooden handle in his hands. The pain that gnawed at him was nothing compared to the torment in his spirit. Perhaps it was the incessant drip of water that echoed through the caverns? Maybe it was the looming darkness that seemed to fill him now? All he had ever wanted was to be a Templar Knight and now that he was, all he wanted was to go home and see his family. Bitterly, he contemplated that a *real* knight could have snapped the shovel handle and driven it through his own heart. On the other hand, a *real* knight wouldn't need to.

He loathed himself. Absently, he fidgeted with the blade of the shovel, scraping it across the wall of sand before him. A tiny avalanche fell away and revealed an odd pattern of swirls and color beneath. He studied the striations against the backdrop of dull yellow. The small section seemed an almost dramatic comparison. Curiosity egged him on. He probed gently at the sand and uncovered more defined shapes and colors; shades of red, umber, and blue appeared in patterns that resembled brush strokes. In the flickering torchlight, the lines began to eddy and roll like the tide on a distant shoreline. He closed his eyes and tried to remember the healing sun of his homeland, the briny twang of the ocean. He could see his father standing at the dock waving him on. He breathed in deeply, only to choke on the acrid vapors of pitch from the torch. His eyes flashed open, as he angrily spit at his own deception.

He cleared away more of the loose sand so that more of the image appeared; a winged figure with its arm outstretched. He looked up. It was similar to the one on the faint marble arch above him. The discovery of the arch the day before had nearly driven Monsieur Lavigne, their leader, insane. He literally drooled, as he ran from group-to-group, frantically shoving them to this one spot. Despite his youth and strength, Jean-Michael's shoulders still ached from the hours of swinging the mattock at the unforgiving soil the night before. The men had stopped exhausted from the effort. He, on the other hand, had pled to remain behind. After the weeks of being underground, he considered he might be going mad. Lavigne eyed him suspiciously before allowing it. When everyone moved to the surface to pray before choking down stale bread and dried mutton, Jean-Michael stayed behind to end his life and the torture of this place. He gave up his birthright to be a Crusader, only to find he was nothing more than a glorified miner.

But at the moment, all of that could wait. His discovery was far too intriguing. He carefully scraped away more of the sand façade and found subtle lines of a magnificent mural beneath the sand. He dropped the shovel and stepped back, so he could see the image clearly. An Angel, stood in the Arch holding a key toward the viewer. Unlike any he had ever seen, its four large points resembled gems protruding on either side of a golden shaft. He moved the torch closer to study the remarkable image in the sand. To his horror, the image suddenly collapsed, falling like an hourglass into a colored heap at his feet. Crestfallen, he stared at the sand. In the dim light, a round globe lay exposed hidden by the mural. He heard his own breath suck in, as the sand continued to sift from the globe, revealing the hollow cavities that had once been home to quick attentive eyes. The sand continued to sift, exposing more of the features until a jawbone dangled precariously from one side.

He squinted in the dim light, drawing the torch closer. His hands trembled as he carefully brushed away loose grains. His ears pounded and adrenaline made his hands shake with excitement. This was something important. He studied the bones, realizing the skeleton was in an odd position, upright, resting on its knees. He stared at it, enthralled. Sand continued to pour away from the bones, and as the loose sand fell free from the cavity, a jewel sparkled in the dim light wedged against the backbone. A blue gem seductively winked at Jean-Michael in the dim light. He stared at it, transfixed. As he touched it, the skin on his hand tingled curiously. Summoning his courage, he reached in and plucked the pecan-shaped gem from its resting place between two of the vertebrae. It felt strangely warm to the touch. He held it up closer in the feeble torchlight, so he could inspect it. A steady hum filled his ears. Deep within the stone, an almost imperceptible gleam winked on as if the stone had awakened. His whole body began to tingle now. He looked at his arm to find the hairs were standing on end. A soft blue radiance grew swiftly in intensity until an ice blue light bathed the cavern. He watched as the cave began to change before his eyes; sand walls around him solidified into alabaster columns and the dirt beneath his feet coalesced into polished marble. His fascination regressed to fear. It was unnatural. He tried to fling the glowing orb, only to find it would not leave his hand. The heat from the gem was so intense that he looked down expecting to see his hand on fire. Instead, he found the skin of his palm was now healed. He looked at his feet in time to see his scuffed worn boots resolved to shiny obsidian leather, while a pearl white tunic replaced his ragged shirt.

The great chamber glowed from every wall with hidden light. In the distance, a figure appeared. It floated toward him. As it drew closer, Jean-Michael stood frozen in place. It loomed over him like a great tree. In the still air, gossamer robes billowed, blown by some unknown wind. His long thin beard almost touched his waist, making his face seem abnormally long. He regarded Jean-Michael severely, staring past his flesh and probing deeply into his soul.

Fear gripped Jean-Michael, as he looked up. He must be dead and this was at the moment of judgment. He dropped to one knee and kneeled as if to the king, steeling himself for what was to come. His head bowed and his eyes shut, he whispered, "Oh merciful, Saint Peter, I know I am unworthy. If you would only allow me passage into our Father's Kingdom."

He missed the merry twinkle in the Entity's eyes. In a voice that reached the core of Jean-Michael's soul, the Entity commanded, "Arise, young knight. You're not dead...*yet*."

Jean-Michael turned his head slightly and half opened one eye as he regarded the figure. He knew there would be a test. He would not be so easily duped. He slowly rose, still not looking up. "What is it you would have of me, my Master?"

"I am not your Master, boy. I am merely a guide. You hold the Sappir. It has chosen you as its new guardian."

Jean-Michael refused to meet the Entity's eyes. "Then what is it that the Sappir would have of me, Master?"

A hint of irritation entered the Entity's voice. "Jean-Michael, look at me, boy."

Irked at being called 'boy,' he held his head high and squared his shoulders. For the first time, he looked at the figure before him. The spirit no longer billowed or glowed. With the exception of the eyes which still glowed eerily, it almost looked normal. He relaxed a bit. "What would you have of me then, spirit?"

"Your fellow knights will return shortly. They cannot know of the Sappir. You are now the guardian. Bury the guardian before you on consecrated ground. I will guide you when the time is right. You have been chosen to carry this solitary trust."

Puzzled, Jean-Michael looked up at him. "How will I know what to do?"

"I will guide you. Take heed of your new powers. They will serve you well."

"Powers?"

His voice trailed off, as the cavernous room before him resolved into a murky catacomb once again. He stared down at the vibrant gem against the healed skin of his hands. In a language so unique, it was not human. The Sappir sang within him. It knew his thoughts. It opened his mind as never before. In the distance, he could hear the crunch of boots coming toward him. Somehow, he knew it was Lord Lavigne. He shoved the gem into his pants. He winced as he dropped heavily onto the sand, striking the shovel handle. Quickly, he clasped his hands together and said, "Be with him, Blessed Mary. Amen."

Lavigne scowled over him with a torch. "What are you doing, boy? Praying that the sand will move itself?"

Jean-Michael rose slowly and stepped aside, revealing the skeleton before him. Lavigne almost dropped his torch. Jean-Michael heard the older man's breath draw in quickly before regaining his composure.

Jean-Michael regarded him serenely. "No, Sire. I was praying for this forgotten soul."

Lavigne pushed him out of the way. As he touched Jean-Michael, it was if a curtain lifted from Jean-Michael's eyes and vision filled him. He stood on a battlefield. Before him, his master straddled a mound of broken bodies. His tunic was bloodied and torn. As he turned to face him, the older man's face was gone, leaving only a blackened skull with eyes glowering like embers from some hellish fire. The once pristine Tudor cross emblazoning his tunic was almost unrecognizable through the blood and gore. A single ruby amulet hung from his neck, radiating and untouched by the carnage. It glowed angrily like his eyes. Even as a bystander, Jean-Michael could feel the tug of Lavigne's amulet against his own—as the fraternal twin to the Sappire Jean-Michael held.

A knight groaned at Lavigne's feet, groping upward as he desperately clutched his boot. His round eyes pleaded in fear. Lavigne never looked, as his sword plunged into the man's side, snapping bone and tearing through muscle like it were paper. Jean-Michael heard the man gurgle and watched as bright red foam bubbled from his lips. His head lolled forward, as a crimson ribbon spread across his chest. From the darkening stain of blood, a frightening image emerged. A long thin face, mouth open in mock, silent laughter and long menacing horns full of jagged spikes. Jean-Michael shuddered. He didn't know the fallen knight, but nothing good could come from this. The vision squeezed him like a vise. His purpose was clear: He must keep the Sappir from his so-called Mentor at all costs.

Jean-Michael blinked and looked up. He could see the irritation in Lavigne's eyes, as he repeated his question. "I said—was there anything with it?"

Jean-Michael ignored the inference to the remains as something inanimate. "Only his bones, Sire." He felt the comforting warmth of the stone in his breeches.

Lavigne looked at him contemptuously. "There

will be many more before this is over, boy. Clear it away and keep digging."

Jean-Michael looked at him, stubbornly. "I would like to see that he has a proper burial."

Lavigne rolled his eyes. "Why, for God's sake? We don't know if he was Christian or Muslim. What does it matter?"

The older man studied Jean-Michael's face. There was a look of resolve he had not seen before. The youth responded, "It matters to me. He died in this place for a reason. With all due respect, Sire, we owe him that much."

Lavigne rolled his eyes again. "I should think you would have seen enough digging. Very well. See to it, then. Do not tarry. We still have much work to do."

Jean-Michael nodded. He worked carefully for the next few minutes, clearing away the soil from the skeleton. He placed the bones reverently on a cart and slowly started his ascent to the top. The wooden cart creaked, as he moved toward the unforgiving sun above. Halfway up the tunnel, he passed the other men. Hollow eyes regarded the bones, as they silently passed. Drained of life they were mere drones in a hive. Jean-Michael couldn't understand why he hadn't noticed it before. The resolve of what had been thrust upon him settled inside of him. He knew he was different now; gone were the petty worries of comfort and fortune. His newfound sense of purpose hardened him. He resolved that history would not remember him, and his family would speak of him only in terms that he had died in the Holy Land. He was reborn a new man.

The chill of night fell upon the desert. Lonely winds swept the hills above them, howling against the vast emptiness of the barren land. The sands formed devil cyclones which danced and skipped across the desolate ground. Despite the anger in the evening wind, Jean-Michael dreamed.

He stood on the warm wooden deck, listening to the waves lap seductively against the side of the ship. Dark-skinned men milled around him laughing and joking in a strange tongue. They walked past him, dropping green leaves on his bare feet. Every spot that a leaf landed, his skin healed. The gentle sun warmed his soul and made him smile, even while he slept. He looked around to find that his was the only white face on the ship. None of them seemed to notice or care. The wind snapped the main sail to attention. He looked to the bow where a handsomely-carved falcon spread its wings to the wind. They faced a smooth emerald green mountain, unlike any he had ever seen.

A cold wind ripped the blanket from him, forcing him awake in the chill of the desert night. The pop and crackle of the dying fire was the only noise in the camp. Men snored around him, exhausted from the hours of digging. Jean-Michael blinked in the darkness, remembering his dream. Silently, he arose, rolled his bedroll, and eased past the sleeping men to the corral. Quietly he saddled a black mare, which stood quietly ~~as if~~—waiting on him. He walked her from the encampment, stroking her side until they were out of eyesight. She never whinnied or made a sound. As he mounted the black mare, he steeled himself for the days ahead.

****

On a distant rock, Lavigne sat with his knees drawn tightly to his chest and watched as the boy disappeared into the night. The young man unnerved him, somehow. The thoughts of him gone were strangely comforting. A crumpled cross tunic lay where his bedroll was. The other men would brand him as a deserter—even a traitor. The oldest of them would attribute that he was too young for the burden of being a knight. Lavigne remained silent. He neither condemned nor defended the boy. Secretly, he pondered. He couldn't remember why he had even selected Jean Michael. Thinking back, it almost seemed like an impulse; one that he never considered until now.

****

Each new dawn foretold another day of unforgiving heat for Jean-Michael. It was like trying to breathe oven-like air, while trying to survive on meager rations of food. And yet, he moved on. Each day, visions led him to brackish water and sparse hidden fronds for the mare. Miraculously, they found shelter among the rocks to protect them from the blistering sun. Each new day, the Sappir led him ever deeper into the hostile desert. Against any logic, they survived. Drained and bleary, they moved on. It was weeks before the weary young man with a gaunt horse emerged at the tall sandstone edifices of the bustling port of Jaffa.

His sword dragged at his side like an anvil; he'd anticipated an ambush at every corner. Yet, he was too weak to lift the broadsword to protect himself. Still the Sappir urged him on. He stopped at a well and gave the mare a drink of cool, clean water. People laughed and talked, and passed him as though he were invisible. He no longer tried to understand how it was possible. Refreshed by the water, he moved on.

The seductive kiss of the sea air reached out to him

and teased him closer to the docks. The mare began to prance. For the first time in weeks, she swished her tail to swat flies. Her head raised and nostrils flared as she sniffed the change in the wind. The fog gripping Jean-Michael's mind lifted. His spirit rallied. A North wind called them closer to his beloved ocean. They rounded a corner to an image which raised a lump in his throat. A sapphire blue ocean stretched for as far as he could see. He stared for a moment, wondering if he had ever seen anything so beautiful. The mare nudged him like a child, urging him on. A long wooden dock lay ahead, with small swarthy men scurrying about loading and unloading.

Jean-Michael's eyes moved from ship-to-ship, looking for a sign—something to let him know that he was in the right place. Several men struggled to move the large wooden wagon. As the wagon rolled away, she appeared before him, floating proudly in the midday sun. Her mast was tall and white; her bow, beautifully carved into a proud Falcon. Her captain ran from the ship, greeting him like a brother. He laughed and wrapped his arms around Jean-Michael, hugging him like a lost brother. His small body only reached the tall Norman's chest. Jean-Michael smiled painfully, trying to pat the little man's back, but found his new friend's bear hug only allowed for minimal movement.

As he pulled away, the captain straightened his turban. He chattered to Jean-Michale like an old friend. Jean-Michael smiled, carefully leading his black mare across the wooden plank. She whinnied nervously, but carefully moved across. An old man sat with Jean-Michael and fed him dried fish and dates, while a young boy stroked and fed his beleaguered mare hay and water. The salted fish burned his raw mouth, but he didn't stop eating. Having survived without eating for days, the fish was like a suckling pig, he crunched into the bones and flesh of the seasoned meat.

He lost track of the days before he awoke one morning to find that his body no longer ached. Happily, he assumed the role of a deckhand. He fished, scrubbed, and bailed water alongside the Arab shipmates. Slowly, he learned their routines and language. He felt the comforting coolness of the deck, while he removed his boots to feel the ocean spray on his bare toes. The salt no longer burned his flesh. The sores of the burning desert heat were long gone. He wiggled his toes in the mist and smiled, remembering what it was like to be on a ship with his father. He heard her creak and felt the pitch, as the tail wind tugged the main sail and pushed her briskly through clear blue waters.

The days turned into weeks and each setting sun found him more content than the previous. Each night cast him into a restful sleep where he dreamed of being a boy on his father's ship. He couldn't be sure what it was that woke him that night. He couldn't tell if it was the wind, the heaviness of the air or some sense that change was beckoning. His eyes were open and his hand went to the stone. It was there, waiting for him. The men all around him were snoring peacefully, dreaming of foreign shores and exotic women—anything but what was about to happen. The roar of the air took them all by surprise. The cyclone struck the mast amidst a maelstrom of splinters and ripped it from the deck like a corkscrew, taking much of the deck with it. Hardened men screamed in fear, while the Captain tried to save the stricken ship. The stress of the ocean and the damage were too great. She began to break up into the rough seas. Young men scrambled to grab anything they thought would help them survive, while older sailors waited stoically for their fate.

Jean-Michael placed the Sappir in his mouth and dove as far from the ship as he could push. He swam hard in rough waters to escape the vortex of the sinking ship, knowing he would drown at any moment. He heard the main beam snap, as the ship groaned and folded neatly in the middle. The rush of water swirled behind him, tugging at him and trying to suck him down with the doomed ship. He struggled to get farther away from the watery grave, kicking with all his might. Slowly, he began to edge away from the whirlpool into calmer waters. Beyond the reach of the collapsing ship, he treaded water while his heart calmed. In the distance, he heard a terrified whinny. The mare was alive and thrashing. He swam toward the sound, hoping to save her. A malicious wave cast him onto a barrel, knocking him unconscious.

He came to in time to see the rising sun glittering across the water in a million points of light. Crates and debris floated and bobbed in the water around him. Jean-Michael found himself draped across a large barrel, only vaguely remembering how he had landed there. He looked over the debris field to see if there were any other survivors. He saw the Falcon face up in the water first and then he saw her. Near exhaustion from treading water all night, the black mare was barely above water. Her eyes were wide and full of fear, but she kept moving. Jean-Michael tied a rope to his waist and dove into the blue water. His body undulated under the water like he had as a child. His father's nickname for him was '*poisson de mer*' or sea fish. Pulling the large timber behind him he moved toward her. She looked relieved to see him paddle toward her. Lashing the rope to a floating timber, he swam back to the barrel. Carefully, he pulled the rope tight under her chest and dove again. In no time, he had rigged a makeshift harness under the mare, easing the drag of her muscular body and buoying her up. The Falcon still bobbed in the water nearby. He dove and paddled it toward the mare. He lashed the final bit of rope to the Falcon's talon, holding them together as one.

He didn't know how long they floated. What few casks of food and water he could find, he shared with the mare. The Sappir whispered to him, keeping him alive. He thought back to his time in the cavern where he wanted to die to end the suffering. Now, he was resolved to survive and he smiled at the irony of it.

It was at dawn when he saw the green mountain in the distance. Steadily, they were drawn toward it. At mid-day, he saw the white sail of the ship looming toward them. Stout red-haired men in longboats tied ropes to them and began to row steadily toward the ship. Jean-Michael came and went from consciousness. He barely remembered them winching the mare from the water. She was too weak to put up a struggle.

He was unsure how long he had lay there, but by the growth of stubble on his face it must have been days. He sat up in a soft bed and found himself staring out of a window at the round green mountain from his dream. A buxom redhead rocked on the porch. She smiled coyly at him through the open window. He smiled back, pushing a shock of thick black hair out of his eyes. His other hand still clutched the blue gem tightly. He stood and walked unsteadily to wash his face. A basin of water rested on a simple wooden stand against the rough wall. He barely recognized his face as his own. He looked at the square jaw, the quick dark eyes, the deep lines in his tanned face were those of his father; he would miss him. Jean-Michael studied the one prominent difference, a silver white streak coursed through his dark hair across the temple. Dipping his hands into the cold water he broke the image. It was time to move forward.

The black mare whinnied in the distance, calling out to him from a green pasture nearby. He smiled and considered that once again he was a stranger in a strange land. And yet, he was home.

Chapter 1

Present Day

A courteous tap resonated on the dark, enormous door. He could barely be heard over the persistent tick of a gold leaf Chinoiserie grandfather clock. He peered up from the quilled notes of the weathered lambskin. He sat back and drew in a deep breath, almost tasting its ancient mustiness. He knew she would not interrupt him unless it was important. She slipped silently into the room like a thief. He rarely saw her smile. It made her pristine face rigid like that of a manikin. Her blonde hair was pulled tight against her head in a bun like an old maid and her business suit hid the supple lines of her body, she appeared almost embarrassed to be so beautiful.

She knew he tolerated the intrusion only because he trusted her and that she wouldn't be here unless it was of the utmost importance. He sighed again deeply, clearing his mind of the manuscript and touched the small furry head beside him. A dainty Persian paw stretched out to touch him from her cushion, tribbling at being awakened. As his manicured nails delicately caressed her behind the ear, she purred contentedly and kneaded the silk threads of the chair's tapestry cushion.

Gretchen appeared small, almost childlike across the vast cavern of the library. Level after level of leather volumes climbed upward, making anyone in the room look small. He opened a single palm to her expectantly and, in a surprisingly soft tenor he asked, "Yes Gretchen, what is it?"

Her voice was precise like her hair. "I have some unfortunate news about your son, Sir."

His eyes rolled and his head shook disdainfully. "What do we need to bail him out of now?"

She hesitated for the briefest of seconds. "I'm afraid it is more complicated than that this time."

He looked at her dourly before opening both hands in a gesture to go on.

Flatly, she said, "He's dead, Sir."

His eyebrows knitted together, forming a deep furrow between his steel blue eyes. He almost sounded irritated as he asked, "How did it happen?"

"It appears to be a drug overdose. The doctor said he didn't suffer."

"Well, I suppose we can be thankful for that. Please see to the arrangements. Does his mother know?"

"No, Sir. We are trying to locate her."

****

"Try the South of France. She tends to frequent the villa in Marseille this time of year."

"I'll request that the Liaison Chief of Staff inform her. He tends to be more diplomatic than the Security Chief." He concurred silently by nodding.

With the subtlest tone of tenderness she could summon she asked, "Will you be able to attend the funeral?"

"I doubt it. I have far too much to do. Ensure it is kept low key. I don't want some gung ho reporter spraying this all over the papers. Use the discretionary account to pay off whomever you need to. If the bribe goes over a half million Marks, employ Mr. McPherson to deal with the problem."

"Yes, Sir." She turned to leave.

He stared at the thousands of volumes surrounding them. Collectively, they captured the most powerful reasoning in mankind's history. Yet, not one of them could tell him how to control one stupid impudent child—his only heir. Not that it mattered now. His thoughts flashed to another unassuming young man in the United States, roughly his son's age, whose destiny was yet to be explored. Ironically, he had far more respect for the American than he had for his own child. The thought struck him. It was time to nudge the American forward to achieve his true potential. "Gretchen?"

She stopped and pirouetted gracefully on a toned calf. "Yes, Sir?"

"At your first opportunity, please call Mr. She'mul and advise him that we need to accelerate our plans with Mr. Wood."

Passively, she responded, "Certainly, Sir." Turning, she made the long trek out of the room.

He rose from the massive desk and stretched his shoulders. It took only a few steps to reach the small, plain door in the corner of the room between two massive bookcases. He removed the shiny brass key from his vest pocket and listened as the tumblers clicked when he turned it in the lock. The small room within was in utter contrast to the luxury of the library. The ugly naked glare of a single bulb amplified the bleakness of the peeling paint and the thick crust of grime on the dated black and white floor tiles. No one had been allowed in this room for over a decade. He faced rows of shoulder height beige file cabinets. A sturdy white enameled steel table with faded red trim and a sturdy uncompromising oak chair sat under the light. Each file drawer was numbered with a year. He went to the oldest drawer and opened it. Reaching in, he removed a dog-eared green file. Carefully, he placed it on the table and spread it open. Numerous pictures were clipped to typed reports. He leafed through the yellowed, worn pictures stopping at an 8x10 photograph close to the bottom. His finger traced the outline of a little boy clutched tightly against an old farmer, as he carried him across what looked like a battlefield. Small flames and long columns of smoke served as a backdrop for the old man and the child. The old man's face was dotted with mud and dark blood, while the child looked almost completely untouched. It was the kind of photo that should have ended up on the cover of *Time Magazine*. And yet, there was only a small press release buried in the business section of the Times. He set the photo down almost reverently on the metal table. No matter how many times he looked at it, the question always intrigued him—how had the child survived the plane crash?

From another file drawer, he removed a more recent police photo of his son. His handsome features bore a striking resemblance to the duke, himself. He placed the photos together and studied the images intently. In one photo the picture of Marty as a small child; ; blonde curls and rounded cherub like cheeks underscored eyes that bore a daunting determination for one so young. In comparison, his son's photograph captured a sullen youth. His disinterested eyes reeked of entitlement.. He tried to find some hint of his-boy's powerful bloodline. There was none.

He gazed at Marty's picture again. It puzzled him. Why did he feel such a strong connection to a child he had never met? The old wooden chair creaked, as he sat back heavily, pondering what lay ahead. Methodically, he put the photos back into order and into their separate files. He nodded to himself, convinced that he had made the right decision to bring the Wood in. It was time to move to the next stage of the plan.

****

Marty stared absently at the droplets of condensation on the brown glass as they snaked their way down to form a puddle on the lacquered surface beneath. He crunched on stale cocktail nuts under the angry glare of the red neon of a *Budweiser* sign. All the while he kept going over reruns of what was probably one of the worst days of his life. He stifled an irritated retort as the bartender asked, "Are you feeling okay, sir?"

Marty tried not to glare at the young man who was probably the same age. A shock of blonde curls on the bartender's forehead amplifying the deep tan made Marty wonder how he managed to keep a tan like that on a bartender's salary. He tried not to seethe, as he responded, "I suppose." He tapped the bottle. "Give me another."

He reached out and slowly turned the near empty bottle in front of him in slow circles trying to forget the memory of her curled up on the loveseat in the morning sun. He knew something was wrong when he saw her. There had been no warning; no indication that she was going to die, other than her being old. They had been together since he was a boy. It was unreasonable to assume she would live forever. But still, she could have given him a sign; a signal that something was wrong. She was only a cat, but she was the only family he had left.

A fresh beer appeared before him. He finished off the wash in the bottle in front of him and sipped on the fresh one. He scowled at the *Hotspot* calendar behind the bar. He stared at the date, trying to remember something. *There is something significant about this date.* It irritated him that he couldn't recall what it was. He quit trying to remember and that is when it hit him. He pushed himself away from the bar and took a deep breath. It was five years ago to the day that Bess had died. The irony, however significant at the moment, would be short lived.

The bartender's quick eyes watched from a distance, as the back of Marty's hand covered his mouth. His head lowered, while his face contorted into an unmistakable grimace. A single tear tracked down his cheek, but he didn't try to wipe it away. The bartender looked toward the other customers and made an off color joke, drawing their attention away from the guy at the end of the bar having a bad day. It was the best he could do for Wood at the moment. He had a feeling Marty's day was going to get worse, though he didn't know how.

Chapter 2

A steady hand carefully drew the blackened steel blade across the moonstone in front of him, it rasped as it slid across the stone. The pungent oil glistened on the dark metal in the dim light. The sound and smell were comforting to him, taking him back to the few quiet moments of his childhood. It was on those rare occasions- when his father had sharpened the blade- that he hadn't beaten him and it was the same blade he used to take his father's life like a thief in the night.

It had set the precedent for how he was to live his life. He lived in the shadows, fulfilling contracts and dissolving into the commotion of daily life. His ruthless skill was unprecedented and his skills eventually carried him to the Death Squads of South Africa where the money was good and the killing was easy. Most were principled people and their families were the kind of people who were not used to dealing with *his* kind of people. He thought back. *Those had been the salad days*. He still missed South Africa.

He set the blade aside, almost reverently. He reached for a blue cellophane packet containing his orders. He studied the dimpled cheeks and the curly strawberry blond hair of the young American. The contract called for a live delivery job this time. It would be more complicated because there was competition in the mix.

He set the packet aside for a moment and picked the blade up again for one final pass across the moonstone. As he drew the blade away from the stone, he picked up a filthy rag which could barely be identified as an extra-large V-neck T-shirt. He slowly wiped the blade clean of oil making the dark metal shine like onyx beneath him. He eased it into a worn leather scabbard and tucked it into the small of his back. He walked across the dirt floor, grabbed the edge of a mildewed tarp and pulled across the ashen corpse lying against the wall, while turning off the bare light bulb over his head. It was time to finish the operation.

****

Gillian stepped back from the bed and did a quick inventory. She knew she would leave something she needed behind. It was inevitable. Neatly arranged clothes, guns, knives, and ammo were in uniform rows. She packed as methodically as she arranged. The memory of the call had given her a chill in the unseasonable California heat.

The voice was as tight as a banjo string. "Gillian?"

Blearily, she tried to focus on the clock. "Yeah, what's up?"

"We have information that they're planning to kidnap Wood."

A surge of adrenaline shocked away the sleep. The single sheet fell away from her T-shirt as she sat up in bed. "When do you expect movement?"

"That's unclear. We're seeing assets coming into Charlotte, but they're still getting organized. I need you to start moving that way. I can brief you in transit."

"I'll be underway in an hour. Check back at 0400." As her hand moved away, the voice stopped her in mid motion.

"Gillian?"

She moved the earpiece back. "Yes, Franz?"

"They've assigned McPherson to this one."

Her jaw clinched while her lips drew into a thin white line. She tried to sound confident. "I'm ready for him," she said.

"Good. Talk to you soon."

The phone clicked on the other end. She rubbed her hand across her face and slipped her muscular thighs over the edge of the bed. She took a deep breath and looked at the nub of her left pinky finger. It still hurt when it was cold. She owed the Scottish bastard one, or at least a half of one.

She slid the zipper closed on the gold and black knapsack and she took a quick sweep of the room. Text books and papers littered the worn enamel atop of the ancient dinette table. The sink was half full of dishes. She doubted if she would see them again. At the moment, they seemed unimportant.

Chapter 3

The evening sky was awash with the radiant hues of salmon and orange which sliced across the Western skies. A gentle North wind grazed the back of Howard's neck like the touch of a lover's hand. Undistracted, he fumed over a small black box. Another soft breeze wafted over him, this time carrying the hint of wisteria. He mumbled and cursed at the splice enclosure, all but ignoring the delectable scent. He mumbled aloud at the box in front of him. "Dadgum cheap housing. When will them boys in corporate learn to quit cutting corners with this foreign crap? I ain't ever going to fix this thing before dark…"

He didn't hear the crunch of gravel beneath him, nor did he see the man at the base of the ladder studying him intently. He struggled with the small box until he had a signal. Smiling, he tightened the last screw on the cable housing and started to descend the ladder, mentally patting himself on the back for repairing the aging system once again. For the first time, he looked down as he descended. The tall dark stranger stood beneath him with a map in one hand and scratching his dark head with the other.

Howard scowled, thinking, *dang tourists, how do I always end up with them? Always asking for directions. Why can no one ever go to a dadgum convenience store and ask?* The man flashed a beautiful white smile, disarming Howard. Though accented, his English was quite clear.

"Excuse me, Monsieur, but I think I am lost. Is the 109 near here?"

Doesn't anyone know how to use a map these days? Howard shook his head as his foot touched the ground. "Sorry, Mister. You're a long ways from the 109. You'll need ta'...." were Howard's final words. The small caliber bullet pitched his head backward, as he crumpled into the soft green bluegrass of the embankment. Without hesitation, the Frenchman gripped Howard by the feet, twisted him around and easily slid down the grassy embankment to the secluded ravine below. He pulled him easily to the bottom of the hill and left him to return to the cable van. Methodically he packed all the repair gear into the van and eased back to the body. He carefully stripped Howard's body, keeping the garment away from the seeping blood. He grabbed the dead weight of the corpse and carried him like a sack of potatoes to the trunk of his Camry. As the Frenchman smiled he looked at his watch. He was ahead of schedule and equipped. Things had gone much smoother than he had expected.

****

Marty stared at a growing pile of bottle caps in front of him. The blonde surfer barkeep seemed irritated that Marty distracted him as he tried to clean them off the bar. Marty kept stacking them in neat columns. When they fell over—it was time to leave.

For the first time in a year, he had been late for work. For the first time, his new boss was waiting on him at the door. Gertrude's death was an omen. When he saw Brice standing in his cubicle, he knew it wasn't going to be something good. Brice was a man driven by spreadsheets and a reasonable rate of return. His job was to bring their operating cost down by five percent which didn't seem to make much sense because they were already operating at a margin of over forty percent. He remembered the conversation:

"Good morning Wood. Decided to sleep in today?"

"Actually sir…"

Brice cut him off with a raised hand. "No problem, just don't make a habit of it."

Marty tore his eyes away from the comb-over to focus on Brice's pudgy fingers shoving a packet of papers into his hands. "Get these back to me by four o'clock. Can you handle that?"

Without any clue as to what he was getting himself into, he responded, "Uh, yes, Sir."

He gave Marty a plastic smile. "Good man. Thanks, Monty."

He was already walking away when Marty muttered under his breath,

"It's *Marty*, Sir."

At three forty-five, Marty's stomach growled. He realized he had worked through lunch. He took a deep breath and went over the adjustments to the packet: updated calculations, reformulated dimensions, inserted code requirements; all in all he had never seen such a butchered report. Despite having to correct half of the work, he had still finished on time. Smugly, he wrapped the package back up and carefully placed everything together so it was ready to be shipped overnight. As he walked it back to Brice, he passed Hal in the narrow hall.

Cheerily, Marty asked, "Are you coming to the

club house tonight, Hal?"

Hal stared hollowly at the speckled brown carpet in front of him. "Not tonight. Got to go home and talk to the wife."

As he moved farther away, Marty could swear he could hear the older man mumbling. He shook his head and eased up to Brice's doorway. It occurred to him that he had never been to Brice's office before now. The newness of the plush maroon carpet stung his eyes and caused him to catch his breath. He blinked hard and tapped on the door frame. Brice peered at Marty over his reading glasses. His comb over was now firmly pasted to his head with Brill Cream. It seemed to coordinate nicely with the thin smile and the wart on his left cheek. "Ah, Wood, come in and have a seat." He made a sweeping motion toward the chairs in front of his desk. "I'll be right with you."

Marty sat stiffly on the edge of the brand new leather guest chair, while Brice carefully stacked a sheaf of papers into the correct order and neatly sequenced them in perfect linear alignment. Marty looked around the room in glimpses taking in the architectural prints, model skyscrapers and commercial buildings. It was all quite angular, to the point of being disturbing. There were no plants or pictures of family. The room was linear perfection. It was like a model office; impersonal and much like Brice himself. Brice finished his arrangement of paperwork and looked up.

Marty started with an apology. "I'm sorry. I didn't mean to intrude, but you said you wanted this by four o'clock. Julie wasn't out there…" His voice trailed off. He felt like a fifth grader in the principal's office.

The corners of Brice's lips turned up, but his eyes

showed no emotion. He was as plastic as a politician. "Not to worry. I gave Julie the afternoon off. Thanks for running it right up here. I like to see a team member who's willing to give a one hundred and ten percent."

Team? One hundred and ten percent? Marty thought Brice was joking for a moment. And then recognized the tone of corporate rhetoric. He mentally shrugged it off and began with an overview of the work. "I double checked all the primary and secondary outfalls. I made one recommendation that the contractor increase the size of outfall #5. It seems a bit under size considering the slope the architect has recommended. It will be more expensive initially, but saves us digging it up under a warranty or guarantee. I made several minor adjustments…"

Marty watched as Brice's eyes glazed over half way through the first sentence. He didn't have a clue as to what Marty was talking about.

"Great job Wood. Sounds like a 'win/win' to me."

More dogma. Marty made a mental note to start tracking the clichés for an office pool. It would be fun for Fridays to see who counted the most *team* references in a week. Brice almost caressed the packet as he placed it behind him on the sheen of the new cherry credenza. He took great pains to space it perfectly on the glossy red finish.

"Martin, I can't tell you how glad I am you have such a great attitude. In the game of life, that is going to carry you very far. As you know, we're being considered for a merger with Wake Engineering, so we're being very careful about head counts and overhead."

Marty forced himself to look straight ahead and

away from the brand new carpet and leather chairs in the room.

"I'm very happy to offer you the opportunity for out placement services with…"

The conversation blurred after that. Marty sat there stunned for a moment, as Brice described "right sizing." It took five minutes for Brice to neatly arrange some forms in front of Marty, with perfectly aligned velum strips at each signature point. In a matter of fact tone he explained the outplacement package and the "benefits" associated with it. Brice's nonchalant tone made sound like he was asking Marty how he liked his coffee. The anal little man was now a shining Star in the Richard Cranium Hall of Fame.

He looked back to the brown bottle in front of him. He took another sip from it careful not to spill any, since he was now officially unemployed and on a budget. He contemplated that his job at Consolidated Engineering was like a bad marriage. He wasn't happy with it, but he didn't quite know how to end it. He considered the possibility and that maybe Brice had just done him a favor. *He is still a twerp though.*

Red faced golfers filtered in. Their raucous laughter filled the room, while cheap cigar smoke swirled in eddies overhead. The noise was starting to give Marty a headache. *Maybe it was time to leave before the great wall of bottle caps is finished.* A sudden jostle and the splash of something cold on his back made him flex toward the bar instinctively. He watched as the goose bumps rose on his arm. It was definitely time to go. He rose slowly from the stool and turned to find himself towering over a small man in a pinstripe business suit. Compared to the sea of ugly pants and polo shirts, the little man was as out of place as a prom queen at a monster truck rally. His face contorted in an animated look of horror.

He stammered, "This bloke bumped into me. I am so terribly sorry…" He jabbed his thumb toward the room full of loud drunks.

His narrow face and unusually expressive eyes made his look of dismay almost look comical. This was truly a fitting end to a real crappy day. With a small half smile of disbelief, Marty raised his hand at the bartender. "Sorry, Dude, looks like five is my limit." He snorted at his own joke. He looked back at the little man. "Forget about it. No harm done."

The little man shook his head. "Please, Sir, this is most grievous of me. Let me at least buy you a new shirt."

Marty shook his head. "Don't worry about it. It's no big deal."

His large eyes looked like he would cry at any moment. "Sir, I cannot in good conscious let this pass. I must do something to make it up to you."

Marty's head cocked slightly, as he listened to the man speak. He changed the subject. "Where are you from, Mister?"

The man stopped for a moment and looked sheepish. "Scotland, originally."

Marty smiled and extended his hand. "My Grandmother Bess was a Scot. What part of Scotland are you from?"

The little man didn't look like he was going to cry anymore. "Dundee; where was your Grams from lad?"

"Ayr; along the West Coast."

He smiled, knowingly. "Aye, I know it well. It's a

beautiful green mountain."

The small man smiled broadly and he raised his glass "A toast to your dearly beloved Grandmother Bess then." Raising his hand, he flagged the surfer dude. "Lad, a couple of pints in memory of his dearly departed loved one."

The surfer dude looked confused. "Dude we don't have anything but domestic beer. And we don't have *pints*."

The little man blinked at him and shook his head. He clarified. "Two glasses of whatever you have on tap."

The surfer nodded with a half-smile. "Oh, yeah. I got ya."

He turned away to fill a pair of glasses. The bartender watched the two cautiously. His mouth easily hid his intelligence, but his eyes could not. The small man turned back to Marty and rolled his eyes. Marty snickered. The man asked "What was her full name, Lad?"

"Bessag Wood. Everybody just called her Bess."

The Scot raised his glass to the room and pronounced loudly, "Raise your glasses to Bess Wood. Mother and mentor to the end."

A loud cheer went up amongst the drunken golfers. "Hear. Hear. To Buzz Wood!"

Marty smiled. It would have pleased Bess to know they were raising a glass to her. No one but Marty and the little man knew what they were toasting. The golfers didn't care, so long as there was drinking involved. The cheers died down and both Marty and the small man sat at the bar. Marty extended his hand. "My name's Marty, Sir. Marty Wood."

"It's a pleasure to meet you Marty. My name's Dick, Dick McPherson."

Chapter 4

Marty awoke, his thick tongue was stuck to the roof of his mouth; his head was splitting. He blinked, his eyes burned. He sat up for a moment, trying collect his thoughts against an impossible ringing in his ears. The room smelled of spoiled meat. He sat up and leaned heavily on one arm; beads of sweat began to dot his upper lip followed by the sudden feeling he was going to retch. This was not good. A cold sweat washed over him like a sudden spring rain. He sat there for a moment and focused on breathing. He hoped some fresh air would clear his mind and chase away the ill.

However, the more he breathed in the rank air the more he realized it was the air making him revile. Change tactics—breath through the mouth. That seemed to help. His head cleared a little. He began to make out his surroundings in the dim light. The earthen floor around him was littered by a hodgepodge of odds and ends. He could just make out a few crudely built wooden shelves and odd assortment of bags and jugs too dirty to identify. He squinted to see if there was some way out. There was something familiar about the room that kept pestering him.

He got up and moved around. A new plethora of smells weaseled their way into his sinuses, none of which were any more pleasing. Slowly he navigated around the room. Occasionally he would bump into various objects in the dark, making him curse silently. His head began to clear making him feel almost normal. The nausea waned along with the ringing. He fought against the sudden anxiety of why he was even here.

He squinted in the dark trying to find a light switch finally making out the thin outline of a string hanging from the joists above. He followed the string up to make out the dim outline of a light bulb. He gingerly worked his way across the room using posts and storage shelves to steady him. He grasped the yellowed string and tugged. He blinked against the sudden glare of the naked lamp. It was a moment before he realized the light was in front of the gray wood of the basement doors. He pushed against them; they couldn't have been more solid than if they had been bricked shut.

He looked around the room. With the light, he could make out the earth floor scattered with old cans, jugs, fertilizer and other oddities. He held his hand to block the glare as he stared at a long piece of canvas along the wall. He eased toward and slowly lifted the edge of the mildewed tarp. A pair of clouded eyes stared vacantly back at him from the ground. The realization ran through him like an electric shock; he stumbled backward catching his foot on the mildewed fabric pulling it toward him as he tried to escape it. He barely stayed on his feet as he scooted backward.

Marty's eyes were wide as he stared at the body in front of him. It was too much, too soon for him to fight. He could not stop himself from retching into the powder dry soil beneath him. He sat back for a moment exhausted. He used his shirt tail to wipe the sweat from his face. He sat for a while with his eyes closed trying to calm himself. The longer he sat, the more his mind cleared.

The events that brought him here formed a collage in his mind: getting fired; the bar; the toast; the odd little Scottish man. What was his name? Dirk? No. Dink? No. DICK. It was with Dick that he had begun to feel woozy at the bar. The odd little man had offered to drive him home. None of the rest made sense. He continued to get the feeling there was something about this basement that was familiar.

He steeled himself to take a second look at the corpse. He pulled his shirt up and over his nostrils in an attempt to block out some of the smell. He crept toward the body as though it were sleeping. He studied the chalky facial features for a moment. Uncle Mal? It had been fifteen years since he'd seen the guy, but he hadn't changed much. He was a train wreck before; he was a train wreck with a bridge collapse now. His wide mouth and puffy jowls had always reminded Marty of a hippo for some reason. Perhaps it was his huge belly that completed the picture for him. Sprigs of thin gray hair sprouted behind his ears like weeds. The top of his head was as smooth as a river rock and about as mottled. It was hard to tell if his T-shirt was filthy from being dragged down to the place, or if it had been that way to begin with. One thing was for sure: this was definitely Mal. He looked pretty much the same as he had when dumped off in the pouring rain on Bess's doorstep when he was ten.

He studied the old man for a moment. There was something wrong about the way his body was positioned. It looked like there was something under him. He was not about to touch him, if at all possible. Marty grabbed a loose rag and made a loop. He wiggled it under Mal's hand and tightened it. With the rag secured, he began to pull on his limp arm. He strained against the dead weight of the figure. Gradually, the body began to move forward. With a flop, the body rolled forward revealing the form of a petite woman beneath him. *Aunt Faye?*

If the couple before him was Faye and Mal, then this must be Barb's basement. He hadn't been back to the farm since Barb had died. *What have I gotten myself into?*

Neither Faye nor Mal had any real sense of ethics. When Barb had died, they had, in one fell swoop, tried to rob him of his inheritance and dump him like a stray puppy into Bess's iron hand. Ironically, Bessie had turned out to be the best thing for him. He shuddered to think how he would have turned out under his Aunt and Uncle's guidance. While crusty and sardonic to most, Bess had turned out to be sweet and patient in her own way. No matter what the circumstance, she was always his fiercest ally. No one messed with Marty more than once. As he looked down at the corpse couple, they looked a lot smaller these days. While the family reunion was heartwarming, it was time to get out of this place. He remembered that Barb's cellar only had one way in or out.

Marty squared his broad shoulders up with the old wooden door. With his size, he was sure he could break it open if he tried hard enough. He just hadn't tried hard enough before. He walked over to the double doors and steeled himself. A quick push and he should be in fresh air. He placed his hands squarely in the center and pushed up. The old oak planks creaked a bit, but didn't give way.

Deciding to focus his energy in one big push, he stepped back a few feet. He would fling himself at the door and hope that he didn't land on his face when he crashed through. Squaring his shoulder up, he threw himself at the door like a linebacker. He slammed into the door with no effect other than the radiating pain down his arm. The door was rock solid and now his shoulder hurt. He rubbed it sullenly and looked up at the windows. They were too small for his lumbering frame to fit through, but he could at least get a little fresh air through them. The windows were only twelve inches tall and well over his head. Looking around, he found a broken rake handle. The window broke easily, allowing the cool evening air to filter in. The breeze carried a hint of lilac and honeysuckle. He closed his eyes for a moment and enjoyed the memory of happier times on the farm. The thought struck him that he was a kidnap victim for some bizarre reason. Stranger still was the huge question mark as to why? He wasn't rich or important. No one would miss him, if he was gone. The thought depressed him.

He shook his head. *Maybe Dick is a serial killer?* He thought this through and found it to be as preposterous as the kidnapping. If he were a serial killer, Marty would already be dead like his aunt and uncle. It was no irony that he was being held at Barb's old farm. *There must be a connection?* Unless he got out of here soon, he was going to find out. It was time to take some action.

The night air cleared his senses enough for him to develop a strategy. For the first time, he noticed the sound of crickets singing in the night. It was comforting to hear something normal. Unless things had changed, there were no neighbor's for miles. He looked around the room for a useful tool. The room was cleared of metal tools. *How considerate*, he thought.

His eyes fell back on a bag of fertilizer and an old kerosene lamp. The idea formed slowly. It looked as though his escape would require some assembly.

He carefully surveyed the door. *Maybe I can blow it open?* He built a rickety structure of old crates and pallets at the door. He hefted several bags of potting soil onto the top pallet, hoping that this would push the energy toward the door and protect him. He was good at building bridges—not so much at blowing them up. He moved quickly onto the bomb.

He assembled the lantern, pill bottle and fertilizer into a crude explosive. A small amount of paint thinner and a pool tablet would act as his fuse. Fishing line and a rusty nail finished the contraption. He carefully placed a bag of potting soil on top of it. He could feel his heart pounding in his ears, as he pulled the fishing line chlorine tablet into the waiting paint thinner to start the chemical reaction.

It had taken him all night to come up with this. The orange rays of sunlight were beginning to peek through the window, as he quickly took shelter behind a bunker of pallets and the remaining bags of soil—and waited.

Chapter 5

The cool night air whistled through the open window of the old Bronco, as it rumbled down the Interstate. The boxy shape, the blotchy worn paint and peeling bumper stickers with *Live Free or Die* belied its potential. Domed pistons, hemi heads and duel distributors made it hum flawlessly down the highway.

She had driven steadily for days. She turned off the throbbing bass of the stereo, as she passed the *Welcome to North Carolina sign*, a welcome sight in the headlights. An hour later, she scanned the back roads lined with corn fields and pastures in the dim pre-dawn light. Their local surveillance contact had witnessed Wood being kidnapped and the location where he was being held. He continued to watch. It struck her as odd that the Scot would have taken him there, but this wasn't a business of second guessing. You proceeded at face value and prepared for the worst.

She eased down the winding dirt road that led to the farm and flipped off her lights. She looked for some place to hide the Bronco, while she moved in on foot. Moments later, she tucked in a cozy hideaway in a fallen section of fence which was only a few hundred yards from the farmhouse. She kept her eyes on the roads around her, as she draped camouflaged netting across the front of the Bronco. The hulking truck disappeared in the backdrop of honeysuckle and wisteria blossoms.

An odd thought struck her, as she methodically worked on the vehicle: She had never technically met her handler, Franz, face-to-face. The rest of the team had, including her father, before he'd died.

It was her father who had drawn her into all this. He had made her the perfect soldier—in his own image—even if she was a girl. She never strayed far from his teaching. It was a curse, really.

When the Bronco was camouflaged and she was securely hidden under a camouflaged net, she looked at her Timex: *0600*. She pulled out her cell and hit the speed dial. Almost instantly, she was greeted by the squeak of Franz's voice.

"Where are you now?"

"I'm in position and waiting at the farm."

"Good. Surveillance is in position on the East side of the property. All is quiet over there now. We are confident Wood is in the basement. We suspect the Aunt and Uncle may be dead." He said this in such a matter of fact manner that it took Gillian aback.

"You're sure they're dead?"

"Ninety percent. Our source saw McPherson move them to the basement a few days ago—and none too gently from what he described."

"So I only have to worry about Wood?" It was more of a statement than a question. She needed the confirmation.

"Correct."

"Do we have any assets in the area?"

"Minimal. You do have some back up assets to help with the extraction."

Swell. Once again she would go it alone. She

would have to make it work. "Does McPherson have any assets in the area?"

"Yes. They have two teams in place and a third on the way."

A chill ran down her spine. "Is there anything else I should know?"

"Yes. The object has not been located." He paused momentarily. "...by either team."

"So, is my objective Wood or the object?"

"Wood. He will lead us to the object."

"Very good. I'll touch base in two hours, if possible. Cell phone will be turned off in forty-five seconds." Even in vibrate mode, it made enough noise to tip off anyone within earshot.

"Understood."

A small chirp indicated that the line had been disconnected. It was a good thing she had years of training for this sort of thing. A girl might get her feelings hurt with a guy continually hanging up on her like that.

****

He barely noticed the clatter of the ice machine across the hall. The bed was lumpy, but compared to some of the snake infested swamps he had slept in, it was comfortable enough. McPherson awoke before the clock ever went off. He checked through his supplies again to ensure that everything was in order; car battery, wires with alligator clips, duct tape, rubbing alcohol, ball peen hammer, rags, plastic sheeting, handcuffs. He smiled, thinking of the pleasure it would bring him.

Everything had gone smoothly the night before. He dosed the lad with GHB and left him at the farm. Since he wouldn't tell him what he needed to know, he would employ more traditional means—torture. It reminded him of South Africa. He whistled a happy tune at the thought of making the boy scream.

It was just after dawn when he eased up the long driveway to the farm house. He backed in to unload the station wagon and retrieve Wood. *After being locked in the basement for a day, the lad should be pliable enough.* He hoped Wood didn't give in too easy and rob him of his fun. Easing out of the front seat, he dropped the keys in his pocket and patted them. Experience had taught him that there was no such thing as being too careful.

He worked his way around the house, surveying the perimeter as he went. His assumption was that his presence had not gone unnoticed. Noting no suspicious dots of reflection from the surrounding wooded area, he felt confident that if he was being watched there weren't many or they weren't very well prepared. He moved quietly toward the basement door and listened. There were no unusual sounds that he could detect. Everything seemed intact. Glancing to the right he noticed the broken window pane. *No surprise there.*

McPherson silently eased the lock off the door, with his foot planted firmly on the door to prevent it from being slung open. Leaving the door shut, he inched away slowly, giving his prisoner time to make a move. Inexperience usually dictated that a prisoner would rush the door as soon as the lock was removed, leaving him (or her in some cases) vulnerable and off balance. Dick liked to wait at least a moment or two in these situations. He couldn't kill him yet—Boss's orders.

Carefully, he moved over to the door and surveyed the seam for movement. Seeing none, he flung the door open and stepped back. Oddly, a duct taped lantern base rolled forward smoking in the dewy grass. *Bollocks*!

He leapt back just in time to miss the full force of the flash and the concussion of the explosion. The flash blinded him for a moment, while the shockwave threw him backward onto the ground. He coughed in the thick acrid smoke eddied in a plume over his head. *Bloody Hell*. He hadn't seen that coming. The kid laid a booby trap for him. He rolled over and sprang up, the blue gunmetal of his Walther gleaming in the early morning sun. He waited and watched, but nothing happened. He shook his head to clear the ringing in his ears and blinked against the burning acrid smoke. He heard a faint cough. The boy wandered out of the basement with his hand blocking the sun and the other waving away the smoke as though nothing had happened.

"That's far enough, Lad."

Marty blinked against the bright morning sun, trying to make sense of it all. There was the little Scottish man with a pistol pointed at him. He stared at him for a moment, gathering his thoughts. McPherson spoke again. "On the ground, Mate."

Marty blinked. He was still a bit bleary from it all. He slowly lowered himself to the ground, with his hands slowly going to his head. The wet grass felt cold against his knees. He thought about how odd the thoughts were before the end.

Dick reached into his pocket and jerked a pair of handcuffs free. "Face down on the ground and spread eagle there, Lad. I don' want to hurt ya, but I will if I have to." His accent was decidedly more Scottish than the night before. Marty guessed the time for pretense was over. All cards were on the table. He tried to stall. "What do you want? I have some money, not much, but I can get more."

It occurred to Dick at this point that the boy didn't have a clue why he was here. This might be harder than he'd planned. The crack of a pistol and the burning in his shoulder were almost simultaneous. McPherson's right arm fell uselessly to his side, while the Walther dropped to the ground with a thud.

Instinctively, McPherson clamped his free hand over the wound, dropped to the ground and darted toward the cover of the basement. He tripped over the debris in the doorway and stumbled forward. He rolled as he hit the ground and came up into a crouching position. The pain from the sudden tumble made him nauseous. A steady throb of raw nerves coursed through his shoulder, threatening to make him black out. He gritted his teeth and scooted himself backward, deeper into the basement.

Like a wounded animal, he moved away from the light and hid in the shadows with a view of the opening. He found some cover in the dim light and scooted behind it. His right arm was useless and had little feeling at the fingers. He reached with his left and removed a .25 caliber backup weapon. He was trapped, but at least he had cover, a weapon and the light to his advantage. Marty lay on the ground with his hands on his head longing for a dead-end job in corporate America. That was when he heard her call his name.

"Wood!" The low, female voice summoned him.

He slowly turned his head in the direction of the voice. He saw her frantically motioning to him to come to her. She wasn't shooting at him. That was a good sign. He heard another noise, it sounded like a gear, or a click, or... *Crack!* The noise popped from the basement like a fire cracker. The grass kicked up a few feet from him. He was a pretty smart guy and it didn't take long to do the math:

Choice A—a gun welding maniac motioning to him to come closer, but not shooting at him; Choice B—a gun welding maniac shooting at me.

Choice A tipped the scale, though he couldn't fathom why. Instinctively, he rolled away from the basement door and kicked it closed as he went. Rolling onto his knees, he raised to a crouching run toward the girl. As he approached, she began moving toward him. It wasn't hard to see the automatic in her hand.

She moved past him toward the basement. Choice A seemed so logical, but now he was confused again. *Why was she going back to the basement?* A few feet past him, she stopped still facing the basement door. Without looking back, she thumbed toward the driveway with her free hand. "I'm Gillian. I'm here to rescue you. Run to the road. I'll tell you when to stop."

He ran like an obedient Labrador toward the road. Tired and still groggy from the drugs, he loped awkwardly, occasionally glancing back to make sure that the girl was still there. She padded along behind him, running gracefully in reverse, but easily keeping up with him. His lungs burned, making him gasp for breath. She breathed easily through her nose and didn't appear to be exerting herself at all.

In glimpses, he studied her. Her short dark hair shown in the morning sun, complementing her olive complexion. Occasionally, he caught a glimpse of dark eyes and full lips which complemented her small button nose. Her no-nonsense cargo shorts and tank tee fit the high end running shoes, but made him wonder who she was. *She's certainly not with the government.* He would have expected anyone rescuing him to be in navy polyester and worn leather shoes.

Gillian padded silently behind Wood, careful to keep pace without running over him. Aside from being a bit loopy at the moment, he looked different than the last time she had seen him—more mature somehow. A shred of doubt in the back of her mind made her wonder whether she had rescued the right guy. She would let Franz figure that out. The upside was that she got to shoot McPherson. And it was a beautiful shot.

They neared the road, so Marty slowed to a walk which caused Gillian to bump into him unexpectedly. Curtly, she said, "Keep moving!"

Martin mumbled a quick, "Sorry" and picked up the pace again. His breathing was coming in ragged gasps, while sweat poured down his face stinging his eyes. He managed to eke out in short gasps, "How much farther is it? I'm really tired."

Her contempt flashed unmistakably in her eyes. He said nothing more, mopped his brow and trudged on. Aside from the growing stitch in his side, he was still glad to be out of the basement. In a low tone, she said, "It's just a little farther."

Suddenly, she tugged his shirt and motioned him toward the right. All he could see was a shrub. *Now what?* Not that it mattered, he was happy for the rest. She moved him into the foliage and motioned for him to sit down. He plopped unceremoniously to the ground and wheezed like an old man under the broad leaves of a sweet gum tree. A light breeze kissed his cheek.

Gillian crouched behind a tree and watched their back with a small pair of binoculars. It seemed like an eternity before she put them aside and stood. Wordlessly, she tugged at the foliage behind them, uncovering a worn Bronco behind the façade of camouflage. He stared with his mouth open at the truck. He said nothing but couldn't help but think that this girl was really resourceful. He sat staring at the Bronco before she raised a single eyebrow at him. "Coming?"

With both hands and the help of a fence post, he hauled himself off the ground. As he flopped into the passenger seat, he uttered the only intelligent question he could think of: "Are you with the police?"

For the first time since he'd met her, she smiled showing two rows of perfect teeth. "No. But I promise you that I've been sent to protect you. We just have to make it through the next twenty-four hours. Do you understand?"

Marty nodded, feeling a little better, though not much. In his mind, he pictured a frog jumping out of a pot of boiling water and into a fire. *A little better* would have to do.

Chapter 6

David Delgado was happy with his alter-ego of Digger. It allowed him a degree of anonymity for who he really was. However, Digger was as far removed from his image as an asteroid is from a quark. His frightening intellect intimidated a great many intelligent people. Though she didn't understand him, his mother loved him without end. But even she wasn't sure how to reason with him at times. He toyed with writing his doctoral thesis on a series of brown paper bags, but he realized that the committee at Southern Cal would have dismissed it as a prank rather than a political statement. In any event, it was taking them two years to understand what he had written, so he decided to take some time off.

Perhaps it was by chance that he had met the strange little man known as Franz at one of his mother's garden parties. The little round man was by no means physically impressive with his unkempt appearance and short, portly figure. Still the beautiful people gravitated around him like a rock star. That intrigued Digger who listened intently from a distance. The little man seemed to light up, as he described the excavation where he'd found ancient papyrus scrolls predating the fall of Rome. Digger stopped listening to the mundane twaddle around him when Franz described a series of complex paradoxical worlds that sounded like a prehistoric version of his thesis on layered quantum dimensions. Interestingly enough, his thesis had not been published yet. Digger watched politely, as the people around him smiled and nodded—even though they had no idea as to what the little man was saying.

Digger had waited until the crowd dissipated before introducing himself. That had been two years ago and he had been working for the bizarre little man ever since. The odd jobs he assigned him were always interesting, albeit strange. Digger never regretted it, though it had drawn him away from home.

Digger had always enjoyed his random encounters with Gillian. She was stoic and acidic at times, but genuine. If he said something that she didn't understand, she minced no words in telling him so. He always knew where he stood with her. They felt no sexual tension, no pretense of something else. Their relationship was clear and to the point where there was no room for innuendo between them. Today, she would be bringing in Marty. That, in itself, was a relief on several fronts. He had watched the farm for days and reported activities directly to Franz. While he accepted the importance of the work, there were limits to how long he could live off of food paste and dodge poison ivy and chiggers. For future reference, he would not bring any more of the roast beef. He didn't care what the boys at NASA said. It was not prime rib in a tube.

He sat reading the National Examiner, waiting patiently for Gillian and Wood to arrive. He had watched her deftly rescue Wood and whisk him away from the farm. It was almost a thing of beauty to watch. He had remained quietly watching McPherson until they were out of sight. When it was apparent that

McPherson was not following, he melted into the foliage, silently retracing his steps back to his bug.

He smiled at the simple delight of the egg-like shape of the yellow Volkswagen; its chrome wheels glistening in the sun, a stubby whale tail on the back and flames spread across the side. He had driven it from California and would drive nothing else. He opened the trunk and used the towelettes to remove the camouflage paint from his face. As he slipped off the next generation Gilley suit/body armor with cool packs, he smiled. The gaggle of old widow women on his block would have been in a tizzy for weeks had they seen him in this getup. But then, it might have given old man McGillacutty a rest from their conniving gossip.

Digger had anointed the old women as the Blue Hair Gang. Each one of the widows worked as deviously as any secret agent to ensnare McGillacutty into matrimony. They were as formidable as mercenaries and the old guy didn't stand a chance.

He swept the car for bugs or tracking chips, thinking that the whole thing had gone too smoothly. Satisfied the VW clear of devices, he spun it around and headed back to the main road. He senses tingled, as he worked his way from the wooded area. He assumed he would be followed, but just as he assumed he couldn't see them.

He swung into the Gas-N-Go a mile up the road. With a Moon Pie and RC Cola firmly in hand, he tapped the touch sensor button on the stereo system and watched as a small screen slid silently out of the slot and adjusted itself to measure Digger's retina. As he munched on the moon pie, he opened his eyes wide. The system scanned him and logged in under his name.

The screen lit up from hidden fiber optic connections in the back. The screen cast an amber glow on his face, as he scrolled through the information while it pinged a remote system. He tapped icons until he reached history tables on the array of sensors integrated into the body of the car. All green bars for the last twenty-four hours. In the event that someone had touched his car even slightly, the history would reveal exactly when and where anyone had placed a tracking device. If the car's sensors detected explosives, it would not unlock itself to allow him to enter. No alerts or warnings crossed the screen, so he was confident that the vehicle had gone unmolested.

He relaxed a little. He was still another ghost in the system. He pulled up his messaging screen and tapped out a quick message to Franz: *G has secured Wood. The opposing team lost their star player. I will rendezvous with them at the Safe House. D*

Digger sipped the syrupy cola and nibbled on the marshmallow cookie the size of his hand. He calculated that Gillian would take the long way to the safe house to make sure that she wasn't being followed. She didn't have all the electronic gadgetry in her Bronco, so she relied on the old fashioned way of losing a tail; plentiful traffic, lots of distance and a dash of cut backs. *How quaint.* He would have to introduce her to the twenty first century someday.

He retracted the computer screen and touched the *audio* button on the system. Selecting *random* would allow the system to compile the music in the order it wished. That suited Digger just fine. The B-52's suddenly blasted the cabin of the little yellow machine. He eased the VW out of the Gas-N-Go and onto the main road, and headed back into town. He didn't see the faded bronze minivan following him at a discreet distant. The Albanians were also good at surveillance. In fact, they were far better than most.

****

McPherson sat on the cool dirt floor, amidst the vomit, clutter and dead bodies, collecting his thoughts. He needed to check in on the developments. He struggled against the fog that continued to threaten to engulf him. He breathed through the pain until the throbbing in his shoulder was under control.

Fishing the cell phone from his right pocket with his left hand proved to be more of a challenge than one would expect. He winced as the fabric draggedacross the raw nerves from the gaping wound in his shoulder. Shock waves of pain coursed down his arm and into his useless hand.

He cursed and continued to fish for the phone. Droplets of sweat rained into the dirt below him. Finally, two fingers wrapped around the tiny little phone and pulled it out. He sat back for a moment, exhausted. The waves of pain were now threatening to nauseate him. He was reaching his limit of endurance, but he could not afford to black out.

He reached into his trouser pocket and fished out a small stainless steel tube. He gripped the red plastic cap between his teeth and pulled it free. He spit the cap into the dirt like a wad of chewing tobacco. Placing the flat side against his injured shoulder, he braced himself as he hit the actuator button on top. With a tiny click, an eighteen-gauge needle pushed through his blazer and shirt, delivering a strong dose of antibiotics, pain killers and coagulants into his bloodstream. The lab called it a smart drug. A brief wave of euphoria swept across him, as the pain killers moved through his system. He knew it wouldn't last. Gradually, the giddiness wore off and for a moment, he felt almost normal.

He flipped open the phone and touched the speed dial. A deep voice with a thick Albanian accent greeted him on the other end. "Da?"

"This is McPherson. What's our status?"

"We are following the surfer dude. Bernard has the woman."

"What is Mr. Delgado doing at the moment?"

"He has left the farmhouse. We are following."

McPherson took a deep breath and focused on the conversation. The drugs were beginning to kick in. "Follow him to his destination and advise me then."

"Da."

The call chirped off. As much as he hated to, he needed to call Bernard. The phone rang only once before Bernard picked up. "Oui?"

"McPherson here. What is your status?"

The Frenchman smirked on the other end of the line. "I have lost the American couple at the moment, but I am sure I will find them again."

McPherson's eye twitched, involuntarily. His voice was tight, as he responded. "How do you intend to find them?"

"I thought I might wait in the center of the town square. I am sure they will drive by and I will follow them."

The muscles in McPherson's jaw tightened painfully as he gritted his teeth. He barked, "I don't care if you have to go door-to-door. *Find* them!"

"But of course, Mon ami." The line went dead. The

Frenchman smiled, as he watched the GPS tracking device he planted on the Bronco move. It would be a while before they showed up here at the safe house. He took his time getting ready for their arrival.

McPherson took a deep breath to calm down. The Frenchman had undercut him on a contract in Algiers and he was not the forgiving type. He called his employer's number. Within two rings, a familiar German tenor came on the line.

"Mr. McPherson, how good of you to check in. Anything you wish to report?" His English was flawless, tinged with just a hint of an accent.

Dick ran through a quick account of the morning's events, careful not to exclude any details—including the gunshot wound. The duke listened quietly, as McPherson walked through the recap. There was a slight pause before he asked, "Was Wood injured?"

"No, Sir."

"Have you called in for medical assistance?"

"No, Sir. Your call was more important."

"Thank you for your loyalty, Mr. McPherson. Who is following Wood?"

"Mr. François is watching them."

"Were there any other members of their team involved?"

"The young man from California. I believe his name is Delgado, Sir."

"And who is watching Mr. Delgado?"

"Gem and Gur, Sir."

"Mr. McPherson, you know I don't refer to my employees by their first names."

McPherson's tone dropped a notch. "Yes Sir, I know, but I can't pronounce their last name…" He sounded like a five year old being scolded.

A patient sigh sounded from the other end of the line. "Once again, Mr. McPherson, it's Bos-kov-ski. In any case, please make sure the medical team is dispatched immediately to attend to your wounds and contact me in three hours with a progress report. Are we clear?"

"Yes, Sir. Three hours, it is." He looked at his watch to verify the time.

With a small chirp from the phone, the other end was silent. His eyes blurred slightly, as he scrolled the contact list. With the touch of a button, he called the Critical Response Team number. It amazed McPherson sometimes at the German-like precision the call center used to handle emergencies. The network of teams with skilled staff could respond anywhere in the mainland US and Puerto Rico within an hour of a call. A young cheerful voice greeted him on the other end. "National call center, how may I help you?"

"Employee ID 973145 in need of medical assistance."

"Thank you, Sir. What is the nature of the injury?"

"Gunshot wound, upper extremity, blood loss." Dick sounded as though he were ordering a pizza. The thought occurred to him that he was on some great pain killers.

"Thank you, Sir. Are you caring for the wounded party and do you have first aid training?"

"Thank you, Dearie, for asking, but I am the wounded party. And yes, I've had some experience with this type of wound before. Thank you."

Unruffled, she responded, "My apologies, Sir. We'll dispatch someone immediately. Do you have a transponder unit?"

"I'm setting it now." McPherson removed the phone from his ear and pressed a small yellow button below the keypad. It began to glow.

"Thank you, Mr. McPherson. I have your signal and we will have a unit there in twenty-three minutes. Do you need any further assistance?"

"Yes. We'll need a cleaning crew at the same location."

"Thank you. For how many today, Sir?" Her cheerfulness annoyed him. He considered finding her and killing her just to wipe the smile from her cherry red lips.

"Two."

"Very well, Sir. They will be arriving as a separate team in one hour. Is there anything else I can help you with today?"

"No. Thank you. That should be quite enough."

"Very good. Have a nice day, Sir."

"Yeah, you too, Lass." He disconnected the call. While he appreciated the thoroughness and efficiency of the Call Center, it made him wonder just how many calls they handled like this each day.

Chapter 7

The duke's smile filled the room, as he returned to the waiting entourage at the massive mahogany table. Staff busily shuttled drinks and treats to each guest invisible to the group. While all were of royal blood, his was the only one with any standing. As he entertained, he watched them carefully, considering which would be suitable for his empire. He could almost taste the greed in them. It would be a means to control them, ensuring his edict. His legal team would manage the flow, as he rarely inconvenienced himself with such details.

Entranced the Countess of Luxemburg watched his every move. She watched as he passed a wisp of a smile in her direction. Almost involuntarily, she arched her back in the seat, opening her ample cleavage to him. In a slow circle, she coyly ringed a glass of red wine with her fingertip and brought it slowly to her mouth. With the tip of her tongue, she grazed the single drop of wine from the pale flesh of her skin, nearly closing her eyes in the process.

The duke allowed himself the momentary distraction, watching as she eased her manicured nail past the lush full lips. His sensibility screamed in protest, as he tore from the vision to focus on the other guests. They would all be his subjects, shortly. He would have more than enough time to explore her uncharted regions then. For now, there was much to be done and he had no time for such distractions. She pouted at losing him and tossed back the glass of wine in a single gulp, making her luxurious auburn locks bounce in response.

The Baron of Ardmore puffed his chest and turned his head up at the duke, looking down his nose as if he were pointing. As he spoke the tinny nasal intonation sounded like his voice would crack at any moment. "Duke, what is your opinion of the Americans purchasing titles of nobility?"

It was a reasonable question based on his insecurity of position. The duke smiled at the Baron like a small child. "Baron, as you know, nobility for us is a birthright. Our ancestors fought as knights and ruled some of the bloodiest periods known to man. Politics usurped our rule under the misconception that people could rule themselves. So perhaps, there are those who feel that they are ready to return to the aristocracy. Perhaps they are disillusioned and are reaching out for what they feel is a better way? I fear, though, that it is nothing more than the mistaken belief that anything can be bought at a price. They purchase titles of nobility for the sake of novelty, with no true sense of the responsibility that it carries. So in the end, they are nothing more than scraps of paper with pretty blue ribbons. They are nothing more than spoiled children." He paused thoughtfully, staring at the vaulted ceiling for a moment. "But, as with children, you can hardly blame them. They are ignorant and nothing more. We must look beyond that and just kill them all." He took a slow sip of wine.

The room was silent. A titter escaped from the Baron, followed by a laugh. Soon, the room had erupted into laughter. Some slapped the table in merriment, while several at the table politely applauded. When the laughing began to subside, a small impish grin crossed the duke's lips. He moved to something lighter all the while wondering why they had thought he'd made a joke.

When his guests were all safely on board the jet and traveling back to their vapid lives, the duke strode purposefully past his secretaries. Both acknowledged him, as he passed through to his office. The surface of the cherry desk was cluttered with maps, scrolls and ancient books. A few surfaces were left to see the rich wood grain beneath.

He settled into the cushy leather chair and carefully unfurled an ancient scroll, covering the one open spot on the desk. He shuffled some papers to the side and tapped a tempered glass embedded in the desktop. With a quiet hum, a silvery monitor glided out of the desk and glowed as it powered up. A keyboard appeared on the glass under his fingertips. He began to key the characters into a powerful program that was part interpreter, part cryptographer. He feverishly followed the yellowed lines of characters in anticipation of what it would reveal. His jaw tightened, as a quiet chirp of a hidden phone broke the silence. The soft amber glow of a glass touch screen radiated from the desk. His lips drew thin, as he acknowledged the chirp. "Yes, Gretchen?"

"Baron Rothberg is on line one for you, Fredrick. Do you have time for him?"

Gretchen Hapsburg was the only person, other than his wife that he allowed to call him by first name. And, he really didn't care for his wife all that much.

She could hear the peevish tone, as he responded to her. "Yes, Miss Hapsburg, put him through."

He touched the desktop to bring up the call. Flawless audio accompanied the Baron's nasally British accent. "Duke Lindenspear, you are in good health, I trust?"

He snapped at the Baron. "Yes, Baron. What is the purpose of today's call?"

True to form, he started with, "The President would be most pleased if he could meet with you to discuss our arrangement. How would you like for me to respond?"

The Baron winced, as the duke asked, "The President of what?" He paused for a moment before stuttering out, "W-why, the United States, Duke."

The duke smiled. "Please extend my warmest greetings to Washington, but I am not in a position to grant an audience at this time. It will be two months at least. I'll have Miss Hapsburg inform you when my schedule is free."

"Very good, Sir. I'll inform Mr. President."

"Baron?"

"Yes, Duke Lindenspear?"

"He does understand our relationship, yes?"

"I'm sure he does, Sir. However, I will clarify it with him."

"Please make sure that he appreciates that my time is precious. With seventy-five percent of his campaign contributions flowing from me, I will let him know when I need to see *him*. You may use those words."

Quietly, the Baron responded, "Thank you, Duke. I will make that abundantly clear."

"Very good, Baron. I'll be in touch." The duke

tapped the glass screen loudly without waiting for a reply. He eased back into the soft leather of the chair, irritated at the interruption over such a trivial matter.

He sighed, leaned forward and considered the scroll. Clearly the notes were from a different time period. They bore the marks of being translated from code into another language. He unrolled more of the text. There were notes all over the margins. He stopped at the worn intricate lines of an illustration drawn in such fine detail that at a glance the characters were almost invisible to the naked eye. He retrieved a large magnifying glass from under a pile of papers and stared at the finely written letters, along the branches of a tree. The hair-like lines had corresponding symbols above them. He stopped. He had seen the symbols before. He shuffled through another pile of papers until he removed an 8x10 color glossy photo of the Ark. With the magnifying glass, he studied the inscriptions along the side of the Ark, alongside the scroll. His jaw dropped. They were the same. *Have I broken the code?* In the scroll, along one entire side of the tree, the symbols correlated with the words and formed a sequence in such fine detail that it appeared to be part of the drawing. He slapped his leg and laughed aloud. The noise sounded odd in the deep silence. The scrolls predated the Sixth Century. However, the notes were Eleventh Century Arabic. *Someone else had tried to break the code.* He keyed the characters into the interpreter program and watched as the sequence evolved before him. At last, he had the code to activate the Ark. It was clear to him now and the sequence of events surrounding the story of this ancient forgotten scroll unfolded. He pictured Saladin high in his mountain fortress, seeking to find a weapon to drive out the white invaders. *What could be better than to use their own weapon against them?* He sent his deadly agents forth to seek the Ark and the means to use it. They couldn't find the Ark, but they had tortured a priest until he had given them the location of the scroll. A century later, Crusaders discovered a cache of jewels in an underground vault, but still there was no Ark. The Arabs had the scroll. The Norman Crusaders had the jewels. It was only now, a millennium, later that the duke had all three save the final gems.

The duke sat back, letting a small self-satisfied smile cross his face, one of smug assurance that he had been right. He sat up straight and his thoughts raced. He realized how tantalizingly close he was to the final piece of the puzzle. When the American led them to the final gems he would finally fulfill his destiny.

He was like a child on Christmas morning and he was too excited to read any further. He wanted to be near *Her*. He stood and walked briskly to the ornately carved bookcase on the far wall. He clicked a small remote from his pocket. The bookcase slid silently into a pocket in the wall, revealing the mirror like chrome of the elevator doors behind it. The doors quietly whooshed opened at his approach. As he entered the car, a multitude of LED lights lit at his approach. Deep within the bowels of the castle, a small Trident class nuclear reactor hummed away providing more power than was feasibly needed. The elevator glowed with seven buttons for him to choose from; three for the stories in the citadel above him and three for the sublevels below him. The workers had labored against the stubborn bedrock for ten years to install the shafts.

The cost was sadly exorbitant, enough to feed South Africa for a year. He had never even asked Gretchen how much it had been. He didn't care.

The elevator chimed to the tune of Vivaldi's Spring movement when he reached the sublevel. As the doors opened, the soft sheen of gold relief formed the full size image of an arch-angel before him. It was so realistic that the angel seemed to reach out and touch him. His one hand reached out, while the other held a mighty sword aloft as though preparing to strike. The construction team had commissioned an artist from Milan to complete the piece. It was, without a doubt, unsurpassed by any of his best work. It was most unfortunate that he would not remain silent about it. McPherson had seen to it that he had died quietly in his sleep.

The duke reached out and touched Gabriel's hand. His touch triggered a sensor behind the gold plating. A section of Gabriel's robe silently recessed, revealing a biometric pad behind it. The duke placed his thumb on the pad, allowing it to scan. The system scanned and verified the duke's thumb print before titanium rods began to sequence open. The process took a full minute to complete. The foot and a half thick door pivoted on a massive hinge, making an opening large enough for a small car to drive through. As he entered a small anteroom in the vault which doubled as an airlock chamber, he moved to the protective suits hanging neatly along one wall. Ultraviolet light filtering glass segregated the chamber from the main room of the vault. He had left nothing to chance when it came to protecting the Artifacts Chamber.

He slipped into one of the self-contained suits and

clicked on a small oxygen pack on his belt. He would hook into a supplied air once inside the vault chamber. He zipped up the suit and turned on the oxygen pack. Walking toward the door to the Artifact Room, he reached another security device on the door. He entered a ten digit cipher to enter the room. The door to the air lock hissed, as it sealed. Within seconds, the airlock began to purge air and replace it with pure nitrogen. The door hissed at him angrily when the sequence was complete. The vault was deceptively large; rooms and chambers divided the space which could have contained a regulation soccer game. While it housed some of the most priceless pieces of unknown treasure, his only interest today was the Center Piece of the chamber. In the center, a black marble pedestal gleamed in dark contrast to the gilded golden chest crested by two solemn Angels standing watch over a carved tree in the middle.

Despite the dim light the chest glowed with a faint blue light. Ancient symbols were etched into the thinning gold plate, dancing in the dim light. He knew the entity within didn't like him and he really didn't care. He would control it, if it was the last thing he did. He stood as close as he dared. Even with his protective suit, the ancient energy within could kill him with a single touch. He knew it longed to do so, but he wouldn't give it the satisfaction. He longed to caress the skin of the artifact with his bare hand; to touch it in a manner that no other man could. He had found a way. Soon, it would be within his grasp.

Chapter 8

For over an hour, Gillian cut back through uneven dirt tobacco roads and obscure shortcuts to ensure that they weren't followed. Confident they were alone, she eased the Bronco toward the safe house to rest and regroup. Little had passed between them during the trip—mainly because she had informed Marty that he was not to distract her while she drove. It needled him being treated like a six year old. In reality, he understood. It gave him time to think. The one question that preyed on him was, *Is she a friend or foe?*

After a long silence, she pointed to a stash of energy bars behind the seat. "Hand me one of those, please? Help yourself, if you like."

Without a word, he opened a bar and handed it to her. He tore the wrapper off a second one and gnawed at it, hungrily. Silently, he handed her a bottle of water from the cooler and took one for himself. The water tasted sweet to his parched lips. The nutrients from the treat made him feel almost normal.

The day was pleasant and he enjoyed the coolness of the morning breeze against the warmth of the early June sun. The air had the delectable hint of honeysuckle. It wasn't long before Marty's head began to nod. As he dozed, she drove on. She occasionally glanced over to make sure that he was all right.

As he dozed, she sized up his lumbering frame. He

was stocky but not fat, tall but not overly so. His round cheeks and button nose topped with strawberry blonde curls made him look angelic as he slept. She caught herself and pushed away the feelings which would make her think of him as anything other than the focus of her duty.

Marty dozed peacefully. For the first time since his kidnapping, he had pleasant dreams. He dreamed of Barb. She stood before him in the old farm house. The room smelled of apple pie and cinnamon. Her eyes sparkled, as she looked at him adoringly. A small beatific smile crossed her lips. She had never failed in letting him know that she loved him unconditionally, as she would for any child. It made him smile in his sleep.

Silently, she pointed to her favorite chair in the living room. His eyes followed the length of her hand to a seat where the soft brown leather of her Bible glowed in the sunlight. It sat on the polished table beside her faded comfortable rocker. This is where she had always been when he came to visit as a child.

The Bible seemed to beckon him. It drew him closer, begging to be picked up. As his hand reached for it, he awoke with a start. The Bronco had stopped moving. Darkness surrounded them, the air was thick and stuffy. In the dark, he heard Gillian's voice. "Stay put, while I turn on some lights." He was good with that.

A single stark light bulb suddenly glared inside the Bronco. Against the glare and stark shadows, he could make out the inside of a garage. Gillian was standing on the step to the house. Marty flinched as the the click of the door unlocking snapped.

She turned to him. Something in her eyes had

changed. They didn't seem quite as hard. Softly, she spoke. It was loud enough from him to hear, but just barely. "I'm going to sweep the house. I'll be back for you in a minute, okay?"

Marty nodded in agreement.

He looked around, though there wasn't much to see. This was probably the cleanest garage he had ever seen in his life. There were no implements hanging on the walls, no work benches, nothing of any kind around him. The walls had a fresh coat of white paint. It almost looked as though no one lived here.

He looked around the Bronco. In the dim light, he could see energy bar wrappers, empty water bottles and pages of type written papers were scattered across the back seat. He looked at the Bronco and then the garage. This was clearly not *her* garage.

Gillian's head popped out of the doorway. She motioned to him and said, "Everything is clear. Come on in."

He eased out of the truck and walked around. His skin felt gritty and the hint of his own body odor made him wince. He looked up at her beseechingly. "Any chance of a shower around here?"

For the first time since he seen her, she smiled. "I think we can probably manage that and some fresh clothes to boot."

The house was neat and well ordered. While nice, the furniture was rather ordinary as was the room. It reminded him of a model home—attractive and impersonal. They scrounged through a couple of rooms and came up with an entire outfit, including underwear. It seemed odd that many of the clothes were his size. *What are the odds of that?* It probably would have frightened him to know the real answer.

The steaming hot water began to peel away the layers of grime and stress. His mind cleared. Of all the weird things that had happened to him, he kept going back to the image of Barb standing before him, smiling. The memory of the Bible burned in his mind, the dream drove his every thought. He remembered back to when he was a child. They'd sat in a tiny chapel on a cool November morning. She stood and handed him her Bible. With an uncharacteristic solemnest, she said, "Take good care of my Bible, Dear. It holds the key to many secrets." It was an odd statement at the time, but he had shrugged it off as some religious connotation. Now he wondered.

He turned off the water and toweled off. He opened the medicine cabinet door to find his brand of deodorant, toothpaste and toothbrush on the shelf. The coincidences were beginning to rattle him. *This isn't normal. It's like they planned his arrival.* He walked out of the bathroom and into the bedroom where he found an outfit laid out on the bed for him. He almost felt human again, as he slipped on a pair of rugged hiking shoes, one of a new generation of lightweight waterproof shoes designed for the urban explorer. They felt very good.

As he walked out, he found Gillian talking to…his bartender? He recognized the new guy from the Green Lake Golf Club House. Now, the alarm bells were really beginning to ring. The young man smiled, as he looked at Marty. He extended his hand. "Hi, my name's Digger Delgado. Welcome to my home."

Marty shook his hand guardedly, as he positioned himself near a window in case he needed to jump.

Digger could read his look of concern. Digger pointed to a chair. "Relax, dude. We just want to talk. You look like you might need to be filled in."

The trio piled onto comfortable overstuffed furniture. It was Digger who opened up first. "Man, do you have any idea what's going on?"

Marty shook his head. "Not really."

Gillian chimed in. "How much do you remember about your grandmother?"

It was Marty's turn to raise an eyebrow. "Which one?"

Gillian responded, "Barb is what everyone called her."

"She was one of the best people I ever knew. She took me in when I was five. My parents died in a plane crash. She died when I was ten. I went to live with my other Grandmother Bess." It was all true, nothing revealing. *Surely, this isn't about money.*

Gillian understood he was confused and suspicious. There was no way he would say anything under the circumstances unless she and Digger came clean first. So, she began. "Let me tell you what I know."

"Your grandmothers held a secret, an important one. I work with an organization that is trying to protect that secret."

Marty looked at her, skeptically. "What? You mean they were spies? What could they have possibly known?"

"Evidently, they knew of some important artifacts that were thought to be lost."

Marty raised an eyebrow. "Okay, I'll bite. What kind of artifacts?"

Digger stepped in. "The old name for it is a Sappir.

We call them sapphires. The one we are trying to find was thought to be one of the original stones brought down from Mount Sinai by Moses."

Marty looked at him, doubtfully. "I thought Moses brought down the Ten Commandments?"

Digger nodded. "He did. But that wasn't all. Part of the Biblical text says he went forth with the leaders of the twelve tribes of the Hebrews and they brought down Sappirs for each tribe."

Marty blinked, looking from Digger to Gillian. He burst out laughing. "Okay, I get it. This is one of those reality shows that are supposed to make you react, right?"

Digger and Gillian looked at each other and then back at Marty. They weren't laughing. They weren't even smiling.

This isn't good. Marty tried to reason with them. "Look, after Barb's funeral, her sister Faye dumped me at Bess's. They left me with a toothbrush, comb, my clothes and that's it. I never saw them again until last night. Bess took good care of me, left me with a pretty decent nest egg, but no secret jewels; nothing more mysterious than an old cat. I got an inheritance and a house full of antique furniture. I really miss the cat."

Gillian prodded. "Did they leave you any clues or messages? Maybe something they said?"

"Nothing. I'm telling you—someone must have confused me with someone else. You've got the wrong guy."

They sat quietly for a moment. Marty considered what they'd just told him. Clearly, Gillian was armed and dangerous. Had she wanted to hurt him, she could have already done that and searched the house at her leisure. The little Scottish guy was clearly after something. He had drugged him and locked him up with his dead relatives. It was clear that something was going on. Marty spoke, thoughtfully. "There is one thing that occurred to me. It may be nothing…"

Digger encouraged him. "Anything is better than what we have now."

"Barb once handed me her Bible and said one day it would be mine with all its secrets. I was little at the time and it didn't make any sense then, but in retrospect, maybe she left a clue in *it?*" He didn't dare mention that it came to him in a dream. They would think he was crazy.

Gillian shrugged. "It's more than we have now. Where is it?"

"Back at the farm house, I guess. That was the last time I saw it. That's been fifteen years ago."

Gillian looked uncomfortable. Digger looked downright sick. The two Albanians parked across the street with the parabolic microphone smiled at each other. The Blue Haired Gang in the front window of the house across the street—peeping at the two Albanians—looked grim. Things were about to happen here in the sleepy town of Green Lake. Rose one of the blue haired ladies, looked at Emma and asked "Tea?"

Emma nodded, solemnly. "Yes, please. That would be lovely." There would be plenty of time to deal with the dark muscular men in the minivan after tea.

Chapter 9

The more he thought about it, the more Marty was convinced that the Bible had to be the key to all this.

Gillian jotted notes, formulating a plan to get them in and out safely. She surmised with a fair degree of certainty that this would most certainly lead them into a trap, and probably result in them being captured. She also knew that it was their only lead. She would wait to inform Franz when they were on the road. He didn't like taking chances. He would try to dissuade her from this and send in an assault team, but there was no time for that.

Digger stood and excused himself to the bathroom. He was quite happy when this was just a surveillance detail. The thoughts of physical confrontation made him ill. Gillian looked at Marty and said, "Let's take a shower."

Somewhat stunned, "But, I…"

"Never mind the coyness, Lover boy. I know you want me."

Marty tried to mask his surprise, but failed. Gillian gave him a devilish smile and winked, putting her index finger up to her lips bidding him to remain silent. Recovered slightly, Marty managed to stammer, "Uh, sure. Whatever, Babe."

She unfolded herself with the grace of a contortionist and took him by the hand, leading him to the bathroom. Inside the small room, she reached inside the shower and turned on the shower. Her face was stoic as she sat on the toilet and began to debrief him. "I am sure we're being watched. We need to develop a plan to get in and out. There is no way we can do this without being seen, so we need to figure out how to do this right under their noses. Would you be a dear and go see if Digger is finished throwing up? When he's finished, wait ten minutes and then come back here."

Marty eyed her curiously for a moment "Why ten minutes?"

With a raised eyebrow, she replied somewhat matter of factly. "I've decided I really do need a shower."

"Oh." He quietly pulled the door closed behind him, quite certain, that he would never understand how a woman's mind works. Crossing through the bedroom, he went to the other bathroom and knocked. "Digger? You okay, man?"

A weak voice from the other side of the door, replied, "Yeah. I'll make it. Be out in a minute."

Hearing this, Marty walked back into the living room and looked at the gentle slope of the antique clock on the mantel piece. It was noon. Five minutes later, Digger walked dejectedly out of the bathroom and sat down in one of the chairs. He sat there for a moment, not saying anything. Finally looking up, he asked "Where's Gillian?"

"In the shower. Apparently, she wants us both at the same time?"

Digger's eyes were suddenly very round. Marty gave him an animated wink and motioned for him to follow.

The Albanian in the passenger seat strained and cursed, trying to see anything through the binoculars. His eyes almost looked wild, as he looked at his brother. "Should we take a closer look? They might escape out the back."

Gur rolled his eyes. "Imbecile. Where will they go without their vehicle?"

Gur responded, indignantly, "Maybe they steal one, how should I know? Do I have to think of everything?"

"What I think is that Mama must have dropped you on your head. All you want to do is see the girl take a shower. Am I right?"

Gem glowered silently in the passenger seat. He cupped the binoculars so tightly against his eyes that he began to see stars. "This is why I hate surveillance. We never get to see anything."

Gur took a more soothing tone. "They will be out soon, you'll see. Maybe I'll let you kill the surfer? You would like that, no?"

Gem smiled, revealing that he was missing his two front teeth. He hated the one they called Digger. The greedy bastard kept the good women for himself. "When we were at sea and came into port, we always had fun. I miss that."

Gur slapped him on the shoulder. "Yes; but this pays better. Besides, we could not be merchant marines all our lives. You know that."

"I know, I know," he said, shaking his head and looking downward.

Gillian toweled off from the shower. She always thought better in the shower. Her mind cleared and she looked at their situation objectively. She knew what they needed to do. She suspected she knew who would be watching her, so it might just work. The knock on the door brought her back to the present. "Just a minute." She hastily finished toweling off and jumped back into her clothes. Her hair was still wet and glistening when she opened the door and motioned for them to come in. The shower was still running.

Shutting the door behind them, she looked at them and said, "Boys, I have a plan."

****

Bernard geared up to climb the utility pole at the end of Gum Street. Howard's Cable Service truck was perfect for the operation. It wouldn't be missed for a couple of days. Howard never knew what happened when Bernard shot him. He had dumped the body near the glue factory. No one would notice it for a long time. If they didn't find him for a couple of days, there wouldn't be enough left to identify after the coyotes and possums got a hold of him.

He climbed the pole with the best view of the house. The two Albanians across from the house should have placed a sign on top of minivan that read *Imbeciles for Hire*. It would have been less obvious. He didn't understand why McPherson insisted on hiring such people. Surely, he recognized his talent.

He could see the four old women in the house across the street, peeping out at the Albanian's van. He would use that to his advantage. He had watched Gillian drive into the garage. The Delgado kid got in an hour before them. Bernard anticipated that they would be there until night fall and then make a break for it. He was patient. He would wait.

****

Gillian walked through the plan twice, each time

having both Marty and Digger repeat it back to her. She looked at Digger and asked, "Any questions?"

Digger gave her a slightly exasperated look and responded, "As *if*. Remember who you're talking to here."

Gillian gave him a quick smile. "That's precisely why I asked."

He pouted. She knew he was a genius. She also knew he tended to read more into a plan than most people. That's why she kept things simple. Marty took it all in. It seemed simple enough. They would have to manage a few loose ends, as they went. Somehow, he thought the plan would be more precise, like on television. He guessed that was just drama.

****

The Blue Haired Gang gathered around Rose's small kitchen table, drinking hot English Afternoon Tea with lemon. The mood was somber. Emma looked at Hazel and asked, "Is Earl working down at the garage today?"

Hazel nodded and continued to sip her tea.

"Do you think Rico is with him today?"

"Well, Hun, you know he is. He never goes anywhere without that dang dog."

"Why don't you call him, and see if he'll come over and talk to those boys."

Hazel looked up, concern filling her blue eyes. "Emma, you know how he is. What if he hurts one of them boys? I don't want him locked up over some misunderstanding."

"Face it, Hazel. What good could they be up to if they're parked on the street watching that nice young man Digger. He's never given us a moment's trouble.

In fact, he came in last week and set the time on my VCR, *without* the manual. Nobody's ever been able to do that. He's such a nice young man. I'm afraid they're going to hurt him."

Hazel rolled her eyes. "Oh, Good Lord, Emma…" With a sigh, she held out her hand. "Hand me the phone."

Hazel held the phone at arm's length, trying to see the numbers. "Anybody got some glasses I can borrow? I can't see the numbers."

Three sets of glasses came at her simultaneously. She chose the closest ones. Picking them up, she looked at Sarah and asked, "Where did you get these? I love the frames." Holding the frames at arm's length and squinting, she asked, "Are those roses on the arms?"

Sarah beamed. "Why no, they're periwinkles. Cute as they can be. Smith's Drug had them in the close out bin for five dollars and ninety-nine cents."

Hazel looked at her, earnestly. "Did they have anymore?"

"Not in pink. They only have blue ones left." Hazel pouted. She loved pink, but then Sarah knew that.

Emma looked pointedly over the lenses of her reading glasses and cleared her throat. Hazel ignored her and carefully fitted the glasses on her nose. Slowly, she punched in the number to the garage.

The phone rang six times before a surly voice answered. "Tilley's Garage."

"Earl?"

"Yes, Mama."

"Sweetie, I need a favor."

There were few things that Earl Tilley cared about enough to drop what he was doing. His Mama and his dog were at the top of the list—and in that order. The phone looked small in his hands, as he hung up. Earl was a man of basic needs and a clear talent for two things: fixing cars and fighting. He had three different divorce lawyers and fifty or so loyal customers to prove it. If his Mama called saying two strange men were scaring her, that was all he needed to know. He called old man McGillacutty and told him that it would be another hour or so before his Buick was ready. He then hopped into the cracked blue vinyl seat of the faded relic of a wrecker and whistled for Rico. Merle Haggard blared through a single speaker from an '87 Chrysler laying on the dash. It strained to overcome the racket of twin straight pipes. The only AM station the wrecker would pick up competed against the wind whistling through the cab. He made the four blocks to Gum Street in less than five minutes.

Earl smiled grimly, as he played it out in his mind. He hoped these boys were player wannabes. In that case, they would be packin' heat. Despite his thick chest and six and a half foot frame, he could move faster than a cat on fire when it came to stripping a weapon from a stranger. It was an easy eighty or so dollars in his pocket, if they were in good shape. There had been many an unfortunate soul who had underestimated Earl's speed because of his size. It was a bad assumption that usually ended up with a broken wrist or ribs.

At the top of the block, he saw the cable truck parked with the lineman at the top of the pole, working on the line. It seemed odd, because it looked like Howard's van. But it sure wasn't Howard at the top of the pole. That would have to wait for now. He had other business to attend to.

A maroon Ford minivan stood out like a red dress at a Baptist Church social on a block where most people drove older Buicks and Chevy's. He killed the big V-8 engine a hundred yards behind the minivan and glided quietly behind van. They didn't even look up. He eased the door open and motioned for Rico to come out. The ears of the ninety-pound black German Shepard stood at attention, as he dropped as silently as a cat from the cab.

A swarthy looking fellow sat in the driver's seat, with a salad bowl contraption in his hand, so Earl moved to the passenger side and let Rico handle the fellow with the salad bowl. Mama and the girls practically had their noses plastered to the living room window like they were seated in the front row for Saturday Night Wrestling. All waited in eager anticipation to see the action. Earl focused on making this quick and clean. He didn't want his Mama seeing him get hurt. That would scare her. He didn't want that. Besides, he knew how the rumor mill worked with them old widow women; one tiny scrape on the arm and the rumor mill would have him in intensive care by sundown.

He patted Rico on the side. The dog looked up, attentively. Earl pointed to the man on the driver's side. His large arm out the window, Earl could see the two headed eagle with odd letters circling it on the deeply tanned shoulder. Had Earl been somewhat worldlier, he might have recognized the Cyrillic letters. As it was, they just looked right funny. One thing was for sure— these boys were definitely not local talent. He was sure they weren't cops, either. It looked like it was time to have a little fun.

Easing up to the passenger side, he was sure to stay far enough behind the window post. As he took a quick glance at the driver, both guys looked a lot alike. *These guys must be twins.* Earl's tone was low and guttural, "Can I help you boys?"

Startled, the passenger lunged backward, trying to grab him through the window. It was not the smartest of moves. Earl caught his wrist quickly and pinioned it against the window post. With his free hand, he curled his fingers into a grapefruit sized fist and rammed the juggernaut into the man's temple. The stocky form flopped forward in a heap.

The other man dropped the salad bowl—looking contraption reached for his waist band. Earl grinned. It looked like he was going to get a little extra beer money this weekend. As the gun cleared his belt, Earl snapped, "Get 'em, Rico." A black blur cleared the window, clamping his jaws tightly on the gunman's wrist. The man yelped in pain. The gun dropped harmlessly to the floorboard. Earl jerked the passenger door open and threw the unconscious passenger to the street. Gem's head struck the pavement like a wet melon. Blood began to ooze under him.

The other man struggled to free himself from the dog, but Rico was still clamped on the man's wrist. His other arm was pinned under a hundred pounds of dog flesh. Earl put a big fleshy hand on the man's thick neck and took his time with a powerful left. Gur went limp and slumped back into the seat. Earl's fist made a wet slapping sound, as he hit him a second time to be sure he was unconscious. Gur's dark head lolled forward, unresponsively.

Earl glanced up in time to see Rose high five his Mama. He allowed himself a sideways grin and went back to the task at hand. When he looked up again, his mom gave him the thumbs up. He winked and smiled, boyishly. Be it ever so humble, there was nothing like a mother's approval.

Earl patted Rico on the head and said, "That's good boy. Let him go." Rico returned a low guttural growl and didn't move.

Earl raised his voice an octave. "Rico..."

Rico gave him a sullen look and let go of the man's wrist. Some indentions were present, but there was no blood. He smiled at Rico and gave him another pat on the head. The dog nuzzled him to be petted some more. "That's a good boy. Yes, he is." He scratched him under the jaw. The Shepard dropped to the ground and padded back to the wrecker, tail high and wagging. Rico jumped into the front seat of the wrecker and lay down. With the excitement over, it was time for a nap. Earl looked around to see if anyone else had noticed the events. The cable guy was still on the pole. He hadn't moved. Given all the activity, that was really strange.

He walked back to the wrecker and opened the passenger door. He gave Rico a quick pat. The dog raised an eyebrow, but little more. Earl reached into the floorboard and picked up a roll of duct tape. He ambled back to the minivan and opened the side panel door. Reaching down, he felt the pulse of the one fellow on the ground. The pulse was strong. He was still alive. He would have a headache when he woke up, but he'd be okay. Earl duct taped his hands together and then his feet. He grunted, as he picked up the stocky little man by his shirt and pants—like a gunny sack—and tossed him in the floorboard of the back of the van. The man was a little stocky, but then Earl had been known to pick up entire engine blocks and move them to the back at the shop. He walked over to the other side and taped the other man's wrists and feet, and pitched him unceremoniously on top of his buddy. He checked the parking brake, shut the doors and moved the wrecker to the front of the van. With experienced ease, he hooked the van up to the wrecker.

When the van was six inches off the ground and ready to be towed, he made his way up the short walk to Rose's front door. He was met by four adoring faces.

His Mama took a tone of sternness. "Now son, don't go and hurt them boys."

Earl rolled his eyes. "Yes Mama. I'll take them down to the woods near the glue factory on 109 and drop 'em off. They'll be all right. They should come to in a couple of hours with a headache, but nothing more. They'll be fine. I promise."

"All right. Thank you, Honey." She leaned up and kissed him on the cheek.

Earl grinned. "Sure, Ma. It kinda breaks up the day, you know?"

With that, he returned the kiss tenderly on her cheek and started back down the walk to the wrecker.

Hazel called after him. "Dinner on Wednesday, remember?"

The response came back. "Yes, Ma'am." With any luck he'd finish putting the starter on Ol' McGillicutty's Buick by day's end. He might even call Thelma down at the cable company and find out if there was a service call on Gum Street. Something about that cable guy still bugged him.

Chapter 10

Gillian stared at the scribbled outline and considered what would go wrong at each phase. With any luck, they would search the house, keeping the body count to one. Two would endanger the mission. And three would be a failure. They would begin the set up two hours before sunrise. She gambled on assumption that any surveillance teams would hold their position until they were sure that she and Marty had found whatever it was that they were looking for. The only drawback was they didn't know what they were looking for. That made her queasy every time she considered it. However, if a Bible was their only hot lead, then she would work through it. She smiled noncommittally at Marty, without dismissing the idea. He seemed so convinced that she didn't have the heart to challenge him.

Digger wasn't quite so green now and he began to joke around a little. Marty rolled an ink pen through his fingers, preoccupied by the things that had happened. Without warning, Gillian shooed them out of the bathroom to finish the arrangements. Her plan was contingent on how much support she could gather in the next couple of hours, which could jeopardize the plan. Marty looked forlornly at Digger and asked, "Dude, is there anything to eat around here?"

Digger responded, cheerfully, "Oh yeah."

Walking to the kitchen, he opened the refrigerator like a game show presenter. Marty was surprised to see a ridiculous selection of his favorite foods. Barbecued chicken, smoked pork chops, potato salad, green bean salad, banana pudding—even his favorite cold beer. He could get used to this. He nodded at Digger. "Dude, that's enough food to feed an army. Were you expecting a NFL football team to drop by, or something?"

Digger grinned. "I never know from one minute to the next who might be coming by or when. I always keep it stocked. I rotate the stock every three days and take it down to the Christian Ministries where they feed the homeless. Those guys down at the homeless shelter will miss me when I'm gone. They eat like kings down there."

"No doubt. This is awesome," Marty said, as he was digging out items. "Can I get you anything?"

"Nah. You go ahead and eat. I'll catch something later."

He sat at the 1970's era bar with an avocado green counter top and commenced to devour a plate of potato salad, chicken and green beans. They watched a Braves game on a flat screen TV in the living room.

Between mouthfuls, Marty looked at Digger and asked, "Can I ask you something?"

"Shoot."

"Have you been watching me the whole time you've been here?"

Digger leaned against the counter and nodded. "Yes."

"How did you know I would be at that bar?"

"I used trend data. You normally play the course

every third Friday afternoon. During the subsequent two Fridays, you go straight to the Club house for beers with the work crowd. My data was skewed, though. You were the only one there. We knew your company was getting ready to perform a structured cost cutting to improve their debt position to avoid a hostile takeover. Since we knew the plan was to cut cost before the close of the second quarter, they would have to make the changes three weeks before closing to absorb the restructuring costs into second quarter financials. Since most employers choose to perform layoffs of this nature at the end of a pay period, and Friday ended your pay period for this month, I guessed it would happen that day and toward the end of the business day."

Marty shook his head. "Man, that's just freaky."

Digger smiled, ignoring the statement, and continued. "I obtained a job as a bartender and scheduled myself for a Friday afternoon. There you were. I watched as McPherson drugged you, put you into his station wagon and then took off to follow you. I've been watching you one-on-one ever since."

Marty felt the back of his neck getting warm. He dropped a chicken bone on the plate, annoyed. "If you were watching me, why didn't you get me out of that flipping basement?"

Digger shrugged, apologetically. "Sorry, Dude. That's not my area. I'm strictly a surveillance geek. I would have gotten us both killed, if I had tried to go up against someone like McPherson."

Marty took a long swig of beer and tried to calm himself. He shook his head. "Man, you guys are scary."

Digger shrugged his shoulders. "That's why I called it in a week ago. That's why they sent Gillian.

She really is the best at what she does."

Marty stared back at the plate of food and shook his head again.

They were silent for a while before Marty asked, "So, are you guys the NSA, CIA, FBI…what?"

Digger looked at him without smiling and said, "We're the ESF."

Marty's brow furrowed. "Okay. I'll bite. What is the ESF?"

"The European Scholarship Foundation."

Marty nearly spit out a piece of chicken. He coughed to the point that Digger feared that he was choking, and he began to move into position to perform a Heimlich maneuver.

Marty waved him off and finished clearing his throat. When he was able to speak, he asked, "You mean there's a school for this?"

"Not exactly. We're a private international agency that's focused on the preservation of historic artifacts. We don't answer to governments, though we do ally ourselves with strategic agencies, so we can get support when we need it. We don't seek to overthrow any political system, just to identify certain key artifacts and get them into credible hands where they can be preserved and protected. Eventually, they end up in museums or places where they're available to all people."

Marty shook his head. This just kept getting stranger. "So, why are you guys called a scholarship group?"

"It's a good cover. We can travel all over the world. We're listed as being non-profit. Most of our agents are students, so airport security doesn't give us a second look. It's the perfect setup. Besides, they pay college tuitions to whatever college you get into."

"Is that why you joined?"

"Me? No, their leader recruited me. I don't need the tuition. It was just something to do."

Marty smiled, wryly. "Must be nice." He went back to the chicken.

Gillian walked into the room. Her hair was still damp. She looked at Digger and asked, "Have you got your usual toys with you?"

Digger rolled his eyes. "Of course." He tried to sound exasperated, but it came out comical. Even Marty smiled, although he didn't know what he was smiling for.

It was Gillian's turn to look exasperated. "Well, turn them on, will you. What are you waiting for?"

"I was hoping for a gratuitous shower scene out of the deal, silly."

Gillian glared at him.

With that, he hopped off the bar stool and walked past her into a small pantry. From Marty's vantage, he could see Digger slide a can of pasta sauce forward, causing the shelf to open like a hinged door and revealing an electronic touch screen behind it.

After logging in on the interactive screen, Digger began to flip through the menu to find the correct program. Finally, he touched one icon, which caused an almost imperceptible hiss to fill the room.

After the noise began to sound, Gillian spoke. "Okay, now we can speak freely."

Marty looked at her, curiously. "You mean—the house is bugged?"

"No, they just sit across the street with a parabolic

and listen to us, as though they were in the room. The hiss you hear is white noise. It screws with their listening devices, so they can't hear us."

Marty nodded, clearly impressed.

Gillian looked at Digger and then at Marty. "Well, everything is set. The arrangements have been made."

Marty asked, "So, what time do we need to be there?"

"Six o'clock a.m."

"What do we do tonight?"

"We sleep. Everything should be fine. They won't make a move on us until they're sure we have something."

"Well, I guess I can take some measure of comfort in that."

"Digger, do we have any eyes outside?"

Digger brightened at this "Of course." He left the kitchen, beckoning Gillian to follow him to the bedroom. Once in the bedroom, he tapped the notebook out of sleep mode. Chicken leg still in hand, Marty watched from behind, as the screen brought up a series of cameras in a grid which monitored the outside. One was focused across the street.

Gillian remarked, "That's odd. The Albanians are gone. They don't normally fly the coop on a surveillance job."

Digger looked somewhat aghast. "How did you know they were watching? I didn't see anything. I scanned everything, I swear."

Gillian took a soothing tone, while patting him on the cheek, reassuringly. "It's okay, Sweetie. It's all part of the game. I spotted them, as we were coming in. It concerns me more that their gone now. That's not what

I would expect. Digger, can these pan and tilt?"

He nodded and began to work the controls.

"Pan up the street until I tell you to stop."

Using a small joy stick, he began to move the camera up the street.

Gillian suddenly told him to stop. Pointing, she said, "Bring this camera to full screen and zoom in on that…"

All the other cameras went away, while the camera in question showed up in full color on the screen in front of them. "Can you see that van?"

Digger replied, "Uh huh."

"There's a pole in front of it. Follow that pole up."

The camera tracked up the pole until it stopped. She could see a pair of gleaming combat boots on the pole in front of them. Gillian furrowed her brow.

"I'll be back," she said abruptly and hurried out of the room.

Within moments she returned from the garage with a compact rifle and a banana clip. Marty's eyes grew wide. He gulped. The color suddenly washed out of Digger's dark complexion. She looked at them and said, "Relax, guys. I just need a better look."

Removing the scope from the mount of the Ruger Mini-14, she moved over to the window facing the front of the house. Easing up one edge of the mini-blind, she verified she could see the van from this vantage. She eased the scope into position and began to survey the person on the pole. She looked for a long time before quietly turning around and sitting down heavily on the couch beside the window. She looked up at Digger and said flatly, "It's Bernard." She sat back, silently thinking. Digger tugged at Marty's sleeve and motioned him back to the bedroom.

Marty felt confused. "So, what's up?"

Digger looked at him, somberly. "Gillian's pretty sure that he's the man who killed her father. If they've sent him, we're in serious trouble."

Marty looked at Digger. "So, what do we do?"

They were both startled by Gillian standing in the doorway. Quietly, she said, "We stick to the plan. Digger, you have first watch. Let's get some rest."

At three forty-three am a young man and woman quietly ran across the back property of the old farm. They monitored the house until they were sure that there was no one else in the house. They moved carefully to the house and removed their dew wet shoes, so no trace would be evident. Slipping up the steps, the man removed a lock pick set from his pocket and worked on the back door. To his amazement, it was open. The woman kept her back to him, watching the surrounding landscape for movement. The Star finder Night Goggles gave her visibility up to a hundred yards.

She watched the foliage move behind them. She zoomed in on the long ugly tail of an opossum, as it slid through the undergrowth and was gone. The night was silent, save the noise of crickets. They slipped into the house and moved quietly upstairs. The girl sat on the floor and checked the rounds in her automatic. It wouldn't be long before Marty and Gillian arrived.

Chapter 11

There was a small knock at the door. Natalie looked up, as her assistant poked her head in the door. "Sorry to bother you. The patient has arrived."

Natalie gave Chou Mae a smile. "Thanks. I'll be right there."

There was far too much to do with FDA trials coming up, but if the CEO considered it important enough to make the call himself and he wanted her to take personal charge of this patient, then she wasn't going to argue. She pushed her glasses revealing large chocolate eyes.

She limped past the dual PhD's in biochemistry and medicine on the wall. She hardly noticed them anymore, which was odd considering all that she had struggled through to get them. Her education had been the simple part. Avoiding the death squads in South Africa had been the trick. But then, Natalie didn't dwell in the past. Her work was too important to waste her time on personal baggage. Or so it seemed...

She entered the small sterile room to find two assistants and a heavily bandaged muscular man. She didn't really look at his face, but went straight to the chart. She carefully reviewed the list of findings compiled by her associates. She had tested her treatment on gunshot wounds. All had been remarkably successful. This one didn't seem nearly as complex as others she had worked on, so she wondered why this particular case needed her attention. The unspoken question nagged her: *What makes this man so important?*

It was then that she looked at her patient. His face hadn't changed all that much. She couldn't recall how many years it had been, but it hadn't been so many that she wouldn't remember the face of the man who'd killed her parents. The sudden pounding in her ears made her realize just how real it still was for her. She had thought she'd been able to stifle that one single horrific moment but at the sight of him, it all came flooding back. A pit of nausea edged its way up her throat despite her will to push it back.

Once again, she was peering through the slit in the wall, bathed in a clammy sweat, she watched helpless as he used a long thin blade to toy with her mother. Her mother strained against the leather straps so tight it looked like they would cut her in two. The heap of her father's lifeless body lay like trash at their feet. She could not imagine the will her mother must have had not to look in her direction and give her away. He had dragged the blade playfully up her arm, asking "Where are the others?"

Her mother shook her head, refusing to speak.

Again, ever so softly he asked. "Where are the others?"

This time, his blade pierced her skin ever so slightly at the wrist. A small ribbon of blood streamed down to the armrest and dropped to the floor, landing with a splat.

Tears of pain and fear streamed down her mother's cheeks, but she still refused to speak. The blade slowly moved up her mother's arm, this time splitting the skin like an overripe grape. Her mother's jaw tightened. Still, she refused to utter a whimper. Natalie watched through her tears, as he methodically filed her mother, each cut slightly worse than the previous. She had clinched her teeth so hard, she thought they would shatter until he mercifully thrust the blade deep into her mother's heart ending it all. The woman had slumped forward, free of the torture at last. Now, that same man sat before her.

Natalie could barely remember putting the chart back, as she moved slowly from the room. The two assistants stared after her, somewhat perplexed. She walked into the hall and slumped down the wall into a squatting position. It was Chou Mae that found her wrapped in a fetal position, rocking back and forth. The small Asian hissed at two orderlies, who lifted her and shuttled her into a vacant room. Chou Mae then shooed the burly men out like hens in the barnyard. She gently took Natalie's hand and sat silently for a while. "Nat?"

She stared at Chou Mae, vacantly.

"You're scaring me, Nat. I don't like that." Chou Mae gave her an impish grin. "My whole future relies on me riding on your coat tails when this system hits the open market. You can't shut down on me now. Tell me, what's the matter?"

The last question filtered through the shock. She blinked at Chou Mae, trying to focus. A tiny voice eked forth. "That m-man in the other room k-killed my parents."

Chou Mae's almond eyes turned very round. "Oh, my God. We have to call the cops."

Natalie grasped her arm so tightly it almost made

Chou Mae wince. She shook her head, vehemently. "No. We can't."

Chou Mae looked confused. "For heaven's sake, why not?"

Natalie's brilliant mind was at work. "That happened twelve years ago in South Africa." She released her grip and moved her hand gently to Chou Mae's shoulder. "Think about it. The CEO called about this man. He has a gunshot wound, so he must be working for someone very important. If I try to have this guy arrested, they'll kill us and this project. Think of the lives that will be lost. Think of the cost in human misery that can be avoided."

"But Nat, they were your parents."

With conviction, Natalie looked at her. "Yes, and as my parents, they didn't give up on what they believed in. I can't change what happened to them, but I can honor them by doing something where they will be remembered. If I go back in there and finish this, we will finish the project and chances are I will save someone else's parents."

Chou Mae shook her head. There was no arguing her logic "You're a better person than me. That's all I have to say."

She gave her a tight smile. "That remains to be seen. Let's get through this first and you can tell me again how great I am over drinks. Maybe then I'll believe you."

Chou Mae shook her head. "Should I assist?"

Natalie's head was high and she smiled, more convincing this time. "By all means, Doctor Chun."

The pair entered the room, walked straight to McPherson and began to probe the wounded arm.

"Hello, Mr. McPherson. I'm Dr. Vergeef. I will be performing the procedure today with the help of Dr. Chun. I assume my team has explained to you the experimental nature of this procedure?"

He winced, as she probed. Sweat beads began to form on his forehead. "That's right, Luv. Some kind of super tonic from what I gather." He looked at her strangely. "Where are you from, Luv?"

She raised an eyebrow and looked coldly at him over her glasses. "Canada. Why?"

"No reason, you just seem familiar."

Natalie pushed back the raw fear with all her might. "We're going to use an experimental procedure called Programmable Protoplasm. We call it PP for short." She smiled. The mention of a body function usually got a snicker from most patients. McPherson didn't smile. He studied her like a lab rat. She steeled herself against the rising tide of panic.

As she spoke, she continued to probe the wound. "Fundamentally, PP uses tiny programmable particles to focus your body's normal healing process. It supplies targeted nutrients and flushes scar tissue at an accelerated rate."

Seemingly unimpressed, he studied a text message on his phone before looking up. "How long will it take?"

"Three hours, including recovery from the anesthesia."

His eyes cut toward her. "No anesthesia."

She was somewhat taken aback by his response, but tried not to show it. She blinked. "Excuse me?"

He looked directly at her again. "I said no bloody anesthesia."

"But the procedure can be very painful, as the nerve endings are reconnected."

"So give me a local."

"Locals don't work very well with this procedure. The protoplasm works so fast that the local is gone before it can take effect."

He leered at her. "So, I guess you'll just have to hold my hand through it, won't you, Doc?"

Natalie was sure her heart was going to hammer out of her chest. Chou Mae rescued her. "Doctor Vergeef will be monitoring every aspect of your procedure. I will be by your side, Mr. McPherson." Chou Mae's eyes narrowed as she gave him a long thin smile. she looked like a Siamese cat, the kind of Siamese that was looking for a pair of shoes for some payback.

Irritated, he responded, "Whatever. Just get on with it."

Within twenty minutes, McPherson was in the procedure room and prepped. Twelve needle electrodes formed a circle around the wound, with a plasma circulator pump moving fluids at a remarkable rate. As the fluids carrying the small programmable cell bodies and the electrodes began to furiously work, McPherson began to sweat profusely, while his breathing and heart rate increased proportionately. Dr. Vergeef nodded to Dr. Chun, who started the anesthesia in with the protoplasm. McPherson was unconscious before he could protest. It was just as well. He would have passed out from the pain anyway.

The beauty of Natalie's system was that her protoplasm could communicate back and forth with a host computer. As it acted as an interpreter with

McPherson's own cells, she could focus the incoming fluids on knitting bones, tendons and muscles at high speed, while outbound fluids carried away contaminates and damaged tissues. It literally flushed damaged tissues out, as it progressed.

By inducing a signal directly into the body, she could send and receive messages to and from her little workers much like a computer program. Usually, her only involvement was to manage the nerve connections at a microscopic level. Once the PP *learned* the uniqueness of the person, they quickly adapted to the repair. In a scant hour, the PP had re-knitted his shoulder to its original condition.

An hour later, McPherson was conscious and impatient. He felt fine. He was needed in the field. Natalie insisted that he wait six hours to ensure that the process had worked.

The bedside phone chirped. It could only be one person. "McPherson." His voice was crisp and professional.

"Good evening, Mr. McPherson," was the response. The tone would have worked equally well had he been calling to invite him to tea.

"Good evening, Duke Lindenspear. Are you ready for a progress report?"

"Why yes, Mr. McPherson. That would be most helpful."

"My understanding from Mr. Bernard is that Messrs. Bos-kov-ski had an altercation with an unknown American. We have lost contact with them. Bernard has taken up the surveillance and another team is on the way."

The duke didn't care about any altercation, so long

as Wood was not endangered.

"Excellent, Mr. McPherson. When the other team arrives to relieve Mr. Bernard, please be kind enough to debrief him and turn the operation over to him."

Damn. He knew that would happen. It was just the opportunity Bernard had been waiting for to assume the reins. "Yes, Sir. I understand."

"Don't sound so glum, Mr. McPherson. I need you here at the castle. What I suspect is that our objective is not in the United States, but here on the continent. I will need your skill here. Do not concern yourself with Mr. Bernard. He will not usurp your position in this endeavor."

Despite his condition, he brightened. "Thank you, Sir."

"Mr. McPherson?"

"Yes, Sir?"

"Don't dally. We have much to do."

"Yes, Sir. I will be there directly."

The line went dead.

McPherson understood that the duke always knew more than he let on. Somehow, he always had the uncanny ability to stay one step ahead of everyone else. It was eerie sometimes. He picked up the phone and touched the speed dial for Bernard.

The phone on the other end was answered almost immediately. "Oui?"

"McPherson here."

"Ah yes, and how are you, Mon ami?"

Dick closed his eyes and visualized a lightning bolt striking Bernard dead on the spot. It gave him a little smile before he went on. "Do you have the other team in place?"

"Oui. They arrived shortly after dark. And it was a beautiful sunset, no?"

It was all McPherson could do not to throw the phone at the wall. He took a deep breath and visualized his hands around Bernard's neck, crushing the life from his body. The thought calmed him again and he enjoyed another little smile. "I wouldn't know, Bernard. I didn't see it." Wryness permeated his voice.

"A pity really. The subtle the hues of red and salmon…it's most lovely."

McPherson's voice was tight, as he asked, "Where are you now?"

"I have found a charming little motel. I have just had an excellent glass of Grenache in my room. I am wearing nothing but a towel. And you?"

Dick clinched his jaw. His muscles bulged until they ached. The heart monitor above his head began to chime due to the elevated heart rate and blood pressure. A young dark haired nurse entered the room, almost immediately. The syringe in her hand carried morphine. McPherson picked up a stainless steel bedpan and flung it at her. The young nurse dodged, as the receptacle clanged against the wall. She quickly backed out of the room never taking her eyes away from him.

He unclenched his jaw and replied far more calmly than he felt. "Fine, thanks. I've just spoken with the duke. I'm to head back to the continent, so the duke has asked me to put you in charge of the operation for now. Do you have any issues with that?"

"Mon dieu; but, of course not, my friend. I would be most happy to do anything to assist you in this great quest."

McPherson rolled his eyes. "Thanks, Mate. I'll be

in touch." Bearing as much as he could, he disconnected the line before the Frenchman could say another word.

Bernard smiled. Nothing amused him more than irritating the little Scot. He was so easily baited. He slid the phone into the pocket of his filthy coveralls and continued to clean the interior to the cable van. Starting in the cab, he worked his way to the back. Methodically, he wiped every surface he had touched. The van smelled of bleach, as he systematically removed finger prints and trace evidence that would link him to the murder of the cable technician. The small battery powered shop vacuum whirred, as it grabbed the particles. He would wipe for prints and drop it in a place where it would be stolen. Thieves had their uses, as well.

The engine strained, as he pressed the van farther into the thick underbrush. At nearly twenty miles away from where he left the body, it would be some time before local police made the connection. By then, he would be gone. When it could go no farther, he shoved the door open into thick green pines. They slapped him, as he pushed his way to the back. He left the door open, creating an invitation to woodland creatures, further destroying any evidence left behind. Sweat soaked his sleeve as he mopped his brow. He hiked back to the older model Camry parked close to the road. Opening the trunk, he stripped the cable company coveralls and shoved them into a bag. The air felt cool and inviting after shedding the extra clothing.

The speed dial on his phone rang the second surveillance team. He waited for the boys from Atlanta to pick up. He had picked them personally. They were a non-descript pair that could leave a Bar Mitzvah and show up at a barbeque and have some elderly aunt pinching their cheeks in a matter of minutes. They were as adaptable as modeling clay. He guessed at their military training. In this line of work, people didn't ask a lot of pushy questions.

The phone chirped. "Boyd here."

"This is Bernard. Anything to report?" Unlike with McPherson, his accent was now practically imperceptible.

"No, Sir. We've taken a distant vantage point to avoid a similar mishap that occurred with the first team."

"Very good. If they leave, follow them. If they split up, let me know immediately."

"Understood, Sir. Should we take any action other than surveillance?"

"No. That won't be necessary. I'll see to any interaction with the subjects."

"Yes, Sir. We came prepared for a long engagement, if necessary."

"Thank you, Mr. Boyd. I will check in within three hours. If you need anything, feel free to call me." It occurred to Bernard that he did not know either Boyd's or the Matthews' first names. It was probably just as well. He didn't expect they would survive all that long.

Chapter 12

The clock glared *4:00 am* when Marty opened his eyes. Digger was still standing at his foot. "Dude, are you awake?"

Marty blinked a couple of times and responded, "Yeah, I'm up." He half-hearted rolled his feet over the side of the bed.

Digger was working on his third Jolt cola. He was so wound up that Marty half-expected him to levitate. Marty, on the other hand, was a slow start in the morning. Still, within a short while, he was munching on a breakfast burrito in the front seat of the Bronco. Gillian sat in the driver's seat, sipping on coffee strong enough to have a first name. Digger eased out ahead of them, striking off in the opposite direction that Gillian planned to take. They hoped the remaining surveillance teams would follow him and draw some of the attention away from Gillian and Marty. It was a small hope, but they clung to it just the same. The Bronco idled down the street, which choked out much of the rumble of the big V-8, but not all. She started off in a direction designed to draw out a surveillance team and give the appearance that they were trying to elude anyone behind them. This was far from the truth.

After a forty-minute ride of zig zags, they finally rolled up the dirt road that led to the driveway of the old farm. Stashing the Bronco like before, they made their way up the road to the old house on foot.

The sky was beginning to glow behind the house, making it a dark shadow on the horizon. Birds chirped in the early morning air. The old farm looked as though nothing had happened the day before. The basement doors were shut; no car stood in the driveway; no signs anything was out of order. Someone had done a grand job of tidying up.

Gillian's gut told her that someone was in the house. Instinctively, she crouched from a distance and pulled out her small pair of field glasses to get a better look. Nothing seemed out of the ordinary, which meant something was. All the curtains in the house were open, but there was no light within. It was dark and silent. They staked out the house for a while to watch for any movement.

Marty sat quietly in an alcove of overgrown hedges. He took a moment to realize that the once neat farmhouse was overtaken by English Ivy. The clapboard siding curled away in places accentuating the curled dots of butter cream paint barely clinging to the wood. The house was falling apart. The outbuildings fared no better. The old silo was covered by kudzu and the barn room was collapsed on one side. Wisteria cascaded through the oak tree in the front yard, filtering down fragrance in the early morning air.

The once picturesque pastures now lay overgrown and neglected. The green of Honeysuckle and moss now replaced the John Deer Green of the '42 vintage tractor in the back. The tires were flat, the seat was missing. Something about that old tractor tugged at his heart.

He broke from his revere when Gillian gently

tapped him on the arm. She gestured for him to follow. Suddenly, she was sprinting silently through the yard to the porch. He felt clumsy running behind her, just trying to keep up. They stopped at the edge of the porch. He tried to slow his breathing, as they strained to hear anything out of the ordinary.

Marty couldn't hear anything over the pounding of adrenalin in his ears. Gillian was even breathing hard. Everything was quiet, except for the occasional coo of a mourning dove. This was just too easy.

Gillian eased up the first two steps. The dilapidated boards groaned and creaked. It made no sense in hiding their presence anymore. She eased up to the door from the side. She never stood directly in front of a door, as she wasn't sure what was on the other side. Trying the knob, it turned so she was able to swing the door in easily. She rolled across the porch in front of the door to gain visibility of the other side of the room. It was empty. Sig drawn, she stayed low, as she eased into the house. After what seemed like an eternity, she motioned Marty to come in. Standing him in the corner like a child, she pointed to her eyes and then to the room next to them.

Gracefully, she eased her way to the next room, leaving him standing in the corner like a five year old. Within moments, she was back, coming from the opposite direction. She pointed up and eased her way to the narrow staircase.

This was the first time Marty had been in this house in fifteen years. His memories were two fold. For one, it seemed much smaller. Secondly, it was much filthier. His Grandma Barb had kept the house neat and orderly. His Aunt and Uncle did not. There were pizza boxes strewn across the small living room, while beer cans lined the stairs to the second floor. Trash littered the floors. The smell of rotten food made him cover his nose with his hand. Or at least, he hoped it was just spoiled food that he smelled.

Most of the furniture was the same—just more worn and tattered. His Aunt and Uncle did little to maintain the house and it showed. Barb's favorite platform rocker was stacked with newspapers, pizza boxes and trash two feet above the seat.

Her prized autographed picture of Judy Garland in full Dorothy costume was crooked on the wall behind the rocker. The dust was so thick, it was barely recognizable. A proverbial straw broke Marty. The fact that Mal and Faye had underhandedly cheated him out of his grandmother's estate didn't matter. The fact that Barb and Faye were sisters didn't matter. The fact that Barb had taken Faye in, and Faye had disgraced her sister's memory was the last straw.

The stress and angst of the last several days punched through and washed over him like a tide. He found himself shaking with anger. Walking over to the chair, he snatched the stacks of discarded papers and pizza boxes from the seat and threw them into the floor. He cleared the cobwebs and dust as best as he could with his bare hands.

Barb had rocked him in that chair when he was little. It represented her very essence and the memories he held of her. All he had were his memories. Everyone was gone, except for him. He stared at the chair beneath him. Cleared of the debris, he moved it close to the window, where it was supposed to be. He sat down and began to rock. The anger slowly began to slip away, as he peered out the window. When he looked up, Gillian was watching him, curiously.

Marty looked back for a moment, "Sorry. It was my grandmother's chair. It means a lot to me."

Gillian nodded, but said nothing. Switching gears, she simply said, "We need to get started."

Marty nodded.

Gillian prompted him. "So, what exactly are we looking for?"

It occurred to Marty that she was waiting for him to tell her what to do. He was so used to her taking charge. He had to pause for a moment to think of what they needed to do. "We're looking for her Bible. It's black and about this big." He held up his hand to show her the size. He smiled wryly and pointed to the pile he just threw to the floor. "It's not in that pile."

That drew a smile from her. "So, where *should* we look?"

Marty gave her a sheepish look. "The last time I saw it, it was right there." He pointed to the coffee table littered with beer cans and gossip magazines.

Trying to be more helpful, he said, "In this mess, there's no telling where it is. I suggest we start in this room, grid it out and work our way to the next room."

Gillian nodded, secretly admiring his logic. "Where do you want me to start?"

He pointed her to the corner opposite him. Like a well oiled machine, they worked toward each other, stacking piles of trash as they went. They found fish hooks, decaying rubber bands and empty liquor bottles, but no Bible. They moved to the next room and then the next. It was two hours before the main floor was searched and nothing was found.

He looked at Gillian. "Looks like we move upstairs, I guess?"

Gillian put her hand on his arm. "There's something you should see."

He raised his eyebrows.

She put her finger to her lips. Then she smiled and patted him on the arm. "Let's take a shower."

She began walking upstairs. Marty shook his head. She sure had a weird sense of humor. Upstairs, the old master bath was everything Marty remembered, with the exception of the two people sitting in the floor. Ironically, the man could have been Marty's brother and the woman was the spitting image of Gillian. Marty opened his mouth to speak, but Gillian gave him the finger to be quiet.

She walked over to the shower and turned it on. She really had a thing for running water. "Marty, this is Doss…" He extended his hand. "…and Cindy…." She had an equally strong grip. "They're our decoys."

Marty stared at both. "Wow. I can see why."

Gillian quietly explained that when the time came, the decoy team would exchange clothing with Marty and Gillian and drive off in the Bronco, hopefully leading the surveillance team away. Digger would then meet them in the woods and they would get away in the yellow bug.

Marty thought. *This might just work.*

She turned off the shower and they exited the bathroom leaving Doss and Cindy silently waiting on the bathroom floor.

Gillian and Marty searched the upstairs, starting with Marty's old bedroom. Marty looked around the room, which surprisingly had not been touched.

Through the dust, he could see the trinkets he'd collected in his youth and had been forced to leave behind. He picked up a small wooden treasure chest and opened it. Inside were the oddities that had been so important to him: Three Morgan dollars, his lucky cat's eye marble, a broken railroad pocket watch that had belonged to his grandfather. These things had been his prized possessions so many years ago. Now, they seemed a part of a forgotten past.

Gillian placed a gentle hand on his arm. "Marty, we've got to keep looking."

He sniffed. "Yeah, I know. I'm sorry. Would you mind searching this room and let me move on to the next one? This place holds a lot of memories."

She smiled. It was a surprisingly gentle smile. "Sure, you go ahead. I'll finish up in here."

He moved to the next room, which must have been Faye and Mal's bedroom. Marty could not imagine anything sleeping in this place. The soiled linens smelled seedy and offensive. More gossip magazines covered in dust. Stained glasses with healthy cultures of mold littered all the furniture. It didn't look like they had washed a single glass in fifteen years. Marty was amazed that anyone could enter the room, much less sleep there. But then, he surmised they wouldn't be doing that anymore.

He moved stacks of magazines and litter into the corner of the room, as he methodically filtered through all the assorted objects and papers. Dust tickled his nose, causing him to sneeze. Gillian entered the room and began to help.

After what seemed like an eternity, Marty plopped onto the floor in exasperation. The task was beginning to seem fruitless. They had searched everywhere, but to no avail. As he leaned back against the bed, it shifted slightly. He hadn't leaned back that far.

Out of curiosity, he pulled up the edge of the yellowed cotton bedspread with two fingers to reveal a broken foot on the bedpost. The bed was being leveled by two stacked books. The one on the bottom with the gold edged pages looked familiar.

Excitedly, he exclaimed, "Gillian, give me a hand here."

Immediately, she was by his side. "Pull these out, while I lift the bed."

Marty gripped the footboard and lifted, while Gillian hastily snatched the books free. The top book was gouged from the repeated moment of the rough edge of the broken foot. The black cover on the book beneath it seemed relatively unharmed. As she turned it over, the gold embossed words *HOLY BIBLE* gleamed back at her. She smiled. "Is this it?"

Despite himself, Marty smiled. Quietly almost reverently he said, "That's it."

She handed it to him. He took it from her and held it. Picking up the edge of the bedspread, he dusted the cover of the Bible, cleaning off the dust and cobwebs that clung to it. A tear formed in the corner of his eye.

Gillian asked gently, "Marty, are you okay?"

The simple question jarred him back to the present. "Uh, yeah, I'm sorry." He wiped his eyes with his wrist. "It must be the dust."

She looked at him. Despite her hardness, she understood. Strangely, she felt a twinge of guilt for intruding on the moment, but time was critical. Giving him some latitude was the least she could do. "I know what you mean. It's going to take a six pack and a half to wash down the dust after this."

He nodded. "Let's see if we have anything helpful in here."

Lifting the well-worn Scripture, he suddenly realized that finding the Book might be the easy part. His grandmother had left more than two dozen bookmarks throughout the text. That didn't even begin to count the church bulletins throughout.

The Good Book was a half-inch thicker because of the markers. *Where should I start?* He wondered.

They sat on the edge of the bed together for a while, looking through each marker and trying to find something to indicate what they might be looking for. Finally, Gillian looked up. "Are you thirsty?"

He nodded. "Yes. I'm dying here."

"Me, too. I'll be right back."

He called after her. "See if they have any crackers or anything."

"Jeez, Dude, what are you, some kind of eating machine?"

He jabbed back, "Uh, excuse me, but some of us eat more than once a week, thank you very much."

She grinned. "Whatever. I'll see what I can find." And she was out the door.

He continued to study the Bible, trying to remember anything that would narrow the search. As he flipped through the text, he came across an old church bulletin from twenty years ago. It was yellowed and fragile. As he read it, his hands began to shake.

Please remember Sister Barbara Wood in your prayers. Her son, Martin Wood Sr. and wife Ann have joined the Lord. Barbara has gone to escort the dearly departed home, along with her grandson, Martin Jr. Memorial Services will be...

The entry went on. This was when his parents had been killed. The plane crash in New York had been sensational at the time. It had taken the lives of everyone on board, with the exception of one small boy. That was something Marty hadn't thought about for a very long time.

He continued to stare at the bulletin for a moment, trying to adjust to the implication of what he'd just read. His eyes drifted back to the Bible. In the only location he had seen in the Text, he noticed a block of scripture underlined in pencil in the margin was *See Pastor Thomason*.

Marty blinked. The pencil marks took his mind off the painful memory. He studied what his grandmother had noted in this section. She had not written anywhere else in the Bible. And yet, she had taken time to underline this passage. *Is this what we're looking for?*

The passage was in the Book of Exodus:

Then went up Moses, and Aaron, Nadab, and Abihu, and seventy of the elders of Israel; And they saw the God of Israel: and there was under his feet as it were a paved work of Sappir stone, and as it were the body of heaven in his clearness.

There it is, the Sappir. But what does this mean? Should I go to the church? He was sure all the people who had been there would be gone, including Pastor Thomason who had been the Minister at the Mt. Sinai Baptist Church. He couldn't recall all the Sunday mornings he had squirmed to get through the lengthy sermons on the hard wooden pews, while Pastor Thomason's soft melodic voice had delivered his eloquent ministry from the pulpit of the tiny sanctuary. The church had been small, but comforting. It always smelled of pine cleaner. Its ancient dark wooden beams vaulted the ceiling, giving a stark contrast to handmade stained glass windows, which flooded the sanctuary with colored light. Scenes of the apostles told the stories, acting as reminders of why they were there. Engraved wooden rails separated the choir from the pulpit.

Barb had always sung in the choir. Her voice was strong and confident. He sat quietly in the pew when the choir sang. Some days, it was if she were singing just for him. It was a happy memory, all except for those unpadded pews.

Gillian walked into the room with two glasses of water, cheese and crackers. "Sorry, I'd have been here sooner but I had to wash the glasses."

Marty looked up, excitedly. "I've found something."

She walked over, setting the glasses down on the now cleared bedside table and sat down beside him. He pointed to the passage in Exodus. "She left a clue."

Gillian stared at the Bible, and then at Martin. Her eyes were quizzical. "Okay, what is it?"

He looked at her confused. "There, on the page, can't you see it?"

She looked back at him. "See what?"

Martin looked back at the page. As he did, the watery thin pencil lines of his grandmother's writing dissolved before his eyes. He rubbed his eyes and looked again. The chill ran the length of his spine, ending up as goosebumps on his arms.

Gillian stared at him. "What is it, Marty?"

"No-othing. C-could I have some water p-please?"

She looked at him, with concern. She didn't know he had a stutter. She handed him a glass of water. He drank the entire glass and handed it back to her. His eyes had not deceived him. He *had* seen something. He just knew it. He looked at Gillian in earnest. "I'm pretty sure I know where we need to go."

She looked at him, dubiously. "Pretty sure?"

"Yeah, I'm sure."

There were moments where she relied on her gut. This was one of them. She nodded and smiled. "Okay, let's go."

Marty tucked the Bible to his chest, hugging it, as they walked together to the bathroom.

Chapter 13

Digger kicked a rock from side-to-side under his feet, as he waited at the car for Gillian and Marty to arrive. He mentally calculated the number of rocks that size to fill the interior of his bug. He had become accustomed to waiting and watching. He normally created mental games to amuse himself. He once calculated the trajectory for a rock launched from earth to Venus, only to find that he was off by .00034567 degrees later. It irritated him at times that he needed computers to help him.

He tired of the game and decided to access satellite information to help with his surveillance of the area. Climbing into the car, he tapped into the Internet from his car's system. He began to call up geo-data satellites to see which ones were transmitting today and which grids were being mapped. He could not commandeer one, but he could grab the image and tweak it according to what he wanted to see. Using the internal GPS system in his car, he determined his coordinates and began to plug the latitude and longitude into the uplink to the satellite. He scrolled through the available JPEG's within the last half hour. The system began to retrieve a series of images from the feeds. After the images were downloaded, he used image enhancement programs on his hard drive to refine the detail.

He sat patiently, as the system downloaded the

enormous files one by one. Minutes later, the hourglass on his screen finally went away and was replaced by a series of thumbnails. He scanned two of the images before the topography began to resemble the area around him.

Using the graphical interface on his computer, he began to zoom in on the one area where he thought he was. He tinkered and tweaked the image until he could clearly see the top of his little yellow bug. Even though it was in monochrome, he still recognized the car. It was beautiful, even from space. First, he scanned north of his location toward the wooded area. He would not be able to see a single person hiding, but he would be able to spot any vehicles. Chances are no one would think to hide their car from a satellite image.

There was nothing to the north of him. He scanned west toward the farm's pasture land. The images of a large building came into focus. He wasn't even aware that there was a building on the other side of the farm. He ran out of range before he ran out of interest. Going back to the east, he looked toward the road he'd drove in on. At the very edge of the image, he detected the front end of a car parked alongside the road. He guessed that whoever was in the car would be their guests this afternoon, if everything went well. Gillian had laid out a trap for them. All that the other surveillance team had to do was to follow them.

Farther up the road, another car waited. Mostly in the shade, the back end stuck out a little. It looked Japanese. *Maybe it is a Toyota?* That, he guessed, would be the other guest they expected.

Digger's heart pounded, as he kept telling himself, *This is the fun part. This is the fun part.*

Marty had to admit to himself that he felt slightly uncomfortable undressing before three strangers. But then, they were too busy removing their clothing to really notice him. It struck him that all four of them had different ways of disrobing. He had never really thought about it before. Doss folded his clothes neatly and handed them across to Marty. Marty followed suit.

The girls must have trained with firefighters. They peeled off their clothes like grape skins. He could not help but catch a sideways glance at Gillian in her skivvies. Her body was lean and muscular. It must have taken years for her to develop her physical condition. Scars dotted her body like a roadmap of events. Some were long and thin, while others were round. None appeared to be less painful than the other. Even so, she was pretty in an unassuming kind of way.

He forced himself back to the task at hand. He slid on the warm jeans and realized that he had never worn anyone else's clothing before. It felt strange. Once fully clothed, Doss and Cindy slipped out of the door. Doss was holding a cigar box to make the escape look convincing. Gillian whispered behind them, "Remember, Cindy has to drive."

Doss looked back at her and grinned. "That's not a problem. Her daddy always said she was the hell gettin'est youngin' he'd ever had." With that, they were out the door and running down the driveway to the Bronco. Gillian hoped to get it back in one piece.

Moments later, the Bronco spun gravel and dirt, as it hurtled out of its hiding place and sped down the road. It wasn't long before Gillian noticed a Camry not far behind them. The small car struggled to keep up, as it sped in pursuit. The Frenchman would have been infuriated to know that she actually slowed down several times to allow him to catch up. Their purpose was to allow him to chase her, but not to elude him.

She eased up behind a pristine 1970 GTO. Its red and black paint gleamed in the morning sun. As she pulled out to pass the car, the driver swerved over, blocking her from passing him. She eased back behind, staying close to his bumper. She secretly smiled. Finally, there was something to make this a little interesting.

Reggie had spent years restoring the GTO. He would be damned if he was going to let some *woman* in a piece of crap Bronco pass him. He grabbed the soda bottle from the cup holder on the door, spit tobacco juice into the container and gripped the wheel. He'd show her.

Cindy shook her head. *Amateurs*. She looked in the rearview mirror to check on the Camry. It was hanging at a safe distance behind her. She would have to time this just right, or the Toyota would be right on her tail.

Doss gulped and looked over at her, nervously. "Is everything okay, Sweetie?"

Without looking at him, she clipped, "Fine." She picked a long downhill slope of the road and edged out again, only to have the GTO driver match her move. She continued to move farther in the left lane and watched as the Detroit steel did the same. Without warning, she snapped the Bronco to the right pulling her back into the right, lane and along the back fender of the GTO. Now, the GTO was in the left lane and she had maneuvered beside him. Reggie wasn't the brightest bulb in the lamp. He was slow to react to the change in his situation.

Doss's knuckles turned white as he gripped the door and waited for the impact. Cindy eased the front end of the Bronco into the rear quarter panel of the GTO. She kissed it so softly that Reggie didn't know that she was even there. She gunned the heavy SUV and yanked it hard to the left. With a sudden tug, the GTO careened into a spin, whirling toward the soft shoulder.

Smoke from the tires boiled from the rear of the GTO, as it moved in a slow arc and then suddenly whipped around, whirling into a one-eighty degree spin. The smell of burnt rubber filled the air around them. Reggie tried to compensate by gunning the engine. It was a classic mistake. Instead of straightening out the car, it made the spin worse. Cindy jammed the emergency brake, locking them in place and allowing the GTO to spin clear. Without seeing the brake lights, the Camry driver was suddenly on top of the Bronco. He yanked the wheel hard to the left, sending the Camry spinning into the soft shoulder.

The small Toyota skidded out of control backward into the brush, along the side of the road. The GTO finally stopped spinning and came to a rest, sideways in the road. She popped the brake off and slowly accelerated past Reggie, without looking. As they passed, Doss looked into the boy's eyes. He shrugged as they went by. He could see the whites of Reggie's eyes and his slack jaw, and snickered out loud when they were clear.

Reggie sat for a moment, staring straight ahead. His knuckles were white on the steering wheel. He looked down at his crotch, which was soaked. He didn't want to think about that right now. He also didn't want to think about the immense wad of tobacco he had just swallowed. He was certain, though, that as much as he didn't want to think about it, he was going to have to—very shortly.

Bernard cursed, as he eased the Toyota out of the brambles. Weeds and dirt clung to the car, dragging as he went down the road. He cursed, as he gunned the small car in the direction of the Bronco.

Cindy slowed over the next rise and almost came to a stop.

Doss stared at her. "What are you doing?"

Her eyes narrowed to an alluring glance, while she gave him a sensual smile. "Waiting."

"For what?"

"Why, the Toyota, Silly." She licked her lips, slowly.

"I thought we were trying to get *away* from the Toyota?"

This time, she rolled her eyes at him. "We wouldn't be much of a decoy, if he couldn't chase us."

Doss shook his head in dismay, realizing that he was just arm candy. Cindy watched as an old man in a Buick pulled out in front of them. *Perfect.* She pulled in behind the Buick and followed at a safe distance. In the distance, she could see the Toyota almost turn sideways, as it crested the hill behind them. Cindy wore a small Mona Lisa smile, as she looked at the traffic coming toward them in the other lane. She would have to be careful, so it didn't look too contrived.

She timed the car in the opposite lane. As it approached them, she pulled into his lane. It was too close for them to avoid. The car began to pull off the road to avoid them. Doss could see the old man in the

Buick muttering, while he jerked the aging car to the shoulder to make room for them pass. Cindy gunned the Bronco, passing the cursing driver in the opposite lane. Doss caught a look at the old man in the Buick. It was McGillacutty. He had prepared his taxes last year.

Doss looked straight ahead. Quietly, he said, "Sweetie, this has gone on long enough. We need to cut this off. That man was a customer."

She gave him a pained sideways look and sighed. "I guess it has been long enough."

"Besides, we have the Ferguson's Baby Shower at two o'clock. We still have to wrap the gifts."

She glanced at her watch. "Oh crap! We've got to get a move on."

He could feel the Bronco accelerate, while the distance between the Bronco and the struggling Camry increased. The Bronco was doing over a hundred when they crossed the Tuttle Bridge. It came off the ground in the dip and skidded sideways into the Iron Jaw Lounge gravel parking lot. Somehow, she managed to miss all the Harley's parked in front and came to a stop a few feet from the building.

They left the doors open, while they hopped out of the truck. The front end pinged from the heat, as they moved away from the vehicle. They plowed through the front door of the biker bar and maneuvered around empty tables to the bar. In the dim light of the smoke-filled room, they could just make out the bartender wiping down the bar. The clatter of a prehistoric air conditioner greeted them.

Sharkie, the bartender, eyed them warily as they came in. At almost seven feet tall on a muscular three hundred and ten pound frame no one challenged him on his turf—that included the likes of Earl Tilley.

Doss looked at Sharkie. "Are you ever going to get that thing fixed?"

Sharkie raised an eyebrow. "Yeah, when it stops running."

He jabbed his thumb at small wooden door marked *Office*. You can change in there. "Clothes are on the desk."

They breezed past him into the cramped office. None of the patrons seemed to notice or care. In less than three minutes, a very different looking couple exited the office. Cindy's brunette hair was now blonde. Her floppy T-shirt was gone, replaced with a sleeveless denim top which showed more cleavage than Doss wanted her to show in public. The cargo shorts were gone, replaced with skin-tight black leather pants.

Doss' strawberry blonde curls were in stark contrast to his now bald head, tanned from hours in the sun. The torn sleeve on the faded *AC/DC* T-shirt worked well with the leather chaps. They both looked right at home.

They eased up to the bar. Without a word, Sharkie slid them each a cold beer. Doss looked up at Sharkie, expectantly. "Are you coming to Mom's on Sunday?"

Sharkie looked at him for a moment, thinking. With a long sigh, he rumbled quietly, "Is it her birthday?"

Doss nodded. "Yes. I've only told you three times."

Sharkie dropped his head. "Dang. How do I keep forgetting that?"

Doss chuckled. "That's why I remind you, Baby Brother."

Sharkie gave him a lopsided grin and nodded. "Thanks." The gravelly response was barely audible.

Cindy cut in. "Has Kathy gone in for her ultrasound yet?"

Sharkie beamed like an expectant father should and his head bobbed up and down. "Uh-huh. It looks like it's going to be a girl."

"Is she excited?"

"Yeah. Me too! I was afraid it was going to be an ugly boy like his father." He revealed a row of pearly white teeth behind the scraggly black beard.

She ignored the comment. "I'm so happy for you guys."

He dropped his head, shyly.

Cindy smiled, reached across the bar and patted him on the hand. "You'll be a good dad. Trust me."

Sharkie gave her a grateful look. Doss kept a watchful eye on the window. As expected, the Camry was in the parking lot and idling beside the Bronco. A tall muscular man with dark hair got out of the car.

Doss gave Cindy a nudge. "We've gotta go. See you Sunday, Bro. Bring those ultra-sound pics, if you can remember them."

The hulk nodded and smiled gently at them. "You guys be careful, okay?"

Cindy raised herself onto the bar and gave Sharkie a warm kiss on the cheek. "We'll be fine. My love to Kathy."

"Uh-huh. You, too."

She hopped off the bar and they moved toward the door. The tall thin man entered, just as Cindy reached the door. She bumped him and didn't look back. Bernard's eyes followed her for an apology. She kept walking. Doss came up behind her. As Bernard turned, he found Doss looking him in the eye.

Doss snarled, menacingly. "What?"

Bernard said nothing. He returned the glare, with a look of disdain and walked away. As he went by, Doss flipped him off. Just outside the door, Cindy was putting on her helmet, straddling an aging Sportster. She looked at Doss, sourly. "Did you have to flip him off?"

He gave her a sideways grin, as he slipped on his helmet. "I didn't *have* to, but it sure felt good."

She shook her head and rolled her eyes. "What a drama queen."

He snickered and eased onto the cushion of his Fat Boy. Not a single patron looked up, as the pair of V-twins roared to life. Sharkie went back to polishing the wooden bar with a rag. Bernard peered around the dark interior for a moment while his eyes adjusted to the dim light. He strode to the bar and sat down.

Sharkie eased down to the stranger. "Help you, Mister?"

Without looking at him, Bernard replied. "A beer, please."

The coldest beer in the county slid toward the Frenchman. Ice fell from the brown glass, as the Frenchmen slid a five across the bar. The cold beer was lost on the Frenchman's palette. But it had been a long morning. Sharkie turned away from the Frenchman and smiled to himself. He thought to himself, *Mister, you've gotta a long wait.*

Gillian and Martin sat in the bathroom for what seemed like an eternity. Marty gripped the Bible like it was going to fly away. He mentally relived the morning's events. He told himself he was under a lot of stress and must have imagined it, but something within him grew like a seed. He couldn't put a finger on it, but he felt different. He tried to convince himself that it didn't have to make sense. It was what happened.

Gillian sat quietly, going over the details of every possible scenario. She considered every possible negative situation. After twenty minutes of waiting, her cell phone lit up. Her tone was low and flat, "Gillian."

"Hey, it's Doss. We dumped him at the bar."

"Any problems?"

"Nah, Cindy had to slow down a couple of times, so he could keep up."

She frowned. "Do you think he suspected anything?"

"I doubt it. I'm not sure how long it will take him to figure out we're not there. It probably won't be very long, so you guys might want to bail now, while you can."

"Thanks Doss. My best to Cindy."

"You, too." With that, the phone chirped off.

Marty looked across at her. "Gillian?"

"Yes, Marty?"

"I know you have a plan and all, but I have an idea."

She paused for a moment, as all her carefully laid plans drifted out the window like dandelion petals on a warm summer day. "I'm listening."

He smiled. "Come on."

They exited the house through a hidden kitchen door into the back yard. This was something she hadn't considered. The door put them on the opposite side of the house and away from prying eyes. Marty led her across a short distance through the overgrown yard and into the forest behind the house. It was here that she noticed a faint path before them. It had been a while since it had been used. The undergrowth came over their shoes, but not much further. They followed the path until the house was completely out of sight. They stomped their way through the undergrowth and suddenly broke through the brush onto an old gravel road.

Gillian looked at him, amazed. "How did you know this was here?"

He raised an eyebrow. "I grew up here. Remember?"

They walked in silence up the road. Birds tittered and chirped over them. A squirrel darted in front of Gillian. She paused for a moment, startled. Marty stopped and looked at her, quizzically, "Are you okay?"

"Yeah, I'm just not used to all this nature."

He chuckled. "It grows on you after a while."

The path was shady and cool, compared to the growing heat of the day. As they walked, she could hear the lapping of water in the ebbing pool just off the path. Gillian pointed to the water. "What's that?"

Bemused, he replied, "It's Green Lake."

The road swayed in and out from the water like a dancer. Lush undergrowth peeped out at every turn. It surprised her at how relaxing the walk was after all they had been through. It peeled the layers of stress away. No one seemed to be following them and the walk was idyllic. The road turned and twisted,and at each turn there was something different to see. As they approached an open section of water, Marty's arm went out, catching Gillian squarely on the bosom. He creased his lips with his finger to indicate silence.

She looked at his hand and then at him. He looked down. It occurred where his hand was. He recoiled like she was a snake. She stood still, listening intently for their attacker. She began to lower herself into a crouch, waiting for the attack. Her adrenalin began to pump. She began to take in everything around them at a heightened level of awareness. She strained to hear someone rustling in the undergrowth, but could detect nothing. So she waited quietly at his side for a moment until she could determine the threat level. Slowly, he pointed to the water. It was then that she saw it. Standing proudly in the water, the great blue egret waited patiently for an afternoon snack in a small pool of water. She moved slowly closer to where Marty stood to get a better look. The bird saw her and squawked angrily, as he lifted off. Its broad wings spread six feet across, as it flapped away. She stared at the departing bird.

Proudly, Marty stated, "That was a blue egret. They're pretty common here, but that's the first one I've seen in years."

With the palm of her hand, she smacked the back of his head. "You stopped us for that?"

She walked ahead a few paces and stopped turning toward him. "If you touch me like that again, expect to end up in a cast. Are we clear?"

He nodded numbly, as she stalked away. A few paces down the path, she stopped again. Marty hadn't moved. She glared at him. "Are you coming, or what?"

Sheepishly, he responded. "Yeah. Sorry."

He watched as a Tiger Swallowtail fluttered past them lighting on the bloom of a Pinxter beside the trail.

He decided to keep it to himself. The path sloped up dramatically, making the climb a bit more of a challenge than Marty remembered. As they walked ahead, he could see the trail lighten ahead of them. He could just make out the shape of a building through the trees.

He led them off the dirt path and into a courtyard of a tall brick building. The green grass of the courtyard was so unlike the path they'd just left. They walked around the corner of the building where they found immense stained glass windows punctuating the side of the building. A hint of a tall spire towered over them in the small courtyard.

She looked at him, amazed. "How did you know about this?"

"Barb and I used to walk this way every Sunday morning, if it wasn't raining."

They continued to work their way around to the front of the building. Marty looked about, lost. She watched him for a moment, before asking, "What's the matter?"

Marty stared at the towering red brick structure. "The Church is gone." He shook his head in dismay. He had been so sure it would be in the old church. They continued around to the front of the building where they saw an elderly man tending to the church sign on the front lawn. The older man turned, startled at the scuff of a shoe on pavement. As he straightened, it became apparent to Gillian that he was a tall man. He was taller, in fact, than Marty. His spare build and kind face was capped with a mop of neatly trimmed dark hair. Silver patches sprouted at his sideburns like snowcaps. His large horn-rimmed glasses framed the deep green eyes, which sparkled in the afternoon sun. Marty was surprised that his appearance seemed to have changed little in the last fifteen years.

To Gillian's surprise, Marty's hand popped out toward the gentleman. "Pastor Thomason, it's certainly a pleasure to see you, sir."

With a broadening smile, the elderly pastor squinted at Marty, as he shook his hand. He blinked in the bright sun at Marty for a moment before cocking his head to one side. "Why, Martin Wood, you've grown, Son. I almost didn't recognize you."

It was unlikely that anyone would. Marty was pleased and amazed at the Pastor's recollection. It made things easier. Somehow, the Reverend always seemed to *know* people. It was uncanny. Gillian stood by quietly, unsure on what to do. Without skipping a beat, Marty took a half step backward and made a sweeping motion toward her. "Pastor, I would like for you to meet my girlfriend, Gillian."

Taking her cue, she smiled radiantly and extended her hand. She could play nice when she needed to. Pastor Thomason took her hand and smiled warmly. "A pleasure, my dear." As he shook her hand, he looked into her eyes, it was like he could see straight through to her soul. It unnerved her, but she didn't let it show.

He returned his attention to Marty. "So, Mr. Wood, I guess you're looking for something left here for you?"

Marty tried hard not to look surprised, but failed. Instead, he gave Thomason a sheepish grin and responded, "I wasn't sure, but I thought *it* might be here."

The old man's eyes gleamed, mischievously. Gillian looked on, mystified. She felt like she had missed the punch-line on an inside joke. Pastor Thomason eased himself between the couple and placed a gentle hand on each shoulder. "Come on, kids. Let's talk about this inside, out of the hot sun."

He led them around the front of the church to the side where a small red brick chapel gleamed in the afternoon sun. Martin smiled. Pastor Thomason looked down at him and winked. "You didn't think we would tear it down, did you?"

Marty looked a little embarrassed and said, "I wasn't sure."

Thomason patted him on the back. "We use it as a fellowship hall during the week and as a pulpit on Homecoming Sundays. It was designated as a historic landmark by the state some years back. I have a feeling it will be here for some years to come." He changed the subject. "So, what do you think of the new sanctuary?"

Marty looked at it, earnestly. "It's beautiful. It must've cost a lot to build?"

"It did. And for that, you should be very proud."

Marty looked at him, quizzically. "I'm not sure I follow?"

The Pastor smiled. "Barb donated the money to ensure it was built."

Marty's jaw dropped. He stopped in his tracks. "Pardon me?"

The old Reverend gently patted him on the back, propelling him forward. "We have plenty of time for that later. You kids look thirsty. Let's go inside and have some of Rose's iced tea. Shall we?"

"Uh, yeah, that would be great. Thanks." Marty hoped he would make sense of all this some day. He had a sickening feeling that he was going to put some therapist's kids through college, though.

Inside, the corridor was dark and cool. It smelled of polish and pine cleaner. The tile floors beneath them shown like a mirror in the dim light. Their feet squeaked on the clean floors, as they walked to the Pastor's office. Thomason poked his head in the church secretary's office and asked, "Rose, would you be so kind as to round us up some of your wonderful iced tea for our guests?"

Rose Tilley looked up. Smiling brightly, she responded, "Why certainly." She looked at the young couple, curiously. It seemed like she had seen them somewhere before, but she just couldn't place it.

The Reverend ushered them into his office and motioned Marty and Gillian to two old comfortable wing-back chairs. The leather squeaked, as they settled back. He studied Marty for a moment before saying, "I guess you didn't know that your grandmother contributed all the money to have the new sanctuary built, did you?"

Marty acknowledged by shaking his head. "You're sure it was Barb? Bess seemed to have all the money."

Thomason gave him a knowing smile and continued "Shortly before your grandmother passed on, she made a rather considerable contribution to the church. Your aunt and uncle stepped up and took over the day-to-day affairs of the farm, and have run it for quite a while, but the Will filed in the County Clerk's office holds it in trust for you."

"She left fifty acres to Faye. Your aunt and uncle have sold off most of the livestock and their portion of the land. The house is yours, but she did put a caveat in the will that let Faye and Mal stay there until they passed." His eyes twinkled, as he said, "That kept them away from you. Barb was shrewd that way. Since they couldn't sell the house or borrow money off of it, they just lived there. But then, I'm assuming you're aware of all this?"

Marty cleared his throat, somewhat uncomfortably, "Well, actually, to be honest, I haven't kept in touch with them the way I should have."

The Pastor smiled innocently. "So, are you visiting with your aunt and uncle, while you're here?"

Marty shifted in his chair. "Not exactly, Sir. We don't really get along that well."

The Reverend smiled and nodded, knowingly. "I understand. The Good Book teaches us to *love* one another, but it doesn't say we have to *like* one another."

Rose tapped on the door, as she entered with tall glasses of tea with lemon. Marty took a long drag of the amber liquid. It was the best thing he had put to his lips all day. It was strong, sweet and as cold as an artic ice flow. *It doesn't get much better than this.*

The Pastor smiled at Rose "Thank you, Rose. Would you be so kind as to close the door on your way out?"

He had worked with Rose for many years. She was the most organized church secretary he had ever known, and probably the worst gossip in the county. What he had to share with Martin was for him, and him alone. The Reverend knew that the tidbit about the near scandalous activity by Faye and Mal would keep her on the phone for the next hour at least. That would be plenty of time to share what he needed to with Marty. *Who knows, it might even give poor old McGillicutty a rest from the Blue Haired Gang for a while?* As the heavy oak door clicked shut, the Reverend turned to face Marty. He wasted no time getting to the point. "Martin, your grandmother was dearly loved by everyone in this congregation. To this day, people still make memorials in her name." The Reverend laced his fingers, forming a 'church and steeple'. He pressed his index fingers to his lips and looked at Marty soberly for a moment for a moment before continuing. "However, there was a side of her that few people knew about; a secret, if you will. I was very fortunate that she entrusted me with her secret. We both knew that some day, fate would drive you to seek me out." He swiveled the old desk chair around to face an enormous antique leaded glass bookcase behind him. He eased open the glass door and removed a small wooden box from the bottom shelf. He slid the small ornately carved wooden box across the desk to Marty. "This box has waited patiently in that bookcase for twenty years for you. It should have been passed on by your father. I'm sorry that could not be, but I am honored that I have been a part of this piece of history, though."

Marty stared at the box, transfixed. It was beautifully carved. The top was adorned with a flared Tudor Cross, while the sides were carved with intricate flowers. Gillian sat quietly, wondering whether she was witnessing history. She wished she knew more about why they were there, or why this was so important. Instead, she considered how easily this artifact had been handed over. Somehow, it seemed so small. She always thought it would be something bigger. She shifted in her chair, nervously. She could feel herself getting edgy from the anticipation of what was in the box. She smiled to herself. All this time, Franz had thought it was locked in some vault or hidden a cave. It never occurred to any of them that it was in the custody of an elderly pastor in a rural Baptist church, without so much as a lock protecting it—whatever *it* was.

The Reverend had held the stone for Barb for twenty years. In many ways, he was glad to be rid of it. But then, there was a side of him that would miss it. All those who touched it were left with a mark so indelible, it could never be stricken from them. He was no different. Transfixed, Marty stared at the box. He seemed oblivious to everything around him, save the little wooden box. The Reverend felt Marty's mind adjusting to the presence of the stone like a series of locks being opened. The stone sang in siren's harmony in a language forgotten long ago. In time, it would tell the story of why he was here.

In the meantime, he would not notice anything around him. It would give him a chance to work with Gillian. As she looked on at Marty, the old man focused on her thoughts. He could see that her mind was fractured by years of the unspeakable horror of killing again and again. It was not his place to be her judge, but it was his duty to be her healer. He could feel Gillian's rising apprehension with him. Instinctively, she was afraid, and yet she needed help so badly. If he did not help her, she would be lost within herself. The old man looked deep within her and saw the struggle. He witnessed the dueling personalities; the conflicts of her past, the uncertainty of her present, and her lack of perception of the future. It was her survival instinct that kept her cold and hard, and focused on the mission. But she was detached, devoid of any true feelings. It kept her emotional intelligence from growing. She desperately wanted to change, but could not seem to break free.

Even at this early stage of their relationship, Thomason could see that she had deep feelings for Martin which she repressed. They were the same feelings she suppressed every time she was attracted to a young man. The preacher could see the demons, as they snapped and snarled every time her heart tried to step forth. Healing her was going to be a challenge. Quietly, he studied her. It was her father who continued to push her at every turn. She was his puppet and he wasn't even living. He sensed no birthday cakes or Christmas trees in her past. She had no close friends and had been robbed of any kind of a normal childhood. At her core, he could see the little girl begging to come out, longing to be released. As he turned the pages of her psyche, he could see the emotional numbness. She was trapped within herself. It troubled him to see in her in such pain. At every turn, her father's formidable will blocked her from changing.

The Reverend could see a path of self-destruction within her. It led to a senseless death to honor a man long dead and forgotten. Joseph knew if she was to face what lay ahead, she would have to be something more than a robot waiting for its next order. This was going to be painful for her, but it was necessary. He saw no other way. The old man chose his next words carefully. In a voice practiced in years of delivering a message from the pulpit, he drew her in. He pulled her attention away from Marty and the box for a moment. "Gillian?"

Mesmerized, she blinked. Her eyes were round and wide, like a child's.

"I know we hardly know each other, but I need to

share something with you."

She seemed distracted, and she nodded distantly.

"I know you and Martin have only been together for a short while now and it is a lot to ask, but you both face some very difficult times ahead. Martin needs you at his side. Is this something you are ready for?"

She nodded like a five year old.

"Make no mistake. This will be more difficult for you than anything you have ever done."

She turned her gaze to Marty for a moment, reassuring herself that it was worth it. *He* is worth it. She turned back to the preacher and nodded. The old man reached slowly across the desk with outstretched hands. He held his large, soft hands open to her, and smiled at her kindly. "Place your hands in mine, Child."

She forced herself to let go, against a sudden crash of alarm bells within her. Strangely, she almost felt compelled, as though she was under a spell. Timidly, she moved her hands toward his. As their palms met, he clamped his fingers closed on her hands. She could not move. A sudden surge of energy came from the old man's fingers into her. It was as though a bolt of lightning coursed through her. A floodgate of emotions welled forth like a dam collapsing. She struggled against the maelstrom of memories, as they wrangled out of the darkness of her subconscious and into the light. Her eyes widened, as fear, awe and anger welled forth, followed by angst, remorse, wonder and love. Emotions flowed through her in a torrent. It staggered her for a moment. She could feel the old man reaching into her mind, probing. She tried to push him away, but he pushed past her like she were a child. She couldn't hide from him. She felt violated. She gritted her teeth in anger, as tears forced out of the corners of her eyes. She would kill him to stop him. Strangely, he was unafraid of her. Her eyes burned, as she focused on the old man's face. His face transformed before her to the face of her father she struggled against. It was only then that she began to see the walls within her. It was only then that she understood her true fear. It was then that she realized that even though her father was long since dead, she still feared losing his respect. It was upon this revelation that the walls began to crack. Calmness ebbed forth like the trickle before the levies break. In the stillness of the morning calm, a peace she never knew existed began to grow and flow through her. It was far different from anything she would have expected.

Thomason watched, as the calm washed over her like a baptism. He smiled. For the first time in her life, she was free. He ever so gently released her hands and leaned back in his chair, exhausted. He sat quietly, radiating his glow outward. Her hands dropped limply back into her lap. She sat back and continued to relax across from him.

She sat for a moment, groggy and disoriented, like she had awakened from a long terrible dream. For the first time in her life, she saw a future for herself. A single tear formed in the corner of her eye, followed by another. She sat confused, trying to understand where the flood of tears was coming from. Thomason pushed a box of tissues toward her. She dabbed her eyes. She could not remember ever crying. She choked, as she managed a small laugh. "You know, this job was a lot easier when people were just shooting at me."

His voice was calm. "Gillian, I know that was hard

for you. It takes most people years to arrive at what you have come to realize in just a few moments. You're a brave young woman. I admire and respect you."

She stared at him in disbelief for a moment. This was the first time anyone had ever given her an affirmation. The feeling was overwhelming.

"You face a dangerous time ahead, but you are both strong. You must trust and rely on each other's strengths. Martin will need your trust to do what he is destined to do. Your fates are intertwined. Never underestimate the power you give to each other."

She blinked at him. She hardly knew this man. *How could anyone know this?* The Reverend smiled and stood. The spell seemed to break. She smiled at him, weakly. "Thank you" was all she could manage.

He smiled at her as a parent smiles at a child. Marty's gaze was frozen on the box. He still hadn't reacted to them.

The Reverend broke the moment by speaking loudly enough for Rose to hear, "Well kids, I need to finish changing the sign out front. I'll give you some time alone. Let me know if there's anything you need."

He placed a hand on Marty's shoulder, as he came around the desk. Marty stirred for the first time since the box was presented. "Let me know if you need to talk, Son."

Marty blinked, distantly "Uh, yeah, okay. Thanks."

The preacher left, closing the heavy wooden door firmly behind him. Gillian sat dazed for a moment. She looked at Marty. "I'm not sure what just happened here? It was as though he was looking straight through me. Do you think we can trust this guy?"

It was like he was seeing her for the first time. She

absolutely glowed with radiance. "I don't see why we wouldn't trust him. Barb trusted him enough to hold the box. He waited twenty years for me to come for it, and then hands it over and leaves. I don't understand how you could demonstrate more trustworthiness, if you tried?"

Gillian nodded. He was right. She tried to sort out feelings of insecurity. It wasn't something she was used to. She shrugged off the feeling and changed the subject. "Well? Are you going to open it?" She looked at Marty like an expectant six year old on Christmas morning.

He grinned. "A bit impatient are we?"

She rolled her eyes, but said nothing. He eased the box toward himself and lifted the cover. The wood was old and dark with age. The unhinged lid lifted off easily, revealing the carefully folded amber silk within. He set the lid aside, laying it carefully on the desk beside the box. He removed the small piece of silk, uncovering the contents of the box. A multi-faceted blue stone the size of his thumb lay nestled in amber velvet. Both stared at the gem and then at each other. He gingerly reached in for the stone, almost afraid he would break it. At the slightest touch of his finger on the jewel, a jolt of energy shot through his arm and paralyzed him. He sat with his finger frozen to the stone, like a block of ice. He sat paralyzed, incapable of speaking or moving. He didn't know what to do.

As he touched the gem, Gillian watched him twitch. She reached toward him and found that her hand could not touch him. Every time she reached toward him, her hand was repelled by some unseen force. She moved her hand up and down his arm, and found his body was encased in an energy field. She relentlessly pushed at the field, but to no avail. There was no reaching him and he was only a foot away. She fought to control the panic, convincing herself that this was supposed to happen. She sat back and waited for the force field to subside.

Marty blinked, while his eyes adjusted to his surroundings. He was no longer in the Pastor's study. He stood in a long hallway. The thick, rich carpet was soft under his bare feet. He couldn't remember how he got here. He certainly couldn't remember taking his shoes off. The hall seemed to stretch without end. Small butler's tables with Tiffany lamps and flower arrangements against the wooden walls with deep rich carpet gave it a warm, calm feel. He looked in both directions. It seemed endless. Solid heavy paneled doors dotted the corridor much like a hotel hall. He stood for a moment, not quite sure what to do. "Gillian?"

His voice fell into the silence.

"Anyone here?"

There was no response.

He opened the door closest to him. It led him into a cave. The sandy soil beneath his feet was cool. The air was thick, with musty smelling smoke. As he strained his eyes against the meager light, he could see a young man ahead digging furiously with a shovel. "Hello?"

The young man took no notice of him. He continued to dig like a man possessed. He threw down the handle and began to dig with his hands. He stopped suddenly and reached forward. Marty could just make out the blue stone in his hand, a stone very much like the one Marty had just touched only moments ago. A sudden flash of light presented a figure before them. The figure of a man seemed to take no more notice of Marty than the young man digging. He listened, as they spoke in a foreign tongue. It made no sense to him. Something about the figure made Marty pause. He backed toward the door he had come in and shut it, leaving him back in the hall.

He wandered farther down the hall. He opened the next doorway into the gray stone walls of a forgotten castle. A large surly man carefully carved on a small wooden box before him. He brushed his unruly red hair to the side, as it fell into his eyes. The box looked identical to the one the stone was in.

"Excuse me?"

The man took no notice of him, but continued to work. Marty watched for a while, and stepped into the hall once again. For what seemed like an eternity, he wandered from one door to the next. Each room was a different period and place. The only consistency was the stone. It was like walking through a living diorama of the stone's history. Finally, he reached a door he could not open. Try as he may, the door remained shut. He sat for a moment, wondering what he should do before moving on. The next door opened easily.

As he entered, he encountered a thin man dressed in white suit who sat comfortably in a large leather chair, reading. His skin was so pale it that was almost translucent. His fingers were long and delicate, as he flicked through the book.

The library was enormous. Books on shelves reached as far up as Marty could see. Marty didn't know such a place existed. He stood patiently and waited for another scene to unfold before him. None did. Much to his surprise, after a moment, the silver-haired man looked up at him. "Hello, Martin, I've been expecting you."

Marty blinked in surprise. Civilly, he responded, "I'm sorry. I didn't expect for you to see… I mean, look, I mean…"

The silver-haired man smiled. "You mean, speak?"

His hand swept to a chair before him, motioning Marty to sit.

He eased back in the comfortable, leather wingback. "Well, yeah. That sums it up nicely."

"My apologies for what must seem like a winding journey to this point. I have no way of controlling what the Sappire will show you or how. My purpose is to help you to understand the responsibility of protecting your legacy."

"I'm sorry. Who are the *Sappire* and what is this *legacy*?"

The man in white chuckled. "The Sappire are not so much of a *whom* as a *what*. They are the Sapphires bequeathed to you by your family. But they are more than simple baubles. The stones were commissioned by the creator and given to the twelve tribes at Mount Sinai. You are bound to the Sappire like your ancestors. You hold within you the morphic memory of every ancestor who has faithfully guarded the stone before you. Your family has protected it from prying eyes, thieves and warfare for centuries. The doors you passed through before me were your ancestors and their contributions to the Sappires' secrecy."

"There was one door I could not open. Why?"

"It was not the proper time for you to open it."

"Will I ever be able to open it?"

The tall man gestured Marty to sit across from him. "Perhaps someday you will, but not this day. Instead, let us discuss the *jewels* for a moment."

"Did you say jewels, as in plural?"

"Yes. There are twenty-four in all. Half are Sappires, half are their lodestones. There is another jewel you must seek that is the mate to the one you now possess. They form a lock and key, of sorts."

Marty looked confused. "A key to what?"

The thin man smiled. "All in good time."

Marty felt lost. "How will I know how to find this other stone?"

"The Sappire will guide you."

Marty contemplated this for a moment. "So this stone will lead me to another stone?"

"Correct."

"So, when I find the next stone, what do I do?"

"That is difficult to say. There is purpose in all the stones reveal. I will help you along the way as much as possible, but there are aspects even I do not know to the stones."

None of this made sense. Marty tried another angle. "So, where do I begin to look?"

"Your trail leads to France. You must follow your instincts there."

Marty sat back, somewhat exasperated. "I don't get any other instruction other than *go to France*?"

He smiled, patiently. "You must realize that what you face is not just the quest of a single gem. There is so much more at stake. What you are about to embark upon is more about the journey than the destination."

Marty frowned. He wasn't big on word games and scavenger hunts.

The stranger's hair seemed to glow now, as he spoke. "Look around you."

Marty looked up. There was row after row of books, for as far as he could see. "All I see are books."

"And what do books represent?"

"Knowledge, I guess?"

"It is important for you to realize that all this accumulated information cannot help you on your path."

He looked at his companion, skeptically. "Well, there must be something here?"

The man stood and walked across the room to him. He touched his forehead. Marty could feel the warmth of the touch, but could not see the small glowing spot left behind on his forehead.

"There are parts of your life that must be experienced to be understood. Books can only be written in retrospect. You are forging ahead on a new path. With that, comes a certain uniqueness to be entrusted to those demonstrate the character necessary to handle the power of the Ark."

Marty felt like he was taking a test that he hadn't studied for. "I'm sorry, but I don't understand."

The thin man smiled. "You will."

Marty blinked. Everything he had ever learned had come from a book, or so it seemed. The thin man continued. "Your perception of the world has changed. Accept it. This is how the Sappir's will guide you. Accept it and move on."

Marty appeared a little troubled. The stranger placed a comforting hand on his shoulder. "Be not afraid. You will become accustomed to your new talents."

Without as much as a warning, the room began to glow with a piercing white light consuming everything around them. Marty squinted against the bright light, only to see it wink away as quickly as it had started. As he opened his eyes, he found Gillian staring at him. Gillian repeated her question. "Marty, can you hear me?"

Marty blinked at her and looked around the room. "Of course. Why are you shouting?"

She stared at his eyes, which now glowed with an eerie blue light. Her voice lowered an octave. "Sorry. You didn't seem to be able to hear me."

He looked all around him. "Did you see it?"

She stared at him, quizzically. "See what?"

"The room, the old man, the bright light—any of it?"

She frowned and shook her head.

He sat for a moment, reliving the experience. It amazed him that she had seen nothing. He looked at her and said, "We need to go to France."

She looked at him, incredulously. "We need to go where?"

"France. You know, they make a lot of wine, wedged between Germany and Spain."

"I know *what* France is. I just need to know *why* we need to go there."

"Because that is where we need to be."

She frowned. "You're not making any sense. Plus, you're starting to weird me out here." She began to shake her head. "I don't need this now."

He was making her feel a trifle unhinged. She wasn't sure when, but at some point she had obviously lost control of the situation. She wasn't sure how to report any of this. Franz would think she had flipped. At this point, she wasn't sure that she hadn't.

Marty smiled. "Trust me. It's what we must do." Gently, he placed his hand on hers. As he did, her eyes glazed over. She began to see what he had seen. Marty let go and watched as she sagged back in the big chair. Her chest heaved, breathing heavily. She blinked several times and then looked up at him. In a small voice, she stammered, "I-I'll make the arrangements. I-It'll take a few calls."

He placed the lid back on the box and slipped it into his pocket. They sat quietly for a few moments before leaving the small office.

****

Hours later, light from the setting sun filtered into the small office, bathing it in amber. Joseph Thomason removed the letter of resignation from his top desk drawer. It was yellow with age, having been drafted years ago and put away. It awaited only a date. Carefully, he wrote in the date and dropped it on his desk for Rose to find. The associate Pastor Ryan was long overdue to assume the duties of the church. He left the study door cracked when he picked up the phone to call Pastor Ryan. He knew Rose would circulate word around the church faster than they could get a bulletin out.

Chapter 14

They made sure they were out of the sonar-like ears of Rose Tilley before Gillian made the call to Franz. The phone rang only once before she heard his familiar voice answer. "Yes, Gillian."

"Sir, we have the target. However, Mr. Wood informs me that there is another piece we need to recover. We need travel plans to France as soon as possible."

"I'll see to it. Is Delgado still with you?"

"I'm calling him next."

"When the three of you are together, proceed to the closest airport. I believe it's Charlotte and I will have everything you need there waiting tomorrow morning."

"Sir?"

"Yes, Gillian?"

"We don't have any travel documents."

"Not to worry. I will have passports waiting for all of you."

"Very good." They both disconnected.

Marty looked at her, curiously. "Are you sure you're not in the military?"

She smiled at him, sheepishly. "No. But I used to be. That's where I met Cindy. Our fathers served in the same unit. It is the only lifestyle I've ever known. She and I served together in the Marines."

"Which branch was your dad in?"

"Most of them."

Marty looked at her, quizzically. "I thought people just served in one branch?"

"Most do. In my dad's case, they put him where they needed him. He was different." She changed the subject. The thoughts of her dad disturbed her for some reason. "Does it bother you that I was in the military?"

He smiled. "You've kept me alive and fed for the past two days. I'm not complaining."

She returned his smile. "Speaking of which, hold that thought for a moment."

She dialed Digger's number. "Hey, Dig. Can you get us out of here?"

She couldn't see it, but she knew Digger was smiling wherever he was. "Of course. You know I live to make your life better."

"Yeah, whatever. Please be careful. These people are very different people than what you're used to."

"I get that. Where do you want me to pick you up?"

She blinked for a second. "Hold on."

She looked at Marty. "Just exactly where are we, anyway?" He smiled at her.

Dourly, she handed the phone to Marty. "Yo Dude, what's up?"

"Where are you guys, anyway?"

He was surprised at how comfortable he felt giving Digger directions. It felt like he had known him for years instead of hours. Digger disconnected the line and calculated the time. By the most direct route, he could be there in ten minutes. But he wanted to impress Gillian with how clever *he* could be. He would show her he could do it her way, with a slight of hand. He scrolled to *Billy* on his phone. It was time to call in the troops.

****

Marty and Gillian slowly meandered to the shade of an old oak. They sat under the canopy of broad leaves, with the small chapel to their back. The freshly painted, white picnic table felt slick to the touch. They waited, sheltered from the warm sun by the ancient oak. A cool breeze soothed the morning's tension. It was the first time they had sat without something looming over them. Silently, both of them tried to rationalize all that had happened. Marty felt numb from the strain of receiving so much information. As he sat, an unexpected vision intruded his thoughts. All else faded, as his attention turned to the vision. His perspective was that of being on the floor looking up, behind two men. He couldn't see either of them very well. His field of view panned around an opulent room, balanced with books and art. He felt the sensation of leaping and then he could see neither face. He could still hear them speaking.

"…the plans are falling into place…should be within our grasp…only a few more arrangements…"

As suddenly as it came, the vision winked away. Marty had a feeling deep in the pit of his stomach that something was terribly wrong.

Gillian broke the silence. "Are you feeling okay?"

He looked at her, warily. "I'm okay, just a little tired, I guess. Thanks."

"How does it feel?"

Marty looked at her, distractedly. "What do you mean?"

"I've never experienced anything like that. I

received a second hand dose. I guess what I'm trying to ask, is, do you feel any different than before you were given the stone?"

His eyes were far away. "I am different. I wish I could explain how, but it's hard to put into words. I feel like a radio. I keep receiving images, but I can't tune them in, if that makes any sense."

Her smile was far away. "I think I do understand. The preacher opened my eyes to a lot of things." Her voice trailed off. That didn't come out the way she wanted. She always felt like she was saying the wrong thing. *Where did that thought come from?*

Marty nodded. "For the first time in my life, I feel like I'm connected to something." He looked down as he spoke. "I felt like I was drifting through life, with no particular purpose to anything I did. Does that make any sense?"

She nodded. "I think so." She really didn't. Her whole life had a purpose. As an assassin, motherhood and apple pie didn't factor in to it.

He looked at her, solemnly. "There's one thing you need to know."

"What?"

"I think we have a spy among us."

That got her attention. Her eyes narrowed, while her voice took a strained edge. "What do you mean? Who is it?"

"I don't know. I just get the feeling that something is not right."

She looked at him. "Marty, this isn't a game. You can't just say something like that and leave it. I must know who it is."

He shook his head. "Honestly, I can't. I only

caught a glimpse of him. I have never seen him before. I saw two people discussing us, but I didn't get anything more. Please trust me. You'll know as soon as I know."

She looked into his eyes. She knew when someone was lying to her. There was no deception in his eyes. There was an uncomfortable silence. Marty sat silently, wishing he hadn't said anything at all. The longer he sat, the more lethargic he felt.

"Marty, are you okay?"

Distantly, he said, "Yeah, I'm okay. I'm just feeling a little washed out."

He looked exhausted. She patted him on the shoulder and said, "Digger will be here soon. We'll get you to some place safe where you can rest."

Marty nodded in acknowledgement. He could hear her, but it was like she was far away. He knew she would look after him. He wasn't sure how he knew this. He just did. They sat quietly for a while on the picnic table. A hint of lilac traveled on the cool north wind. The oak tree rustled and swayed in the afternoon breeze. Everything was quiet save the chatter of cardinals arguing over food and territory. Marty's head nodded forward. Gillian guided him gently into her lap. He was asleep before he ever touched her leg.

Chapter 15

Digger eased the VW onto the main road and headed back toward town. He watched the stoic pair tailing him in a faded green Ford Explorer. They were just within sight. A shiver of nervous excitement washed over him, as he anticipated how he would elude them. He hoped that it wouldn't end too soon.

He fiddled with the radio, as he continued north toward West Bend, as the Explorer followed at a discreet distance. Within minutes, traffic began to increase, as the town of two thousand swelled from work traffic from the surrounding county. Digger coasted into ever-present runway lights of the Snack Shack, where a small contingent of foreign cars surrounded the building. Several were bugs, like his own. Others were tricked and toned in various states of assembly. The cast of characters was as diverse as the vehicles they touted. Little Richard's the banana yellow sported red stripes front to back to the whopped and chopped profile. Jersey Nick's bug rested on wide profile chrome wheels that cost more than the car itself. Billy Slade looked quite plain on initial inspection. Yet, he received a weekly noise citation because of his sound system.

Jimmy, the owner/cook, yelled over the speakers at the parking spots. "You boys gonna order, or run off all the other paying customers?" He slung hamburgers to the tunes of the Beach Boys, wishing he were with them.

Digger glided into the vacant spot and hopped out to a chorus of yells and cat calls. While he cut up, he kept a watchful eye on the high tight pair across the street at the auto parts store. He leaned against his car and started the pitch. "Dudes, are you up for some games?" Nods and grins reflected their eagerness for anything out of the ordinary. A shadow fell over Digger, as Little Richard eased up beside him and leaned against the bug. His towering stature loomed over Digger, his clothing strained to contain his powerful physique. However, it was his shrewd eye that set him apart. He glanced discreetly at the stone-faced men across the street. He pegged them the moment he saw them. Those men were far from anything this little town had seen, much like his friend Digger. "So, surfer boy, do I take it we are going to toy with those nasty white boys in the green cracker box across the street?"

Digger gave him a small sideways grin. "Cracker box? You do know my parents drive an Explorer, right?"

Richard smiled back. "Well, I'm sure *they* make it look good."

"Okay Dudes, this is what I want to do..." They all gathered around and tittered like a bunch of debutants.

Fifteen minutes later, Digger washed down the last of his cheeseburger with a chocolate milkshake. He was truly going to miss this place. The small clutch chatted and laughed in the warm afternoon sun. The pair across the street waited patiently, while the group of boys took verbal gabs at each other. Digger's yellow bug was the last car to ease out of the lot and into cross town traffic.

Even in such a small town, it was becoming difficult to follow him as factory workers began to commute home. Digger drove carefully with no sense of urgency, as he cut down a side street. The green Explorer tailed him doggedly, trying to keep the gap closed as much as possible in the traffic. Digger slowly accelerated, opening the gap up a bit. Before the surveillance team realized it, they were at a disadvantage. The Explorer driver accelerated, trying to close the distance when a red Volkswagen turned in front of them, cutting them off. Throwing caution to the wind, the Explorer shot past the Volkswagen only to find a yellow VW coming at him from the opposite lane.

The passenger in the Explorer cursed under his breath. "Watch it, Boyd, they're playing some kind of game here!"

Boyd glanced at the weapon in his partner's hand. "Matthews, whatever you do, don't hit the Delgado kid. I don't care about the rest of them, but we've got to have him alive."

Matthews glared at him. "Yeah, I know. Christ, I miss Iraq."

Boyd nodded, glumly. Matthews jabbed his finger at a cross intersection ahead. "There he is," he barked, pointing to a yellow bug which shot across in front of them two blocks ahead.

Boyd slammed on the brakes, as another VW cut in front of him from a sidestreet. Matthews was becoming visibly agitated by the cat and mouse game. He fidgeted with the gun. Boyd accelerated the Explorer. Instead of trying to pass the car in front of them, he closed the distance, ramming the smaller car in the rear. Using the weight and power of the bigger SUV, he gunned the motor and pushed the smaller car off the street and through purple pansies and the picket fence of a meticulous front yard. The car lurched to a bumpy stop just before hitting a large white oak. Billy's eyes were wide and his face was pale, as they passed him.

Boyd leered at Matthews. "Man, that felt good."

Matthews sneered back. "Hell, yeah."

There was no pretense now. They powered ahead, closing in on Digger's yellow VW. Digger quickly jogged the wheel into the service entrance of a strip mall. Both vehicles careened through the maze of dumpsters and truck trailers, along the back row of buildings. Digger slalomed the VW back and forth, missing trash containers and orphaned shopping carts by mere inches. Boyd drove with abandon. He pushed the heavy SUV through the channel like a snowplow, leaving a trail of collateral damage in his wake.

Digger eased the car closer to the wall. Matthews lip curled into a sneer. He had the rookie now. He eased closer to the VW, crowding the small car closer to the wall. Suddenly, they were free of the alley, as they reached the end of the complex.

In one deft move, Digger cut sharply to the left and jammed the brakes, skidding to a stop. The Explorer shot past him, only to see Digger's head turned, smiling at them as they passed. Matthews hit the brakes, cursing loudly. As he crashed past the barricade he pressed the pedal harder only to find there was nothing to stop them but air. For a split second Boyd and Matthews were weightless floating in space. One second later, their journey ended with a sickening crunch of bending metal, as the behemoth landed at the bottom of an enormous sink hole.

Digger reflected, as Billy sipped on a chocolate milkshake. "It's supposed to be the biggest one in the state, you know." Nick's head had bobbed in agreement. Thinking back to that moment, Digger couldn't have agreed more. This was truly the biggest sink hole he had ever seen. He eased the bug into reverse. Heading back down to the main street, he raised his hand to Richard as he drove by. The young man responded with a smile and signed *peace*. Digger eased the VW south to go pick up Marty and Gillian.

It was Boyd who managed to drag himself from the passenger seat and to scratch and claw his way to the top first. It was every man for himself at this point. He cursed and muttered, as he struggled against the slick red clay. He grabbed at roots and rocks, struggling to pull himself up. Even with years of military training, the climb proved to be a challenge. Muddy and mad, he muttered to himself, as he hauled himself from the hole. "If I get my hands on the little twerp…"

He reached the edge of the opening and grabbed blindly over the edge. His hand slapped something that felt like a shoe, only bigger. He gripped it and pulled up. As he slowly pulled himself forward, he found that he had indeed grabbed a rather large left shoe of a rather expensive pair of Italian loafers.

He stopped to let his eyes follow the loafers up the tree trunk leg and out of sight to the face above. Boyd didn't wait for any witty dialog. He reached for his Beretta in the small of his back. He never made it. There was a sudden enormous pressure on his wrist, as a hand the size of a small ham gripped him firmly. Another hand (or foot) pushed his face into the asphalt. It didn't matter. Either way, it hurt. He couldn't move.

He didn't think that was possible.

He could feel himself being relieved of the Beretta.

He heard Matthews grunt, as a size nine and a half Nike connected with his jaw. A second later, there was a thud as Matthews landed back on the top of the Explorer fifteen feet below.

The Brown Italian loafers had a deep baritone voice. "Who's paying for the damages to my friend's car?"

Jeez. Boyd wished he had the gun back, so he could shoot himself. They would never get work again, if this got out.

****

Marty stood on a short stool, as he finished washing the last of the mixing bowls and spoons while dinner cooked in the oven. The kitchen smelled of roast and potatoes. His stomach growled, begging for just a taste. Bess came in and placed an affectionate hand on his head. She bent over and kissed him on the top of his head. He looked up at her and smiled.

Cupping his cheeks in her soft hands, she reached over and gently kissed him on the forehead. "I don't know what I've done to deserve such a sweet-natured grandchild. It's been a long day for you. Why don't you go to your room and take a little nap before dinner? I'll get you up when it's time to eat, okay?"

With a small beatific smile, he nodded and climbed down from the stool. Obediently, he headed off to his room with his little gray companion bounding at his feet. Marty considered that Gertrude liked nap time a little too much, but then she was a kitten.

He crawled into the bed and fluffed the oversize down pillow before he lay back in the bed. The sheets smelled fresh from being outdoors. He lay back and enjoyed the smell. Evidently, Gertrude enjoyed it as well, as she sniffed all around him on the bed. He lay back with his arms behind his head. As he did, Gertrude chirped and nestled happily against his side. Occasionally, he reached down to scratch her behind the ear. She sounded like a small motor boat beside him.

This had to be heaven. The aroma of roast and potatoes, mixed with the freshness of the bed. Gertrude was happily oblivious to all but his company, as she curled contently next to him. Peacefully, he drifted into a nap. He dreamed of being back on the farm. Barb was standing beside him, smiling just like always. She pulled him close, hugging him like she hadn't seen him in a while. He squeezed her back. He thought to himself, *it is all been a big mistake. She isn't really dead, after all. Everything is going to be just like it was before.*

Barb smoothed his hair from his eyes. "Hello, Pumpkin. Have you been a good boy?"

"Oh, yes. *Very* good. You would be proud."

"I always have been, and always will be proud of you."

"When can I come stay with you again, Grandma?"

"It will be a while before we're together again, Sweetie."

"But why, Grandma?"

"Well, because there is much work to be done yet. You'll have to trust me. It's all going to work out and I'll be waiting on you."

The dream shifted. Now, Bess was standing beside Barb. Bess's hand rested comfortably on Barb's shoulder. Both women smiled at him from above. He was confused for a moment. It was as though she were reading his mind, Bess sat on the bed beside him. She reached down and affectionately squeezed his hand. "Sweetie, it's okay. Everything is going to work out fine. You'll see."

The small affirmation from his grandmother was all he needed to make him feel better. Barb and Bess looked at each other. Barb nodded her head in silent agreement with Bess. Bess looked at Marty and said, "Marty, we have a very special gift for you." She opened her hand to reveal a beautiful blue sapphire in her hand. It glowed as it floated just above her palm. She held it out to Marty. "This blue stone can change the world. It is important that only special people know the secret. Do you understand?"

He nodded.

"It is a very special stone. It will speak to those who are gifted enough to hear it. Do you understand?"

He shook his head.

"Remember when we talked about the birth of the Baby Jesus at Christmas? This is just like the Star of Bethlehem for the Wise Men. It will lead you to where you are supposed to go. Your mind will be clear and help you see people for what they really are."

His little head bobbed up and down that he understood.

Bess closed her hand over the stone and opened her fingers once again. Like a magic trick, the stone was gone. Marty laughed and clapped his hands. "Do that again."

They both smiled at him. Bess murmured, "He is such a dear child."

Barb continued, "We wish we could go with you, but we must stay here."

Each woman took turns leaning down to kiss him on the cheek.

Their kisses were warm. His little arms reached up and clamped around each of the old ladies, squeezing them to him. For the first time in as many years as he could remember, he felt at peace. Everything would be okay. And then his tiny arms were empty and they were gone. He heard his named being called in the distance. *Is it time for dinner already?*

Again, he heard his name softly. It was a woman's voice, but not that of either grandmother. He felt a gentle hand on his cheek, a gentle stroke and then, "Marty, it's time to go."

His eyes opened with a start. He straightened to find himself in Gillian's lap. He blinked, trying to orient himself. Digger's yellow VW was easing into the lot in front of them.

He looked at Gillian. "I'm sorry, did I drift off?"

She smiled at him. "Only for a little while."

He struggled to remember the dream, while coping with the fact he had been sleeping in her lap. He was awake now.

He stammered slightly, "I'm sorry, I didn't mean to…"

She smiled, placed her finger over his lips, and her eyes smiled at him. "It's fine. You needed the rest."

He looked at her. Somehow, she looked different. It was as though he were seeing her for the first time.

She hopped off the table and said, "Come on."

Digger already had the passenger door open for them. Excitedly, he said, "Guys, you should have been there. It was awesome!"

Marty opted to hop in the backseat, leaving the front for Gillian. She piled in next to Digger. She could tell he was excited. "Okay, so tell me everything..."

They jabbered excitedly back and forth. Marty sat in the back, quiet, staring out of the window. He sat, wondering who the stranger was inside him. He refused to dwell on the madness of this, so he focused on the one thing he could trust—Barb. It was evident to him that she was conveying a message in his dream. Barb had always jokingly told him that he had been granted the *vision*. This was the second time she had guided him through a dream. The message was not as direct this time, so he would have to figure out its meaning. Whatever it was, he needed to figure it out sooner rather than later. The clock was ticking.

Chapter 16

He waited in the dingy bar for twenty minutes before it became obvious that his quarry had eluded him. The Bronco was still there, but there was no way they were hiding in the small bar. The American cash he flashed for information met with nothing more than sullen stares and a few growls. Considering his options, he opted for a discreet exit and eased out of the bar into the bright sunshine outside.

He hit his cell phone again, trying to check in with Boyd and Matthews. The phone kept going to voice mail, meaning the phones were off or they were. It was hard to tell. As much as he hated to admit it, he had failed. He paused for a moment and took a deep breath before dialing McPherson with the news. "McPherson."

"Bernard here, I've lost them."

"Understood. Disengage and fly directly to Charles DeGalle Airport. We'll follow up with further instructions there."

"Oui." The phone chirped off in Bernard's ear.

The call left Bernard feeling odd. McPherson seemed strangely unconcerned over the phone, almost distracted. This was surprising, considering how tightly wrapped McPherson was. Nothing distracted him. Something was up.

McPherson ended the call and looked at the duke. "Master, I implore you, may we kill him *now*?"

The duke's tone of voice was similar to that of a parent with a small child. "No, Mr. McPherson. We may still have use for him."

McPherson's eyes dropped down and he mumbled in response, "Sorry, Sir. I guess I just a little put off at the moment. Those blokes have failed and I'm not there. It's very disturbing."

The duke smiled empathetically. "I know, Mr. McPherson. Soon, this will all be behind us and we'll be able to laugh over a couple of bitters. You know, we make quite good beer here."

McPherson brightened at the mention of them sharing a drink. "I'm looking forward to that, Sir."

It was the first time the duke had ever mentioned any sort of social setting. He felt privileged. The duke really seemed to be taking a shine to him.

"Thank you, Mr. McPherson. That will be all." The duke turned his attention back to the manuscripts in front of him. The cavernous room was suddenly as silent as a tomb. The small Persian beside him cleaned herself and purred. Dick quietly eased out, leaving the duke to his research. He was whistling a happy tune by the time he passed Gretchen's desk. She looked at him coldly, as he passed. Hired thugs—she hated them all.

****

The neon marquee winked sporadically like a dyslexic Morse code. It wasn't an issue, so long as there were clean sheets and plenty of hot water. Bone weariness engulfed Marty, as Gillian counted out twenties to a haggard, gray-haired night manager. There was a selection because it was the *slow* season. Though, Gillian couldn't imagine a rush any time of year. She paid for two connecting rooms in the same bungalow.

Marty and Digger bunked in one room and she in the other. Gravel crunched under the tires of the VW, as they pulled up. The Pancake Palace across the street painted an ugly glare on the night sky, as the sign boasted *Here to Serve You 24/7*. It was the closest thing to a restaurant they were going to get. Eloise sauntered up to the table. An unfiltered Camel dangled from her lips, causing her to squint to keep the smoke out. It was a practiced looked, one that had taken her thirty years to perfect, along with her indifferent attitude.

Marty never noticed the layers of coffee and mustard stains. His rapt attention was focused on a delicately balanced inch-long ash, which hung precariously from the tip of the Camel. He held his breath, afraid it would fall on Gillian and incur some sort of deadly martial arts blow, spanning some life and death struggle with the local authorities. As it was, Eloise noticed his fascination and flicked it into the floor, so he could order his pancakes without incident. Gillian's order of cinnamon French toast seemed far less dramatic. Digger, on the other hand, earned an icy look from Eloise, as he smiled pleasantly and ordered a chef's salad. Eloise eyeballed him with her good eye before stating flatly, "Hun, we don't do salads here."

He sighed and settled on scrambled eggs and dry toast. She sloshed coffee in all three cups, which turned out to be surprisingly good. Digger got in one more jab by opting for a glass of ice water, causing Eloise to walk muttering none too quietly about *Yankees* as she swayed back to the counter. Digger inspected the glass suspiciously, but said nothing before taking a sip.

Eloise jammed their ticket on the pre-Korean war order carousel and swung it around, so Marv could see it. Marv made great pancakes even when he was dead drunk, which was convenient, since he usually was. The threesome ate quietly at first, but began to perk up with surprisingly excellent coffee and food, though Digger did find a bit of shell in his eggs. Marv took another drink and sat back down on a milk crate in the kitchen. Eloise went behind the counter and joined him.

The electric clock was slightly fast, but not so much that it could not undo the lateness of the hour. The twenty-four hour *SuperMart* was a haven for shoppers and drug dealers in the middle of the night. They would need supplies for the trip and the sign at the front door promised the *Hottest Deals Around*.

By the time they made it back to the room, Marty was almost asleep before he touched down on the pillow. Gillian opted for second watch, leaving Digger to watch the first part of the night. Marty was, after all, still under their care.

Digger pulled out his black bag and set up a surveillance system for the night. Carefully, he placed small RF pen cameras at strategic locations inside and out. Nothing could get in without him seeing it first. He yawned, as he waited for his laptop to boot up and bring the cameras online. He watched the screen, fighting the urge to close his eyes. So far, the only threat had been from a stray mongrel, which cocked its leg on his bug. He felt a gleeful sense of satisfaction, as he pressed the remote and sent a quick zap of static resulting in a yelp and a thin whiff of ozone. The canine limped into the night, with his tail between his legs to nurse his offended privates. Digger snorted in the room. No dog was going to pee on his car while he was watching.

After a quiet three hours, Gillian instinctively

awoke and relieved an exhausted Digger. She rubbed her eyes, as she moved the laptop through the connecting door to her room. She looked over at Marty who snored peacefully never noticing the change in guard.

The digital readout of the clock glared *4:30* when Marty's eyes flew open. His mind raced and his back was soaked in sweat. The thought of the flight ahead caused his mouth to go dry. Nauseated, he padded to the bathroom to splash water in his face. After what he had been through in the last several days, a fear of flying seemed a bit ridiculous. However, no matter how absurd it seemed, it was very real and very much making him reconsider the trip. He stood in the bathroom door and stared at the locked door to the outside. He could leave and they wouldn't know. He could go back to his old life, find another job and put this all behind him. His eyes moved slowly back to the stone. His mind went back to his dream of Barb and Bess. He remembered the feeling of comfort, as they watched over him, protecting him. The feeling of comfort washed over him. With it, came the resolve. Here in this fleabag motel in the early morning calm, he resolved to finish this. Whatever he faced, it was bigger than him; bigger than all of them.

Digger breathed peacefully in his sleep in the double bed beside Marty. He quietly made his way to the dresser. He carefully slid open the top drawer, so it would not make a sound. He quietly eased the box from its resting place and carried it back to his bed. Sitting cross-legged in the middle of the bed, he carefully removed the top. The silk inside seemed to move and dance in the meager light of the room's single lamp.

The silk rustled ever so quietly in the stillness of the room. He could almost hear it whisper to him "Yes, Yes" as a lover would in the night. Somehow, the Sapphire looked different now. In the dim light, the color seemed richer, fuller. The facets seemed to sparkle and glisten, beckoning him. Now, it was as beautiful as any stone he had ever seen. It almost enticed him to want to caress it like a new bride. He shivered with excitement at the thoughts of holding it. Perhaps it was the light, but he could almost see it glow in the deep recesses of the stone. He carefully set the box down in his crossed legs and gently removed the stone. He cradled it in his palm, gently expecting some sort of singularity appearing, or a tunnel filled with light opening before him. Nothing happened.

He closed his eyes and dropped his head, dejectedly. Perhaps he had been too eager to want it to change him; to provide his with something more than his mundane life. He stopped feeling sorry for himself for a moment and felt the change around him. Something was wrong with the room. He opened his and found he was no longer in the motel. The table before him was worn from years of use. Its cherry finish was worn through in spots. Long lines of bookshelves contained thousands of hardbound volumes. Ladders hung from both sides of the room to access the upper shelves. The antiquity of the room rose to his sense of smell. Soft golden wood tones glowed and made him feel welcome. His gaze traveled up, only to find the soft tones of a fresco depicting rolling hills of green pastures dotted with plump sheep.

Across from him was a leather wingback chair. The aged leather was buffed to rich brown hue from the many years of use. Tiny cracks appeared in the leather from ages of use. He looked around him to see if he was alone. There was not even a hint of sound, save the resolute tick of a century old grandfather clock. The clock struck the half hour and chimed once. Marty was fascinated by the room. Behind him, an ancient door handle turned slowly and the door creaked in protest, as it opened.

The tall man glided in effortlessly. His white beard was cropped short against his face. Marty smiled at the old man. He was the same as before. He felt strangely at ease with the old fellow.

He spoke. "Hello, Martin. How nice of you to visit."

A thought struck Martin. "Where exactly am I?"

"You haven't moved. You are precisely where you were five minutes ago."

Now Marty was confused. "I'm afraid I don't follow?"

"You are still in Room Two of the Starlite Motel."

"Then why does this look like a library?"

"Because that is where you are going."

"I'm confused."

"I will be your guide on your journey. The room you seek will look much like this."

"Why can't you just tell me where to go?"

"Because what you seek is not as important as what you will find along the way. Life is funny that way. Any journey you take will not be a simple beginning and an end."

"So, I will find something, then what?"

"Then you must find *her*."

"Who? Gillian?"

"No. Rachel."

Marty sat back, heavily. He suddenly felt lost. "Who is Rachel?"

"She is the one who needs you."

Marty stared at him, blankly. "I'm sorry. I don't want to appear stupid, but I'm lost."

The old man smiled. "Your history is riddled with versions of her. Many were handed down before there was written language. I'm sure you've heard of Moses and the Ten Commandments?"

"Of course."

He smiled and continued. "Your Bible speaks of a magnificent chest of gold, gilded with angels and holds the power of God, true?"

Marty looked at him, suspiciously. "You're talking about the Ark of the Covenant."

"Yes, the vessel is imbued with Devine power. That power is Rachel."

"So Rachel is God?"

"No. She is a servant, as am I."

"So, you're an Angel?"

"No. I am a guide."

"So Rachel is the Spirit of the Ark."

"Yes, she is a link between our realm and the others."

"You mean, like, between Heaven and Earth?"

"Let's just say it's not quite that simple, but yes, Heaven and Earth would be realms, as are many others."

Marty's brow furrowed. "People have been searching for the Ark for centuries. How do you expect me to find her?"

"She is not lost, but merely hidden. If you seek the

man, he will take you to Her."

"Man? What man? I don't understand."

"The man who holds her. He is a ruthless man, one who would use her for his own purposes. He seeks to use her power to bend the natural order of things for power and greed."

"Is he Satan?"

"Oh, no. Satan seeks your soul. This man seeks only to subvert the balance of things. His mind is small and petty. He sees himself as a conqueror of that which he does not understand. He is an emperor of ignorance."

Marty scowled. He was starting to miss his cushy nine to five desk job. He wondered when he would wake up in the mental ward, with a Thorazine drip. He quietly contemplated before asking, "What is my role in all this?"

"You are the guardian of the Twelfth Stone. Your destiny foretells restoration of order to this realm."

This sounded way bigger than anything his High School Guidance Counselor had told him. In fact, he couldn't remember his Guidance Counselor's face at the moment. He phrased his next question, carefully. "So, am I supposed to save Rachel from this maniac?"

"I suppose. In a manner of speaking, you could call it that. You must return her to the Sacred Place; to where she came from when she first entered this realm. That is where she will be the most powerful, the place where she can defend herself."

He looked at the tall man. "I don't suppose you could give me any hints on how I'm going to do that?"

"You will know what to do when the time is right. You must be ready to rely on your friends when the time comes."

Marty drew a blank on the idea of *friends* helping him. "What friends would that be, exactly?"

The old man smiled. "Those you travel with, of course."

"You mean Gillian and Digger? I'm not so sure I trust them."

"Trust your instincts. Your heart should be your true guide, not your eyes."

Marty considered this briefly and responded, "So what do I call you?"

"Peter will do."

"So what will happen in the end?"

"No one can say, really."

"Does that mean you can't, or that you won't say?"

Peter smiled. "It means that you're thinking in terms of the universe as being a system of absolutes. I'm afraid the cosmos doesn't work that way. Martin, I assure you that there are limitations even in my realm. Please be patient and realize there is a bigger picture here."

He hated it when people called him *Martin*. "Funny, that's what my boss said right before he fired me. I guess we both know how that turned out for me."

Peter responded, patiently, "All turning points test your mettle. While they are painful at times, they happen for a reason. It was the starting point for you and all that has happened. Would you have left everything behind so easily had it not been for that?"

Marty pondered the statement.

Peter pressed on. "You must include your friends. Have faith they will not abandon you."

"So, what do I tell them? That my *pet rock* told me

of a quest. They'll think I'm crazy."

"Convince them to hold the gem. It will help them understand."

"When should I do this?"

"Gillian will be entering the room any moment. I would not delay in telling her. She is a far stronger ally than you think. One other thing, Martin, the Sappir affects everyone differently. The experience will be different with all three of you."

"Affects?" His voice was an octave higher than he would have liked.

"Calm yourself. No harm will come of it. You have dormant energy locked within you. The Sappir is the key."

"Care to give me a hint as to what they will be?"

"Your mind's eye will be awakened."

Marty raised his eyebrows. "Pardon?"

"There is no time to explain. Be patient and you will understand. Follow your dreams and visions. It will feel odd at first, but you will adapt. One final thing…"

"Yes?"

"Gillian is in the room with you. It's time you explain to her."

Chapter 17

They moved to the other room. She looked at him, alarmed. "Please say you're kidding?"

Marty tried to look convincing. "I know this is strange, but you're going to have to trust me." He didn't even try to explain about Rachel. She was having enough difficulty believing that the stone had *spoken to him*.

She eyed him, skeptically. "You know if you had told me that two days ago, I would have cuffed you and stuffed you in the trunk."

Marty looked at her, patiently. "I know. I didn't believe it myself at first. He said I needed to let both of you hold the Sappir."

She shook her head. Emphatically, she said, "Absolutely not."

Marty gave her an imploring look. "Why?"

She sighed. "I'm not going to endanger his life. He's trained to do surveillance. He's not trained to adapt in the field. Besides that, he's my friend. I can't risk putting him in harm's way."

The response stung. He was an outsider. He pleaded, "Look, I know we haven't known each other very long, but I promise that I am sincere and I'm pretty sure I'm not crazy. I really questioned whether I should tell you. I decided to trust you. All I'm asking is that you return that. Is that so much to ask?"

She looked at him hard and long. It was clear that he was serious. He confided in her when he knew she would not believe him. He did it on faith that she would see the truth in what he said. She bit her lip, as she considered their situation. She considered what had happened in the church. This was beyond anything she had ever experienced. There was a twinge of guilt about being so stubborn, which made her realize that she *was* a different person now. If she had changed, then maybe there was some truth to what he was telling her. She was conflicted because of her wanting to protect both of them. Now, she faced a decision of having to protect Digger from the uncertainty of the situation they were in. It was both confusing and aggravating. She wished she could go back to not trusting anyone and shooting people she didn't like.

Marty could see her struggling with the conflict. He tried to give her an easy out. "Look, I'll put the stone on the dresser and leave the room. You can lock the doors behind me." He could almost see her mind working. "You can do this on your own terms. When you're ready, just pick it up and relax. It doesn't hurt. If it works, you'll know I'm telling the truth. If it doesn't work, you can fall back on plan A and drop me off at the closest psyche ward with a note around my neck and take the rock to your boss. You can't lose."

Stoically, she considered him. Marty readied himself for cuffs and a gag. She hated to admit it, but she knew he was right. She sighed and let the angst of trying to fight it go. "All right, you go into my room. I'll lock this door."

She slid a gleaming .45 caliber pistol from under her pillow. Marty's eyes grew large. That was not something he had considered. There was a smooth click, as she dropped the magazine into her hand. In one fluid motion, she ratcheted the slide, ejected the unspent round and caught it before it hit the mattress. Marty didn't try to hide that he was impressed by her skill. "Wow."

She looked at him drolly, as she thumbed the round into the magazine and handed it to Marty. "If this is some drug-induced hallucination, I don't want any *accidents*."

He nodded. Inwardly, he wondered what kind of an experience would lead her to think that way. He quickly decided that some things were better left unknown. He tried to smile, bravely. "I'll be right here, if you need me."

She arched an eyebrow at him, but said nothing as she closed and latched the door behind him. As he went through the door, she slid a chair over and wedged it under the knob. She still wasn't sure if she liked the idea of this. If nothing happened, they could move on. She walked to the dresser and opened the wooden cover. She inspected the gem closely, to see whether there were microscopic spores evident. It shown brightly in the box and looked ordinary enough. Perhaps it was a bit larger than ones she had seen in the past? It was the size of her thumbnail and shaped like a pecan.

She grabbed a towel from the bathroom and gingerly picked up the case, like the stone had just come from an oven. She eased the box into the bathroom and placed it on the counter next to the sink. She placed her finger along the drain and inspected the opening to see how wide it was. Satisfied that the opening was smaller than the stone, she turned on the water and waited for it to get hot. If there were some pharmacological or biological agent on the stone, it would be gone shortly. Cradling it carefully in the towel, she washed it for a full minute with soap and running water. The water was so hot that it made her wince. As she turned the water off, she was confident that any nerve agents were washed away. She toweled it dry and carried it back to the bed. She sat in the center of the bed, cross-legged. If there was any chance she was going to fall under some *magic spell* she didn't want to fall physically.

She placed it in front of her. It glittered in the dim light. Carefully, she reached into the towel. Her hand hovered over the glittering jewel for a moment, while she weighed the sanity of this. She shook her head at the absurdity of the moment, reached down, tossed the gem up and deftly caught it. It was warm from its bath and didn't feel particularly amazing at first touch. She sat for a moment with it, while nothing happened. She sighed, feeling a little silly. Just as she had suspected, an overactive imagination had been exacerbated by some real-life drama. It was going to be difficult to tell Marty. He had seemed so convinced.

Cupped in the palm of her hand, she climbed off the bed to return the stone to the dresser. The sensation was as palpable as an electric shock. As her foot touched the floor, the coolness of the tile floor passed through her like a wave. Slowly, her gaze traveled to the floor. The familiar gleam of polished white tile loomed as never before. A smell rose up from nowhere. The tang of boot polish and mothballs suddenly filled her nostrils. A chill edged its way up her spine, as she looked up to find the expanse of her old Fort Bragg barracks. The familiar long rows of steel bunk beds spread out, each with a neatly rolled mattress centered precisely in the middle. Strangely, calm washed over her.

The door latch at one end of the barracks clicked hollowly through the open room. It creaked, as it opened. The Master Sergeant strode briskly through the door, walking straight up to her. Without thinking, she was locked at attention by the time he reached her. He returned her salute and walked past her, without saying a word. He snatched a nearby chair and draggedit toward her. Swinging it around, he sat with the chair back toward her, his arms folded over the top. His first words rang out like a hymn. "As you were, Kelly."

She dropped into a parade stance and relaxed, but only slightly. This part she understood.

He began a little less formally this time. "So Gillian, what are your thoughts about all this?"

"Permission to speak freely, Sir?"

The Sergeant smiled. "Permission granted."

"It's a cluster, Sir. We have insufficient ground troops, unreliable Intel and inadequate equipment for this mission."

He nodded in agreement. "Would it be safe to say your mission objective has been compromised, given your current situation?"

"Yes, Sir. I would." She responded, without drama or pretense.

He smiled at her. "Let's see if we can undo some of the damage a bit, shall we?"

Gillian quit play acting and sat back on the bed, cross-legged. This wasn't her unit. He wasn't her sergeant. He was tall and white headed, his hair tightly cropped. His stripes were three up and three down, with the gunnery symbol in the center. It was odd. She didn't recognize any of the ribbons on his chest. She thought she knew them all. The name on the uniform was *PETER*.

She quietly asked, "So, am I to assume that I am now part of the lunatic fringe?"

His smile was unexpectedly radiant. "Not quite, my dear. You're quite sane."

The epiphany struck her that this was what Marty had been experiencing. She began to understand his reluctance to explain. It was only at this moment that she appreciated his odd statements and peculiar behaviors were due to something far more unusual than she could have imagined. A twinge of regret crossed her mind. She had clearly been too hard on him.

The Sergeant smiled at her. "He doesn't blame you, you know. He was hesitant to bring you into this. I had to convince him that this was necessary."

Her eyes slanted at Peter. "Pardon me?"

"You're feeling regret about being so hard on Wood?"

She frowned. "You know what I'm thinking?"

"Of course, my dear. This is all in your mind, my bailiwick."

Peter could see the sudden chill of fear, as it passed over her. She tried unsuccessfully to control it. He opened his palms to her. "Rest easy, Child. You're in no danger here. In fact, my purpose is to ensure your safety and success on this endeavor. I want you to have some faith in your mission here."

"Faith? I'm afraid that *faith* is not something I tend

to rely on."

He smiled, slyly. "We hope to change that."

Her response was non-committal. "So what are we doing here? You seem to have all the answers, so why do you need me?"

Peter considered her for a moment before continuing. "Events are transpiring as we speak that require your unique skills."

She looked at him wryly. "I'm afraid the preacher robbed me of the whole *skills* aspect yesterday."

Peter looked at her, sternly. "No, quite the contrary. He prepared you for the changes in your life. He just healed some old wounds to help you. Without that, you could not move past who you were to who you need to be."

Bitingly, she replied, "I wasn't aware that I needed to be anything other than what I was. Maybe I didn't want to move on?"

He looked at her, patiently. "We both know that's not true. For the first time in your life, you do not feel empty. It was painful, I know, but sometimes it is necessary. Gillian, I'll get to the point. I realize you want a specific step-by-step plan that is precisely timed and sequential. I can't give that to you. I can assure you, I will be with you every step of the way. But you will have to adapt as you go. Your objective now is to rescue *Her*."

Gillian blinked. His statement caught her off guard. "Excuse me, who is *Her*?"

"That isn't important at the moment. Martin will be able to explain that later. Our time here is short, so let's focus on your ability to defend yourself."

Finally, it was something she could relate to. She

smiled. "Trust me, this is where I know what I'm capable of."

Peter gave her a wicked smile, "No. I don't believe you do."

Peter reached across and touched her forehead. His hand glowed for a moment and he drew it away. She felt no different. From the doorway, a fly entered the room and angrily buzzed around them. It flew in slow circles before landing on Peter's elbow.

He pointed to the fly for a moment. "This fly has an enormous power within it, which you can tap into. But you must learn the true nature of the power and how to harness it."

She gave him a skeptical look and thought, *Fly Power? Who are you trying to kid here?* She tried to remain patient and listened.

He smiled, seeing her doubt. "I once knew someone long ago named Thomas. He was a lot like you. Now, focus on the energy of the wings of our little friend here. Watch him, as he takes flight."

As the fly left Peter's arm, it seemed to move in slow motion. Gillian blinked, involuntarily. She questioned herself, as a world of iridescent bands of light flowed through the room like the currents of a hundred streams. Bands of color intensified closer to the source of energy. It was like watching the insect fly into a wind tunnel. She watched as the bug changed color in front of her. Dabs of red turned to orange and finally yellow at the tips of the wings.

Peter's voice seemed distant. "Focus on what you can see."

Her fascination caused her to forget what she was doing. The fly seemed as though it were flying in slow motion, as it buzzed through the barracks. It maneuvered through the currents like a canoe on the rapids, avoiding the stronger air currents in the opposite direction and riding the winds to its destination. She began to sense when the motion would change so she could capture and redirect it at will.

Peter smiled, satisfied with her instincts. "Good, you're a natural at this. Now, see if you can borrow a small portion of that power and focus it on something you wish to move?"

She focused on a whisp of air in a tiny pink strand. She concentrated on balling the small string of air into a concentrated orb and moved it against the fly. Its tiny head disappeared inward and the insect fell to the floor. She blinked. "What happened?"

Peter sighed. "You must use the energy sensibly. You are not using a hammer. This is more like delicate surgery. Let's try again."

Another fly entered the room and landed on Peter's arm. As it took flight, she followed the flow of energy as it created movement. Again, she concentrated on *borrowing* a small amount of energy. Slowly, she released it on the fly and it began to slow. A small strand of electricity flashed by, as a crooked blue line distracted her from the release of air current. Her momentary distraction caused the air *ball* to release all at once, hammering the small fly in one unchecked energy ram. It flew backward across the room, falling dead as though struck by a fly swatter.

He looked at her, dourly. "You killed it, again."

She looked at Peter, determinedly. "I can do this. Besides, it was just a fly."

He held his tongue. "Try again. This time, don't let

anything distract you. Release the energy slowly. Focus on controlling it."

A third fly entered the room. This time she did not wait until it landed before she began to *bank* the power from the wings. Carefully, she released the energy back onto the fly. Its tiny wings beat furiously, and yet it did not move through the air. She held it motionless in mid-air. It buzzed angrily, as it tried to move forward. Yet, it remained in stasis. She continued to capture tiny bits of energy and redirect it on the insect. Suddenly, it fell to the floor dead.

She looked at Peter, defensively. "I didn't do that."

He smiled. "A fly has a very limited life span to begin with. With you using its own energy against it, essentially you doubled the rate at which it aged. It simply died of old age."

"And you're okay with that?"

"You didn't intentionally kill it. It simply expired."

She sat back smugly, considering the implications of her newfound talent.

Peter continued, "Energy is all around you. It can be borrowed from almost any source that you can visualize and capture. It will take time for you to master your gift."

"Gift? I thought you gave me the power?"

"No. It was always there. I merely opened your eyes to it."

She looked at him, curiously. "Is this a dream?"

He smiled. "You make it sound like dreaming is a bad thing. The reality of it is that what lies within your dreams, lies within you. They are doorways to your intuitive self. Soon, you and I will be apart, but you will still have your new ability. That is not a dream. That is real."

"Will I ever come back here?"

"That is difficult to say. This place is unimportant. The world you return to is critical to the stability of the system. Your gifts are important, but they are only a part of what you are. Rest assured that you will reach deep within yourself to face the challenges ahead. Your world and many other worlds are dependent upon you and your friends."

She sat quietly for a moment. Ribbons of iridescent energy around her began to fade into the background. In the stillness of the moment, she accepted her fate. She looked at Peter and said, "I suppose this is goodbye for now, then."

Peter stood and returned the smile. "For now, go in peace."

She felt a great wind rise around her. The barracks crumbled and dissolved into it, leaving her in a maelstrom of debris. She closed her eyes tightly against the wind. A moment later it died as quickly as it began. As she opened her eyes, she found herself seated in the middle of the motel bed. The stone sparkled and winked in her hand. She carefully returned it to the box. Picking it up, she got off the bed and carried it to dresser. As she placed the box on the dresser, she noticed the dead fly on the clean surface before her. They were definitely not in Kansas anymore.

Chapter 18

Digger stood in line, patiently waiting to purchase tickets for the movie. There was the usual murmur in the crowd. The conversations ebbed and flowed like the tide. He smiled at the excited titter of teenage girls and watched as parents tried to calm excited little ones.

It was an older building, but it was clean. Still, the carpet on the floors was beginning to wear thin in spots, making it dull. Because the theater was in a mall, they wound pass hair salons and shoe shops. The moviegoers watched, as Pearl's Hair Salon busily teased hair and clipped curls. The shoe repair man next door haggled with a patron on resoling a pair of shoes. The smell of popcorn mingled with hair gel. For some reason, it had a familiar smell like he was back home in California.

A small trim blonde politely squeezed between the couple in front of him and eased up beside Digger. She comfortably slipped her hand in his. He looked down at her. She practically glowed, as she smiled up at him. Digger kept smiling and looked back up the line. It had moved three inches since the last time he looked.

Her blonde hair fell over one eye, making her look coy. Every guy in the mall would have been thrilled to have her on his arm. And she was on his. There seemed to be only one problem: he didn't know who she was. He wasn't going to let it spoil the moment.

She looked at him and asked, "Where are we going after the movie?"

"I don't know. What do you want to do?" Some things never changed.

She smiled. "What if we go get something to eat? I hear there's a new place out on Highway 66. It's all chrome and glass. All the waitresses are supposed to be on roller skates."

"Cool. Let's do that." He didn't know where Highway 66 was and he didn't care, so long as she was with him. He was thrilled and amazed that she liked him. This was wonderful. He heard his name over the intercom in the mall. He didn't react. It had to be a mistake. No one ever paged him at the mall.

She curled her arm around his and stood close. She smelled like roses. When she smiled at him, everything about her smiled. He couldn't remember a time when he had been this happy. They paged his name again. This time, it was a little louder. He would just wait this one out. *Maybe there's another Digger Delgado in the mall?* Suddenly, the mall began to shake. The stores collapsed around him and his new love evaporated like a puff of smoke. Grumpily, he asked, "What?"

Gillian looked a little sheepish. "Sorry. It's time to get up."

He ran his hand across his face, took a deep breath and looked around for a second. His brain began to put it all together. *North Carolina; motel; some kind of rock*—begrudgingly, he accepted he was back in the real world.

He mumbled, "Another ten seconds. That's all I needed." He rolled his legs over the side of the bed. He still had his clothes from last night on. Sometimes, these field operations left something to be desired.

Gillian considered him with a degree of anticipation. Marty was leaning against the dresser. He rubbed his eyes and asked, "Is everything okay?"

Gillian smiled. It wasn't as nice as the blonde had smiled, but it was okay. It meant everything was all right. Both had a strange look about them, though.

She started with, "We need to talk."

That was how his last girlfriend broke up with him. This was never a good way to start a morning. Marty handed him a fresh cup of coffee. It was just the way he liked it; one sugar and two Hazelnut creamers.

He considered Marty for a moment before speaking. "My coffee is perfect. How did you know?"

Marty smiled, noncommittally. "Doesn't everyone drink coffee that way?"

It was too early. He let it go. Gillian sat on the bed next to him. Marty pulled up a desk chair beside them. He started to feel a little hemmed in.

Gillian opened the conversation with, "I need to show you something."

His eyes were open. He heard the sound of her voice, but in retrospect he wished he had paid closer attention. Digger sipped his coffee, careful not to burn his mouth and tried to blink the sleep from his eyes. "So, can this wait until after we've had breakfast?" He tried unsuccessfully to tone down the sarcasm.

Gillian responded, "Not really."

He rolled his eyes in response. "Oh all right, what is it?"

Marty excitedly bubbled out, "Well, we found this jewel…"

Digger half-listened. When Marty finished, he

sighed. "Oh, all right. This had better not be some kind of practical joke. You do know I can rewrite both your personal credit histories, so you can never buy anything on credit, don't you?"

Gillian looked him in the eye. "Dig, I'm serious. You can't understand this until you see it." Something in her tone made him look at her seriously for the first time.

"Okay. I'm with you. Let's do this."

Gillian led him into the next room. She sat him in the middle of the bed. The whole thing felt very much like a grade school sleep over. Marty handed him the small wooden box and said, "When we leave the room, open the box and pick up the stone. Don't be afraid. It won't hurt you, but you need to be prepared. It's going to be very different from what you're used to."

Digger gave him a contemptuous look. "Dude, I'm from California. You'd be amazed at what I'm used to."

Marty smiled, but said nothing. He thought to himself, *Dude, you haven't seen this.*

The room was quiet and dim. A single lamp lit the bed. With the doors closed, Digger shook his head, carefully placing the box on the bed in front of him. He removed the lid and inspected the contents. For a moment, he considered laying down for another twenty minutes. They wouldn't have to know.

The stone was so dark blue, it almost looked black. It appeared perfectly benign sitting in the box. There was no glowing sphere, no chorus singing, no thunderclap. In fact, there was nothing particularly dramatic about the stone at all. It seemed like a somewhat crudely cut black rock. He didn't see what the big deal was. He lifted it and placed it in the palm of his hand. Nothing happened. He yawned and closed his eyes, rubbing them with the back of his hand. He opened eyes to find the motel room was gone and in its stead his old college physics auditorium. He closed his eyes again and then opened them to see if it had changed back. It didn't. This was definitely his physics auditorium. He was alone in the cavernous room. The quiet was a little unnerving.

The door in the back of the hall clicked hollowly and swung in, as a white-haired professor walked in. He looked a bit disheveled, even though he wore a cardigan sweater. Half of his shirt peeked out from under the sweater. His hair went in all directions. His reading glasses rested on the tip of his nose, threatening to fall off. And yet, even with his unkempt appearance, there was no mistaking the quickness in his eyes. There was something about them. He peered over his glasses at Digger. "Ah, Mr. Delgado, would you be so kind as to help me with today's problem?" The professor walked toward a whiteboard the size of a football field.

"I am Professor Peter. You can just call me Peter, if you like. Would you care to join me at the blackboard?"

Digger corrected him non-confrontationally. "Whiteboard."

The professor peered over his glasses at Digger. "Excuse me?"

Digger looked at him earnestly, as he stood. "It's a whiteboard, Sir."

Peter turned to face the board and smiled. "So it is. Semantics... Don't get bogged down with them."

Digger proceeded to the whiteboard and stood beside the professor. He gave Digger a sideways look and asked "Have you heard the one about the two black holes that walk into a bar?

He looked at him, politely. "No, Sir. I don't believe I have."

"One black hole asks the bartender, 'Say, have you got the time?'"

"The bartender holds out a cigarette and says, 'Sure, pal. Tell you what, you give me a light and I'll give you the time.'"

The professor laughed heartily at his own joke.

Digger gave him a pained grin. "No, Sir. That's a new one."

The professor wiped tears from his eyes, as he peered over his glasses at Digger. "So, for today's problem, we are going to use religion as the denominator and science as the numerator."

Digger stared at him. "I'm sorry. Those terms are like apples and oranges, aren't they?"

"How so?"

"You're asking to mix discrete terms with non-discrete terms?"

"Hmmm. You're correct. Why is that a problem?"

Digger looked confused. "Well, there can't be a solution to problems of that nature."

The professor smiled. "Very good! So let's get started, shall we? How did life begin on Earth?"

Digger looked at him confused, but answered the question. "Well, I guess we evolved from simpler life forms."

"That's a sound hypothsis. What did the simpler life forms evolve from?"

Digger felt like he was taking a test that he hadn't studied for. As disciplined as he was in physics, he was lost in biochemistry. He played along just the same, hoping it would lead somewhere quickly. "Simple single celled organisms formed and evolved."

"Good. So, these single celled organisms are made up of what, exactly?"

"Various proteins, amino acids, water, trace minerals..." He trailed off, not knowing how to finish the response.

"Fabulous. So we have this great big pot of chemical soup floating around the planet and out pops the preliminary forms of life on the planet?"

Digger eyed him warily, trying to understand where the conversation was going. "I'm pretty sure there is more to it than that."

Peter pushed him a little further. "I'm sorry. What did we leave out? The planet was this large melting pot of gases, liquids, vapors and so on. Everything mixes together and life occurs."

Digger pushed back a little. "I think it's safe to say that there was some sort of catalyst to cause life to begin. One theory is that some extra-terrestrial influence such as a comet or meteor may have introduced the necessary elements."

"So, if you mix all the materials like amino acids, water, minerals in the right proportion, a life form should just pop out, correct?"

"I'm pretty sure that there's more to it than that. If it were that simple, we would have figured out how to re-create life already."

"So you're saying that science has not adequately explained how life began."

"Not yet. I mean, we can recreate amino acids in the laboratory, but we can't combine them to form

DNA. That's the challenge of discovery."

"When do you think that humans will be able to solve the puzzle?"

"That's difficult to say."

"Would you say the occurrence of life is a series of random events?"

Digger stuck doggedly to his position. "It seems unlikely. However, that is the only conclusive data we have to this point."

"So you're saying you would rather believe in a theory of random actions than a planned event?"

Digger would not be baited so easily. "I believe in what the facts tell us. That is all I can do."

The Professor smiled, cagily. "Do you feel there is a desire to know the answer to that question?"

"Without a doubt, most people want to know," he responded a little testily. "Honestly, though, we both know that this is something I cannot solve, so why am I here?"

Peter nodded, agreeing with some unseen presence, and then responded, "To prepare you."

"For what?"

"Something your facts can't explain."

Without a word, Peter walked away from the board and sat in the front row. He sat, waiting. Digger was confused by the odd little man. He didn't understand the whole discussion they had just had. Peter smiled, knowingly. He baited the lad intentionally to force him to think outside of his box.

Digger recalled that Marty and Gillian had both said the experience of the stone was unique to the individual. This must be his personal twist. As he pondered what to ask next, the door across from him opened and she entered the room. He stared at her in disbelief. He watched as she flipped her hair. Her eyes sparkled unnaturally, as she moved toward him. Her smile was as radiant as he remembered. It was the same blonde from his dream. He could feel his heart hammering in his chest like an anvil. His palms felt sweaty, if that was even possible in this place.

She wore a simple pattern pink dress with tiny white flowers. The open bodice accentuated the curve of her slender neck and shoulders. It struck him as odd that she was barefoot. Her bare feet were browned and tan with pink edges to the toes. It was a summer tan. Her skin glowed in a healthy radiance. Digger thought to himself, *I've fallen asleep again. If Gillian wakes me up this time, I'll strangle her.*

She walked up to him and took his hands in hers. She giggled, as she said, "Don't worry. She can't wake you. You're not asleep."

Digger's eyes widened slightly. She knew what he was thinking. It unnerved him slightly. He quickly pulled himself together and responded brightly. "So, I guess we missed the movie. Is dinner still on?"

Her accent sounded Swedish. She looked at Peter. "He's very quick, don't you think?"

Peter shook his head and smiled at them both. "Yes, my dear. He's very quick, indeed."

She turned back to Digger. "We might have to take a rain check, there, Slugger." She placed a single finger under his chin and traced his jaw line. Her touch was almost electric. "My name is Rachel."

He smiled. "I'm Digger. But then, you probably know that."

Her smile broadened, as she moved closer. She

stood close. Her lips were tantalizingly near. It was all he could do to concentrate. He swallowed hard.

She hated to break the mood, but it was necessary. She turned and sighed solemnly. "Digger, we need your help."

Trancelike, he continued to smile. "Sure, anything you need."

"I need you to help me escape."

His smile remained unchanged. *It seems like a silly game, but it should be fun, though.* He playfully continued, "Okay. So what do I need? Magic rope, enchanted beans, energy balls, what?"

Rachel and Peter exchanged looks. Peter looked at Digger, gravely. "Digger, I'm sorry, but this isn't a game. Rachel chose you because you are uniquely capable of understanding her complexity. Your intellect, your personality, and your history singled you out among all others. Your friends Martin and Gillian are equally gifted in different ways. Together, you form a powerful trinity. It will take something as unique as you three working together to free Rachel from the duke."

Digger looked at Peter, confused. "If I need to rescue her, how can she be here with us now?"

Digger took her hands in his. They were soft and warm. She smelled of lemon blossoms. She seemed real enough. He looked deep into her eyes. Digger could feel the conflict raging within her like a storm. It was strange, as she seemed so calm on the outside. Rachel could sense him reading her angst. It made her pause for a moment. She realized she was seeing her own emotion through the eyes of another. She dropped his hands and stared across at Peter. Her thoughts reached out to Peter. *How is he able to read me that way?*

Peter responded telepathically, *They are His creation. There are many layers.*

It isn't supposed to happen this way.

It is not our place to say what is to be.

She looked back at Digger. He gently placed his hands on her shoulders. He smiled at her with his eyes. "Don't be afraid for me."

She blinked. Humans never failed to amaze her.

Digger continued. "What do you need me to do?"

For the first time in a millennia, she felt a twinge of fear, though not for herself. "You're sure you can go through with this?"

Digger looked at her, slyly. "You're not a ghost, are you?"

She giggled and made an arc with a barefoot toe on the floor in front of her. The carpet moved like sand under her foot, making a trough in the floor. As her foot resumed its position at her side, the floor resumed its natural condition. "Not all the time."

Peter had never understood this type of banter. He stepped in, almost abrasively. "She can assume any form she wishes when she needs to. However, the essence of her being is contained within the confines of the vessel. The duke continues to experiment on how to control the Ark and assume control of her. Her power is limitless by mortal standards. She can level entire cities—even mountains."

Digger nodded. "The City of Jericho comes to mind."

Peter and Rachel looked at each other, somewhat taken aback.

Rachel was the first to respond. "How did you

know that?"

Digger raised an eyebrow. "From the Bible story, of course."

She blushed. "I forgot about that."

"I am curious, though. How is it possible that any human could use your power in this day and age?"

"Remember the instrument of God for the Hebrews? I was guarded closely as a secret for many centuries. It was only when I was hidden for the safety of all Tribes that I was lost. I was accidentally found by one of the duke's people, so he has spent the last forty years studying me like an insect. Your friend Marty will find the final key for the duke to release me. Once that happens, he will control my power. That will be a disaster for all of us."

"I don't understand. How can he figure something like that out? Everyone who knew anything about it has been dead for centuries."

"True. The stone you hold is called a Sappir. All the Sappir are embodied with intelligence. The Sappir has unique effects on every person it touches. The duke has been able to read and understand certain ancient texts that were previously considered undecipherable."

Digger looked a little confused. "But I thought Marty had the only stone?"

She smiled at him sadly. "No. There are many more. The duke possesses all but the twelfth stone."

Digger pondered this. "So can't we just hide it from him?"

"He has almost limitless resources. He would torture and kill each of you to find it. You, Martin and Gillian are the only ones who can stop him. But it must be at the right time and the right place."

"So what do I need to do?"

"Go back and follow Martin. The Sappir will lead him to me. All three of you play an important role. You must act as one. That is the only way that any good can come of this."

Digger pondered for a moment. "Why am I so special?"

Peter and Rachel smiled at each other. She responded, "That is the question that all men ask and the answer lies within you. It will reveal itself when the time has come."

She took his hand and held it gently against her bosom. His hand and her bosom began to glow. "You have a part of me now. The power you need is the power you will have. You're a good man, Digger Delgado. Never underestimate that."

Digger nodded, still not wanting to go back. He slowly removed his hand and took hers. He raised it to his lips and gently kissed it. His eyes said more than his lips could. He closed his eyes and drank in the moment. When he opened his eyes, Marty and Gillian were sitting beside him on the bed. They formed a small triangle. Digger blinked for a moment, trying to orient himself.

Gillian reached out and gently touched his hand. "Hey, are you okay?"

He stared at her for a moment. "I'm fine. I just need a minute."

Marty nodded. "Take all the time you need. We've been there."

Digger nodded, absently. He placed his fingertips to his lips. His fingers smelled of lemon blossoms. Marty reached over and touched Gillian's hand, motioning her toward the door. She nodded and silently slid off the bed like a cat. She looked at Digger and said, "We'll be right outside, if you need us."

Digger nodded, absently again. All he could think about was Rachel. Marty and Gillian eased out the door.

A few thousand miles away in a cavernous vault, a spirit entity pondered on the human she had just met. She thoughtfully floated in a room of her own creation. She stared through a picture window at a cloud of gas and dust near Alpha Centauri, as it shifted and rolled in the solar wind. She considered the dilemma that she now faced. She was beginning to experience the human emotion of love. It was unfamiliar to her. She did not understand it. It felt almost...painful. Michael and Gabriel had not designed her to have emotions, or to make choices. They had designed her to do as she was bid. Now, she was faced with both. If Digger were to come here, he could never leave. She stared for a while longer at the gas pocket, thinking about the future.

Gillian studied Digger's surveillance system for a moment and decided it was safe enough to go outside. She stepped into the cool morning air, with Marty in tow. A symphony of crickets sung in concert into the night air. The freshness of the morning air washed away the cobwebs, leaving them refreshed. As they walked, Gillian eased her hand into Marty's. He said nothing but smiled enjoying her touch. It was odd for Gillian. She had never had the desire to walk and hold hands with anyone. And yet, it felt completely natural being here with Marty. It made no sense. She didn't dwell on it. She just enjoyed the moment. They walked silently, neither of them wanting to spoil it with mindless chatter.

After some time, she looked up at him and asked, "So, what did you see?"

"A Librarian. How about you?"

"Drill Instructor."

They walked for a while longer before Marty volunteered. "I'm being drawn to France. I don't know what to expect. Peter told me it would come to me when it was time, but I don't know what that means."

She smiled at him, encouragingly. "None of us do, Sweetie. We're going to have to play this, as it comes. It's all intuitive now."

It was the first time she had ever used a pet name with anyone. It came out, without thinking. They quietly walked in the quiet cool of the morning. Gillian suddenly stopped, realizing that they had walked for several blocks. They could see the first light of dawn. Birds were beginning to wake, chirping to celebrate the new day.

A sudden chill coursed through Gillian's spine. "We need to be getting back." With that, she dropped his hand and performed an abrupt about face.

Marty rolled his eyes. *Women*. He didn't think he would ever understand them.

Chapter 19

Bernard's phone met with out of service or voice mail with every other team member. It was a foreboding sign, one that hinted failure—possibly worse. Aggravated, he navigated his way back to the farm to verify no one was there. It was all he had left. The dilapidated structure appeared as dead on the inside as it was on the outside. He turned the car off and sat gazing at the gray wood that was in desperate need of paint. He contemplated his next move. He knew McPherson would gloat, and he considered any conceivable option to avoid that. After what seemed like an eternity, he resigned to the fact that the mission was a failure and that he needed to catch the next flight to Paris.

The first hues of dawn made the night sky glow in its wake, as he eased through a small town in the middle of a road to nowhere. In the delicious coolness of the morning, the air through the open windows was heavy with the smell of honeysuckle. A single traffic light glowed like an angry red eye, daring him to glide through it even with a clear absence of traffic.

He sat under the ruby red light, surveying his surroundings more out of habit than deliberate action. The erratic blinking of the half-lit motel sign cornered his attention for a moment. He looked across the parking lot of the Starlight Motel. Considering that it must be difficult for any motel to stay in business when there are no tenants, he noticed that there were virtually no cars in the lot, except for one. Bernard smiled. It didn't look like he would be making that call to McPherson just yet.

****

Gillian felt her stomach involuntarily knot up. At one hundred feet, she could see that the door to Room #3 was slightly askew. Even from a distance, she could see the door pitifully sagged on one hinge. She stopped in mid-stride, putting her forearm on Marty's chest, nearly causing him to lose his balance. He looked at her arm and then at her. Her eyes said it all. The change in the air was almost palpable. He was pretty quick to evaluate their situation and realized he was more of a liability to Gillian than an asset. He touched her shoulder gently, pointed to himself and then to a small thicket with trees. While she did make an elaborate affirmation of what he was indicating, he could sense that she appreciated that he made a quick decision and acted on it.

Marty hunched down and ran toward the trees, as quietly as his lumbering frame would allow. He looked around cautiously to see if there was anyone on the street lurking or lying in wait. There was no one within sight. So, he vaulted to the nearest tree with low branches. Once in the thicket, he assessed that he could probably get a higher perspective on things. Grabbing the lowest limb on a sweet gum tree, he grunted and clambered up the tree, scraping his arms as he went. If they wanted him, they would have to come up after him.

Gillian's gaze darted all around her. She took

mental snapshots of everything. The area was quiet, with the exception of the broken door standing ajar. She considered that it might be a trap. She reached down and pulled the Sig free from her ankle holster—thankful she had the presence of mind to grab the magazine and the weapon before she left. These were some strange times indeed.

Easing around the door to Room #1, she listened for any unusual noise from within. The room's prehistoric air conditioner suddenly clattered loudly, drowning out any chance of her hearing any sounds of a struggle inside. She began to work her way around the small building, occasionally looking over her shoulder. She eased around the building to find a row of small windows along the back where the bathrooms were located. She eased up to the first window. It was locked. The next window bore the same result. If she broke a window coming in, it would give away her position. She worked her way around to the front of the bungalow. She carefully moved back to the door that was ajar. She would have to chance coming in that way.

She picked up an empty drink can from the side of the building, as she came around. She eased up to the door on Room #3. Using the drink can, she pushed the door open and tossed the can. Nothing happened. Taking a quick glance, she saw nothing in the room. With the grace of a cat, she leaped, and tumbled into position. The Sig was poised in front of her. There was no one in the room. She eased her way through the connecting room with the same result. She was alone.

In a flash, she realized that Marty was alone and exposed. She quietly eased outside. Marty was nowhere in sight. A cold feeling crept into her stomach. A hoarse whisper cleared some of the butterflies. "Gillian?"

She looked up and saw him in the tree. His hulking frame desperately clung to the branches. They would all laugh about this later, but for now, she said, "It's okay. Come on down."

He shinnied down the tree, somewhat awkwardly, and landed on the ground. "Is Digger okay?"

"He's gone."

"Where?"

"Good question. Let's go look at the surveillance footage and see if we can answer that."

It took the pair five minutes to figure out the software and find the frame where Digger had disappeared. Their answer entered the room in the form of one Bernard François. Marty heard Gillian suck in her breath at the sight of him. He had out-maneuvered them somehow and she didn't know how. She watched with growing distress, as Bernard entered the room and left a few minutes later with Digger draped across his shoulder like a gunny sack. Something small and square was held firmly in his other hand. He strode out of the motel room and into the darkness. They sat there for a moment, taking it in.

In a small, almost subdued voice, Gillian finally asked, "Where do we go from here? I was so focused on protecting you. I never considered Digger or the gem…" Her voice trailed off. She stared at her hands, they had failed her.

Marty placed a gentle hand on her shoulder. His voice was calm his resolve evident. "There is one aspect these people, whoever they are, have failed to consider." She looked up at him, not prepared for what she saw. His eyes almost pulsed from a light within. His jaw was square, and his look unwavering. "We are connected in a way that they cannot understand. It's time to get our friend back."

In that purest of moments, she saw him in a new light. In an inexplicable moment of reckoning, she cast aside any doubts and believed in him. It went against every instinct that had forged her sense of survival. It was, conceivably, the most irrational thing she had ever done. Were the circumstances not so dire, she might have relished the moment. There was no time for that now. Hope edged its way into her voice. "You're right. How do we begin?"

Marty smiled. "You go ahead and start packing. I'll let you know where we're going in a minute or two. Okay?"

She mustered a weak smile and said, "Okay," as she began to stuff gear into the duffel bag.

Chapter 20

The air in the trunk was stuffy and smelled funny, road kill kind of funny. Digger was not in his happy place. He banged his head, as the car swayed in and out of curves. He slid helplessly, fighting against the duct tape that bound his hands and feet. He breathed slowly through his nostrils and tried to push the tape from his lips. He tried to piece together what had happened through the montage of blurred images. It confused him because he was sure that they had slipped the surveillance teams. No one had followed them. There were no tracking devices on the car. He didn't understand how they had been found. At this point, the *how* was not nearly as important as the *what*.

The side of his head pounded from being struck. His body began to cramp from the confinement in a trunk designed for a donut tire. Between the stuffiness, the warmth and the stress, Digger dozed off for a moment. He dreamed he was jostling in the back of a buckboard wagon. He could hear the guttural growl of hungry wolves chasing the wagon. A single horse whinnied and strained to pull the wagon faster to stay ahead of the hungry pack. Its body was lathered and slick with sweat. Its eyes were wide with fear at the smell of the snarling wolves behind him. Digger struggled to raise his head and look ahead. Small dust clouds wisped past the driver's tan duster and into the wind like smoke on a blustery day. His Stetson stayed glued to his head with a single leather cord, which struggled against the wind. The horse needed no urging to move faster. And yet, the driver continued to slap the reins, egging him on. The driver looked over his shoulder and yelled, "Dude, are you okay?"

"Marty? How did you get here?"

"It's a long story. Do you know where you are?"

Digger looked at him for a moment in disbelief. "I'm right here."

"In your dream, yes. But do you know where you are in real life?"

Digger considered the statement for a moment. "In a car trunk, I think. That's all I know."

"Okay. We're coming after you. Don't worry."

He gave him a wry look. "Worry? Why should I worry?"

"You know what I mean."

The car went over a bump, causing Digger to bang the sore part of his head against the trunk lid. He awoke to throbbing pain and the glow of brake lights. He could feel the vehicle slow down, as it went over rougher terrain. He could just make out the sounds of people talking. He heard the crackle of a walkie-talkie. He strained to move closer to the fender to listen. He heard the sound again. It sounded like a police radio. *A police radio? Maybe they're being pulled over?* He shimmied away from the fender and rolled onto his back. He bent his knees as much as he could in the confined space and kicked at the fender wall, making a small thud. A stab of pain from the side mounted light made him realize that he wasn't wearing shoes. He ignored the pain and continued to kick. He stopped for a moment and listened. He heard voices which suddenly went silent—deadly silent.

Don White had only been on duty for an hour. The fight he had with Marybeth was still fresh in his mind, as he approached the driver's side to ask the tall fellow about the busted tail-light. The tinny *clink* of the hammer was the last thing he heard, as the silenced Glock fired a single round between his eyes. He crumpled in a heap where he stood. It seemed like an eternity before the trunk finally opened. Digger sighed in relief, as the dark-headed man in a brown uniform shirt peered in. Without so much as a word, the Deputy reached in and yanked Digger up out of the trunk by his clothing. He unceremoniously dragged him to the police cruiser and hurled him into the backseat, like a bag of potatoes.

Unaccustomed to such behavior, Digger lay in the seat bewildered for a moment. He had anticipated more professionalism from a man of the law. He straightened himself up in the seat in time to see the uniformed man throw the half-naked body of another man into the trunk of the car in front of the cruiser. A chill crawled its way up his spine and down his arms causing every hair on his arms to stand on end. He had awoken from a bad dream into a nightmare.

He practiced his breathing exercises to calm himself. He closed his eyes and pictured his *happy place*. As he watched the sunrise over Malibu, the head of the dead man popped out of the sand in front of him. He opened his eyes to stop the image. In the early morning sun behind a bright gilt-edged cloud, sunbeams burst from it. It was possibly the most beautiful thing he had ever seen. He hoped it was not the last sunrise he would ever see. If it was—at least it was a nice one.

****

Marty sat, with his eyes closed on the bed. He concentrated on Digger. He looked through Digger's eyes at the sunrise. It was beautiful and scary—all at the same time. Marty could see a tall dark-headed man wiping down a bronze Toyota in front of them. He watched as the man put the car in gear and pointed it off the road. It idled over the edge of the embankment and plummeted into the ravine below. There was no fire, no explosion, just a pillar of steam from a busted radiator. The man turned and smiled at Digger, as he walked back toward a patrol car.

Digger turned his gaze back to the scene in front of him. Bernard smiled with a sense of satisfaction, as he walked back to the patrol car. Saying nothing, he eased in, throwing a black duffle bag on the floor beside him. He adjusted the seat and mirror without a word. As he eased the car into gear, he flipped off the light bar and slowly pulled the car onto the road. It should be several hours before anyone noticed the Camry at the bottom of the ravine. Hopefully, he would be out of the country by then.

Gillian sat down beside Marty on the bed. His eyes were out of focus. She placed her hand on his arm. Her touch was like an electric shock to him. He jumped, startled by it. She pulled back, reflexively.

He opened his eyes and looked at her. "He's in the back of a patrol car, headed south."

She was startled by his eyes, which glowed more intensely now with flashes of eerie blue light. She stammered, "H-How do you know that?"

Distantly, he replied, "Because I can see the sun is coming up on the driver's side."

"That's not what I meant. How do you know where he is at all? We don't have the stone."

"I don't need the stone. I can see him."

She stared at him.

He looked toward her, but didn't look at her. His voice was clear. "It's the man we saw on the camera. He has stolen a police car and uniform. Digger is in the backseat, tied up."

She quit trying to rationalize it and simply asked, "Can you tell where they're going?"

"They're going toward the airport."

"How do you know?"

"There was a road sign. He's going in that direction."

"That's good enough for me. Let's go."

Hopefully, they would make to Digger it in time.

Chapter 21

Ordinarily, Marty would have been petrified, had he seen Gillian pushing the Volkswagen faster and faster while talking on the cell phone. Instead, he was tuned out to what was going on around him, and watching everything that he could to help Digger.

Her responses were clipped, as Franz methodically fired questions at her: "Where are you now? Is he injured? Has there been gunfire?" Franz's voice was calm, with the detachment of a pollster. When she interrupted with a question, his calm was like that of a therapist. This was a typical situation update for them. She carefully listened to his instructions over the whine of the engine and the squall of the tires, repeating them back to him to ensure that nothing was lost in translation. They were to go to the airport after they collected Digger. A plane would be waiting on them there. It all sounded so simple over the phone.

Digger would have cringed, had he seen the limits she pushed the Volkswagen to. Even with his life at stake, he would have shivered at the smell of hot rubber and the smell of the brakes. The small four cylinder whined in protest, as she again took it to the redline. Slowly, they began to close the gap—unbeknownst to Bernard. Marty sat rigidly beside her. His eyes had a weird glow, as he spoke in a monotone voice. Every few seconds, he would adjust their route to intersect with the patrol car ahead. She had long heard the rumors of CIA *remote viewing* but had dismissed them as voodoo ops. That view was changing rapidly, as Marty sat beside her. He was quite rigid and his voice was right out of a Vincent Price movie.

Marty would explain it to her later, but for now he watched the entire scene was surreal, like he was in a hot air balloon high overhead. He wasn't sure how he was doing it, but he could see both cars from the air. Periodically, he would tell her where to turn. From the corner of his eye, he would suddenly have flashes of small game such as rabbits or field rats. Fortunately, *eyes* were staying true to what he needed.

He realized that they were passing the location where the car had gone over into the ravine. He blinked and turned to Gillian. Flatly, he said "Stop."

She blinked at him for a moment and continued to drive. Again, he stated more firmly, "Stop." She let her foot off of the accelerator and crammed her foot on the brake, almost throwing Marty into the dash.

Staring straight ahead, he said, "Pull over to the shoulder. Careful. There's an embankment."

She coasted over to the shoulder and slowed to a stop.

"Back up."

She put the Bug in reverse and moved back up the road on the shoulder. There was no other traffic on the road yet. She could see the plume of vapor curling from below the grade of the roadway. As they got closer, they could see the outlines of a car at the bottom of the embankment. Marty looked at her, his eyes glowed brightly. "You must call this in. It will be worse for the family, if they have to search for him first and then find him dead."

She gave him a sideways look. "Find who dead?"

"The police officer in the trunk, of course. Haven't you been listening to a word I've said?"

"Yes, but I thought you were talking figuratively."

"No. Call 911, *now*."

The shrug was almost involuntary. "Okay. Suit yourself." She handed him the phone.

Smoothly, he lied to the 911 operator. "...flat tire...car down the embankment...no I don't know if there's anyone in the car...steam or fire..."

The dispatcher assured him that there would be a car along in a few minutes. He knew they would be long gone. There was nothing they could do for the fallen officer. He looked at Gillian and said hollowly, "Let's go. Straight ahead. There will be an airport marker. Follow it."

She felt the goose bumps rise on her arm and move to her legs. Gillian wasn't sure at what point she had stopped calling the shots, but she knew without a doubt, that she didn't like it. Regardless, of her feelings of the situation, she moved on. Within two minutes, she saw the airport marker and followed it. Marty was back in his zone. She liked it better when people were shooting at them.

****

Al McGillacutty eased the champaign 1968 Buick Riviera down the road, enjoying the crisp morning air. It was the same trip he made every week. He smiled over the thought that Earl had been able to return his beloved Riviera so quickly. For over a decade, he had been coaxing the life into the ancient air conditioning system on Sunday mornings. Normally the roads were deserted. It was most curious when the chocolate brown patrol car topped the hill from nowhere and dropped in behind him hard and fast with his lights blazing. He looked down. He was barely at the speed limit, much less over it. He knew every deputy in the department, and they knew him. There was no reason to delay him and yet there it was, as big as life.

Bernard eyed the Riviera ahead and hit the gas pedal. The patrol car had been an impromptu change. Now, it was time to make another. Out of county patrol cars stood out, but he did not want to stand out. He pushed the powerful engine to catch the ancient Buick and flipped the switch on the light bar. He fiddled with several switches until he triggered the siren. After a quick blare, he quickly shut it off to avoid drawing unnecessary attention to himself. The Buick eased to the shoulder in front of him. Gravel crunched under the tires, as he eased to a stop.

McGillicutty studied the patrol car in the rearview mirror. It was an older model Chevrolet, indicating a younger officer. It looked like Deputy White's car, but it wasn't Don White driving the car. Instinctively, he left the Buick in gear with his foot on the brake. The officer's approach was odd. He looked around him almost ignoring the old man behind the wheel, focusing instead on the tree line in anticipation of an ambush. The rising sun glinted off of his dark glasses as he finally looked in McGillicutty's direction. "Could I see your operator's license, please?"

McGillicutty gave him an odd look. While his accent was odd, no sworn officer ever asked for an *operator's license* around here. He smiled at the officer glancing at his name tag as he did. The chrome tag

White glinted in the morning sun. The old man tried to keep his composure. He knew Don White and this fellow wasn't him. Al had survived two tours on the front lines in Korea by following his gut and using good old-fashioned horse sense. Right now, his gut was telling him that something was terribly wrong. He smiled disarmingly and squinted at the officer. "What say Sonny?"

The old man's mind worked, furiously. *Officer White's* hands were in front of him, with his thumbs tucked in his belt. While terribly theatrical, it meant he would have to reach for the gun. The distinctive basket weave of the Sam Browne belt looked like White's rig, which meant it was a safety holster. They could be tricky if you weren't used to them. It would be all the time he would need.

Bernard repeated the request louder. "Your operator's license, please." The accent was a little heavier this time.

Bernard waited. He would shoot the old man, as he turned.

"All right, all right…you don't have to yell…"

He reached toward the dash and he heard the click of the thumb snap on the holster. He didn't wait. He jammed his foot on the accelerator. The V-8 roared, as it spun sideways, almost knocking over Bernard and showering him with dirt and loose gravel. Bernard grabbed the weapon and yanked, almost pulling the whole rig up with it. The gun was still firmly in the holster. He cursed and pushed the weapon forward, releasing it from the stiff leather. McGillacutty heard the *crack* of the automatic and the instantaneous *thunk* of bullets, hitting the old steel body. The shooting stopped and McGillacutty peeped up in time to see the Buick hurtling toward a ravine on the opposite side of the road. He yanked the wheel and eased off the gas. It was enough to change direction. The old car groaned under the demand, but held steady as it smoothly eased back into the right lane. He peered in the rearview mirror, only to see the officer's back. He was not facing the opposite direction. Al decided to sort it all out later, but for now it was time to put some distance between them. As he sped down the road, he considered that between the two weird guys Rose had told him about and some foreigner posing as Don, it was clearly a weekend for the books.

****

"Gillian, I know this is going against all you instincts, but please trust me on this. You don't need to use your gun."

She took her eyes off the road for enough time to give him a *have you lost your mind* look and then it was back to the road. "Sorry, I don't do that. I do what I do, instinctively. It's not a matter of choice. Hocus Pocus doesn't work for me."

"You can and you must. You will fire. The Frenchman will fire. Some innocent bystander will be hurt. You must try to use your power."

"What if I don't do it right? I've only done it once and that was like being in a dream. What if I imagined it? What if I was in some drug-induced high? I can't take that chance."

He placed a gentle hand on her arm. "I know you can do it. I believe in you."

She scowled. "I appreciate that. I really do. But this is war. You don't win a war with happy thoughts.'

His eyes were beginning to return to normal, enough so that she could see the sadness in them. "The war has ended. You must begin anew. Sometimes, belief is all you need."

Deep within her, it was fear that still lurked; fear that he was right; fear that she would never be the warrior that she was. However, it was anger that responded, "That doesn't work for me. I've got a Sig and I plan to use it."

The VW practically left the ground, as it came over the small rise and arrived at a scene from the movies. A uniformed officer was standing in the middle of the road, his pistol blazing at an aging Buick wildly careening away. Gillian jammed the brakes and spun the wheel deftly causing the car to skid around sideways. The squall of tires caused the officer to turn and face them. The scene unfolded in slow motion, he removed his glasses. His eyes slanted and his mouth turned in a menacing leer, as he recognized Gillian behind the wheel. His weapon never lowered, as he took new aim at her. At last, it was his chance to eliminate the American woman -once and for all. Not *all* Frenchmen were Lovers.

Gillian tried to control the swerve, so that she could draw her weapon and return fire. The small car refused to respond the way that she wanted it to. The car half-skidded and stopped, so that she was only partly turned. She was in a bad position to return fire. He, on the other hand, was in a perfect position. *Crap!*

Bernard didn't wait. He fired the first round. She reacted, as she had been trained to do. Only this training had not come from the military. The world around her began to slow. She watched the white hot energy at the tip of the barrel. She watched the glowing red bullet travel toward her, faster than she would have believed. She struggled to redirect the energy back on itself. She marginally succeeded as the speeding bullet slowed, microsecond-by-microsecond. It got closer, it was slow enough that it struck the side of the car at about the speed of thrown rock. As it pinged a small chip of paint and fell to the ground. Gillian hardly noticed. She was already concentrating on the next round fired by Bernard. She concentrated on his finger tightening on the second round. Somehow, he seemed ridiculously slow in his movements.

The second round exploded from the barrel and began its long slow journey toward them. Now she was able to focus all of her energy on the second round. She redirected the bullet's energy back on itself. It fell to the ground, halfway to the car. Bernard hardly realized what was happening, as he fired a third round. This time, she held it in the barrel letting it spin, furiously heating and expanding the metal tube. The choked barrel would prove catastrophic for the final round.

Gillian waited now. Bernard squeezed the trigger one final time. As she waited, the millisecond seemed like an eternity. In the fleeting moment before the end, she watched the flicker of confusion in Bernard's eyes. She sat and simply waited. She watched the kaleidoscope of color, as the heated gases and shrapnel exploded in the center of the barrel, snapping the slide and pushing it backward in a shower of energy and debris. For the first time in her life, she watched the slide pierce Bernard's forehead in slow graphic detail. The energy snapped his head back for an instant before he finally dropped to his knees, crumpling into a heap.

Even though she hated him; even though he was trying to kill them, she felt no sense of satisfaction from this. She blinked and found herself back with Marty and Digger in real time. A single tear formed in the corner of her eye. For the first time in her life, a pang of regret touched her. Marty said nothing, but simply placed a comforting hand on her shoulder.

Chapter 22

It took hardly any force on the razor sharp carbon steel blade to free Digger from the gray tape binding his wrists. Marty caught Digger and steadied him, as he wobbled from the confinement and nerves. He guided his friend to the comfort of the bug, as Gillian methodically cleaned the patrol car of fingerprints. Second nature, born of years of experience, dictated her patterns to leave no trace evidence to follow. Normally, she would plant trace evidence for the forensics people to find. She liked to use blonde hairs, torn Minneapolis bus stubs and broken shards of imported Scandinavian glass. But today, time was of the essence. This crime scene would undoubtedly get a lot of scrutiny since a fellow officer had died. A good cleaning would have to do. Bernard would undoubtedly get the blame. While a weapon malfunction would be attributed to his demise. There should be no follow up, other than to inform the family. She retrieved the small wooden box from the front seat and handed it back to Marty. She met his eyes. They were both thinking it, but he was polite enough not to say 'I told you so,' and she was smart enough not to bring it up.

In less than a half-hour, the small section of back road would be swarming with police officers, ambulances, fire trucks and men in dark suits with solemn countenance. But for now, it was the trio of friends and one body.

They piled in the VW and buzzed down the road. Gillian's driving was now under Digger's careful scrutiny, so she drove closer to the speed limit and much less erratically than when she was trying to find him. He still gave her an occasional frown when she cornered too fast, but said nothing. The chatter among them ranged from the amusing to the virulent, but none of it involved the morning's events. They pretended to be on a normal morning spin, even though there was nothing normal about what they did. After a few moments, the small car was strangely silent, as they each contemplated what would happen next.

****

Maria De La Hoya put the phone back in the cradle and stared at it for a moment. She had been in government service for most of her career, but she had never received a call like that. A crisp female voice greeted her. "I'm calling for Site Supervisor De La Hoya?"

"Speaking."

"Please stay on the line for the Deputy Director."

De La Hoya tensely waited for the unprecedented call from a superior high up on the list.

"De La Hoya?"

"Yes, Sir?"

"Did you receive the packet?"

"Yes, Sir."

"Please open it now."

"One moment, while I remove it from the safe, Sir." She lied. It sat in front of her on the desk. "I'm opening it now, sir." She ripped open the seal.

She dumped the contents on the desk. Inside she

found a banded pack of a hundred dollar bills, passports bearing the Diplomatic seal, and gate instructions. She read off the inventory to the Director.

"Good. How long have you been with us, De La Hoya?"

"Five years in TSA. I spent the previous fifteen in Army Intelligence, Sir."

"Good. Then you understand the nature of sensitive information. You will have three young people coming in that will match the descriptions in the passports. You are to remain on your post until they arrive. Understood?"

"Yes, Sir." She cringed at the thought of waiting forever for a bunch of spooks to show up. It always spelled trouble.

"Good. Follow the instructions on the gate information. There will be a private plane waiting. Ensure that they board that flight without incident. Is that understood?"

"Affirmative, Sir."

"Good, good. You will tell the female in the team that *Franz sent me*. Understood?"

She parroted back, "Franz sent me." She bit her tongue to keep from responding with a smart ass comment about secret handshakes or decoder rings to the Deputy Director. Statements like that could prove to be career limiting.

"Very good, De La Hoya. How long have you been a Supervisor?"

"Three years, Sir."

"This conversation did not occur. No leaks on this and maybe you'll be here for another three years. Are we clear?"

"Crystal."

The line clicked and went dead. Her gut told her that the orders were from higher up—possibly even from the Secretary himself.

De La Hoya fidgeted, trying to get caught up on the paperwork covering the gunmetal gray desk. It had been two hours since the phone call. She had to call her neighbor to pick up her daughter from school. She was starting to get irritated. She had three years of combat experience, spoke four languages and was respected by some of the top intelligence officers in the Army. Now, she was in a holding pattern because some bureaucrat was nervous about travel arrangements. Her patience began to wane when the knock came at the door.

Gillian looked around, making sure she was out of camera range. She unloaded the Sig and wrapped it in a clean towel, while her fledgling team kept a look out. Placing it in the spare tire well, she lifted three matching overnight bags and handed them back one-by-one without looking. She slammed the trunk shut, as she called Franz. "We're at CLT and proceeding into the main terminal building."

After a minute of silence, she hung up the phone. "We're to go straight to the TSA supervisor's office."

Both young men blinked at her and then at each other. Marty found his wits first and asked, "You're sure that's what he said?"

She was only partially successful at not giving him a dour look. "I know it sounds insane, but the TSA will be assisting us."

Digger shook his head. Having escaped capture only a short while ago, the thoughts of walking straight into a paranoid stronghold and turning themselves in seemed nutty. In retrospect, he concluded that talking to rocks was as well, so he held his tongue. Gillian patted herself twice for hidden weapons. A concealed weapon in an airport would make this a very short trip.

She took point in the airport and wasted no time in finding a uniformed officer. After a few indecipherable radio exchanges, the screener personally escorted them to the office. The screener rapped on the door waiting for her superior to acknowledge.

De La Hoya barked through the door, allowing the screener to hold it for them upon arrival. She regarded the trio severely because for their beatnik college appearance, but said nothing disparaging. When only De La Hoya could see her, their escort rolled her eyes as she backed out of the room. De La Hoya concentrated on maintaining her icy exterior.

Gillian extended a hand. "Kelly, Gillian Kelly."

"De La Hoya." She was greeted by a confident handshake and she returned it. It was one more suited to a soldier than a student.

Maria quickly sized up Gillian. She had the earmarks of a professional: quick eyes, physically fit, strong, callused hands; the kind of professional you wouldn't want to be on the receiving end of. She looked Gillian in the eye. "I was informed by my superior to provide any necessary support until you board your flight. I was also instructed to provide you with the contents of this packet." She handed Gillian a freshly sealed manila envelope.

Gillian regarded the packet for a moment and asked, "Would you happen to have a place in private where I can examine the contents with my colleagues?"

Maria smiled inwardly at the term *colleagues*.

"Feel free to use my office. I'll step outside. Let me know when you're ready." She paused for a second before finishing with, "Let me urge you to expedite your evaluation of the material. There is a plane waiting for you."

Gillian smiled, unruffled. "We'll only be a moment."

Maria returned it with a tight smile of her own. She was going to be a lot happier when these people were on their way. She stepped out of the office and waited just outside the door.

Gillian ripped open the package and dumped the contents onto the now clean desktop. She thumbed through the contents, jabbing out passports and money as she went. Marty stared at the cash. "What's this?"

She smiled. "Traveling money."

Each stuffed documents and money into various pockets, as Digger cracked the door. "Officer De La Hoya?"

She walked past Digger and Marty, regarding them for a moment with cool disdain. Neither was military and both seemed like nice kids. She wondered how they got hooked up in all of this. With a mental shrug, she looked at Gillian, "Okay, Ms. Kelly, if you and your friends would follow me, and please keep up."

De La Hoya managed to stay to the side of the trio. She never exposed them to her back. Gillian admired the officer's poise. She clearly had professional experience. In fact, they weren't that dissimilar. In and out of twists and turns, De La Hoya walked quickly and confidently through the winding terminal. Never once going back through the main terminal, they navigated through the bowels of the airport. There seemed to be a cipher lock at every turn. It would be impossible to go back the way they came in. Gillian kept track of the turns as a habit. Still, she didn't think it would do her any good. They followed narrow corridors that were dotted with cramped antiquated offices full of disillusioned masses of schedulers, planners and logistics people of every type—none of which even acknowledged their presence. They felt invisible.

Gillian stopped, as they reached another cipher at the end of the narrow hall. De La Hoya coded in the cipher and allowed Gillian to enter, only to have Marty place a hand on her shoulder. "Hold up."

Gillian looked at him. "What's the matter?"

"Something's wrong."

She glanced sharply back at De La Hoya. He shook his head. "Not her. There's someone out there."

De La Hoya bristled at him, "Sir, I assure you that there are no boogey men on the other side of that door."

She pushed past them into a dimly lit baggage cavern. There appeared to be no one else in the room, but there were hiding places at every turn.

Maria was now ahead of them. She waved them on and said, "Come on, people. Let's go. We've got a plane waiting."

Gillian let De La Hoya get a few steps ahead before she paced herself beside Marty. Instinctively, she trusted Marty's instincts. Quietly, she inquired, "What's up?"

He looked at her, gravely. "We're walking into an ambush. I can sense it."

Digger listened but said nothing.

A hulking baggage handler popped up out of nowhere. A startled Marty jumped. Digger nearly wet himself and Gillian was two seconds away from taking him out when De La Hoya looked back and said, "Hey Ernie. What's shakin'?" She kept walking, without waiting on a reply.

Ernie raised his hand in a silent acknowledgment. His crush on Maria was evident to everyone except her. He smiled at the three behind her. *They must be important friends for her to bring them through this area. No one is allowed back here.* All three smiled and waved back. Ernie thought, *They seem like nice people.* He went back to loading luggage for US Air to Philly, making sure he checked each tag for the TSA seal. The auditors wouldn't catch him on that again.

Using another code key, Maria opened the gate in front of them, which led out of the baggage area. She moved ahead down the narrow sheet metal corridor to the hangar complex. She didn't wait to hear the door click behind them. Without stopping, she did a brief look to the rear to ensure that all of her little ducklings were still in tow. Satisfied all three were with her, she continued down the tin hall at a deliberate pace. She had things to do, and they appeared to be keeping up. She stopped for a moment at the end of the tunnel, so they could catch up. The sudden burning sensation above her right breast felt painfully familiar. It had been years since she'd felt that kind of pain.

She looked down to see the broadening red stain across her white uniform shirt. She staggered back a step before crumpling into a heap. It was like all the energy left her. Her eyes began to blur, as everything seemed to slow down around her. Her mind drifted for a moment. She looked down at the blood stain. It covered half her uniform now.

She stared at the red, wondering how she would get the blood stain out. They were only issued four new sets of uniforms a year now. They had to keep them up. Budgets were tight this year.

Armand waited patiently in the hangar. Quite honestly, he was a far better thief than an assassin, but times were tough for a hired gun. He took any work he could get these days. With all the expatriate terrorists running amuck, there were too many free agents in the field. The labor market was flooded with cheap killers willing to blow up a school bus of kids for a pack of smokes. Accessing the hangar, stealing a size fifty-two coverall and making himself look like he belonged was easy. Shooting the dishy broad in uniform was a bonus. His instructions from the Scot were clear. *Follow and observe*. If any of the kids appeared to do anything weird or supernatural (whatever that was), eliminate them and bring the gem to his boss. It seemed simple enough, though he had trouble deciphering what he had meant by *supernatural*. He had watched from a distance as the gun blew up in the Frenchman's hand. All the while, she stared at him like she were willing it to happen. It was at that point that he decided that the situation was *supernatural* enough. It was time to collect the gem and cash in.

Digger headed back to the door to the baggage area. The door had a code key on both sides. He turned to face the others, his face a deathly shade of pale. They were trapped.

Chapter 23

Gillian grabbed De La Hoya by the collar and pulled her back, scanning as she moved. She looked back at Marty and said, "Get her out of here." She watched as Marty struggled under the load of De La Hoya's dead weight. She didn't have time to worry about that.

Gillian popped her head out, trying to survey the scene without compromising her position. This was urban warfare. This she understood. he called back to Marty. "I need some eyes here, Pal." She made small cat-like movements up the corridor.

Marty moved in close behind her, trying to follow her example. Halfway up the length of the corridor, he stopped and slid down the wall to the floor. He relaxed, as he eased onto the concrete floor. Gillian stopped and gave a quick backward glance. She watched as his eyes had begun to glow. She turned her attention back to the front of the tunnel. She hissed back to Marty, "Are you picking anything up yet?"

She noticed the change in the tone of his voice, "You'll have your visual in a moment."

Forty-eight hours ago if someone without electronic surveillance equipment had told her that, she would have thought them insane. Right now, she was happy to have him. "Let me know when you have something."

"Will do." His voice was detached and ethereal.

Marty called out to Gillian. "It's an older man in a gray maintenance uniform. He's walking toward us."

Gillian nodded. The older gentleman seemed to be in no hurry. In fact, he looked almost nonchalant.

"Are you sure it's him? He doesn't look like he has a gun?"

"He's your shooter. He has a pistol in his right pocket."

She stepped out and faced the man directly. He didn't seem concerned nor, did he react like she would have expected a trained killer to. He didn't try to hide or conceal himself. He was either the most confident hitman she had ever met, or the most stupid. He looked at Gillian and smiled. Removing his hand from his broad coverall pocket, she saw the narrow frame of an older Walther PPK slip from his pocket. The long tube of a silencer pointed straight at her. "That's quite far enough, Missy. Why don't we go back down to the ally for a little privacy? I'll make it quick and painless for you and your friends."

Gillian considered him carefully. She wasn't in a practice of underestimating her adversaries. It was unfortunate that her adversary was. She responded, civilly. "Look, I know it seems like the odds are in your favor at the moment, but believe me it is in your best interest to just walk away. Don't ask any questions. Just leave."

Armand snickered. *She must think I'm stupid.* "In case you hadn't noticed, Honey, *I'm* holding the gun."

Her eyes turned to ice. "So, do you plan to talk me to death?"

"I hit the security chick over there at a hundred and

fifty feet away. Unless you can cover forty feet in two seconds, I don't think you have a chance." *Screw it. She's not going to talk her way out of this. She must think I was born yesterday.* He stopped, and leveled the gun at her chest.

She spoke, calmly. "This is your last chance, Mister."

"See you in Hell, Sister." He squeezed the trigger. It seemed to be stuck. He squeezed harder. His finger was beginning to hurt. Beads of perspiration began to pop out from his forehead. She seemed to be getting closer, but she wasn't moving. He was. Unnoticed by him, a large vent fan in the garage behind him began to slow. Slowly, his feet dragged along the rough concrete. He placed his other finger on the trigger and squeezed harder. His hands began to shake from the strain. He tried to back up only to find that he couldn't. As he moved his feet backward, he seemed to move toward her faster. He began to panic. The woman was as serene as an alpine lake.

Digger stared at Maria, trying to control the panic and remember the only first aid course he had ever had. His memory struggled with the data. He recited the treatment for bleeding to himself, *Direct pressure, pressure points, elevation.* There was no mention of sucking chest wounds in Mrs. Tannenbalm's fifth grad Health Class. He searched his pockets for anything. His fingers closed around the money and several napkins from last night's restaurant. *Napkins ought to do it.* He pushed the wad of napkins over the wound. The blood seemed to slow its christening effect on her uniform but was beginning to pool beneath her. He eased her up and found a much larger hole in her back. *The bullet must have gone straight through. Oh well, it's only money.* Maria stirred. Her face was turning an ashen color. Her eyes lolled back. He swallowed back the fear.

Rolling her onto her side, he tore the back of the shirt open. Wiping his hand on his pants, he put his palm over the wound. It slowed the blood flow considerably. The waded-up napkin fell off her chest. He placed his other hand over the wound. With one hand on each side of her body, he seemed to slow the flow of blood. However, even with the wounds covered, she seemed to be slipping from him. He was going to lose her. He looked up for Marty and Gillian. They were doing what they could to keep the shooter at bay. There was no other help. He was alone in this. It was in desperation that he closed his eyes and reached out. *Rachel?*

Nothing happened. He concentrated harder. *Please, I need your help.*

Silence.

Rachel, please!

The response was calm. *I'm here, Digger.* The blackness began to lighten. He was in a vast empty void, filled with a soft glow of golden light. In the distance, someone was approaching him. It seemed to take no time and she was with him. Now she was in front of him, smiling. *Yes?*

In desperation, his thoughts tumbled out. *The girl I'm with. She was trying to help us. She was shot. I think she's dying. I don't know what to do.*

Rachel pouted. *In the arms of another woman and you want my help. Honestly, Digger, how am I supposed to trust you?*

He cut her off. *She's going to die!*

She placed a soft hand on his face. *She'll be fine. Trust me. Let's have a look see, shall we?*

Digger opened his eyes. Maria's breath was rapid and shallow.

He could hear Rachel in his mind. *Hmm. I like her hair. Maybe I ought to change my look. What do you think?*

A little aggravated, he thought, *Can we focus here? Please?*

For Heaven's sake, Sweetie, it's just a bullet wound. It's not a bad one, at that. It missed a main artery by a mile.'

Without warning, Digger could feel an odd warmth coursing through him. It followed his arms to his hands. As he looked at his hands, they began to lighten and glow, as did Maria's wound. The bleeding seemed to stop immediately. Maria's color began to improve.

See? She'll be as right as rain in no time. Is that all you needed?

Yes. Sorry. I just get excited when people are dying on me.

He closed his eyes and she was there. She placed the tips of her fingers under his chin and drew him near. She kissed him ever so lightly on the lips. The scent of flowers followed her. *It's okay, Sweetie. It just means you care. I wouldn't want you any other way.* She winked and was gone.

Digger smiled. She was so cool. He cradled Maria's head on his leg,

Maria's eyes fluttered open. Her head was splitting and her mouth was as dry as a Baptist church social, but she was alive. The blonde kid, *Delgado,* she thought—was hovering over her like an expectant father. He smiled. *That's good*, she guessed. He asked her something. She didn't understand at first. She shut her eyes and took a deep breath. Her chest was sore, but the burning was gone. She closed her eyes again and rested.

A few moments later, her eyes flew open. It had been a horrible dream. She stared down at her chest. The uniform was covered in blood, but the place where the bullet had entered had a round white scar, but nothing more. It wasn't a dream. It had really happened. *This can't be.* She looked up at the blonde kid again. He was kind of cute. He spoke again. This time, her brain registered the question through all of the ringing. "How are you feeling?"

"Like the floor of a cross town bus. Other than that, I'm here. Do I have you to thank for that?"

He evaded answering the question. "I'm just glad you're back with us. You gave us quite a scare."

He seemed sweet and quite clueless. She had knocked on death's door before during the Gulf War. She knew the score. She also knew that there was no Corpsman alive that could spontaneously heal a wound.

Digger looked at her, earnestly. "We need to get you to a doctor. You need fluids."

"Give me a Dr. Pepper and some ibuprofen, I'll be fine. I've got to get you on that flight."

"One thing at a time, Officer." He smiled again.

Armand tried fervently to get the weapon to fire. The harder he tried, the less effective he seemed to be. His ice calm demeanor melted as a rising tide of panic washed over him. His feet seemed to be floating now. He could stop himself from getting dangerously close to the girl. Hand-to-hand combat had never been his forte. *It looks like it's was time for Plan B*. Giving up on the pistol, he opened his hand and let the Walther fall to the ground. He tried to ignore the pain in his finger. Reaching into the opposite pocket, his hand closed on a compact stun gun and waited to get closer. Suddenly, he stopped moving. He didn't care. He was going to finish this. He started running toward the girl. After all, she was half his size. *How tough can she be?* When he was only a few feet from her, he yanked the stun gun free and leveled it with her neck.

She shook her head, as though she were being patient with a child and said softly, "I really wish you wouldn't do that."

He leered at her, the little twit. He lunged forward with the stun gun, only to find that she wasn't there. *Okay, so she is pretty quick.* He whirled around and grabbed her arm. Gillian half-smiled. She clamped her hand on his wrist, pushing it upward. As gracefully as a ballerina, she nearly pirouetted under his raised arm, so that now he was behind her with his wrist firmly locked in her grip. Pain radiated the length of his arm, as the stun gun fell uselessly to the ground. In one fluid chopping motion, she drove his arm toward the ground like an axe handle and pulled it back up in a whipping motion. He watched as his legs sailed up over his head. An instant later, he thudded with a gut-busting slam to the ground. He lay there, wheezing for air. Gillian twisted his wrist neatly into a lock which, in turn, forced him to involuntarily suck in air from the pain. She rolled him over to his stomach, handling him like a calf in a rodeo. Neatly, she folded his arm into his back and pinioned it there. One side of his face was crushed against the tarmac. The other side of his face peered upward through one eye like a flounder. She gave him a dimpled smile and said, "Out please."

He lashed out, verbally. "What the hell are you talking about, you stupid cow?"

Pain coursed his arm like an electric shock. He managed a strangled gurgling noise and screaming would have taken too much effort. The pain eased up marginally, as she eased up on the pressure on his wrist.

His head cleared for a moment. Panting, he pleaded, "What? For the love of God, just tell me what tell me what you want."

She looked at him, civilly. "That's better." The pain subsided. "Move your other arm out and throw the stun gun away."

At this point he had forgotten that he even had the thing—not that it would have done him any good in this position. He managed to work it out from under himself and throw it away. Sniveling, he pleaded, "Can we go back to the part where we both just walk away from this? Please?"

She shook her head, as she stared down at him. This man, of whom she knew nothing, was incredibly lucky. Had he met her the day before, she would have had no compunction in killing him as he lay there. But, as fate would have it, she was a changed person. Instead, she milked him for information. "Who sent you?"

"Some Scottish guy named McPherson."

She twisted a little harder. "Okay, okay, he works for some German called *the duke*."

"The duke of what?"

"I don't know. I swear. His name starts with an L. It's Duke Lindenspoke, or something. He wants some damn jewel you have."

"What were you supposed to do?"

"I was supposed to get the rock anyway I could."

She was surprised by his candor. He was obviously not one of their more devoted employees. "What were you supposed to do with *the jewel*?"

"Take it to him in Germany as soon as I had it. He was going to pay me the rest of my fee."

"And your fee was…" her voice trailed off.

"One Million US. That was just for the gem. If I brought you back alive, it was two. I figured I'd retire you and stick with the easy money. Let's face it. You would do the same thing."

The comment stung, as she realized he was probably right. "I admire your honesty."

"Can I go now?"

"I think you should know that I'm getting out of the business. So today is your lucky day."

He leered back at her with one eye.

With a devilish grin, she quickly struck him in the temple with her elbow. With the suddenness of a light switch the rotund little man went limp. She let go. She looked down at his boots and quickly pulled them off. When she finished with his bootlaces, he resembled a calf in a roping contest. His hands and feet well tied and then strung together, rendering him immobile. The rotund thug lay unconscious and was probably better off that way.

Marty found himself watching both scenes, as though he were in stadium seat looking down. He kept watching to ensure that no other intruders were present. When it was evident that the little round man was the only one, he returned to the corridor. Gillian had things well in hand, so he returned to Digger to help.

He eased over to Maria and asked, "Do we try to move her out of here."

Her eyes fluttered open at the question. She eyed him for a moment, considering what to do, and said, "Go inside the baggage area and get Ernie. Oh, and bring me something to drink."

Marty nodded and looked at the code lock. "What's the number?"

It took less than a minute to find Ernie and face the behemoth in the secluded area. Marty was big. Ernie, on the other hand, was huge. Standing a head taller than Marty and seventy-five pounds heavier, he was not fat, just big. Marty quickly explained that Maria was hurt and was asking for something to drink. Ernie quickly moved to a small break area where he grabbed a sports drink. He and Marty moved back to the hangar access. Even though Ernie said little in the exchange, he paled slightly at the thought of Maria being hurt.

Ernie desperately wanted Maria to like him, but he knew he was slow. She would want a man far smarter than he. Being faced with her rejection, he kept his distance. Except for the occasional head nod, he didn't think she knew he was alive. He eased into the hallway, with Marty in tow. Digger had her sitting up. Her color was still a little pale, but seemed to be improving at an amazing rate. At the sight of the blood, his hands began to involuntarily tremble. She's really hurt. *I have to get her to a doctor.*

Maria recognized the panic in his eyes. She managed a weak smile and reached out with her hand toward him. "It's okay, Ernie. It looks worse than it is. Honest."

He held her hand, timidly. It was a moment he had

always dreamed of. "Maria, we've got to get you to a doctor. You're really hurt."

His skin turned from pale to a growing shade of red and his eyes narrowed at Marty. Maria placed a gentle hand on the side of his face and turned him toward her. "It wasn't them, Ernie. Someone else did this. They saved me."

He calmed, slightly. She looked him in the eye. "I'll go to the doctor in a little while, Ernie. We have something to do first. Okay?"

He eyed her, dubiously, wondering what could be more important than her health. "You're sure about this?"

"I'm sure. Trust me. It'll be okay."

He still looked unsure. He cracked open the sports drink and held it to her lips, careful not to give her too much. She started to put her hands to the bottle and he firmly put her hands back down. Gently, he held the bottle to her lips while she drank, all the while coaching, "Not too fast now…That's it…Nice and slow… Let's take a little break…"

Marty smiled. For such a large man, he was incredibly tender. Gillian approached the group. "How are things down here, guys?"

Ernie eyed her, warily.

Gillian looked at Maria drinking and looked at all the blood on the cement and her uniform. She let out a low whistle. "You've lost a lot of blood. We need to get you to a medic."

Maria looked her in the eye. "Not until you're on that plane and gone from my airport. Not a second before."

Gillian rolled her eyes. With Ernie's help, she tried

to stand. It was all she could do.

Ernie looked down and said, "I'll carry you. It'll be okay."

She looked him in the eye. "Are you sure about this?"

He nodded, somberly. "Yes, Ma'am."

Gently, he cradled her in his arms and asked, "Where to Ma'am?"

Maria gave him the briefest of smiles. "Corporate Charters, F terminal, please, James."

Ernie gave her a confused look. *She must really be hurt. My name isn't James.*

Instead, he responded, "We'll need to get a cart. That's too far to walk."

She nodded in agreement. "Let's try the Delta hangar."

The little troop started walking toward the tarmac again when Gillian stopped. "Hold up, gang. Marty, how's it look?"

Marty stopped behind them. He stood there vacant and swaying for a moment. "It's all clear. Let's move."

Ernie knew he wasn't smart, but these people were strange. As Gillian moved them forward with a hand signal, they walked past Armand who was beginning to stir. Maria looked down at him and asked Gillian, "Is that the bugger who shot me?"

Gillian glanced back. "Yep."

Maria looked Ernie in the eye and said, "We'll take care of him when we come back through."

Ernie growled at Armand. It was low, deep and guttural. A broadening involuntary stain appeared on Armand's crotch. For the first time since she left the office, Maria removed a radio from her belt and started barking orders. Armand would not be alone for long.

Gillian took point and continued to move them forward. Maria watched her from her vantage point of being in Ernie's arms. She had skill. There was no doubt in her mind about that. Her head was always moving as she performed deft movements to ensure that they were clear at blind corners. Maria directed them is short concise commands: "Right," "Left," "Forward ten meters." In no time, they were loading onto a club car in the Delta hangar. Ernie eased out of the hangar and down the concourse.

It was a short ride to a non-descript white hangar, simple block letters signifying, *Corporate Services Hanger*. Two smartly-dressed pilots in white shirts and black ties greeted them with the crisp air of professionalism. While their Finnish accents were noticeable, their English was impeccable. They greeted the group and picked up the bags without asking. Marty held the case with the stone, firmly in his hand.

Gillian reached out and took Maria's hand. "I'm sorry you got hurt. I never dreamed someone would attack us in the airport."

Maria managed a weak smile. "Not to worry. I'm fine. We'll have that fellow locked away for a very long time. You guys take care. I hope you're able to do whatever it is you're planning."

Gillian smiled, but remained silent. She turned and disappeared into the terminal.

Maria looked at Ernie. Quietly, she said, "Home James. We have a criminal to interrogate."

Ernie gave her a confused look.

"Drive me back to the main terminal, please." He nodded in understanding. She leaned over and rested against his hulking figure. She stared at her hand where Gillian had palmed ten crisp one hundred dollar bills and suddenly felt very tired.

Chapter 24

The duke scribbled notes in a worn leather journal with a cheap blue pen as he studied the characters on the yellowed scroll under an intense LED-lit magnifier. Carefully, he touched the lambskin with white cotton gloves to keep the oils from his skin from smudging it. While the long forgotten phonetics on the ancient script had confounded the brightest scholars in the world, the duke could hear long-silenced native voices speaking to him as he read.

Franz silently eased into the room. The duke looked up inquisitively and then back at the scroll. "Hello, Mr. Shemu'el. What news do you have for me?"

"All three boarded the plane and are enroute to Orly. As far as we can tell, the jewel is with them."

"Good. So they're coming to us."

"Yes, Sir."

"Well played, Mr. Shemu'el. Pitting both sides against each other was a master stroke...although it seems to have taken forever. I must admit there were times when I had my doubts. But you did pull it off."

He smiled. "Not bad for a *second rate* archeologist from Tel Aviv, no? There is still much to do once they arrive. The contact with the stone appears to have affected them, or at least that is what I surmised from Mr. Castille's last report."

"And how is our pet rat?"

"Incommunicado at the moment, I'm afraid. I haven't heard from him since he entered the airfield."

"It doesn't matter. He served his purpose. Just like a dog in a fox hunt. He flushed them out to where we want them. In a few days, we can begin the next phase. Please wrap up any loose ends with Armand, would you?"

The use of a first name never bode well for anyone in the employee of the duke. It indicated their tenure was up, and their life.

"I'll see to it, Sir."

"Excellent." He continued to study the text in front of him, concluding their conversation with, "Do inform me when we have the twelfth stone."

Franz took his cue. "Of course, Sir." He backed out of the door.

****

The painted gray cinderblock walls of the antiquated holding cell smelled of urine and dirty socks. Since the expansion, this area was only used when they needed to isolate someone from the general population. Unlike most areas, this one had no camera. The cell door was on a single lock system. No one noticed the tall young guard with blonde hair as he entered cell D-12 with a tray of food. Armand looked up as he entered. "It's about damn time."

The guard didn't look at him, as he set the tray down. He lifted the cover to reveal an empty plate and a small stainless tube atomizer lay in the place of the food. Before Armand could say a word, the guard had administered one quick spray from the atomizer. Armand discovered that while fully conscious, he was quite paralyzed. The guard took his time removing the large syringe of potassium chloride solution. Armand watched helplessly as the guard pushed up his sleeve to find a vein. Unceremoniously, he jabbed the needle into his arm and emptied the contents. The tingling sensation spread across the back of his neck and toward his chest like a lazy tide on the shoreline. The tingling washed over into his chest and resulted in a sudden crushing pain that radiated its way from his chest to his arm. As numbness filled him, blackness began to tunnel his vision until all he could see was the passive young face of the man watching him die.

Ten hours later, Armand Castile was found unresponsive in the holding cell. In the subsequent autopsy, the medical examiner would rule that the subject Castile, Armand had died due to an *acute myocardial infarction*. He did not elaborate as to the cause. Case file NCCR 051022-058 was closed without fanfare or interest (other than that of the Sheriff's office who was always concerned when a prisoner died in custody). No next of kin was available for disposal of the body so in accordance with regulations his body was cremated and placed in a concrete vault with his name and date of death. In the end, no one would really care what happened to Armond Castile.

Chapter 25

Marty sank back into the seat's soft white. It was a welcome change from the day's events. He concentrated on the Sapphire, Gillian, Digger's yellow VW—anything to take his mind off of the fact that the seat was attached to an airplane. As the pilot pulled the steel door closed, he felt his stomach began to twist into knots. He knew then it was going to be a long flight.

Gillian surveyed the cabin around them. She was the first to notice the crisp young Asian flight attendant approaching them from the rear of the cabin. Her tight navy blue skirt and powder blue blouse was as crisp as a new dollar bill. She approached them, smiling. The tightly woven bun of hair never wavered, as she bowed deeply to them. "Hello, my name is Coco. We wish you a pleasant journey. We will depart shortly. Kindly fasten your safety belt."

Even with an accent, her English was flawless.

Gillian recognized her Macanese accent and watched her every movement. As the young attendant politely backed away, she stopped and pondered the young woman. Then she turned her attention to Marty for the first time since they had sat down. His face was pale as paper and a fine layer of sweat dotted his upper lip. The panic in his eyes was almost palpable. She placed her hand on his. It was cool to the touch. "What's the matter, Sweetie? First time flying?"

He breathed out slowly. Not a muscle moved. Only his eyes moved in her direction. Tightly, he said, "Quite the contrary. The last time I flew, the plane crashed. Everyone died but me. I haven't been on a plane since. I thought I would be okay until the cabin door closed."

She smiled sweetly at Coco. "Can we get a bottle of water for my friend?"

Coco scampered off to the galley for the water.

She could see he was fighting his fear with everything he had. She patted his hand, reassuringly. "Everything's going to be just fine. This is one of the best aircraft in the world. Our pilots are Finnish. They are unsurpassed as pilots. We'll be okay, trust me."

He breathed through his nose and studied her face for a moment. He tried to fight the waves of panic. Her deep brown eyes were reassuring. Her composure began to ease his angst just a little. He took another deep breath and sat back. "Better make that a Scotch and water."

She leaned across and kissed him. "Now that's the spirit."

Digger held up his index finger. "Hey, what about me? I got a splinter this morning."

Gillian poked him with her finger. "Cranberry juice and Vodka, as usual, I presume?"

He giggled, girlishly. "Am I that predictable?"

She grinned at him. "Well, yeah, you are."

She looked to the front of the cabin where Coco was pouring Avian into a clear cup. "Coco, we need to change that, please."

Patiently, she looked up from the tiny galley.

"Make that one Scotch and water, neat; one cranberry and vodka on the rocks; and one Seven &

seven. Thanks."

With a smile, Coco nodded and turned back to the galley. She seemed quite unflappable.

Digger looked at her, curiously. "Who's the Seven and Seven for?"

She rolled her eyes. "Me, dummy."

Gillian watched, as Coco faced forward into the cockpit and asked the pilots how long it would be before they began to taxi. The short interchange was in German to which the pilots responded in kind. There was more to Coco than met the eye. She would have to watch her. The drinks arrived shortly. She placed the correct drink in front of each one of them. Marty noted a small resistance to the acrylic cup, as he lifted it from the table in front of him.

Coco smiled at his curious look and simply said, "They're magnetic. That way they don't slide around."

He looked at the bottom of the tumbler to see the small round disk embedded in the tumbler. "Humph. What'll they think of next?"

He drank half the tumbler in one gulp. Gillian eyed him, as she sipped her drink. Marty took a long breath and visibly relaxed. He finished the drink off and handed it back to Coco. She had barely set Digger's drink down when Marty said, "That was perfect. Could I have another, please." She smiled dutifully and shuffled off again.

Moments later, she was back. She moved gracefully against the sway of the airplane, as it taxied. As she handed him the second drink, he asked, "This is an excellent Scotch. What is it?"

She smiled. "It's a Glenlivet thirty-year-old special reserve."

He smiled. "I didn't know Glenlivet had a thirty-year-old reserve."

She smiled, demurely. "They do for the right people."

He sipped the next tumbler a little more judiciously, taking in the musky odor and the crisp smoky flavors. It was Bess who had quietly educated him on the subtleties of Scotch when he was old enough. She was partial to Bowmore, while he tended to like Glenmorangie. They both liked Glenlivet. It had been her most carefully guarded secret in the small Baptist community. They only *tasted* on days when Irene was off and Bess always double washed the glasses.

Marty was well into his second drink before his nervous edge began to wear thin. Coco showed up, appeared with a heaping tray of hors d'oeuvres. Marty's eyes bulged at the tray of Goose *Foie Gras*, imported Dutch Goat's Milk Gouda, and smoked duck slivers ringed by handmade sesame crackers. He hadn't thought about how hungry he was until the smells from the tray tickled his nose and reminded him they had not eaten that morning. There was no encouragement needed for the trio to dig into the tray. Marty savored the tangy richness of the duck for a moment before swallowing and popping a dangerously full cracker with foie gras. Another gulp from the tumbler and it was empty. Another one was in its place before Marty could ask.

Coco watched their camaraderie and took pleasure in experiencing their laughter. It was not something she had done in many years. Digger poked Gillian in the arm. "Man, I was mad at you in the motel. I was having this awesome dream about Rachel, and right in the middle, you woke me up."

Marty sniped in mock jealousy, "Jeez, Dude, I got some weird old guy in a library and you end up with the babe... What's up with that?"

Gillian punched Marty in the arm. All three tittered at the inside joke. Coco could not help but give them a quizzical look. Gillian smiled disarmingly and whispered to her, "Video game." She nodded and politely smiled, as she backed toward the galley, all the while thinking, *Enjoy it now guys. Enjoy it now.*

The cabin fell silent as the passengers were lulled by the gentle hiss of the airplane, the alcohol and sumptuous food. Marty was rocked into gentle sleep. His dream carried him far away to the sheer edge of a rugged granite cliff. The winds whipped and tugged at his body, as he surveyed the diorama of green rolling pastures surrounded by neatly tended vineyards and punctuated by clumps of evergreen hillocks. The wind beckoned him forth. He stood motionless over the drop. He should have been petrified, but there was no sensation of fear hardening the pit of his stomach, warning him to back away from the edge. It was an odd sensation. He should have been afraid. In that moment of calm insanity, he did what should have been impossible for a normal man—he jumped.

He fell, exhilarated at the magnitude of gravity pulling him downward. He hurdled toward the serenity below him, feeling the delicious mixture of falling and the freedom of flight. His arms outstretched, every nerve tingling, the earth raced toward him at an alarming rate. And in that long descent, he began to level into an awkward glide. He lacked the finesse of a creature of wings. And yet, he was as airborne. He felt the continual unyielding draw of the earth, while he glided effortlessly above the trees. He turned and rolled, relishing the freedom of flight. A small village loomed on the horizon. He glided to it, as though drawn by some hidden force. Amidst the chaos of the courtyards below him, a peaceful stone church beckoned to him. He eased over the stone wall surrounding the church and landed gently on his toes, crunching the gravel beneath his feet.

The sensations of flight made him feel odd being grounded again. He wanted to return to the air. Yet, even with the thrill of having just flown like a bird, he could not overcome the magnetism of the small chapel. He wondered what drew him to this place. He walked slowly toward the chapel. The façade was simple, almost primitively crude, and yet an aura clung to it like a cloak. It differed from any church he had ever seen. He stared at the skull and crossbones so prominently displayed below the crucifix and wondered, *Did pirates come here? And why were they in the mountains? None of this makes any sense.*

He climbed the chapel steps, not knowing what or who to expect. He was surprised by the wizened old man who stood waiting on him. His wool coat was frayed and tattered, adorned with patches making it a mere remnant of what it once was. He smiled kindly at Marty, revealing that he had only a few teeth remaining. His voice rasped in a foreign tongue that Marty couldn't understand. He listened carefully, but could make no sense of it. He shuffled up to Marty, gently took his elbow and led him inside the ancient chapel.

His feet scraped against the uneven flagstones of the vestibule. Through filtered colored light emanating from stained glass windows, he was able to discern the uniqueness of the small room. Unlike anything he had ever seen, the carvings and features spread throughout in an array of symbols. His gaze moved from the figure of a beautifully carved stone angel to a waste high figure of Lucifer beneath it. Even in the dim light, Lucifer's face was garish and frightening. Its mouth gaped in a permanent howl. Its eyes bulged out in a piercing, grotesque stare. No matter where he stood, it seemed to follow him. Cautiously, he moved closer to the statuette to inspect it in more detail. A chill raced up his spine as the figure's head slowly turned toward him. Marty found himself instinctively backing away from the statue. He looked around for the old man—only to find that he was now alone with the abomination.

The stone demon leaped from its small pedestal, its feet clattering of stone against stone. It made a trail of stone chips as it lurched forward. The creature settled back on its two forked feet and hunched down, seemingly unable to move. It wheezed and hacked, coughing itself to life. Marty crept toward the small figure in morbid curiosity. He crept closer and closer until the demon was within range. With lightning speed, the statue grabbed his leg with a tiny stone claw, catching him with a steely grip that made him wince. The cold began to creep up his leg from the claw. Marty tried to snatch his leg away only to feel the monster's grip tighten.

Gnarled brittle wings unfurled from its back, which began to mechanically beat. Fearing the worst, Marty raised his hand and sent it crashing into the back of the small figure. His blow centered squarely between the wings on the hunched figure below him. To his surprise, the demon released his leg and began coughing forcefully at the floor. On the third retching cough, a stone emerged from its mouth and clattered across the floor. Unlike Martin's Sappire, the gem was a large yellow diamond. The walnut sized gem winked and sparkled in the waning light. The demon froze in position, just as suddenly as it had started moving The diamond lay at Marty's feet.

Wary of his stone adversary, Marty slowly watched its lifeless eyes as he bent over. Its jagged teeth appeared weathered and worn and completely devoid of life. With the gem firmly in hand, Marty backed away from the stone figure. The diamond was not particularly attractive, but it was quite fat with a degree of intricacy around the edges that seemed atypical of any gem he had ever seen. As Marty scrutinized the stone, a hand clutched his arm making him jump. The old man smiled apologetically and looked down. Marty scowled at him and opened his mouth to scold him.

Old watery eyes regarded him, pleadingly. In plain English, he said, "Marty, it's time to wake up. We're here." The old man sounded a lot like…Gillian.

Chapter 26

A slight nip in the night air greeted him, as Franz keyed in the security code to the gate lock. The classic wrought iron gate swung open smoothly on automated hinges. He eased the Range Rover through the gate to the charter terminals at *Aero port D'Orly Sud*. He eased down the access road to a small glass and chrome building. The small office was tucked away from the hustle and bustle of Air France and other commercial airlines. The small non-descript building had been the portal to France for some of the most famous personalities in Europe.

Franz glanced at his watch. He was twenty minutes early, assuming the Finnish pilots were on time. But then, they were rarely late. A young female customs agent waited inside the terminal. She wore the position with pride, with her uniform pressed and her head held high. Despite the show, it was more of a formality than a screening process. Franz exited the Range Rover and moved over to the terminal, where the young woman patiently waited. His French was passable, as they spoke. He knew she spoke English, but it was polite to speak in French. The French could be appeased by acknowledging their superiority.

The trio exited the plane on the tarmac, with Coco waving farewell to them in the morning air. It was one o'clock am, as they walked into the terminal. Between the seven hour flight and the six hour time difference, it was late—even by Paris standards.

Gillian wondered how they would arrange for transportation at this time of night. It was possible that they might catch a cab. They entered the terminal building to find only two occupants; a young customs agent and middle-aged portly man. The customs agent smiled and greeted them, cordially. "Bon Jour, welcome to Paris."

Gillian responded with an equally bright smile for being on such a long flight and having as many drinks as she had.

"Passport, please."

Three passports were extended almost in unison. The young woman scarcely glanced past the diplomatic seal, as she stamped them in quick succession. Gillian was caught off guard by the ease of their exchange. There were no questions and no more than a brief smile, as she bid them "Adieu." Quite to their surprise, she left the terminal, leaving the trio behind with the short, portly man. Digger and Gillian exchanged surprised glances.

The portly man stood slowly, smiling at them. He extended a hand to Digger, who smiled. "Franz, it's been a while."

It was now Gillian who was caught off guard. She had never met the voice on the other end of the phone, while Digger was treating him like an old friend. She was both amazed and a little perturbed. Franz turned to Gillian and smiled. He reached out and greeted her with a hug. It caught her off balance for a moment. She managed to bring up her arms limply, without actually returning the hug. As Franz broke from the embrace, she smiled—not quite sure how to respond, considering the nature of their relationship.

Franz smiled broadly, as he turned to Marty with an outstretched hand. "Martin, it's certainly a pleasure to finally meet you."

Marty stared at him. It seemed funny for some reason through the haze of alcohol, "Yes, Sir… likewise."

Franz smile broadly at the trio. "You kids must be tired. I have some rooms booked for us in Marias. Let's get you checked in and get some rest."

With that, he moved between Digger and Marty, putting his arms on each young man's shoulder. "So tell me about your trip guys," he said as they walked out the terminal door. Gillian trailed behind them, trying to sort it all out.

Chapter 27

The hotel lobby felt cozy for a large hotel; cream colored curtains complemented the dark wood of the crown molding. Golden light emanated from alabaster sconces mounted to the wall, giving the room a welcoming glow. Hunter green carpet set with floral borders gave the room the feel of an English garden without the bugs. This was not the first time Franz had entertained guests at Le St. Paul, and his gratuities were reasonable and frequent. The staff was always happy to see him, even when his entourage was so clearly American. Jean Claude, the portly night clerk, smiled warmly, and greeted them like long lost relatives. "Bonjour, Monsieur Shemu'el. It is so good to see you again."

Franz's tired eyes made him look bulldoggish, as he smiled. "Precisely why I keep coming here, Jean Claude. It's like coming home to family, without all the drama."

Jean Claude slid three large antique looking keys across the desk. "As was intended, Mon Ami. We have prepared the rooms you requested."

"Were you able to hold the adjoining rooms facing the courtyard?"

"But of course. We placed the American tourists on the street side. They will never notice."

Marty, Digger and Gillian exchanged quiet smiles

behind Franz.

"Excellent."

Jean Claude eyed the Spartan array of luggage. "Shall I call the night porter to assist you to your room?"

Franz smiled. "I believe we can manage."

"Very good. Then would you like a wake up call?"

"That won't be necessary."

The pre-war elevator smelled of brass polish and lemon oil from the wood panels. It hummed along, as they stood in awkward silence to their floor. Each one of them shared a common goal for a completely different reason. Franz's pudgy jowls settled into an unassuming smile, as he looked at each one of them in fleeting glances. He tried to assess the trio's mood. Inwardly, however, his stomach was twisted into knots. His ploy to smoke out the gem was a calculated risk. Now, he must deliver as promised or suffer at the hands of the duke; a man who was neither patient, nor forgiving.

Digger beamed, quite happy to be in Paris again. His penchant for the Paris night-life lifted his mood in anticipation. Marty appeared haggard and drawn. The stress of the flight and his sudden random out-of-body experiences had put him on edge. Marty could not predict when he would lapse into another experience and he worried whether it would occur at an inopportune time. Gillian remained stoic, focused on protecting her little entourage. Experience would not allow her to drop her guard. The ease of the trip put her on edge. Aside from the encounter with Armand, there had been virtually no complications to their travel. That wasn't something she was used to.

Their floor was peaceful at the late hour, and Franz scooped the room between Marty and Gillian.

Gillian looked at Franz. "Do I need to check the rooms?"

He smiled. "No. No one should know were here. It's safe."

She looked at him grimly. No one should have known they were in the safe house in Green Lake nor should they have known when they arrived at the airport, but they did. There were too many coincidences. As it was, she held her tongue and entered her room without looking back. Marty smiled, cordially. "See you guys in the morning guys." Digger and Franz raised hands in unison, as they all adjourned through separate doors. With the door securely locked behind him, Marty took a quick look around his room. As with the lobby, the room glowed amber, as it reflected off the deep wood tones of the paneling around him. The room smelled heavily of cleaning fluid and lilac. It was an odd combination. He looked around, curiously. The mini-bar was well-stocked with a variety of popular liquors. Most he recognized, but some he did not. The refrigerator was stocked with a half-dozen bottles of Badoit, locally bottled water. He smiled, for some reason, he thought the French only drank Perrier.

Right now, though, his interest was not in beverages. He was exhausted. All he wanted was to clean up and get some rest. He dropped his bag on the bed, which didn't appear to give at all. He didn't care. He could have slept on the floor at this point. He kicked off his shoes, flipping them into the corner, and fumbled for the switch in the bathroom. As he punched the switch which predated the cold war, the bathroom flooded with stark white light which contrasted the soft glow of the bedroom. It was like walking into the center of a light bulb. He squinted for a moment until his eyes adjusted. He stripped his shirt, dropping it to the floor, and let the sink faucet run until it was as cold as it would get. It was surprisingly brisk and almost immediately melted away some of the cobwebs. He breathed in the water, clearing his head of the long trip. A light rap on the door made him pause. *Now what?*

Muttering, he pulled his shirt on and moved to the door, as another light tap sounded. There was no peephole, so he quietly set the security latch and stepped away from the door, easing it open. Gillian stood there. In bare feet, work out shorts and a baggy tee, she looked as sexy as any woman he had ever seen.

He tried not to look surprised, all-the-while knowing that he was probably failing miserably, basedon the smirk on her face. He removed the latch and swung the door wide. Her eyes sparkled mischievously, as she asked, "Expecting trouble?"

He snorted. "Well, yeah, as a matter of fact."

"Can I come in?"

He tried to think of something witty; something to make him sound interesting, but knew it wasn't going to happen. She looked too perfect, he was too tired, and the mood could be shattered far too easily. So he stepped back and bowed with a sweeping motion, closing the door behind her. Without the slightest modesty, she said, "Let's take a shower."

Damn. I just knew she was going to say that...

The motion sensor for the hidden fiber optic camera watched Gillian enter Marty's room from across the hall. When the door closed behind her, the camera stayed fixed on the door and poised to capture future movement. A control room a country away recorded the event.

Silently, Marty followed her into the bathroom, not quite sure what to expect. She shut the door and turned on the shower. Throwing two towels on the floor to sit on, she motioned for him to sit beside her. With their backs against the tub, she cocked her head and looked at him gravely. "When we were at the church, you said there was traitor among us. I need to understand how you know that and who it is."

Marty nodded. "I'll tell you what I saw, but please realize that I don't have control of the vision. It's unpredictable." He closed his eyes and concentrated on the vision. "There were two men talking. I was behind them. I couldn't see either one of them clearly. One man was seated at this huge desk. He spoke with an accent, like German or something like it. He was telling the other man, 'Bring them to me.' The other guy responded with, 'I'll take care of it, Duke'. This *duke* fellow told him, 'You were smart about how this played out. Do you think they suspect anything?' The next thing they say is garbled. I tried to understand them, but couldn't make it out. I really got the idea that they were talking about us, but I can't be sure of it."

"Then what?"

"You woke me up."

She sat there silently for a moment. "You're sure it wasn't just a dream?"

"I can't be sure of anything at this point, but my dreams are somehow different. But it felt like the time I dreamed of Bess telling me about the stone. It's hard to explain, but I can feel a difference between my dreams and the visions I'm having. I know that sounds crazy."

She looked at him, sincerely. "If you had told me this a week ago, I *would* have said you were crazy. Right now, you're the best intel I've got. You're sure he called him *Duke*?"

"Yeah. I'm pretty sure."

"The guy who ambushed us at the airport said someone called the *duke* had hired him."

"Should we ask Franz?"

She slowly shook her head as she were still thinking about it. "No. We keep this between us. If we don't know who we can trust, then we trust no one."

Marty's stomach twisted when she said that. They sat silently for a moment. He smiled at her. She gave him a quizzical look. "What?"

"Nothing…it's just something about you. You remind me of Bess."

She raised an eyebrow. "I remind you of your deceased grandmother?"

He knew he would say something stupid. He scowled and shook his head. "No, nothing creepy like that. I always admired the way Bess was straight and to the point. I always knew where I stood with her. You're like that."

This time, she was a more good-natured. "So you're telling me I'm too direct?"

He stuck to his guns. "No. You're direct and to the point. Just like her. I really admired her. She was a strong person."

She studied his eyes. She didn't meet many honest people. He was so innocent, so pure. He returned her gaze with the comfortable ease. Something panged deep within her and she struggled against her true feelings for him. She wanted him, but unlike the usual *throw away* romances, it was much deeper, much more personal. It scared her. Marty could see the conflict in her eyes. He knew it was dangerous for them to be involved. Yet he couldn't help but wonder what it would be like.

He moved so that he was facing her. He reached out and gently took her hands. She didn't resist. She looked at him expectantly, not quite knowing what he would say or do. He smiled at her. Her response was impulsive. She flushed and looked down, bashfully.

"Gillian?"

She didn't look up, but murmured, "Yes?"

"You are everything I would want in a woman. You're smart, you're resourceful..." Her gaze rose to meet his. "You are the most amazing girl I've ever met."

Her eyes widened, her breathing quickened.

"There's nothing I would like better than for us to disappear into the night. But we both know what would never happen. We have to finish this, but when it's over I want to be with you."

She gave him a wicked smile. "I'll just bet you do."

He snorted. The only sound in the room was the shower running behind them. They held hands and sat on the tile floor. It was Marty who broke the silence. "Gillian?"

"Yes?"

"I don't know about you, but my butt hurts."

She laughed. "Well, I think it's pretty evident that you have some Bess in you, too."

He laughed. "Yeah, just not in the right location at

the moment." She gracefully scissored her legs up off the floor, pulling him toward her. They walked arm-in-arm to the door. Instead of opening it, she flipped the latch, locking it securely. She turned, meeting his gaze. The soulful look said more than an hour of talking. Marty tried to keep from skipping, as he went back into the bathroom to change into a pair of shorts. There was no need to be presumptuous. His heart was pounding, as he came back into the room. The room was a silky darkness, as he eased into the bed next to her. She smelled like baby powder. Next to his, her body was almost hot to the touch. He reached toward her, as the sound of her snore nearly startled him. His arm stopped in mid-air and retreated. He smiled, as he laid back. It was a complement, really. She didn't trust many people enough to sleep with them. It was a good sign. He listened to her deep comfortable breathing for a moment before drifting into a peaceful slumber.

At the front desk below, Jean Claude made a mental note to ask Franz why Americans used so much water.

Chapter 28

The air conditioning vent gently pushed the curtains aside, allowing daylight to wink through the heavy drapes and teasing Marty awake from a deep sleep. He reached out to find the other side of the bed empty. She was gone, but he detected the hint of baby powder on the sheets beside him. Lost in thought over the previous evening, he cupped his hands behind his head and stared at the intricacy of the medallion over his head. He kept drifting back to where she was curled against him; her leg over his, her arm over his chest, breathing in and out in a deep peaceful slumber. He wondered how long it had been since she'd slept that soundly. Nothing had happened between them. And yet, he lay there reveling in the moment. He yearned for her touch, but there was far too much at stake at the moment.

He took his time making his way downstairs. He sat in the dining room, munching on golden-buttered croissants and marmalade when Digger wandered in in nothing more than shorts and a T-shirt, yawning widely. He seemed completely unmoved by his surroundings. Tufts of hair zigged and zagged in every direction, making his appearance comical. Unfazed by the pair, a waiter dutifully poured coffee into a clear-stemmed cup. Marty watched, as the cream eddied through the dark rich liquid. Digger stirred the mixture immune to the visual symphony of the mingling liquids. He sipped the dark liquid, gingerly. "Man, that stuff's stout."

Marty smiled, with one side giving him a rather lopsided look. "Yeah, I'd hate to see their Espresso."

Digger grunted in acknowledgement and continued to sip. Franz entered the room, his eyes bright and his smile broad. He joined them at the table. "So, Lads, did everyone sleep well last night?" He looked at Marty and smiled.

Marty wondered if Franz knew. He smiled pleasantly and said, "Best night's sleep I've had in days…literally."

Franz chuckled. "I don't doubt it."

Gillian glided in, as radiant as the morning sun. She paused to fill her own cup of coffee and coasted like a figure skater among the tables dotting the room between them. Her fingers brushed along Marty's back, as she moved to her chair. Franz was talking to Digger, but his quick eyes didn't miss the gesture.

She waited for a moment before asking, "So guys, what's the plan?"

Three sets of eyes turned to Marty. He suddenly realized that they were looking to him for an answer. "We're looking for a church. It would probably be best if we could go to a library or somewhere with a church archive, but I believe I could probably recognize the church. It was very unique."

Franz smiled. "Well, that's easy enough. But I must warn you: There are thousands of churches in this region alone. If you have a photograph, perhaps we could show it to someone?"

Cautiously, Marty replied, "I'm afraid the *photograph* is in my head. But I will recognize it when

I see it."

Skeptically, Franz nodded. "We're in walking distance from the best historical library in Paris—The Hotel de Lamoignon. If you can't find what you need there, I have friends in the Academic world we can ask."

Marty smiled. "Sounds like a good starting point."

Digger looked up from his coffee. "Dudes, you mind if I sit this one out?"

Gillian patted him on the hand. "You go ahead and catch some beauty sleep, Sweetie. We'll get you when we're done."

He smiled, gratefully. His eyes were bleary and his normally smooth face was covered in stubble. She wondered if he had made it to bed at all.

Franz seemed a tad eager. "Okay, so I guess we're all set."

Marty took another sip of coffee before standing. He tried to look more confident than he felt. He didn't have a clue, as to what they would look for in the library, but he was hoping that it would all work out.

The morning was bright and new growth on the Parisian trees shimmered in the cool morning breeze. Throngs of morning pedestrians showed no interest in the trio, as they maneuvered through the crowd. In less than three blocks, they faced the imposing façade of the Hotel de Lamoignon. Thick white walls surrounded the tall featureless walls through a towering archway, making it resemble a fortress rather than a library. Once past the arch, Marty found himself staring at the sheer splendor of the garden in the spring. Pink roses bloomed with abandon, as did dozens of other flowers he could not identify. They entered the great hall where

Franz left them in search of a curator. It seemed only moments before he waddled back with a tall gangly youth in tow. The pair was painfully odd; Franz with his short dumpy stature and curly balding hair, while his companion stood a head taller, a mere wisp of a young man. He flipped a shock of straight black hair from his eyes, as he approached the couple. He spoke to Franz in French. While he occasionally flipped his hair, his tone was that of a man directing but not helping. Patiently, Franz negotiated with the young man, trying to keep his tone civil, while the youth sighed and rolled his eyes, disinterested. Sensing he was at an impasse, Franz reached into his wallet. Anticipating a gratuity, his thin lips curled into a thin smile; the kind of smile reserved for victory.

The smile fell, as Franz produced a thin gold business card and handed it too him. Marty watched with fascination, as the docent's demeanor dramatically changed. Nervously, he smiled. In perfect English, he said, "This way please."

Marty's and Gillian's eyes met in utter astonishment. Franz extended his hand for the card back. The young man returned it, dropping it like it would burn him. Marty found it curious, but then the whole exchange struck him as such. He couldn't imagine what could possibly be printed on a business card to garner such an attitude change, nor had he ever seen anyone take back a business card. He made a mental note to get one of Franz's cards later. There had to be something really amazing for a card like that. As they walked, Franz gradually steered the guide to Marty.

With narrow eyes, he glanced at Marty, guardedly.

"What is it you seek, Monsieur?"

"I'm researching period chapels. I came across some pictures of an unusual chapel I would like to find. There was a skull and cross-bones at the entry. Do you know of any chapels like that?"

The young man raised an eyebrow and curled his lip in what looked like a half-smile. It was hard to tell. "This way, please." He moved into the lead. They traveled down long hallways and cut across short hallways leading back to longer halls. The longer they walked, the less inhabited the area around them became. They walked for several minutes, without speaking. Their feet clicked hollowly on the marble floors. They crossed into roped-off areas that were not accessible by the public. Gillian kept track of the number of cameras in the halls. The frequency was steadily increasing.

Franz smiled at Gillian, disarmingly. "You're in good hands. I'll meet you in a few minutes." Suddenly, he veered down a connecting hall and disappeared in the maze of artifacts.

Gillian walked behind the docent by a few paces. She sized him up. His long bony fingers were stained with nicotine, his sallow complexion and long sleeves hid the tracks on his arms. She would have guessed Heroin addict. If he gave Marty any trouble, she would find a quiet corner out of camera range and snap him in two like a twig. She allowed herself a tiny feral smile, when the realization struck her that she would die for Marty. It was something she had never felt before; something different, something quite scary.

Marty looked back at her quizzically . "What?"

Her eyes glinted, mischievously. "I'll tell you

later."

He smiled and then returned his attention to the young man. It seemed as though they had been walking for hours, when in fact they had only been traveling for a few minutes.

Gillian muttered. "Jeez, maybe we should have left a trail of bread crumbs."

Marty smiled back at her.

The curator looked back, expectantly. "Pardon?"

"Nothing. Are we almost there?"

"Oui. It is only a short way now." The young man caught the look in Gillian's eyes and he quickened his pace. They moved down a small side hall and stopped in front of a door capable of fitting a Mini Cooper through it. Yet for all its size, it was actually quite plain in comparison to the rest of the surroundings.

The curator removed a clunky iron key from his pocket and carefully twisted it in the lock. In an age of smart chips, it seemed odd that with all the priceless artwork around them, they secured a room with books. The young man proceeded into the room and began to flip on lights at a bank of switches. Soft light bathed the room, except over the carved mahogany reading tables where reading light illuminated the deep luster of the wood. It was cool and quiet. The smell of polish and old leather greeted them as they entered which was soon overcome by the scent of antiquity. This hallowed refuge was not open to the public. It was only for special guests or special occasions. Richly carved bookshelves stretched twenty feet to the ceiling, making three tiers of shelves accessible from balconies stretched around the cavernous room. The volumes stored here were both ancient and rare, many of which were the last known copies in existence. Beautifully crafted bindings sang of a different time, when the written word was reserved for the most elite. It was a trove of neglected thought, preserved only for the novelty of what it represented, not for what it contained. Gillian heard a small gasp from Marty, as he sat at the nearest chair. The curator looked at him, curiously.

Gillian moved quickly to his side whispered, "Are you okay?"

Without a word, he nodded his face drained and his lips tight. She placed a reassuring hand on his shoulder. The curator walked over to a pedestal table centered in the room and tapped the table top, awakening a computer hidden within the glass top. A white glow made the docent's face look hollow and garish, as the terminal awoke. The young man spoke aloud to no one in particular, describing how the catalog system worked. "It is in a basic search engine which uses the Dewey decimal system to provide the location. You should be able to navigate a computer. You should have no problems."

Marty wasn't listening. His gaze drank in the room like a parched mouth. This place was the exact room from his vision with Peter.

"I have formatted the system for English to make your search easier…"

Marty looked at the young man. "How many books are in here?"

For the first time since they had been with him, he smiled. His teeth were perfect. "There are over two hundred thousand first editions in this room. Many date back to the Sixteenth Century. Many were rescued from the book burnings of the Third Reich."

Marty looked at him, earnestly. "They're beautiful."

The young man seemed pleased and gave him a respectful nod. "Merci, If there is anything else I may be of assistance with, please ring the chime by the door. I will be with you directly."

Marty looked at him, curiously. "Are there any conditions that we should be aware of?"

The young man regarded him with a hint of surprise. "Pardon? What do you mean?"

Marty struggled for the right words. "Are there any books we should not touch?"

"No Monsieur. You may take as many books as you like. Consider this your personal library."

Marty looked at Gillian. For the second time, they were caught off guard. Nodding at the young man, he said, "Thank you. You've been very helpful."

The young man smiled again. "Oui, Monsieur. It is my pleasure. If you need any further assistance, please do not hesitate to call." He pointed to a square green button on the wall by the door. "I will be paged." He opened his blazer to show them a digital pager on his belt. "Adieu."

Without awaiting a response, he was gone.

Marty looked at Gillian. "What kind of a place lets two complete strangers into a room full of books worth more than the GNP of a small country?"

Gillian shook her head. "Sometimes, it's better if we don't know."

"I guess you're right."

Gillian walked straight to the computer. "What search criteria should we start with?"

Marty looked up. Distantly, he said, "Skull and bones, Chapel."

Without looking up from the terminal she said "Sixteen thousand, two hundred and ninety one hits. Top hits, Notre Dame Cathedral, Skull of Descartes, Trinity Chapel…" It was very similar to an internet search engine. As she scrolled through the screens, she looked up to find that Marty had not moved from his large leather chair. "What's up, Marty?"

The sound of her voice brought him back. He smiled at her. "This is the same room that I first met with the Peter in. It even smells the same."

She considered this, carefully. "Does this mean we are supposed to be here?"

He looked up. "I would say so. Or at the very least, we should find some information that will help us find what we need to know."

She stayed on the objective. "What about the hits?"

"I'm sorry. What were they again?"

Patiently, she replied, "The top hits were Notre Dame Cathedral, Skull of Descartes, and Trinity Chapel."

She studied the screen, while Marty began to move about the room. One book drew his attention like a moth to a flame. The binding glowed beckoning him. Slowly, he crept toward it, almost he were afraid that it would disappear.

Gillian was continuing to scroll down the list. "Wait, here are a few more… Roslyn chapel. No wait… that's in Scotland." She was fixated on the monitor and didn't look up.

The rolling ladder moved smoothly on well-oiled tracks. Marty climbed, transfixed on the volume. He barely remembered hefting it from its resting place. The tall leather bound volume was located over his head. It was the size of a World Atlas and about as heavy. Moving the volume to the table where Gillian was seated, he carefully he laid it down beside him.

She looked at him, crossly. "Honey, if we're going to find this book you need, we can't look for it one at a time."

He opened it to the title page, *Le History de Rennes de Chateau* published in 1925. He carefully flipped through the pages until he stopped and stared at a full size lithograph.

Quietly, he said, "That's it. That's where we need to go."

She squinted at him. "You're sure? Don't you want to look some more?"

He looked at her drolly. "I'm sure." He pointed to the center of the lithograph.

She found herself looking at a skull and cross bones in a stone arch. She shook her head. "Man, that's just weird."

He stared at the page. Without looking up, he said, "Yeah, welcome to the wonderful world of Martin Wood. Every time I look up, something bizarre happens. I think we're going to need that French guy, unless you can read this." Carefully, he turned the yellowed pages, his nose wrinkled at the dust.

Gillian didn't respond, but simply strode cat-like to the green button on the wall and punched it like a sparring dummy. She asked him, "So, how did you just *know* which book it was?"

He shrugged, as he looked up. "I know this won't make any sense, but it stood out to me. It was like the only book I could see."

Within moments, the young attendant entered the room, with Franz behind him like an expectant child. The pitch in Marty's voice rose slightly, as he tried to contain his excitement. "Can you interpret some the transcript for me?"

"Oui, Monsieur."

Marty began turning to pages and pointing. The young man droned in English. Marty furiously scribbled notes trying to filter through the young man's accent. He stopped him only occasionally to make sure that nothing was lost in translation.

"So does it say anything about a statuette of the Lucifer? "

"Oui."

"Stop there."

The young man looked up.

"Does it say where the *Lucifer* is?"

"It is not very clear, but it appears to be inside the church, beneath an angel."

Marty patted the young man's shoulder. "That's perfect. Thank you."

The young man looked strangely gratified by the gesture. "Oui, Monsieur. Is there anything else?"

"Where is this place?"

"It is North of Marseille. Do you need a map?"

Marty stared at him for a moment. "You have that?"

"Of course. We can plot it from here?" He began tapping at the computer keyboard.

Marty looked up to find Franz staring at him. As Marty looked back, Franz smiled disarmingly.

The Docent called for his attention. "Will you be

taking the book with you Monsieur?"

"No, thank you. I have all the information I need."

The young man was noticeably relieved.

Marty looked at Franz. "We'll meet at the hotel in one hour. We'll check in with Digger."

Gillian stared at Marty. Suddenly, he seemed to be in charge.

Franz nodded, awkwardly. "Of course. One hour."

Marty smiled. "We'll be there."

****

Marty's mind raced at the prospect of finding the church. There was so much to do; so many important details to consider. Yet, his one prevailing thought was of her.

On a whim, he snuck a kiss on Gillian's ear lobe. She giggled and pulled away. "That tickles."

He grinned, impishly. "Well, if you think that tickles…"

The elevator stopped and the door opened. The old man eased carefully over the threshold and reached back for his wife. She stepped through the doorway and regarded them both, suspiciously. Her starched white hair was pulled tightly into a bun, while her piercing hazel eyes silently communicated that she was in no mood for monkey business. The elevator hummed, filling the car with an awkward silence. Marty felt like teenager who had just been caught by his parents making out—or far worse, his grandparents. The little old man said nothing and jabbed the floor button. The old couple seemed to relax when Marty and Gillian smiled pleasantly and greeted them with, "Bon jour." The car chimed for the third floor. Both Marty and Gillian hurriedly exited the car. The elderly couple stayed on the car, as it went down. As soon as the door shut and it moved away from them in unison, they burst out in laughter. "Wow talk about your awkward moments."

She smiled at him. "You were so busted."

Her arm linked comfortably in his, as they took their time walking to Digger's room. She hated to break the moment, but it was necessary. "I'll get Digger moving. You go ahead and pack up your stuff, and we'll meet back at Digger's in twenty minutes."

He nodded. "Aye, Aye, Captain. Digger in twenty."

Gillian turned to walk away. Marty caught her by the arm and swung her easily back to him—all-the-while hoping she wouldn't use some obscure martial art and render him unconscious. It was so spontaneous, making it alien to him. He pulled her to him and met her luscious lips in a wet passionate kiss. Her body responded, wrapping him in a clinging embrace. Pent up desire burned unchecked between them for a moment, as Marty wondered whose idea this had been. He gave up on logic and yielded to her hot embrace. His hunger for her crept down his spine like the flood gates on a dam lifting. She did not hesitate, or push him away. They remained locked in an eternal kiss until the chime of the elevator wrenched them back to the moment at hand. They reluctantly peeled apart locked in a gaze that screamed for more. Marty smiled, as he looked down at her. "I don't think we properly said goodnight last night."

Her cheeks flushed red, as she bit her bottom lip. "We have some unfinished business, you and I. We'll finish this later."

He nodded. Paris or not, they both knew, there was no time for this. He cleared his throat. "Yes. Later."

Her look was smoldering. "Yeah. Later."

Slowly, they backed away, neither wanting it to end. But both resolved that this was not the time. With every bit of resolve he had, Marty turned and walked away. He knew that their time together would be fleeting, and that their time apart would seem like an eternity.

Chapter 29

The one thing Digger never left behind was his laptop. He was surprised and pleased that his notebook detected a strong signal and had dropped him right into the internet. He smiled, as he opened a note from Billy:

Yo Dude, that was one hairy ride. What a total deal. Richy Rich popped one of them knuckle heads and dropped him back into the pit. We called Five Oh and split. Be cool. Later.

It was typical Billy. His dialog was a visual snapshot of him in life, full of enthusiasm and moving forward to the next adventure. The curious thing was that he didn't mention that anything else unusual. Neither did the other three who wrote him. In a small town, stolen cars, high speed chases and dead bodies would be all anyone would talk about for days. And yet, there wasn't even a whisper in chat from his other friends. It made him pause. A knock at the door rousted him from his revere. He peeked through a crack in the door to unveil a radiant Gillian on the other side, waiting to be let in. He gave her a sideways glance. "What's up with you?"

She ignored the question. "How soon can you be ready to leave?"

With a flip of his hand, he stared at his fingernails from afar. With a fake yawn, he covered his mouth with the back of his hand, pretentiously he said, "Oh, I don't know…a few days, perhaps? French women are oh-so-complicated, you know. I really don't know how I'll fit them all in."

She playfully backhanded him on the belly, as she pushed her way into the room. "Yeah, whatever. Really, Dude, when can you be ready?"

He gave her a dour look. "We've been here less than a day. What's the hurry?"

"Marty has a lead on a town south of here called Rennes le Chateau…something about a church. We need to go there."

His eyes narrowed, as he studied her. "So, how are you and Mr. Wood getting along?"

Her toe betrayed her. She unconsciously traced it over the carpet, as she spoke. "He's fine, we're fine… everything's just fine. Now get ready."

He reached out, caught her wrist and spun her toward him. "Spill it."

She looked at the floor. She never could lie to Digger. "I kind of like him."

"Is that *like*, as in, share an ice cream cone or is that *like*, as in share a cottage at the shore?"

She squirmed a little. "I'd say we're past the ice cream but not ready for the beach. I wouldn't mind a nice cozy evening, going over some old issues of Guns 'N Ammo. So there it is, I said it. Are you happy?"

He smiled and pulled her toward him in a hug. "I always knew you'd find the right guy. He has a good heart, you know."

"Yeah, I know. I'm just not used to that."

"Well, maybe after all this, you can hang up the old cloak and dagger and settle into a *normal* life. You know picket fence, puppies, apple pies…stuff like that."

"What century are you living in?"

He grinned. "Clearly, not this one. I'll be ready in ten minutes."

****

In less than an hour, the Range Rover was headed south for Orleans. Franz drove with Digger beside him, giving Marty and Gillian the back seat to themselves. Franz seemed oblivious to the couple. Digger decided to keep it that way.

"So, Franz, any new finds under the Weeping Wall?"

Their conversation spun off from there. Marty and Gillian snuck their hands together at any opportunity. Their conversation flowed like a stream. Slowly and steadily, they began to realize that even with very different backgrounds, they shared many of the same views on music, books and politics. It surprised Marty at how comfortable he was telling her things about himself that he would never tell anyone else.

Occasionally, Digger would steal a glance at the back seat. He watched, as she happily laughed and talked. Her fingers caressed the back of Marty's hand. The move was subtle and subconscious. Digger smiled, thinking that they were perfect for each other. Seeing her carry on a normal conversation that wasn't laced with words like *operation, mission and objective* was a blessing. She seemed very different. He thought, *She deserves this.* For the first time ever, he could see genuine happiness in her eyes. Marty was certainly at ease.

Gillian realized somewhere around the second pit stop near Nevers that she didn't have a clue as to how long they had been on the road, or even where Nevers was. It surprised her that she didn't care. It seemed like such a simple thing, but for the first time in her life she was not considering a *mission critical* timeline. It would be another hour before Marty told her his favorite joke involving a camel, an old Arab trader and two bricks. She nearly shot soft drink through her nose. Her snorting laughter drew Franz's and Digger's attention. Marty assured them that "it's nothing" which made her laugh even harder.

It was nightfall when they rolled through the ancient gates of Rennes le Chateau. A hush fell over the cab of the Range Rover. Franz eased over the rough cobblestones to park in an empty lot. All the cars were gone. There was no one left. Even the attendant was gone. A gust of cold mountain wind reminded them that it was not summer here yet. It made them shiver, as they exited the vehicle. They walked in pairs through the calm of the deserted streets of the tiny village. The distant bay of dog was the only thing that challenged the whistling of windswept evergreens. Were it not for the occasional amber light peeking from behind drawn drapes, it would be difficult to tell whether the small village was inhabited at all. Marty strained in the dim light of a lamppost to find a landmark. The narrow cobblestone streets seemed familiar, but his perspective was off. He wished he could look from above. After a few minutes of walking, Marty spied the familiar spire piercing a newly risen moon. "That's it," he whispered excitedly, pointing in the direction of the steeple.

The trio followed him faithfully toward the landmark. They walked down narrow alleys and across dim dirt pathways in vacant lots. The spire beckoned them, as they drew closer. A cool breeze made Gillian shiver. It wasn't so much the chill of the wind, as it was the sense of foreboding in the air. It was an intangible warning for all those capable of perceiving it. Instinctively, she looked behind her, not knowing what she was looking for. Small hairs on the back of her neck stood on end. She remained vigilant in rear guard in her head, her eyes in constant movement. *All this is just too easy.*

As they cleared the corner of an ancient row of shops, the walls of the small chapel loomed before them. Marty followed the wall in the dim light to the arched courtyard entrance. He stopped at the sight of the crudely carved skull and bones at the keystone of the entrance. His voice was so low that it was barely discernable over the wind. "We found it. This is the place."

The windows were like ink against the windswept courtyard. A small hand-painted sign of *Fermé* clattered against the door. The small group huddled next to the stone wall out of the wind. Marty posed the question. "So do we try to find someone to let us in, or what?"

Franz volunteered, "We might find a caretaker. Let's take a quick look around. If we don't find anyone, we can come back tomorrow."

They all nodded in agreement. Marty and Gillian walked around one side of the chapel, while Franz and Digger navigated the other. The light was dim under a waning moon. There were no street lamps to warm the path around the church. The grounds were deserted. The small group met on the opposite side of the church and rejoined. Quietly, they walked as a group back to the arch. Marty spotted the oddly hunched figure sitting in the darkness, waiting for them. Marty was sure he had not been there before. As they drew closer, he raised himself slowly, painfully. Marty knew him, he recognized him from his dream. He smiled and raised his hand. "*Bon jour*."

The old man said nothing, but smiled and nodded in return. Everything had been so clear during the dream. Marty cringed when he realized he didn't know what to do beyond a simple salutation. Franz stepped from behind and placed a hand on his shoulder. Smiling, he eased past Marty. "Allow me."

Franz's French was as fluid as a river. He smiled and began a lengthy dissertation about their reason for the late-night excursion. The old man occasionally nodded, showing that he understood. But still he offered no response. Gillian remained in the back, her gaze moving about. The little man seemed harmless enough, but her flesh felt prickly, like the air was charged with electricity. She sensed a trap and readied herself for it. The old man's gaze left Franz for a moment. He looked directly at her. Her ears rung, it was like there was a fire alarm in her head. In that instant, she saw it; the soulless void in the old man's eyes. She saw the cold dark energy swirling around him. There was something very wrong about him; and that he was the *only* one that could guide them. It was a classic dichotomy. The only person who could help them was also the one who would betray them. The old man returned his attention to Franz. Gillian steeled herself for what lay ahead.

Franz slipped a Ten Euro note from his pocket and handed it to the old man, who silently stuffed the bill into his coat pocket. He turned slowly and carefully moved up the steps toward the main door. From the angle he was standing at, Marty caught a brief glimpse of an evil little grin on the old man's face. In the dim light, he shrugged it off, attributing it to shadows and an overactive imagination. Without so much as a word, the old man twisted the knob on the door and swung it open. It wasn't locked. Franz wore a pained look. Marty couldn't tell if it was because it was too simple, or that he had just wasted five minutes of explanations and ten Euros for nothing.

The heavy wooden door silently swung wide on well-oiled hinges. The old man pushed a switch that even predated him, bathing the room in the glare light of a single bulb hanging in a tarnished brass fixture overhead. Marty's mind raced. In the light, he could see their guide more clearly now. He wore a tattered old coat. His bald head had wild sprigs of gray hair sprouting over the ears. The old man's watery, hazel eyes seemed to stare right through him. The group quietly spread out in the vestibule of the church. The harsh light cast deep shadows, making the figures in the small room look garish. A sudden breeze pushed its way through the open door and caused the overhead light to swing back and forth, making the statuettes appear animated and alive. Marty spied the figure of Lucifer and timidly eased toward it. The others were busy gazing about the room taking in the eclectic collection of pieces.

He stood before the squatted demon. Its hideous face gave him the willies. The last time he had encountered this thing, it attacked him. While it showed no outward signs of an unnatural life, he was still cautious. He summoned up the courage and reached inside the mouth, hoping that the gem from his dream would fall into his hands. There was nothing here.

Marty swallowed hard. If they had come all this way to find nothing, it would be a very long trip home.

He began to examine the figure more closely. He could feel goosebumps rise on his arms and crawl up the back of his neck. He stemmed the growing panic that threatened to overcome him. He cautiously approached the statue in the dim light. He couldn't see the figure's back in stark light, so he blindly ran his finger between the wings. He could feel a narrow crevice like a seam. He felt past the seam to the opposite side. The small ridge felt like a button. *Could it be that simple?* He pushed in the center of the ridge to hear a faint click and a small rattling sound. The mouth of the devil clicked, allowing the jaw to drop from hidden hinges. He eased his fingers into the cavity and touched something soft in the hole. Carefully, he removed the object wrapped in soft cloth. Marty looked up and around the small vestibule. The old man was nowhere to be seen. Softly, he said, "Guys, I found something."

All eyes were riveted on him. He opened his palm to reveal a small object wrapped in cloth and tied like a bundle. Carefully, he untied the string to reveal another gem. Its primitive facets sparkled, like lightning in the dim light.

Excitedly, Franz exclaimed, "I think it's a diamond! May I have a closer look?" His stubby hand pushed forward.

Marty slowly placed it into his hand. Franz reached into his pocket and removed a jeweler's eye piece. As he examined the stone, he murmured, "It's incredible… just incredible."

Marty shivered. The room felt cold now. He could

see his breath. He noticed the door was still open and the old man was gone. While the others were engrossed in the stone, Marty strode over to close the door. As he reached the door, he stuck his head outside to see if the old man had stepped out. He felt it, before he saw it. The steel blade pressed against the side of his neck. A familiar voice was more chilling than the cold steel pressed against his flesh, "Hullo, Mate. Let's take a walk, shall we?" McPherson stood there in the dark, hard and unyielding, unfazed like he had never been injured.

Chapter 30

The short hairs on the back of her neck stood on end. *Something's wrong.* Her head snapped around. "Marty?"

The old man stood stoically, leaning in the doorway. Gillian moved toward him like a panther. He neither moved, nor changed his expression. Her eyes narrowed, suspiciously.

"Where is our friend?"

He shrugged his shoulders, noncommittally.

Her eyes narrowed to slits, as she barked, "Franz!"

Her tone tore him away from the stone. Irritated, he responded, "What?"

"I don't see Marty, I don't speak French and I don't trust the old goober here. Get over here and make with the language, so we can figure out if there's a problem."

He sighed and walked over to the pair. "Honestly, my dear, I'm sure the boy is quite fine. Where could he have gone? He was right here just a moment ago." He smiled wanly at the old man. "Where did the young man go?"

The old man simply pointed to the stone arch leading out of the church. Franz stepped outside and caught the glint of the small dagger in the door frame, a lock of strawberry blonde hair caught firmly under the tip. He snatched the blade so quickly that he almost cut himself, while the strands of hair drifted away in the wind. Deftly, he slid the knife up his sleeve before Gillian could exit behind him. Gillian stared at Franz. Even in the dim light, he seemed paler than before.

Franz asked the old man again, "Which way did they go?"

The old man pointed to the gate. Gillian nudged Franz. "Where *is* he?"

Franz injected an octave of bravado in his tone. "Have no fear. We will find him, my dear. I promise."

Digger stepped outside. Gillian looked at him, expectantly. He looked more serious than usual. "What's up, guys?"

Franz worded their situation carefully. "It would appear that our Mr. Wood has gone missing. I'm afraid we don't have an explanation."

Gillian raised an eyebrow. "So why are we standing here? Let's go find him."

Franz eyed her somberly for a moment. "Gillian, we have what we came for. Our first priority is to get this jewel into the right hands."

She stared at him, as though someone had just kicked her in the stomach. She couldn't believe what she was hearing. "Are you suggesting that we leave without him?"

"I don't see how we have a choice. We don't know where he's gone or why. We can't simply wander around in the dark, calling out his name. We must stick with the objective and try to figure this out later."

Gillian looked around. "I say we get the old man and beat it out of him."

"No, my dear. We can't simply beat it out of him. I'm not sure he would tell us, if he could. He appears to be mute."

Gillian squinted, as she looked around. The old man had disappeared again. "Trust me. I can get it out of him."

Franz suddenly appreciated that this must be what it's like to be a lion tamer; constantly trying to keep the wild instincts in check. He changed his tactic to placate her. "Maybe he just needed some time to think and wandered off? We'll walk back to the car and wait. If he's not there, we'll get a room here tonight and look for him in the morning. I'm sure he's fine."

Gillian realized she might be overreacting, given the circumstances. Franz was not aware of her relationship. She needed to keep it that way. Gillian eyed him severely, but said nothing more. As much as she hated to admit it, Franz was right. They simply couldn't wander around the dark trying to find him. She braced herself to fight the sinking feeling that something was terribly wrong. She would have to remain focused on finding another way.

Digger chimed in, optimistically. "Maybe he's already waiting for us at the car?"

Franz looked relieved. "Yes. Let's go back to the car and see if he's there."

They walked into the night, leaving the church door open and the light on. As they walked through the arch, the door silently swung shut and the room went dark.

****

It was a modest inn on the edge of town. Franz beat on the door until a bleary-eyed night clerk opened the door for them. They were fortunate. There were three adjoining rooms available. Digger noticed that there were no other cars in the lot, except for theirs. They were the only ones here. The night clerk fumbled about, half-awake. He was clearly not used to having visitors this late. He wobbled a bit, as he removed ancient keys from the slots behind him. Irritably, he asked, "How many nights?"

Franz smiled, amiably. "One night."

The clerk made no attempt to hide his rolling eyes. As they were turning to leave, Gillian decided to ask the clerk a question that was needling her. She stopped. "Excuse me."

The clerk raised an eyebrow. "Oui, Mademoiselle?"

"Is it possible to have the caretaker open the chapel after visiting hours?"

In reasonable English, he replied, "No Mademoiselle. Never."

She skillfully lied. "But we saw an old man earlier. Does he live near the chapel?"

The clerk eyed her, suspiciously. "This man, what did he look like?"

"He was a short man, balding with gray hair. He wore a gray wool overcoat with a lot of patches."

The clerk's eyes widened and the color in his face drained. "That man you describe sounds like Monsieur Reisebeau, the former caretaker. Seeing him is not possible."

"But why?" she asked, innocently.

"He was murdered fifteen years ago. His body was found outside the church. It was very tragic, very upsetting. An American visited him the night he died. The American was never found by the police."

Gillian made a noncommittal nod. "My mistake

then. Thank you."

"Oui, Mademoiselle."

Gillian watched the clerk's hands shake violently, as he pulled a bottle of wine from under the counter. He cupped a chipped glass with both hands, as he gulped greedily at the dark red liquid. His shaking was calmed only marginally, as he poured another before they reached the door.

Deep contours of the form in the bed lay strangely still. On first glance, the bed was occupied but was also as cold and empty as the heart of the killer. Gillian sat quietly in a chair in the corner of a dark room. Her heart was no longer empty. Now, it was simply torn in two. Her knees were tightly tucked under her chin, as she watched the door. She couldn't decide which unsettled her more; the fact that Marty was missing right from under their noses, or that, a ghost had orchestrated the whole thing. Despite the warmth of the room, she shivered. The gentle tap on door made her start. She gracefully unfolded from her chair and, with unusual abandon, flung open the door. She began with "Marty?" and stopped before she could finish.

Digger looked a little startled. Sheepishly he asked, "May I come in?"

Wordlessly, she stepped away from the door, walked back over to her chair and tucked her knees against her chin. He looked at her, earnestly. "We need to take a shower."

She didn't move from the chair. "I don't have one."

He looked around. "Oh…"

Even in the dim light, she could see the uneasiness in Digger's eyes.

Quietly, she asked, "What's up?"

"Franz wasn't entirely truthful with us."

She eyed him warily in the dim light. "Why do you say that?"

"I watched him from a window in the church. He palmed a knife when he walked outside. And he dropped this…" He held up the small locket of hair.

She reached over and tugged the chain on a tarnished lamp with a Tiffany shade. He heard her in a breath as she saw the lock of hair. It was Marty's.

She looked up. "Franz was with us. He couldn't have taken Marty, himself."

Digger summed up the courage to voice his suspicion. "Who do we know that loves to use knives?"

She looked at him aghast. "That's not possible. He's got to be laid up in a hospital somewhere. I got off a clean shot on him. Besides, how could he have found us?"

Digger's eyes were serious. "More importantly, why did Franz lie?"

Digger gravely continued, "There's only one way to get to the bottom of this. And I think you know what that means."

Her eyes narrowed. They were both thinking it. Quietly, she said, "Go to your room. I'll let you know when to come out."

He swallowed hard and nodded. She stood, as Digger was getting ready to leave. He studied her for a moment before pulling her to him in a hug. "We're going to find Marty. I promise."

She fought back the tears and hugged him in return. It was the first time she had looked to anyone for comfort. "This has turned into such a mess," she whispered.

He held her at arms-length, so he could look her in the eye. He tried to look encouraging. "We're connected, the three of us. That can't be broken. We're going to find him."

She blinked and wiped the tears from her eyes. She gave Digger a choked out laugh through the tears. "Funny. That's what Marty said when the Frenchman kidnapped you."

Digger smiled. "Then it must be true."

She laughed through the tears. "It must be."

She took a deep breath and steeled herself. She was no good to Marty, if she fell apart on him. She set her jaw and wiped her eyes. She resolved herself to find him. A different Gillian looked Digger in the eye and said, "So, let's get this party started."

Digger smiled. "That's my girl." He knew she would never give up and he pitied anyone that got in her way.

She pulled his face toward her and kissed him gently on the forehead. "Thanks."

He snapped his fingers and swiveled his hips. "Ain't nothin' but a thang, gurl-friend."

She laughed, as she wiped away the tears. "I think you've been hanging out with the *Sistas* a little too long."

As he went out the door, he grinned. "What-ever do you mean?"

Smiling, she eased the door closed behind him. It appeared that Franz had some real explaining to do.

Chapter 31

Marty couldn't believe he was on another airplane so soon. This one was almost identical to the one he had come to France on. The only difference seemed to be the crew, and his traveling companion. He had really thought that McPherson was dead. And yet, there he sat across from him, virtually unscathed. He toyed with the idea that he had a twin? Had he not loathed him so completely, he probably would have asked how it was possible. As it was, he sat in silent loathing, perplexed.

The drive from Rennes le Chateau to Carcassonne had been short and uncomfortable. McPherson had taken no chances. He'd handcuffed him and stuffed him in the trunk of a long black BMW. It was very plush, but no matter how nice, it was still the trunk. Now, he shifted uncomfortably in the white leather seat of the plane. He looked at McPherson and held his cuffed wrists. "Hey, be a pal. Where am I going to go?"

McPherson sneered at him. "Not likely, Mate."

Marty realized that he had little hope of escaping. His decided that his only hope was to try to reach out to Gillian to let her know he was okay. He could hope for little more. He didn't know where he was going. Their flight attendant was a robust young man who looked like a cage fighter—not a flight attendant. In a thick German accent he asked, "Would you care for some food or drink, Sir?"

He looked for a second to see if he was serious.

"Sure. Some Coke would be nice. Just make sure it has a straw."

Marty looked across at McPherson who wore a smug little smile.

The flight attendant asked Marty, "Would you care for some hors d'oeuvres?"

Marty's eyebrows rose, as he looked at the young man. "No thanks, I seem to be a bit tied up at the moment."

The young attendant's poker face never changed. "Very good, Sir." He marched back to the galley.

Marty was trying to decide if the young man was really that thick when he arrived with the Coke in a glass with a straw. He held the drink and the straw up for Marty to comfortably drink from it. Evidently, this was a full service kidnapping. The upgrade was nice. Marty wondered if it extended to the toilet facilities, as well. He decided not to push it.

The flight seemed incredibly short. No sooner had Marty finished his Coke when they were landing. Under a blanket of darkness, the airplane gently touched down and eased into a private terminal. Tiny beads of rain peppered the windows, as they moved within sight of the small cubic bunker-like building. Marty strained to read the sign through the cold misty rain *Willkommen nach Innsbruck. Austria, home of the Winter Olympics*, he thought. He'd always wanted to come here. It seemed a bit anti-climatic at the moment. McPherson nudged him from behind. "Keep moving Mate."

As they hurried across the tarmac toward a sleek black helicopter twenty yards away, he could just make out the warmly-lit block wall of the terminal building. It was almost invisible in the night, except for the glowing running lights. McPherson pushed him again to keep pace, as the door to the Agusta Westland opened for them on cue . They were not even seated when the whine of the motors began its slow moan, powering up. The pair of blonde pilots looked like twins, as they chatted through the preflight checklist. From what little Marty could see of them, they looked a lot like the pilots on the Gulfstream. *There must be some cookie cutter approach to choosing pilots in the organization?*

The interior was not what he would have thought. He had always envisioned helicopters as having metal bench seats and a metal floor like a military aircraft. He sat back on his cuffed wrists in a cushy bucket seat, while McPherson strapped him in. The seat was almost as nice as his recliner in his small apartment in North Carolina. The thoughts of his old life made him smile, wryly. McPherson noticed the smile. However slight, he leered back. "If you're thinking that your chums are going to bail you out again, forget it. They'll probably be dead before you touch down."

Marty regarded him, coldly. "What would you know about *chums* Dick?"

McPherson snorted, but didn't respond to the question. He closed his eyes and said a silent prayer for his friends. It seemed odd. He couldn't remember the last time he had prayed. It felt strangely comforting. The pilots were oblivious to their passengers. It was only when they were preparing to lift off that one of them glanced back to ensure that everyone was buckled in. He said nothing, but returned his attention to the cockpit when he was confident that they were secured.

Within minutes, they were airborne again, heading away from the lights of the city below.

As they flew, the storm intensified. Torrents of wind and rain battered the tiny craft mercilessly. Marty felt the helicopter lurch and then his stomach. The pilots fought the tempestuous gusts. Strangely, they seemed unaffected by any of it and joked, laughing while they battled the aircraft. The helicopter made a sudden drop. Marty felt the strain of the seatbelt against him. It held him snugly in place and kept him from beaning himself on the bulkhead. An uneasy feeling washed over him: if they were to crash, he would die with handcuffs on. It was not the least bit comforting. Their flight time was a mere twenty minutes which felt like twenty hours. As they landed, the winds began to calm—if not the rain. On their descent, Marty could make out the enormous spires through the mist and rain. The spires were reminiscent of a Disney creation; or perhaps it was vice versa. They passed a series of buttresses and stone orifices that channeled the rain, waterfalls of rainwater made it appear as though structure were draining. Even in the mist and dim light, it was an impressive medieval castle. As the rotors became silent, all they could hear was the whistle of a cold north wind cutting across the firs surrounding the estate. It was Marty's first whiff of an Alpine forest.

McPherson unbuckled him and spoke for the first time since they had been airborne. "'Ere's where we get off, Mate." He put a secure hand under Marty's arm and guided him toward a pair of massive wood doors. Even in the dim night, the structure was striking. Hidden lights cast a golden glow through the now-misting rain along the base of the structure. Long shadows in the dim light made it look massive and unending. Tall arched windows were unrivaled by any church he had ever seen. As they moved toward the massive carved doors, they silently opened massive hinges. As they entered the vestibule, the doors appeared minute in comparison. With the touch of a button, a tuxedoed-doorman closed the doors behind them.

McPherson moved them swiftly through the vestibule, almost leading them into a trot. A short hall separated the vestibule from an even larger marble chamber, with massive columns sprouting intricately carved marble arches. Marty practically skipped over the rich orange hews of the Italian marble floors. Every footfall clattered hollowly, as they passed through the chamber. Marty caught glimpses of scattered works of art, one of which was most certainly a Van Gogh. McPherson's grip tightened on his handcuffs, as they moved on from the chamber into a plush paneled hall. The thick Karastan carpets deadened their footfalls. Marty sensed a flurry of activity behind the walls. He could not explain why he felt there were people watching them, but he sensed that something or someone was there.

After what seemed an eternity, McPherson stopped before a paneled door. He opened the door and pushed Marty forward. He stopped Marty at the door and held his manacles tightly from behind. In what seemed like a split second, the cuffs were off and Marty was pushed off balance into the room. The door slammed shut behind him and the unmistakable click of the tumbler sounded. Marty smiled to himself. He wondered why they were locking him in. He couldn't find his way out of this labyrinth. He rubbed his aching wrists and looked around the room. The main room was larger than his condo. The fourteen-foot ceiling was a graceful fresco of blue skies and puffy white clouds, with tree branches and birds along the edges. It was like looking up on a warm spring day. The room was divided into functional zones; one for entertaining, one for business and one for reading. Each area was furnished with contemporary furniture balanced with priceless artifacts for contrast; ancient Chinese jade carvings adorned rose wood tables. A Chippendale Escritoire Desk with the finest watermarked bonded paper was laid out, ready for a quick letter to a dear friend. Built-in cherry bookcases framed a fireplace large enough to roast a pig. A dozen different flower arrangements were scattered throughout the room, with a comparable number of tiffany lamps. The walls were a series of tailored panels covered in Chinese silk and gleaming with gold *fleur de lis* patterns. The wallpaper alone was probably worth more than his annual salary. A small bar was tucked discreetly in the corner with a dozen different liquors, including a bottle of Glenlivet. While tempted, he thought better of it. He moved toward the windows. He could just make out the iron bars through the stained glass. It didn't look like he was going anywhere tonight.

An enormous sleigh bed awaited him. The cover had been turned down and a mint awaited him on the pillow.

He ran his hand across the coolness of the silk linens, wondering if he were being kidnapped or coddled to death. Even at his six-foot-two-inch frame, he had to hop onto the bed. He kicked his shoes off. Each landed with a *thunk* in the floor. He laid back and closed his eyes. It was time to make some calls.

****

The delicious combination of cool wet sand between her toes and warm sun on her skin felt delicious. She looked down her brown toes, as they wiggled in the sticky white sand. She smiled at the deep maroon of her toenails. They were just the right color. Satisfied, she smiled at them. They strolled along the edge of the surf, looking out over the breaking waves of aquamarine water. The surf seemed to rinse her free of pain and guilt, as it washed over her feet. She said aloud, "I hate my thighs. They're too big."

A familiar voice responded with, "I think they're perfect the way they are."

She turned to face her love beside her in the surf. His strawberry blond curls tussled by the ocean breeze. "You really think so?"

Boyish dimples materialized, as he smiled. "I'm sorry, but I can't seem to find anything wrong with your legs, or anything they're connected to. Call me crazy."

She giggled. "Okay... Crazy."

He flashed a lopsided grin.

Dreamily, she asked, "Where are we, Sweetie?"

"Someplace safe. I wanted you to know I was okay."

She locked her arm around his hip and pulled him close. "Can we stay here for a while?"

His hand fell comfortably to the small of her waist. He pulled her tight against him and kissed her head, tenderly. "As long as you like."

A delectable ocean breeze teased her nostrils. She closed her eyes and drew it in. The beach was theirs. It was different than any shoreline she had seen. A large cranberry sun sat on the horizon, purple tinted sands sparkled and danced in the setting sun, and silver crests on topped the azure blue waves. She opened her eyes and looked at him. "I'm dreaming, aren't I?"

He said simply, "Row, row, row your boat…"

She smiled and looked back at her toes.

He continued, "I need to know something, though."

She pouted. "Must we talk shop so soon?"

"Sorry. McPherson led me away at knifepoint. I'm in a castle near Innsbruck. The funny thing is when we flew here, the plane was almost identical to the one we came to France on. I get the feeling that Franz and Dick are working for the same person."

She looked up at him. Her eyes were a lovely shade of violet and deeply serious. "That makes sense. Digger said Franz lied to us when he was asking the old man where you went. I suspect it means he knows more than he's telling."

"Don't underestimate him. These people have the kind of power to make us disappear."

She gave him a wicked little grin. "Yeah, I know. But you see, in this particular snake pit, I'm one of the snakes. Franz knows me. He knows what I'm capable of. I think I'm pretty sure I can get him to cooperate."

Along the edge of the ocean, the skies turned a lovely shade of amber, cresting the now orange setting sun. Clouds crossed over a deep backdrop of violet. She looked up at Marty. "It's so beautiful. Did you create that for me?"

"O, speak again, bright angel; for thou art
As glorious to this night, being over my head,
As is a winged messenger of heaven

Unto the white upturned wondering eyes
Of mortals that fall back to gaze on him
When he bestrides the lazy-passing clouds
And sails upon the bosom of the air."

A tear formed in the corner of her eye. "That's beautiful."

He smiled. "Romeo and Juliet; Act Two Scene One."

She wrapped her free arm around him and pulled him tighter, wishing they never had to wake up.

****

Had he been able, he would have noticed the ugly red glare of the digital clock which read *5:00 am* to remind him of what time he first noticed the horrible pain in his jaw. It was like a toothache, but worse. Half-asleep, he tried to move his hand toward his jaw when he realized he couldn't move his hand at all. Adrenaline surged through his system, as his eyes popped open. All four limbs were securely tied to the thick wooden bed posts. In the darkness, he could only see the outline of her shape over him. However, her scent was unmistakable; musky, yet enticing. Had he not been scared senseless, he might have been aroused. He could feel her hot breath on his ear, as she whispered in sultry voice, "Where is Martin Wood?"

He strained futilely at his bonds. "My dear, have you gone mad? Untie me this instant, so we can discuss this civilly. I know you and Wood have developed some sort of relationship, but this is sheer madness." His eyes adjusted to the dark, he could see her eyes. They were two narrowed slits, glittering in the darkness.

"Wrong answer." She laid the dagger beside him.

Franz relaxed, thinking she would release him when, to his dismay, she picked up a hand towel and dragged it slowly along his belly toward his mouth. Fearing what she would do next, he clamped his mouth shut. He could just make out her sneer in the dim light. Without warning, she slapped his bare stomach with an open hand. As he yelped, she stuffed the towel in. His eyes bulged in panic. She picked up the blade and let the cold metal slide innocently along his side. She watched as small bumps of flesh came to attention on his fat little belly. He tried to move away. Despite the coolness of the room, beads of perspiration bathed his body, as he frantically shook his head and made gurgling noises into the towel. She watched his nostrils flare, while panicked breaths labored through the small openings. Tears traced a slow path over his round cheek and into his ear.

She studied him for a moment. The blade reached his hand where it stopped. Her free hand moved so quickly, he never saw it. She gripped his pinky finger in an iron grasp. Ever so slowly, she inserted the blade under the nail and into the soft tissue beneath. Agony wrenched a muffled scream into the towel, as he writhed in pain. He rocked back and forth, trying to break free. She turned the blade slightly. His eyes grew wide and his nostrils almost closed, as he sucked in air. Suddenly, she withdrew the knife and sat back. A single drop of blood dripped from his finger to the sheets below. She watched, as his sweat-slick body relaxed back onto the bed. His gaze still darted back and forth. Moving the blade away from his hand, she laid it beside him on the bed. She reached down and pulled the towel from his mouth.

He lay there, panting. "Y-you don't understand. He'll kill me."

"Trust me, dear Franz. I *do* understand. But what you need to ask yourself is—do you want to die slowly being tortured to death, or quickly and cleanly by McPherson's bullet with your name on it? It shouldn't be too hard to find a castle one hundred kilometers East/Northeast of Innsbruck."

Even in the relative darkness, she could see his eyebrows knit in confusion. She lowered herself closer to his ear and whispered huskily, "If you don't take me to him, I will rent this room, put out a *Do Not Disturb* sign on the door and take you apart one small piece at a time."

He swallowed hard. "I'll take you to him. Please… just don't hurt me anymore!"

She whispered softly to him. "Okay. But remember, play nice. You don't want to get on my bad side. I'm sure there are lots of cozy rooms between here and Innsbruck."

"I-I understand. I wouldn't d-do that."

She stood and moved to the foot of the bed. Lithely, she moved between the posts at the foot of the bed. Almost seductively, she caressed his naked foot. The blade chimed as she sliced the rope from his foot with blinding speed. She moved like a cat, one that was playing with its prey. She slid the knife back in the leather scabbard under her pants leg. It felt good to be back in the game.

Franz looked at her, disdainfully, "May I at least be allowed to dress before we leave?"

"By all means."

"In private?"

"Don't flatter yourself. I've seen bigger raisins."

He blushed. She could see it even in the darkness. Within a few moments, they were standing in front of Digger's door. Franz knocked softly. Much to his surprise, Digger immediately opened the door. Digger dropped his bag at Franz's feet. In his best British accent, he said, "I say, Jeeves, would you be so kind as to stow that in the boot?"

Franz wondered which was worse; being killed by the duke, or being mocked by insufferable Americans all the way there. Neither option seemed very palatable.

Chapter 32

Marty awoke to the smell of lilac. Confused, he wondered if he was still dreaming. *You aren't supposed to smell in your dreams.* He drew in a deep breath and stretched. Still clothed, he was under the covers. He sat up and threw back the covers. As he did, he came eye-to-eye with a small dapper man standing beside the bed. Dressed in the standard attire of a valet, he looked like he had been strapped to a board. His English was crisp and clean like his uniform. "Good morning, Sir."

Marty yawned, rubbed his eyes and blinked. The dapper man wasn't pointing a gun at him. That was a good sign.

He mumbled, "Mornin'."

The little man looked around, as though there were someone else in the room. He whispered to Marty, "Are you from Tex-ass?"

Marty snorted, "Nah man, a might farther north."

He didn't wait for a response and walked to the bathroom, which was no exception to the rest of the suite. All of his essential grooming needs were already laid out for him in perfect order. He wondered if Brice was hiding under the bed. He smacked his lips and rubbed the rough stubble on his chin. He felt grimy for some reason. He contemplated how to broach the subject for a change of clothes, only to find them laid out for him as he walked back into the bedroom. Again,

Marty struggled to see the downside of the whole kidnapping scenario. He quit trying to reason it all out and grabbed a navy polo shirt and a pair of khakis. He looked at the thin little man and asked, "Underwear?"

The valet replied, "Behind the door in the washroom, Sir."

He nodded and meandered back to the bath. He gave the shower the once over and realized that it was big enough to wash his car in. Hot water began to peel away the layers of slumber. He stood there, soaking in the steam and letting the hot water wash across his back and shoulders. He thought about what he should do next. Knocking out the valet and stealing his uniform was out of the question. The man was half his size. He decided to play it out and hope Gillian would find him in time. As he stepped out of the shower, he felt like a new man, only to find the valet waiting patiently with a towel. He smiled at the little man nervously and said, "Thanks, Guy, I've got this." He took the towel from his hand.

Unperturbed, the small man responded, "Very good, Sir, Will there be anything else?"

Marty smiled. "No, thanks anyway." He wondered what he had in store after this. He wandered back out to the main room, dressed but barefoot. Shoes were laid out in a variety of styles. He chose a comfortable pair of Italian loafers. They were possibly the most comfortable pair of shoes he had ever worn. Marty realized he didn't know the man's name who had been so dutifully attending to his every need. With a polite smile, he asked, "My apologies, Sir, but I'm afraid I don't know your name."

The valet seemed confused for a moment. He

wasn't used to a guest trying to get acquainted. He responded "It's *Hans* Sir. My name is Hans."

Marty extended his hand. Hans timidly extended his own. Marty grabbed the little man's hand and shook, vigorously. "It's a pleasure to meet you, Hans."

Hans' eyes grew large. No one ever touched the hired help. The American was clearly insane. Marty continued to smile, as he asked, "So what's on the agenda for today, Hans?"

Hans responded quietly, "Breakfast with the Master, Sir. I am to escort you to the Small Dining Hall."

With a degree of false bravado, Marty said, "Tally ho then. Let's be off, shall we?"

Wide-eyed, Hans blinked at Marty.

****

Anna inspected herself in the mirror. She smoothed her blonde hair to ensure that there were no strays. She turned side-to-side. There were no wrinkles in the perfectly tailored uniform. Her uniform was starched to the point that it almost wouldn't bend. The new Butler, Klaus, had briefed each of the staff, individually on the arrangements. The American would be coming to breakfast. There were to be no mishaps. She had not seen this much excitement since President Dubrovsky of the Russian Federation had visited more than two years ago. *The American must be important for the duke to take breakfast with him.* She practiced her curtsy once again in the mirror, hoping that the move would please her master.

****

The *small* dining room turned out to be a misnomer by most standards. The room was as big as his high school gym. The rich walnut table was big enough to play shuffle board on. Flower arrangements of plump orange tiger lilies dotted the table in several locations, giving the room a smell of polish and flowers, like a funeral parlor. There were only two place settings. A small army of servants feverishly worked along the edges of the room preparing coffee, tea, juices and other beverages Marty couldn't identify.

With innocence, Marty looked at Hans. "So, Hans, which seat would you like?"

Horrified, he responded, "Oh, no, sir. I couldn't possibly do that."

Marty shrugged his shoulders and replied, "Okay, see you on the racket ball court in about an hour."

Hans looked confused, bowed slightly, and backed away from him. Marty snickered, as he sat. He had hardly gotten settled in the chair when a blonde angel approached him. In perfect English, she curtsied and asked, "Coffee, sir?"

"Sure."

"Cream or sugar?"

"Yes."

"Whipped?"

He paused and smiled. "Just cream and sugar will be fine. Thanks."

She curtsied again and moved to the side bar, where several urns were set up. She returned to the table a moment later and waited patiently until Marty tasted it. The aroma was seductive. It was amazingly strong and yet it lacked a certain bitterness, which added a perverse irony to his current situation. "This is the best coffee I've ever had, what is it?"

She stared at for a moment, surprised at the

politeness of one of the duke's guests. She smiled radiantly when she responded, "Kopi Luwak. It is flown here daily from Manila."

He nodded and smiled, enjoying the sweet richness of the flavor. *I could get used to this.* He looked over the brim of the cup in time to see a polished man walking briskly toward him. With an athletic grace, he covered the distance quickly. His coal black hair was kissed with a touch of silver at each ear. Crystal blue eyes moved constantly, giving nothing to chance. His mouth was framed by an envious cleft chin, yielding a rugged handsomeness. The royal blue tones of his Armani blazer accented the razor sharp crease in his khakis. It gave him a finished, relaxed look. Marty instinctively stood as he approached.

He smiled, as he closed in on Marty. Double rows of pearls greeted Marty when he smiled. In a smooth tenor, he greeted Marty openly, "Ah. Good morning, Martin. Duke Frederick Lindenspear. Please call me Frederick."

Members of the staff exchanged glances. *No* one had ever heard such an informal greeting from the duke.

Marty extended his hand in greeting. With an easy smile, he responded, "My pleasure, sir."

The duke's grip was firm and assertive. But then, so was Marty's.

Fredrick made a sweeping gesture with his hand as an invitation to sit. "Have you eaten yet?"

"No, Sir."

"Anna, dear, what do we have for breakfast this morning?"

She looked a little confused at first. The cooks always prepared the duke's meals to order—no matter what they were. She thought it was some kind of test; one that she was about to fail horribly. The rest of the staff stood rigidly along the edge of the room. She approached the table with some uncertainty. Marty sensed her fear, but couldn't understand it over such a simple question. He intervened. "This may seem silly. I know it's not traditional German food, but I would love some pancakes." He asked innocently, "Do you have those here?"

The duke smiled, broadly. "Of course. In fact, we have a wonderful German Apple Pancake, if you're game?"

"Sounds grand."

The duke gestured with his hand. "For us both, please, Anna."

She curtsied and practically ran from the room. Another young lady stepped forward with a cup of prepared coffee, placing it on the table. Without looking, the duke picked up the cup and began to sip. The subtleness of it didn't miss Marty's quick eye—just as the blazer the duke was wearing.

At first, the crest, resembled a coat of arms. After a closer examination, he realized that it was very different than any he had ever seen. A ruby red gold crested shield armed with a golden battle axe and pike crossed. In the center, a black skull with piercing red eyes glowered, as a white snake emerged from its mouth and wrapped around the smooth surface. The phrase *Novus Ordo Seclorum* ringed the crest. Marty stared, locked in a moment of deja vu. The duke's quick eyes noted the interest in his crest.

"It means *A New Order of the Ages*. It is my heritage and my curse."

Marty's eyebrows raised a notch. "Curse?"

The duke smiled sadly. He changed subjects. "So Martin, what do you think of my humble estate?"

Marty took a guess. "It's the most eloquent example of sixteenth century I've ever seen."

The duke laced his fingers and pushed his index fingers under his chin. "What makes you say that?"

"The bastions display an unusual amount of cornice work reminiscent of the Water Castle near Salzburg. The Arcade seems too ornate for work before 1500. It's clear there have been several period changes. I would say the most recent being nineteenth century."

The duke smiled, as he regarded Marty. "Most impressive, Martin. So are castles a hobby?"

Marty returned his smile. "I would say more of a curiosity. Being American, we don't really get a sense of that sort of depth of history from our homes. This is really quite fascinating."

Marty could almost hear Bess snort a continent away. She had informed him that two semesters of European Architecture were a waste of money. His doggedness on the issue had eventually paid off and she agreed to pay for the classes *against her better judgment*. He had always planned on making a sabbatical and castle hop one summer. This wasn't exactly what he had in mind.

The duke sipped his coffee. "Martin, I won't waste your time with some infantile charade. You have something I want. I cannot begin to explain to you how valuable it is to me."

Brazenly, Marty responded, "What makes my Sappir so valuable to you?" He gestured around him. "My guess is it is no more than a bauble in comparison to all that you have."

The duke smiled, tactfully. "I'm afraid that you misunderstand me. Your Sappir is not some trinket for display in some dusty museum. It is part of an intricate system that forms a key to an ancient lock."

Marty sat back in a surprisingly comfortable chair. "So, the stone is part of an array of some sort?"

The duke studied Marty for a moment. He was used to people who feared and patronized him. This young man was very different. Wood intrigued the duke, more so than anyone he had met in a long time. "Quite right, Martin. It is part of an intricate system. The gem you possess has led you to yet another stone, which completes the array. The diamond Franz is so dutifully bringing here—as we speak—is one of twelve."

Marty pressed him. "Once the twelve are together, what do they do?"

There was a long pause on the duke's part. "You know of the Jewish relic known as the Ark of the Covenant? Yes?"

"Yes. I know of it." It was an understatement, to say the least.

"The twelve stones form a harmony of sorts which will unlock the Ark."

"So you plan to control the most incredible force in the history of mankind?"

The duke shifted in his tapestry seat. His knuckles whitened slightly. The fingers were still interlaced, but visibly rigid. Ice cold blue eyes regarded Marty. "You seem to be quite at ease with all of this. Perhaps you don't believe me."

Marty shook his head. "No. I believe you. We

wouldn't be having this conversation, if it weren't true. It's too fantastic. So, would it be possible for me to see it?"

The duke's hands relaxed. He chuckled. The lad wasted no time. "Perhaps after we eat. You can't make history on an empty stomach, can you?"

With remarkable precision, a small army of staff began arriving with more food than a garrison could eat. There were platters of seared Polish sausages, eggs Florentine, steaming pancakes, dark breads smelling deeply of cinnamon, butter, jams, honey.

Marty's stomach growled at the prospect of food. He hadn't eaten since noon the day before. He hoped it was polite to dig in since that was what he intended to do. Before he could make a move, the duke was instructing the staff to portion him out generous helpings of food from several of the platters. Anna stood by Martin's side, patiently waiting for instructions. Marty watched the duke for a moment, shrugged and followed his example. His plate began to fill before him. Clearly pointing was acceptable, if directed at the hired help.

Marty pawed at the plate like a ravenous dog. Anna hovered over him and catered to his every whim. The duke watched Marty and Anna playfully banter back and forth. Beneath the Armani blazer, his neck began to redden. The same wench had pushed him away a year earlier. He had overlooked the incident at the time as youthful ignorance. Now, he watched with interest, as she poured over his young guest, taunting him and throwing the incident in his face. He smiled and joked throughout the meal. All-the-while, the memory festered within him like a boil; an abscess that would not be ignored. He finally felt the rich tug of emotion that he had long desired. Yet, the emotion was not what he would have expected. Anger and jealously rose like the mounting tide within him and they would not be contained.

****

Marty studied his host, curiously. For a man who clearly wielded supremacy with ease, he seemed surprisingly down to earth. As they ate, they discussed baseball. Strangely, they liked the same teams and vigorously shared a conversation about who had been traded and how that was going to affect the defensive strategy. Time flew, as they ate. While the purpose in Marty being here was clearly on both their minds, it was Marty who finally broached the subject. He took a sip of coffee and sat back. He didn't mince any words as he opened with, "If I might ask, why is it so important for you to open the Ark? Surely, whatever secrets it held are long gone by now."

The duke stopped eating and sat back. He delicately wiped the corners of his mouth and regarded Marty for a moment. "Open it? I have no intention of opening it. What if the Ark is not just a storage box? What if, instead, it is a reliquary?"

Marty acted ignorant. "I'm sorry, I don't understand. You mean something that holds some sort of secret?"

"Not just a secret, but energy; unbridled primitive energy from the dawn of time. It is something that has not been seen in a millennia."

Marty pressed him. "So what will you do with that kind of power?"

The duke's jaw tightened. He was not used to

being questioned on his intent, or anything for that matter. He fought his rising temper. Marty watched the duke with interest. He could sense he had struck a nerve and assumed he had pushed him too far. He fully expected the duke to evade the question. He was surprised when the duke asked, "Marty, did you ever play games as a child?"

He was a bit confused by the question, but he played along. "Of course."

"Do you play them now?"

"Well, no. It's kind of boring. They're too easy."

Smiling, the duke nodded. "That is precisely my point. It takes a team of twenty-seven highly skilled lawyers just to keep track of my holdings around the world. My banks hold more operating capital than the entire GNP of China. I collect politicians like most people collect coins. I move them like chess pieces just to see what happens. Controlling this world is child's play to me."

"So, this is all because you're bored?" Marty blurted before he could stop himself.

Oddly the duke didn't seem offended. "I prefer to think of it as my destiny is not being fulfilled. When you win every time, it is time to change to another game."

"You mean—start over?"

He smiled and nodded. "Precisely. Do you like history?"

It was another odd question. "It's not one of my strong points."

The duke smiled, comfortably. "No matter. History is always written by the historian who writes the most popular point of view. Hence, the accounts are subjective to the ruling class at best. There is an ancient sect of Judaism that studied a form of religious mysticism. They used an analogy to represent the different elements of mankind called The Tree of Life. The elements are represented as spheres known as Sephira. Each sphere represents a basic element of life: spirit, air, fire, water, and so on... But there was a secret sphere, an eleventh. It was known as Da'ath, the secret Sephiroth. It was the forbidden place; the place of the ultimate understanding."

Marty nodded, politely. He had no clue as to what the man was talking about.

The duke went on. "I have studied physics and religion for decades. I have plotted a path to the forbidden place. All I need now is the vehicle to carry me there."

Marty blinked. There was a fine line between madness and genius. He was pretty sure that the duke had just strode across it. He wished Digger were here.

Slowly, he asked, "So you believe you can open some kind of wormhole to this place called *Da'ath* with the Ark?"

The duke's eyes sparkled with excitement. "Precisely."

Marty took a long breath and a sip of coffee.

The duke's eyes were twinkling with excitement. "Here, let me show you something."

He removed a small wooden box from his blazer pocket. It was not unlike the one Marty had. Carefully, he removed the lid and set it to the side. He lifted the stone gently, like it is was it were a tiny bird egg, and placed it in the palm of his hand. Almost immediately, it began to glow. Within a few moments, it burned brightly in the duke's hand, like an ember from the fire. As it glowed, it grew. Finally, it was the size of a golf ball. Without warning, it began to levitate above the duke's palm. The staff moved back, closer to the walls, some noticeably disturbed. Without taking his eyes off the stone, the duke called out, "Anna, dear, come here for a moment."

Nervously, she responded to his side. "Y-yes, Sir."

"Hold out your hand, my dear."

Nervously, she extended her pristine palm forward. The stone floated from the duke's hand to hers and floated there for a moment. She seemed entranced by the small glowing sphere. The duke extended his index finger and pointed at the stone. With a quick downward movement of his finger, the stone passed quickly through Anna's hand, stopping just beneath it. The resulting hole in her hand was cauterized and free of blood. Marty heard her gasp, as she pulled the useless hand to her bosom. A smell of burned flesh filled the air. Her eyes were wide and her mouth agape, as she slowly backed away from the table. The room was dead-silent, while the staff stared on in horror. Like a cat watching a small bird, the duke quietly followed her movement from his chair. At two meters, he pointed to the stone again which still hovered silently above the table. His finger pointed to her heart. Before she could react, the stone pierced her bosom through her crossed hands and stopped.

Horrified, Marty watched as her eyes rolled back up into her head. She dropped to her knees and fell straight forward. The silence in the room was broken by the crumpling thud, as her body collapsed to the floor before them. She was dead before her blonde hair touched the floor. Marty's eyes were riveted on her form on the floor. He sat in stunned disbelief, staring at the girl who had just moments before been serving him coffee. The duke turned back to Marty. His eyes were narrow slits and his mouth was twisted in an evil smile. His finger directed the glowing sphere back to the table and straight toward Marty's heart. It flew at Marty at lightning speed. Before Marty could react, it stopped mere centimeters from his chest. The duke looked on, curiously. He moved his finger back and moved it again toward Marty. The stone stopped again, going no closer toward him. The duke sat back in his chair, nodding. He pointed the stone back into its box. The duke placed the small lid back on the box and placed it back into his pocket, as though nothing had happened. He looked at Marty and confided. "It's as I suspected. The stone has no power over another Stone Bearer."

"Excuse me?"

Marty stared again at Anna's body in the floor.

"Our stones cannot be used against each other."

Marty fought the urge to jump out of the chair and run.

The duke smiled at him. "Sorry for the unpleasantness, but it really was quite necessary."

Marty managed a weak smile and a nod. Without speaking, he reached for the coffee cup. He tried to control the shaking of his hands, as he turned it to his lips. The cup clattered against his teeth to the point that he was afraid he might chip a tooth. He put it back down. Mad or recklessly brilliant, he had to stop this man. The closer he stayed, the better his chance to stop him. Opportunism was now his strategy. Resourcefulness and cunning would be his tools.

Marty looked up, as the duke snapped his fingers. Two men in black jumpsuits walked toward them. The blood drained from Marty's face. He watched as they hefted her up and dragged her unceremoniously from the room. He steeled himself as he looked up at the duke. It was all he could do to muster a simple sentence. "I'm sorry. Where were we?"

The duke smiled at the response. Perhaps he had been right in following the boy's progress all these years. Unlike the milksop son of his, he was satisfied that at long last, he had a worthy protégée.

Chapter 33

Gillian was perched in the back seat of the Range Rover. At the first inkling of trouble, the long blade would run through the upholstery of the passenger's seat and pierce Franz just above the left kidney. Franz knew what she was capable of, just as he knew she was right behind him.

Digger could see the drained look in his face and the white knuckles as he clinched his fists in his lap. He silently wondered if the little man would make it to the castle without dying of a heart attack first.

In the ominous silence of the vehicle's cab Gillian watched Franz like a cat. Franz was petrified of making any movements that would make her think he was up to something. His throat was dry, but he didn't dare clear it. After what seemed like an eternity, Gillian's voice was tight when she finally asked the question that hung over them like a dark cloud. "Would you like to explain why you double-crossed me?"

Franz started to turn his head, so he could see her.

"Eyes straight ahead." Her voice snapped like a whip.

The venom in her voice even made Digger afraid to look back. Like a gorgon, he wasn't sure if he would turn to stone. It was a side of Gillian that he had never seen.

She could hear the strain in Franz's voice, as he

began. "It began with the boy's father. He was the original stone bearer. Nothing we said would convince him to turn it over. We tried paying him, threatening him—even including him in the discovery. He wouldn't change his mind. Quite unexpectedly, Malcolm, that's Martin's father, died."

Her voice was low. "He died, or did you help him die?"

Quickly, he responded, "No, I swear to you, we had nothing to do with his death. He and Martin's mother died in a plane crash, one in which Martin himself miraculously survived. That's when we began watching Martin. We thought that if we watched him closely enough, he would lead us to the final stone. Over time, he didn't seem to show any knowledge of the stones, so we approached Martin's aunt and uncle to spy on him and his grandmother. That backfired when the uncle accidentally killed the one Grandmother on the farm, trying to drug her and get her to tell him where it was. We made it look like an accident to give them time to search the house. Since Martin didn't seem to know anything, they left him with his other grandmother, Bess. They assumed that the old woman must have hidden the stones on the farm. They searched for years, trying to find a single stone. We didn't know Wood held two stones."

She asked, almost accusingly. "So why did you suddenly change the strategy? And why send that viper McPherson? You know what an animal he is."

"It was an unfortunate means to an end, my dear. I had always planned on exercising the option of capturing Martin to force him to tell us what we needed to know. The longer we watched, the more evident it was he didn't know anything of his *inheritance*. The duke has become increasingly more impatient. Since we have not made progress with locating the missing stones by waiting and watching, we had to do something more aggressive. Grabbing Wood was our last effort to locate the stones. Your team was in place to give him a comfort zone…to make him feel protected, while we tried to extract any information from him under duress. The assumption was that his grandmother left him some clue about his legacy."

She could feel the heat on the back of her neck. Franz was lucky she still needed him. If he weren't taking them to where they needed to go, she would have killed him on the spot. Her voice was tight, as she asked, "What legacy?"

"The legacy of the stones. He is the Stone Bearer. His ancestors recovered them during the Crusades. His family has sheltered them from wars and theft for generations."

"So, what are they? What makes them so special?"

"That's complex. We think they're the key to something larger."

Digger looked at him, calmly. "You mean you want to control Rachel?"

Franz's heavy jowl dropped. He was speechless for a moment before he stammered out, "W-what did you say?"

Gillian intervened from the back seat. "Digger, Sweetie, that's enough. Franz has had a long day. I don't want to kill him right now. If he knows too much, I'll have to. Okay?"

Gillian could see Franz's neck muscles tighten, as his face blanched. They had rattled him. She smiled for the first time that day.

Digger looked back at her. "Sorry."

"It's okay. You pay attention to the road, okay?"

"Yeah, probably better that I do." The statement was followed by another long silence.

Gillian considered what Franz had told them. Franz had never been a good liar. He knew it. She knew it. Gillian looked down at her left hand for a moment. McPherson had cut off half of her pinky finger under the pretense of trying to obtain information he knew she didn't have. He had tortured her for the sport of it. At some point, she would have the opportunity to repay the debt. She forced the aspect of revenge from her mind. The only thing she could concentrate on now was rescuing Marty from the clutches of a mad man. She owed him that. A worrisome question nagged her. *Why did they bother taking Marty at all? If the stones were all they needed, then, why is he still important to the duke?* That made no sense. There was more to this than Franz was telling them. The strategy formed, as she spoke. "How would you like to keep your miserable life for a while longer, Franz?"

"I'm listening." He sucked in his breath, as the blade nicked the nerve just under the skin.

"I don't care about a bunch of stupid rocks. Do we understand each other?"

He stammered, "I-I believe so."

"Right now, all I care about is getting Wood out of this mess. I owe him that."

"I understand you must feel you owe this young man a debt for all the misfortune. It's not your fault. You shouldn't feel guilty. You couldn't have known."

Her free hand swung over the seat and clinched his

neck in a vice-like grip. She pushed the blade in a little deeper and spoke in clipped tones. "Cut the crap. I don't feel guilty. But I do feel responsible, so here's what we're going to do. We're going in. We're going to find Wood. We're going to get him out. Are we clear?"

Franz struggled to breath. He managed to eke out, "C-crystal."

Without a word, she released him and sat back, plotting how to handle McPherson.

****

He smiled, confidently. "When can we see it?"

The duke returned the smile. "You waste no time."

Marty regarded him, steadily. "Time is not something I have the luxury of right now."

The duke nodded, pleased at his perspective. "I couldn't agree more. Let's go, shall we?" With that, he stood. Servants scurried to move the chairs away from both of them. They chatted like old chums. As they left the great dining hall, an army of servants busily cleared the table and sideboards behind them.

****

Christian and Gunter stared at Anna's body in the service hallway. Christian reached down gently, using a monogrammed linen handkerchief to cover her face. A tear fell to the white linen below, dotting it with a wet spot.

Gunter placed a hand on Christian's shoulder. Quietly, he said, "I will inform Gretchen about her sister."

Christian nodded. He cradled Anna in his arms for a moment before tenderly setting her down. She had always been so full of life. He didn't understand why the duke had killed her. But then, he rarely understood why things happened the way they did in this strange, evil place.

Chapter 34

It was past noon when the Range Rover crossed the border into Switzerland. The SUV chimed the *low fuel* alarm. The silence only exacerbated the irritability everyone felt from hunger and tension. Gillian sat obstinately, unwilling to even allow them to slow down much less stop. It was Digger who finally convinced her that they had no choice. In curt snippets of conversation, they chose a practically empty café in the deserted streets of a tiny ski village. Andermatt was a tourist haven during the ski season. The only people remaining were locals enjoying the quiet of the off-season.

They found a quaint restaurant nestled comfortably in a traditional chalet. The brasserie wore old world charm like a favorite pair of shoes. The smell of wood cured with a century of tobacco smoke greeted them, as they walked into the dim light of the tavern. The sound of techno pop filtered from the kitchen in the back. A young woman arrived at the table right away. Her white blonde hair was woven in traditional braids, which stood in stark contrast to her *Verve* sweatshirt, which hung loosely on her body and faded blue jeans. With a courteous smile, she greeted them in broken English. Gillian and Digger stared at Franz, as he responded in flawless Swiss. The girl looked relieved. Franz rattled on as he made no pretense by ordering for the three of them. Gillian shifted in her seat, uncomfortably. She would have been happy with a power bar and a bottle of water. She wanted to get back on the road. Franz shifted in his seat in awkward silence; Digger looked at the open beams and thick wood furniture, wondering just how old it really was. Gillian watched Franz with the fixation of a hawk watching a rabbit.

After what seemed like an eternity, the food was presented with little fanfare. Even Gillian could not dismiss at how beautifully it was displayed, given the meagerness of the clientele. In typical Swiss-style, heaping plates steamed with unusual looking dishes. With artistic flair, each of them had large shallow bowls ringed with painted spring flowers and raised patterns along the edge. Despite her urgency to go on, Gillian found her stomach growling at the prospect of diving into the plate before her. She poked at it with her fork and looked at Franz. Non-commitally, she asked, "What exactly is this?"

Franz gave her a tired smile. "Wurstsalat. It's a salad with field greens, sausage, cheese and roasted potatoes."

Digger poked inquisitively his bowl. "And this?"

"Bircher muesli. It's oats, cream, cinnamon and apples."

Digger gingerly bit into it. After the first nibble, he was committed and dug in with enthusiasm.

After several bites from her dish, Gillian pointed to Franz's bowl. "What are you eating?"

"Zurcher Eintopf. It's pork shoulder, onions, potatoes and carrots." She made a face at the thought of onions and continued eating.

The young woman placed a steaming pot of hot tea

on the table. After seven hours of tense travel, the food was a welcome relief. Not a word was said, as they plowed through the food. As wonderful as the meal was, it could not squelch the pallor of silence that loomed over them.

Chapter 35

They walked leisurely through the hallways, chatting like old friends. Oddly, they shared several similar interests, which caught Marty off guard. Marty wasn't sure what to expect in one who was clearly so powerful. He seemed charming for someone who had committed cold-blooded murder only minutes before. Marty was beginning to wonder if he was being too naïve. As they walked, he noticed little things at first. Paintings from the Renaissances period, marble sculptures, and crystal chandeliers were so tastefully integrated that they just belonged there. At every turn, he would notice something different. The duke began to notice his distraction. "So, you like my home?"

Marty nodded. "I've never seen anything like this. It's amazing. How long has it taken you to collect all of this?"

The duke smiled. "My family acquired wealth well before the Napoleonic Wars and have continued to amass what you see through the centuries. We have been both strategic and fortunate, without a doubt. It is unfortunate, but my son took it all for granted. He has squandered his life on drugs and women, and debased his birthright before his end."

Marty looked at the duke for a moment. A man so driven by control could not contain his own child? There was a noticeable sadness to his voice. Sincerely,

Marty said, "I'm sorry you've lost your son. Has it been very long since he passed?"

Without breaking stride, the duke responded, "It has been two weeks." He smiled an aristocratic smile and said, "So I guess I shall have to live forever, or at least until I have produced another offspring suitable to take my place. That is, unless you would like to be my heir…" He looked at Marty, slyly.

Marty assumed he meant the statement in jest, but he wasn't laughing. He blinked at the duke, giving the statement a moment to sink in. He thought fast. "Let's discuss it over dinner, shall we?"

The duke laughed and stopped walking. They stood before a full-size, neoclassic portrait of a young man. His face rigid, the chin slightly aloof, his eyes looked to something in the distance. A large beautiful Burmese waited patiently at his feet. The duke reached toward the young man and depressed a wooden medallion in the paneling beside the portrait. "At dinner then."

With a faint hiss of air, the painting disappeared into a wall pocket, leaving behind a thoroughly modern, brass elevator door. The duke placed his signet ring into a small depression in the door frame. The elevator chimed open. Marty studied the insignia in the depression. The All-Seeing Eye formed the inset, for which the signet ring fit perfectly. The duke gestured for Marty to enter the elevator car before him. He stood beside Marty, as he keyed in a nine-digit cipher on the keypad before him. The doors silently slid together in the middle and the car began to descend. This was the first elevator Marty had ever ridden where there were no indicators to reference how far they had traveled. There was no way of telling how far they had gone down. But, as they exited the car, there was the unmistakable feeling of coolness from the subterranean chamber around them. They stood before a glass chamber, with environmental suits neatly hung inside.

There was a soft hum in the room. Marty had to concentrate on what the duke was saying to hear him. "Sealed chamber... Nitrogen used to prevent oxidation... Ultraviolet light filters..."

He struggled to concentrate on what the duke was saying. Marty watched him don the environmental suit and followed his example. Fredrick reached across and helped him secure the various zippers and Velcro flaps, and attached air lines. Patiently he flipped on the electronics until Marty could suddenly hear him through the tiny speakers in the suit's helmet. Even in the suit, the hum seemed to be getting louder. The steady sound now threatened to drown out all of what the duke was saying. Marty felt disoriented, as he moved forward. His feet felt as though there were suddenly weighted. He struggled to move, as he slogged at every step. Even at the short distance between them, it was becoming a chore to keep up with the duke. The duke seemed oblivious to his struggle. As they entered the Artifact Room, Marty had to stop walking for a moment. His vision began to tunnel. He struggled against it, but had no choice but to take a deep breath and close his eyes for a just moment. For a moment, he wondered if the duke were somehow drugging him through the suit. Suddenly, it all cleared. As quickly as it had started, it stopped. The fatigue, the hum and the disorientation all stopped. It was quiet. Relieved, he opened his eyes only to find he was no longer in the chamber with the duke. He faced a familiar wooden door. He smiled and shook his head, as he turned the knob and walked in. The library was almost a place of comfort now. The door swung quietly shut behind him. He looked around, expecting to see Peter, but he wasn't there. From a distance, she came skipping playfully toward him, a precocious eight-year old with blonde curls and Cherub like cheeks. As she skipped, she hummed a little tune to herself. It wasn't a tune he recognized. She made her way down the long narrow room. Her hair bounced as she skipped and her smile was infectious. Without thinking, he found himself returning it. She skipped to him and wrapped her tiny little arms around his waist.

"Uncle Marty, it's so good to see you. It's been so long!"

Oddly, he knew he didn't have a niece, but the warmth of her hug made him want to believe. She backed up a short distance and took him by both hands. With a deeply dimpled smile, she chimed, "I just knew you'd come."

He found himself smiling without thinking. "I've really been looking forward to meeting you, Rachel."

She tugged at his hands, pulling him toward a royal velvet settee where they sat side-by-side. He studied her deep azure eyes for a moment. "Why are you afraid of him? You know he can't harm you."

It was her turn to study his eyes. She looked past the shell of his body into his very soul. She was greeted by an ancient spirit; one that had been tempered by many lives before. Confidently, she confided in him. "I have seen his savage hunger for power. He is a frightening mixture of arrogance and hollowness. He has no perception of empathy or remorse. He is like the child who would pull the wings from a butterfly just to see what would happen. He will experiment with my power just to see where it would lead him—without any consideration of aftermath of the world around him."

Marty pressed on. "True, I have seen that side of him, but don't you have any control over what happens with your power?"

Her eyes changed from blue to a deep olive green. "Sadly, I am only an instrument. As with a lock and key, once he has opened the portal, I have little control over what I am commanded to do. With the correctly spoken phrase or intonation, he could order me to do unspeakable things. But his commands must be clear and in the language of the ancients. I cannot be used against another entity such as myself. I cannot be used to change the fabric of time or space." Her small impish face turned deeply serious. She placed her hand on his. He could feel the warmth of the tiny hand. "I can be used to destroy matter and open existing portals."

"But he already seems to control this world. What more is there for him to do here?"

"It is not this world that he seeks to dominate. He seeks other worlds to conquer. And he will not stop at that."

Marty shrugged. "Any ant can have dreams, but at the end of the day, he's still an ant. I don't understand how he can travel to another world and dominate an alien culture?"

She gently patted his hand and shook her head making her blonde curls sway. "The same way he did here...lies, deceit and misinformation."

Marty tried to conceive of how it was possible. "But aren't you too powerful for a single man to control? He can't simply command you to do his will, can he?"

She tried to simplify her response, so he could understand. "Think about a magnifying lens in the sunlight. If you focus the lens in the sunlight into a single concentrated point of light, think of the effect it has on your tiny ant. Now, think of me as the lens, and the Supreme Father as the sunlight. The duke only needs to adjust me to do whatever purpose he needs of me. I cannot use my power for myself. Any human with the will and knowledge can control me to whatever means suits him."

"Wouldn't God stop him, though? I mean, he could intervene or something, right?"

"He could, but I doubt He would. It's the whole issue of free will. He won't interfere unless the duke threatens the whole system. If it reaches that point, He would extinguish this universe like a matchstick to prevent Fredrick from infecting the others."

"You make it sound like He would just wink and we'd be gone."

She nodded, without smiling. "Something like that."

"So you're saying the fate of the universe lies in my hands?"

"Not just you. You have friends. Together, you form a powerful Trinity. Frederick cannot hurt me, but he can destroy everything around me. If he destroys the people of this planet, I no longer have purpose."

Marty gave her a sour look. "Please tell me this is more than self-serving on your part?"

Her little face was deeply innocent. "I am tied to you all. The loss would be immeasurable."

He studied her eyes, trying to understand. They changed from green to an almost black violet. "I don't understand what you mean?"

She placed a tiny hand on his cheek. "And you cannot, at least, not at this point. Some day, you may."

"So, now what do we do?"

"I need you to trust me. This will not be easy."

She placed both tiny hands on his temples. He could see the mountain top where they would go; flashes of images of things that would come disturbed him. She removed her hands. "Can you do this?"

As he looked down, he sighed, not daring to let her see the tears in his eyes. Quietly, he nodded. He breathed deeply to steady himself and looked back into her eyes. She stood up on the settee and gently kissed him on the cheek. "Know that I will be with you. I know this scares you, but it is the only way."

He nodded.

She hopped down off the settee and took his hands in hers. "It is time to go."

Quietly, he nodded, and stood.

She smiled up at him, still holding his hands. "Please believe in me. I will protect you. Your path leads to Jebel Madhbah. Close your eyes."

Again, he closed his eyes, as she continued to speak. He opened his eyes to the hiss of a demand valve, as it supplied air to his suit. The duke was slightly ahead of him in the vault. The chamber was bathed in amber light. Marty didn't know if he was ever going to get used to this. They moved carefully into the lit chamber. Even in the subdued light, he could see the details on the Cherubs, as they approached. It was smaller than he imagined. Columns supported each corner, and each column was magnificently carved. Each looked similar, but he could see intentional subtle differences. The sides were dimpled and beaten flat by ancient hammers; an intricate relief of a tree with hanging spheres in the center. The edge along the bottom was worn and ragged in places. Thin strips of gold were missing, revealing the dark ancient wood underneath.

He stared at it. It was truly the most incredible thing he had ever seen. The only thing he could think about were Rachel's lingering words ringing in his ear: "Remain strong. The pain will linger only for a moment before you die…"

Chapter 36

Jozef stood quietly with a two day old copy of the Prague Post. The big Czech liked reading the copy in English. It kept him polished on his use of the Western tongue. He never knew when he would have to use it next. The paper served two purposes today, current events and camouflage.

"I have to go to the loo."

Her eyebrows knitted together, as she eased out a long sigh. She regarded him for a moment before responding, "Oh, very well."

Digger's eyes widened, slightly. Gillian watched him squirm slightly before Digger weakly volunteered, "I guess I can watch him."

Gillian gave him a sly grin. "That's okay. I can handle this. This is Europe, you know."

He blinked at her. "I'm sorry. I don't follow?"

She rolled her eyes. "They have unisex restrooms here. I'll keep an eye on him. You finish your lunch."

Digger looked relieved and somewhat confused, all at the same time. He was really bright, but a little naïve sometimes when the conversation strayed too far from Quantum Theory. He returned to his food, plowing away at the last of the bowl. It had turned out to be quite good. Gillian looked Franz in the eye. "Let's be straight with each other for once, shall we? One funny move on your part and I will take a great amount of personal pleasure making sure that you suffer immeasurably. Are we clear?"

He regarded her warily. "Crystal. You know you don't have to be so insufferable about all this."

Her eyes narrowed and the blood drained from her lips, as they thinned. "Just move," she said, tightly.

Feeling that he might be pushing his luck, Franz did not try to press her anymore. Standing, he straightened himself out and moved toward the back of the restaurant. Gillian was a stride behind him. The lavatory was small, even by European standards. It was one toilet with a hand basin outside the door. Still, all the fixtures were immaculate and the room smelled like tulips.

Franz gave Gillian an imploring look. "I'm not going to hang myself. May I at least close the door? I promise, I won't try anything."

He reached into his pocket. Removing the keys to the Range Rover, he handed them to Gillian. "Here, take my keys. Where could I possibly go?"

She pushed him into the room and carefully looked over the walls and ceiling. There were no vents, windows or doors for him to slip out. She doubted that he had the gumption to kill himself.

"All right, but make this snappy."

"Quite civil of you." He feigned a weak smile.

She glared at him. "Don't push it."

She pulled the door behind him. Something in her gut made her uneasy. The room was at the end of a narrow hallway. There was no other exit, with no way out. She stood there, radar on, watching and waiting. The floors down the hall groaned under footsteps, as someone approached from the end of the hall. A massive dark-haired man rounded the corner and headed toward her. He smiled, disarmingly. Her body tingled from the adrenaline rush.

The man asked. "Is the WC occupied?"

Despite herself, she stared at him quizzically, "Pardon?"

"The water closet, is there someone in there?" The big man was still smiling politely.

"Oh, yes, quite sorry. He should be out in a minute."

"Thanks."

He eased past her and stood a short distance away to wait. He nonchalantly leaned against the wall and removed the newspaper from under his arm. His attention turned toward the paper and seemed to pay little attention to Gillian. She relaxed a bit.

With her back to the door, she turned her head and rapped on the door. "Are you almost done in there? There's a line forming."

"Almost."

She heard a tiny *click* which was followed by an almost immediate burning sensation on her belly. Looking down, she struggled to focus on the small silver dart sticking out of her abdomen. She looked up to find the big man standing beside her. Her body seemed paralyzed, as did her mind. She watched absently, as he reached out and put his hands on her shoulders. His broad face smiled down upon her. Almost gently, he said, "Here, let me help you." He guided her body to the wall where she began a steady slump downward. She was unconscious before she reached the floor. The big man removed the dart from her and placed it back in a small titanium case which fit neatly back in his pocket.

Still drying his hand on a clean towel, Franz opened the door. "You young people have no idea what havoc you're..." his voice trailed off in mid-sentence. His gaze scanned up to the Czech and then down to Gillian. Wordlessly, he dropped to his knees and placed his fingers on her neck. He sighed quietly. There was strong pulse, albeit somewhat erratic. His gaze climbed until he found the massive face before him. "What did you use?"

His tone was disinterested. "Trolamine, fifth generation."

The color drained slightly from the old man's face. "Idiot! You could have killed her."

Jozef rolled his eyes. "Honestly, don't you keep up with anything other than your rocks, old man? The side effects of fifth strain are no more than a headache and a nosebleed. She'll be fine." He reached down, picked up Gillian like a bag of grain and hefted her to his shoulder. "We must go. The duke grows impatient. We have played this game long enough."

"What of the young man?"

"He's already loaded in the car."

"Car?"

"Surely, you don't think I'm going to drive that piece of junk you call transportation to the estate, do you?"

They were halfway down the hall when Franz asked, "What about the restaurant staff?"

"They decided to take a break." He sneered to himself, as he said it.

The pretty blonde waitress lay behind the polished wood of the bar. Her face was pure and unblemished, her blue eyes now fixed in a permanent gaze which complemented the awkward angle in her neck.

****

Jozef dumped Gillian into the trunk of the large black sedan. He liked the older car because he could fit two people in the trunk without having to cut them up first. It was pretty convenient at times. He rearranged Digger's feet, so Gillian would lay flat on the floor on her side. He took a moment to rearrange the unconscious victims, so that they were on their side.

Franz watched in disbelief, as he fussed with the pair as though they were luggage. There were few people in the street, but anyone could see what they were doing if they wanted to. He was becoming more agitated by the moment. "Could you hurry, please?"

Jozef gave him a dour look. "This is what I do, old man. Don't tell me how to run my business."

"Yes, of course," he replied, weakly.

Comfortable that the duo were arranged properly for the ride, the big man slammed the trunk lid and moved to the driver's seat. Franz sank into the plush black leather on the passenger seat and stared straight ahead. One hundred meters away, a backup team lay poised with rifles. They were invisible against the surrounding foliage. They silently waited for the first indication of trouble. Not even a bird chirped, as the long black sedan eased out into the street and purred down the road.

The sun cast long shadows of the firs along the private road to the Castle Lindenspear. The piercing edifice skewered the cloudless sky, gleaming like black ice against a backdrop of azure blue. It winked in and out of the trees growing more ominous each time they saw it. They eased past a small contingent of armed guards at the final gate and proceeded away from the front entrance to a more private entrance along the east wing of the castle. McPherson stood stoically, hands crossed in front of him like a hangman waiting for the next condemned man. The car had barely stopped when he opened the door for Franz and motioned for him out. "Let's 'ave it then" he said, holding his hand out.

"Have what?"

"Don't get cheeky. Just 'and it over."

Franz reached into his pocket, withdrawing the oval diamond. He dropped it in McPherson's waiting hand. McPherson patted him on the cheek, none too gently. "That's a good lad." He turned and strode into the castle, leaving a detail of heavily-muscled men behind to help with Gillian and Digger. He hesitated in the half-open doorway. "Get your guests cleaned up. We all meet for dinner in two hours with the Governor, 'imself. I suggest you look presentable."

Franz lips were a thin line. He had eaten many meals with the duke. The Scot's impudence irked him, but he let it go. Dinner would be a civilized event. There would be no surprises. After that, there was no way of telling. He had seen many a man terminated after a meal.

Jozef reached in the trunk and removed Digger like a piece of luggage. He was no gentler with Gillian. Neither seemed the worse for wear, other than the thin line of drool from Digger's to the floor of the trunk. Gillian was still out cold. Franz motioned for the guards to assist. One of the guards barked orders into a radio. Within moments, men in black jumpsuits appeared with wheelchairs. A minute later, Gillian and Digger were on their way to separate attended rooms. As they were wheeled into luxurious suites, the drug began to wear off. Gillian sat on the edge of her bed. She looked up at the attendant, who had to be the missing link in a starched white uniform dress. She wondered if the frau understood English at all. She wracked her brain for a phrase that would work. "Sprechen Sie englisch?"

Without smiling, the attendant replied. "Yes, I speak very good English."

Gillian sighed. "I have a very bad headache. Do you have aspirin?"

"One moment."

She picked up the phone in the room and rattled off several terse phrases in German. She lay back on the pillow and covered her eyes with her open palm. A moment later, the attendant was standing over her. She had a wet towel from the bathroom in her hand. She gently lowered Gillian's hand and placed the towel on her forehead. "Der Doctor will be in shortly." The towel felt wonderfully cool and inviting against her skin.

Gillian nodded. It was all she could do. She napped for what seemed only a moment before she awoke to find a portly, little man with a round face and glasses holding her wrist. He looked down and saw that her eyes were open. He smiled. *He seems like a nice man.*

He spoke softly. "I am Dr. Ostermann. You were given a drug to sedate you. I need to give you a shot to counteract the sedative. This will sting a bit, but you will feel much better, I assure you."

She nodded, but did not move.

"I need you to roll over, please."

She blinked, but did not move.

Ostermann looked at the stout attendant and asked, "Frau Schmidt, could you help me for a moment?"

She moved quickly for such a large woman. Gillian thought she smelled lilac when the woman was near. The little man filled a syringe with some unknown glowing green substance. Without looking, he said, "Roll her onto her side, please."

Frau Schmidt grabbed Gillian with an iron grip and flipped her like a Marlin. The move left Gillian nauseous and the room spinning. She felt the back of her pants being jerked down. Sting would not have been the word she would have used. At first, she felt a tingle of nerves in her buttocks before a burning sensation began to radiate up her spine and into her back. This guy must have been a harpooner on a whaling ship. Frau Schmidt pulled her pants up and she was rolled back over. Frau patted her on the arm. "You should feel better in a couple of minutes."

Gillian didn't see how that was possible. Twenty minutes later, she was sitting on the side of the bed. All traces of the headache and nausea were gone. If she lived through this, she would have given ol' Doc Ostermann a hug. But that seemed like a remote possibility at the moment.

Frau Schmidt watched on. "Dinner is in forty-five minutes. Please ready yourself."

Gillian looked at her. "I'm not on the menu, am I?"

Frau Schmidt looked confused, but said nothing. Gillian smiled, as she got up unsteadily and meandered into the bathroom.

Chapter 37

Gretchen stared at the square blinking cursor on the screen. A streaming bulletin ran across the top of her computer screen like a stock ticker: *All American guests are on site now. They are assigned to general quarters. They are to be escorted at all times. Any irregularities must be reported immediately.* She sat stared at the computer screen. She was too stunned to think. *Her little sister was dead.* Anna was sweet and naïve. There was nothing the duke could say to justify what he had done. Deep within her, she heard the whisper. It was indistinguishable at first, but it grew louder and called out to her: *He knows. You must act.* Mechanically, she stared at the screen before her. She eased the cherry desk drawer open before her, never once dropping her head to indicate that she was looking for something. Her hand clutched a small remote control from the drawer and placed it into her lap. She knew precisely where the security team placed the camera in her office. Deliberately, she had arranged her desk so the security team could not stare at her all day. There was nothing prudish in her actions. The privacy was necessary for other reasons. She pressed a small red record button on the device and began typing dutifully for five minutes without stopping. She stopped for a moment to look at what she had typed. She turned off the recorder. She reached over and began to shuffle through the paper on her desk. As she reached for one page, the rest tumbled to the floor in a mess. She cursed a small oath and began to pick them up. She angled herself to give the camera an unobstructed view of her ample cleavage, as she shuffled the stray pages off the floor. She straightened up and went back to look at the screen for a moment. As she did, she pressed the loop button on the remote. All they would see her do for the next thirty minutes would be to type and read her screen. The maneuver gave her a window of privacy. There were no cameras in the duke's personal office. Her brother Felix had spent an entire year designing and overseeing the entire security system. He was her only living relative right now. It could not be defeated by anyone from the outside, or so they thought. It was their sense of arrogance that would play in her favor. She knew more about the system than the security team did. She was also a master at manipulating it.

During installation, Felix had given her the remote, so she could help him experiment with it. It was forgotten to everyone but her. He had been instrumental in raising them. Guilt ate at her now with the thought that she was betraying his trust. But then, she rationalized. It was bigger than the both of them now.

She didn't bother closing the door behind her, as she entered the duke's office. She confidently strode across the room to a full size portrait of Frederick the Great, the duke's namesake. She touched a hidden button in the molding of the frame. With a quiet *click* the portrait swung open, revealing the large stainless steel safe behind it. Gretchen smiled wryly, as she opened the safe. She considered the irony that the egocentric duke idolized his namesake, Frederick the

Great.

Deftly, she opened the safe and reached inside. She reached past the rare coins and bundles of cash to remove a small wooden box. Careful not to disturb its location, she cautiously opened it where it sat. Inside was a small deep blue Sappir. Removing it, she reached into her bra and removed its twin, placing the replica back in the box. She closed it and placed the real stone in her brassier; It felt strangely warm to her skin. Carefully she set the box back in the safe.

It had taken the gem cutter in Amsterdam a month to find the correct rough stone and to cut it to her specification. It had been a difficult task. It was unlike any other he had ever seen. The ancient lapidary was an oddity. It represented a great deal of complexity which was unknown during the period in which it was cut. While the Gem cutter was perplexed by it, he reproduced it, nonetheless. The finished piece was flawless.

She walked briskly back to her office and to the wall across from her desk. She pressed a section of the molding in the panel and heard the release of a latch inside. The large wooden panel slid easily into a cavity behind it. Two dimly lit tunnels branched off from the doorway. Today, she would be using the servant's tunnel.

The security team had commandeered many of the broader tunnels for placing guards at strategic points throughout the facility. Their readiness teams could respond to any point in the castle, within seconds of being notified. For the most part, they hung out and played cards. It was a boring existence that hinted of adventure, but resulted in none of it.

She moved quietly through the dimly-lit corridor to the chamber where the American girl was being kept. She eased the panel to the room open. The American was not in the room. She could hear the shower in the bathroom. It was perfect. Her *Dienstmädchen* stood primly, towel in hand, waiting on the girl to finish. Unnoticed, Gretchen watched the female valet for a moment, making sure that she was not moving. Again, she used the remote to record a loop of the woman. Much to the surprise of Frau Schmidt, who whirled at the sudden intrusion she entered the room. Recognizing Frau Hapsburg, she immediately bowed her head. Gretchen's cutthroat politics were legendary in the castle. It was enough to make Frau Schmidt squirm, unquestioningly.

Gretchen looked at Frau Schmidt, severely. Curtly, she asked, "Why haven't you provided fresh flowers for our guest?"

The older woman stared at the fresh flowers on the bed stand and stammered, "But I…"

"Go find fresh flowers and don't return until you have them in a crystal vase!"

Frau Schmidt swallowed hard and quickly shuffled from the room, closing the tunnel panel shut behind her. Gretchen strode past the massive posts of the canopy bed and into the spacious cream-colored bathroom. She made no pretense of modesty. There was no time for it.

Gillian opened the frosted glass door of the shower to find herself face-to-face with a beautifully sterile looking woman. Her face was unreadable, as Gillian toweled off her glistening body. Gillian made no attempt to hide from her, as she enjoyed the slight roughness of the thick terrycloth towel. She looked the woman in the eye before asking, "Is there something I can get you?"

In perfect English, Gretchen responded, "I think I may have something you might want, Ms. Kelly."

"Call me Gillian, please."

"Very well, Gillian. I think this might help you." She dipped her hand deep within her cleavage.

Gillian arched her eyebrow. "Sorry, Toots, I don't swing that way."

For the first time, Gretchen's face formed a slight expression as she furrowed her eyebrows and scowled at her. Wordlessly, she tugged the stone free and offered it with an open palm. Gillian's gaze locked onto the object without thinking. She moved her free hand forward; it was like Gretchen were holding a scorpion. As soon as Gillian was close enough, Gretchen plunked it into her hand. It had been a long time since Gillian had been at a loss for words. She furrowed her brow, as she looked from Gretchen to the jewel. "How did you get this?"

"That is irrelevant. What's important is that the duke does not know the stone he has is a counterfeit. You hold a bargaining chip beyond value. Please use it wisely." Gretchen looked at her watch. "I must be getting back."

Gillian stared at the stone. When she looked up, the woman was gone. She finished toweling off, holding the stone tightly as she did. Fresh underwear had been laid out for her. She took the stone and placed it in her own bra. Sometimes, the old tricks were the best tricks. She had been searched thoroughly before she came in. They would not suspect she had anything hidden, or so she hoped.

She walked out to find Frau Schmidt waiting for her. Several outfits were laid out on the bed for her. She looked at the worsted wool dress and white linen blouse and snorted but said nothing. Frau Schmidt eyed her. She grabbed the least offensive outfit offered, a pair of khakis and a short sleeve mock turtleneck. There were four pairs of sensible low heels and one pair of flat loafers. The loafers would have to do.

Frau Schmidt led Gillian unescorted through the castle to the main dining hall for dinner. She considered her surroundings. As they went she picked out items along the hall: the catch on the rosewood panel; *it was probably a hatch to a secret room*; a miniature camera embedded in an eighteenth century sconce; an infra-red laser hidden in the doorframe. She saw the magnetic sensor on the frame of the hanging painting and the motion sensor a few feet away, but missed the painting itself. The subtle pastel overtones of Monet, himself, were lost to her.

She could sense the eyes on her by all the surveillance equipment, but she wasn't going to make it obvious that she knew. They entered the dining hall from a side door. As she looked across the room, it occurred to her that it was the same size as a hockey rink. She wished she were playing hockey right now versus this dangerous charade. Frau Schmidt maneuvered her to a specific seat. The room was quiet, except for the staff shuffling behind her. Digger and Franz entered from another doorway shortly after her. Digger was seated beside her. She leaned over to him and whispered, "Are you okay?"

He grinned. "Beautiful. I don't know what kind of pharmaceutical cocktail I had going there, but if they every start selling that over the counter I'm buying stock."

She grinned. It was the same old Digger. His cup was perpetually half-full. One of the servants opened the door on the west wall for a distinguished gentleman and a dapper young man. They smiled and chatted, as he walked across the room. McPherson padded along behind them like a cur waiting for scraps. He looked none too happy. A chill went up Gillian's spine. As McPherson looked at her, he gave her an evil grin. She tried to ignore him and pay attention to the two he had entered the room with.

The distinguished looking man wore refinement like a comfortable pair of shoes. His clothes were tailored; his hair, teeth and grooming were perfect to the point of being artificial. He stood ramrod straight inches above the young man beside him. She looked closer at the young man. There was something very familiar about him. Her jaw dropped when she realized that it was Marty. He looked like he had just walked out of a Scotch ad.

He looked up and saw her. Smiling broadly he walked across the room to her. "Hello, Love." Taking her hand, he leaned forward and kissed her on the cheek. She was too stunned to move. As he did, he whispered, "Trust me." in her ear.

She smiled falsely, as her open hand popped against the side of his face. It sounded like a rifle shot in the room. The room paused of activity in a moment of awkward silence. "That's for wandering off and making me worry."

Marty looked a little flustered and mumbled, "Sorry. It won't happen again."

The duke covered a bemused smile with his hand, but calmly carried on like nothing had happened. He looked Gillian in the eye, as he spoke. "Allow me to introduce myself. I am Duke Fredrick Lindenspear." He extended his hand. She gripped his hand like a lumberjack and pumped it like a machine. She caught a tiny involuntary wince on one side of his neck for just an instant. She hoped it hurt.

The duke smiled graciously as he released her quickly hand, "So, is it an American custom to slap your lover?"

Gillian felt a little foolish. Pent up angst had gotten the better of her. She would never have let her emotions drive her before. Franz sat. Although his face was stoic, he squirmed mentally. The room was a powder keg of upheaval. McPherson stood behind them like a dog straining against a weak rusty chain. With a snap of his fingers, the duke instantly defused the situation. The staff stood by nervously until the order. Now, they swiftly descended upon the guests with cocktails and appetizers. Marty sat stiffly across Gillian. While he was resolved to see this out, he was torn that she would not understand. It was like she knew what he was thinking, she subtly winked and flashed a flicker of a smile which quickly dissolved, as she instructed her attendant as to how she wanted her end cut of filet mignon. Marty relaxed, as he ordered the filet of sole. The Scotch and soda burned the back of his throat, as he drank it quickly and signaled for another.

The table hummed with activity, as food and drinks flowed in and out like the tide. In the midst of the beehive, Digger could contain himself no longer. Without warning, he stood and faced the duke. "So why are we here?"

Everyone stared at him in surprise. The duke settled back comfortably and interlaced his fingers, which peaked gently on his lips. "That is a complicated answer, Mr. Delgado. I will not insult you with pretense, since all the components I require are in place. You are all aware of certain aspects, but not clear on the grand scheme as it were. Today culminates an operation that has been running for over twenty years. Tomorrow could very well change the course of mankind, as we know it." He opened his hands toward the three of them. "You and your friends have ushered in the final pieces of the puzzle."

Marty watched with keen interest to see if the duke's candor would extend to his friends. Digger continued his role play of a dippy California playboy. "So is this a miracle cure, or some plan to save the rainforest?"

"Nothing so mundane would interest me, Mr. Delgado. My plan is a bit more auspicious than that. In my experience, if you give mankind a golden ring, they will work it until they have turned into lead. I have no desire in solving the world's problems. Had I, they would have been solved by now. Instead, I will give them something else to consider. Perhaps then, they would solve their own problems and move on. What if we introduced them to a new world order—one that was integrated with our own in a single social hierarchy?"

"I'm sorry… I'm afraid I don't follow?"

"You may dispense with the play acting Mr. Delgado. What if I found what could be described as a quantum doorway?"

Digger sat and dropped the childish naivety. "So are you suggesting you've found a wormhole?"

"More to the point, I have found a means to create a wormhole. I have discussed my findings with several top scientists and theologians. They considered the information too vague and unreliable to be predictable. I fear that some of our greatest minds tend to succumb to mediocrity, if they did not propagate the concept."

Digger cupped his chin with his hand and tapped his index finger on his lips. "So the experts wouldn't validate your findings?"

"More accurately, they laughed at the concept."

"So, if I was to surmise, I would say that you have a hypothesis and now you need a means to test it?"

"Quite the contrary. I *have* the means to test it. Now comes the task of doing so. There is only one way. Someone must go through the portal to the other side."

McPherson moved forward from the wall and presented the duke with the final stone. The duke smiled, as he caressed it in his hand. It was warm and smooth to the touch. Without looking up, he said to no one in particular, "My family has sought this for eight centuries, since the age of Lavigne."

He finally looked up. With a distant look in his eyes he said, "Thank you, Mr. McPherson. Now, would you be so kind as to ready us for a voyage to the Middle East? We leave for Jordan in the morning."

"For how many, Sir?"

Without looking up, he murmured, "All of us, Mr. McPherson. All of us."

McPherson was crestfallen. He had hoped there would be killing to be done tonight. Perhaps the duke will allow me to sacrifice them in the Middle East?

Then I could throw their bodies off of the side of a mountain and watch them fall out of sight. The fantasy cheered him. As he left the room, everyone could hear him whistling a happy tune. No one wanted to know why.

****

It was late, as they walked back to their rooms holding hands with two attendants following closely in tow. It was a chaperoned first date. Gillian thought it was sweet in a demented kind of way. She gave him a sly sideways glance. "You really had me worried back there."

"Me? He is good looking and all, but he's really not my type. You needn't worry."

She gave him a tiny frown for being so flippant.

They reached his room first. He smiled. "Care to come in for a night cap?"

She looked deep into his eyes. She cupped his face softly in her hands and said, "I thought I lost you. I was dying at the thought of it."

Hans and Frau Schmidt looked at each other, wondering what to do.

Behind the walls, men in black jumpsuits buzzed angrily back and forth like agitated wasps, preparing to protect the hive.

Marty put his arm around her and drew her to him. Her lips were warm and willing. The closeness of her body lit a fire within him. Her wanton embrace fueled it. Hans cleared his throat. Marty could have cared less.

Men in black jumpsuits paced like chained junkyard dogs. Snarling against an invisible chain, they ached for the opportunity to jump the Americans. A tiny earpiece held them at bay. "Hold your position.

Engage only on my command."

Marty drew away, slowly. Gillian rested her head against his chest, as she wrapped her arms around him. He looked over at Hans, smiling. With a loose hand gesture to Frau Schmidt, he said, "Feel free to do the same."

Frau Schmidt's thick neck turned red.

Digger snickered from behind. "Get a room, you two."

He put his chin on the top of Gillian's head. "It looks like our chaperones are getting impatient."

She whispered, huskily. "Just one more kiss, please?"

Men in black jumpsuits waited, poised to burst the secret opening in the wall and pounce cat-like on the pair. They waited like track stars for the start gun to sound. In anticipation, their taut muscles rippled beneath black uniforms.

This time, his arms cradled her close to him. They swayed in unison in the moment. Hans gently put his hand on Marty's shoulder. "Please, Sir, we must go. It's for you own good."

Gillian was the first to break away. She moved slowly, her eyes never breaking contact with his. Hoarsely, she said, "In the morning…" It was all she could get out. Her voice was thick with emotion.

Marty caught the tear in her eye. The baseball size lump in his throat threatened to strangle him. It was all he could do to manage a smile back. "Until then…" was all he could manage. His voice was barely above a whisper.

Hans opened his door and ushered him in before they could embrace again. Frau Schmidt shooed Gillian down the hall, all-the-while wishing she could leave the young couple together.

Men in black jumpsuits slunk back to their listening posts, tails between their legs, despondent at the lost opportunity.

Chapter 38

She questioned herself as to why she was even doing this. Perhaps it was that she had never had any real relationships outside of family? Perhaps it was that she was grieving over her dead sister? Perhaps it was an intuitive urge to right the many wrongs she had orchestrated? For whatever the reason, her next action could not be undone. On this hallowed eve of destiny, this final night that everything would be normal in the castle, she chose to do something against her master's wishes, something so wrong that she would probably die horribly for it. Unlike Anna, who died quickly and cleanly, she would not be afforded such luxury. Hers would be a death of agony and pain. And yet, she still proceeded. Her step hastened, as she approached door number 312. Its numbers faded, its finish worn, but it was still quite legible. The stoic figure of a coal black tunnel cat sat unmoving at the threshold of the door. The staff only fed the creatures occasionally to keep them alive. Otherwise, they remained forever hungry and hunting. Almost all of the creatures were feral. They'd lived for centuries in the dank narrow corridors hunting rats and mice with little to no human contact. She stopped at the door and stared at the animal. Its eyes glared back, challenging her to make the first move. It was an omen that she would face many fears in the coming days, and this was but the first. She tried to shoo the animal away only to have it hiss and growl at her. Stoically it posed like a guardian at the doorway. Gretchen kicked at the animal only to have it spit at her and move a few feet away. It was as though the animal were protecting the room. The hairs on Gretchen's back stood on end, but it did not deter her.

Gillian sat quietly in a chair, her knees were tucked under her chin, as she stared out of the darkened window before her. Tears streamed across her cheeks, dampening her blouse. Long ago, she had resolved to herself that she would die alone in some hell hole. She had accepted that. Soldiers don't dwell on it. They focus on survival. It was what made the soft comfort of the room wrapped in despair such a bitter pill now. She was finally ready to abandon her hollow existence and give her life meaning, only to have it stripped away before she could consummate her feelings. She bit her lip, as the tears flowed a little heavier. It was probably the first time since she was ten that she had been distracted. There was a faint click as the catch opened on a secret panel into the room. A silent black figure glided unnoticed into the shadows behind her.

****

The attendant had finally left. The room was silent, save the steady tick of the mantel clock and the occasional pop and crackle of the dying fire in the hearth. Marty stared at the ceiling, as the light wiggled and squirmed above him from the mellowing fire. The whirlwind of events swirled in his mind; Gillian in the back of the Range Rover, the Ark, Gillian kissing him, the Library, Gillian…

Sleep would be impossible tonight. He heard the faint click of a hidden tumbler, as he sensed someone had entered the room. The shadows from the moonlight danced and swayed. He could tell where the shadow ended and where the assailant began. He controlled his breathing and waited. Adrenaline pounded in his ears. He wondered if it was McPherson. Most likely, his attacker would strike at him from his side of the bed. Slowly, quietly, he eased his legs from under the silken sheets. It would be easier than coming across the bed. He waited. His mind was on alert. There were alarm bells ringing in his head. The assault did not come as expected. The assassin came from the opposite of the bed. He drew back his hand, ready to strike when the familiar scent stopped him. "Gillian?" he whispered.

A delicious finger drifted across his lips, followed by an engulfing kiss. His hand found its way from her head to her bare back. They rolled over and he dragged his lips down her neck to her bosom. He felt her draw a sharp breath. He leisurely worked his way back to her waiting lips. She kissed him, hungrily. Impatiently, she pushed her body against him. He could sense the yearning in her touch as she clawed at his back. They rolled, almost falling out of bed. She giggled, as they worked their way deeper into the silk sheets. Lathered in sweat, their bodies almost stuck together from the suction. He savored every delectable moment that she racked her nails gently down his chest. They rolled again, as her powerful legs drew him tightly against her. They capitalized on the direness of their situation. Overcoming any awkwardness of a first experience, there was only passion left. The hour they spent together felt like moments. Marty lay back, twitching from exhaustion. He drank in her intoxicating scent which permeated the air around them. She nestled against him, purring with contentment. For the briefest of moments, he drifted off into a delicious slumber. As he slept, she watched his chest rise and fall. Ever so gently she touched the soft curl of his hair and felt the silkiness in her hand. Marty dreamed of the soft touch of her lips to his. He was unaware of her silently slipping from their bed. Moments later, his eyes flew open only to find her gone, like a cloud in the night. He lay there, contemplating if this had been another dream. He wiped his face. As his hand rested on his stomach, he felt the moisture she'd left behind. He smiled and fell back into a contented sleep.

****

The cramped hallway was empty except for a half-starved black cat that purred, as it rubbed against her bare leg. She affectionately scratched behind its neck and felt it quiver in her hand. Naked, she padded back to her room.

****

Digger lay awake in his bed. His mind drifted to home. He missed California and his parents. Seeing Gillian and Marty together in the hallway reminded him of his mom and dad. After so many years of marriage, they were still very much in love. He was happy for Gillian and for Marty. He loved them as friends, as he did with most people. So, it pained him to consider Franz's betrayal. His world tended to be more polarized, more black and white. There were good guys and bad guys. Suddenly, the good guys weren't so good anymore and the duke didn't seem like such a bad guy. This would all be easier if he were calculating an orbital path around a halo of dark matter in the Horsehead Nebula. So much for the good old days, he thought.

Despite being so wound up, he suddenly drifted into an almost coma-like sleep. His dream carried him far away into the deepest of space. From a vantage point never experienced before, he suddenly changed his perception of what space was. It was like a vast neighborhood of celestial bodies. He whistled to a vast wormhole, which in turn wagged a long conical tail like a puppy. A massive red gas giant drank swirling red superheated gas like a cocktail. A white dwarf invited Digger over. It all seemed so civilized, so well-ordered. The physics of what he had only seen in degrees and equations now suddenly felt like a comfortable community. He slept contentedly like a child. Across the voids of space, Rachel saw his lips turn up in a smile. She smiled to herself. She knew she had made the right choice in him.

****

It was just before dawn. Rock Thrushes warbled and chattered in the early morning air. Hans placed his hand gently on Marty's shoulder. "Sir, it's time to rise."

Marty rolled over, grumbling, "Jeez Guy. Five more minutes."

"I am terribly sorry, Sir, but we are on a tight schedule this morning. The plane leaves in thirty minutes."

Marty rolled onto his back and rubbed his face with both hands, trying to clear the cobwebs. Grumbling, he said, "Thirty minutes? What's the rush? It's not like Jordan is going anywhere." He swung his legs over the side of the bed and walked naked to the bathroom. Hans tried to take no notice of him, as he walked.

Frau Schmidt quietly entered Gillian's room to find her already in the shower. In most cases, she was lucky to find her wards out of bed by noon. Hurriedly, she made the bed and laid out her young charge's outfits on the bed.

****

McPherson sipped on the strong black German coffee. He had worked steadily through the night, making all of the necessary arrangements. He assigned squads and squad leaders to the logistics of traveling to a foreign country. Advance teams had moved ahead to local coordinates. Local leaders had been bribed handsomely, or intimidated by kidnapping loved ones. Heads of state were found and instructed. More money would flow into the region in one night than they would ordinarily see in a decade. There was no pretense of discretion. There was no resistance to anything they asked.

The *Transportation Team* mobilized and deployed almost immediately. The hardened strike force team deployed like a small army to the region, fanning out like an invading army. There was no resistance and none of the usual pushback by the locals. Two sleek black Comanche Helicopters waited on the Castle's Helipad. This would be enough for the onsite team and the duke's *guests*.

The duke was already prepping his specially-trained clerics screened from thousands of religious scholars. The small group of eight was tasked with moving the Ark. No others would do. Each man was shaved and ritually cleansed in the esoteric ways of the ancients. Each of them held fiercely to their vows of chastity. None mingled with any of the duke's staff. Their existence on the grounds was barely known and their backgrounds were a complete mystery to all but the duke. All were unwaveringly loyal to the duke who saw to their every need.

The Ark was carefully packaged in a container of lead crystal. It was both beautiful and necessary to fly the Ark in an aircraft. Without proper protection, its emanations generally destroyed most aircraft communications systems within seconds.

Franz sat miserably in his room. He had no attendant. He waited for the armed guard to arrive, so he could be moved to the aircraft, or at least that's where he hoped he would end up this morning.

At precisely five-fifty AM Gillian, Marty, Digger and Franz filed down the long corridor toward the Helipad. This time, there were no attendants pampering them, only silent men in black jumpsuits keeping them in tight check all the way to the helicopters. Marty and Gillian discreetly linked their fingers, as they walked. She smiled up at him. Her face glowed in the early morning light. For what time they had left, Marty was glad it was with her. Digger seemed uncharacteristically distant. Gillian assumed it was nerves. She couldn't blame him. Franz never looked up. He resembled a five year old who had been sent to his room.

A mere fifteen minutes later, the helicopter turbines throbbed, as they lifted the group high above the castle and turned west toward Innsbruck. It was a far smoother ride than Marty's first trip, but the sudden ascent left him with the feeling that he'd left his stomach on the ground. The flight was short and uneventful as they hustled from the Comanche to a long slender tube of the custom-built EADS supersonic jet. The hardened outer layer of the aircraft was ballistic-resistant and more maneuverable than any commercial aircraft in the world. Complete with military grade phosphorus tracers to lure away heat seeking missiles and encapsulated escape pods, it was far beyond anything Gillian had ever seen.

They settled into the quiet comfortable cabin, while the duke was secured in a segregated chamber with the group of mysterious clerics. No one was allowed into the area. Marty and Gillian smiled, as Coco appeared with trays of breakfast treats and coffee. Digger stared straight ahead, without touching anything. He smiled at Coco and tenderly touched her hand. She was startled at the gesture, but said nothing and simply stared at Digger for a moment. Sadness filled his eyes. He nodded almost imperceptibly. Gillian watched as her face drained of color for an instant before returning to normal. Without speaking, she walked away trancelike. Gillian munched on a croissant and resolved that this was going to be one weird trip.

Chapter 39

He watched helplessly, as the looming black figure glided steadily toward him in the dim light. He couldn't move. He couldn't cry out. He was paralyzed, as the form moved toward him like a predator to its prey. Its ebony skull was dotted with piercing red orbs where there should be eyes. Patiently, it moved toward him. There was no need for the creature to hurry. It knew there was nothing the old man could do to stop him, nowhere he could hide. It grew, as it neared closer, becoming so large that the room could barely contain it. Its intent was clear to the old man. It would drag him to a blistering hell, where the torturers were unbiased. They hated all equally. He would live in an eternity of pain, a purgatory without judgment. It was the worst of all possible ends, one reserved strictly for faithless Holy Men.

The old man sensed the creature before he saw him. He prayed. For the first time in years, he reached out to God. His body was powerless to move, but his mind was a locomotive of thought. In that moment, he could not utter a prayer. He came to full term with his anger toward God for taking the treasure from them. In that moment of powerlessness, he only asked for forgiveness and readied himself to have the flesh ripped from his body, as the monster delivered him into Hell.

A golden warrior appeared from the shadows. Both

the old man and the demon were surprised by his appearance. He stepped between the creature and the old man. He wielded a single sword of fierce blue light. The young warrior's head was crowned with ringlets of golden hair and his breastplate glowed blue like his sword. He held the sword before him, as he stepped into the path of the demon. In the voice of a thousand lost souls, the creature howled furiously, sputtering red flames from its mouth in an effort to intimidate the young warrior. Unabated the young man stood his ground. The demon swiftly circled trying to out-flank him. As it moved, the prince parried with lightning speed. The beast bellowed again in frustration. The old man could smell the brimstone from its breath. The young warrior smiled. The creature lunged at the young man. The blade moved so swiftly that the old man could hardly see it move. It cleaved the demon in two. Black puddles formed on the earthen floor where the ground shook and opened up. The black featureless ooze melted into the chasm before them. Finally, its angry, wrathful eyes were all that remained, they followed their every move until at last even they slipped away and the earth healed itself, sealing them away.

Smiling, the man turned to him. He reached out and caressed the old man's cheek. The old man sighed in relief and touched the warmth of the warrior's hand. The young man reached out with the back of his hand and faced the old man. The old man prepared to kiss the hand in respect when he saw the rich blue of the amulet drop suspended from a chain in the knight's hand. He cupped his hand to receive it. The jewel ebbed and glowed, as it lay in the palm of his weathered hands. He felt his throat tighten with emotion, as the Sappire sang to him in a language forgotten before the birth of mankind. He looked up to thank the young prince, who was gone like a puff of smoke in the wind, leaving only the warm blue stone as evidence of his presence.

Gasping the old man sat upright in the bed. He sat for a moment, panting, his body drenched in cold sweat. His mind was still replaying the images of the dream. The face of the young man still burned in his mind. It was the most powerful prophecy of his life. All was coming full circle. The children were returning home. He swung his feet over the edge of the wooden bed and sat for a moment, steadying himself. The bed creaked, as he rose. A full moon through the hut's tiny window lit the way to the small wooden table in the center of the room.

The wooden match sputtered and hissed, as he struck it against the table's rough wood. The warm glow from the lantern allowed him enough light to see the ancient key hanging loosely around his neck. He pulled the leather cord and took the key in his weathered hands. The tumblers clicked open, as he twisted the key in the lock of an ornate wooden trunk which rested beside the table. The trunk stood in stark contrast to the room itself. The black wood was delicately carved with roses in each corner. The rose designs merged creating an oval frame in the center. Within that frame, there was an amazing carving of a vast temple surrounded in tall columns. At the entrance, a heavy arch bore a carved angel its arms outstretched. In each hand, it held an object; a skull in one hand and a dove in the other.

He pushed open the heavy lid, which groaned in

protest from not having been opened in ages. Inside, he pushed aside yellowed scrolls and looked for a small wooden box. His hands trembled, as they caressed the engravings on the lid. Tears formed in the corners of his eyes when he opened the case to the emptiness within. The tears fell to the dimples in the empty satin below, turning it darker. The children soon would be home.

Chapter 40

The gate was roped off with large signs in several languages that stated, Closed for Repairs—Authorized personnel only. The Queen Alia International Airport was usually cramped for space, so the hastily closed section slowed the traffic to a hideous crawl. Controllers scrambled to keep the airport on schedule, as connecting flights began to back up in a landing pattern. People sat on the floors and on every available surface. Children ran and played, while their parents argued with ticket agents trying to catch another available flight.

None of it seemed to matter to five-year old Songee, who played hide and seek with her new Iranian friend. She slipped past the bold red satin rope with sign in Arabic reading, Section Closed: Keep Out. Giggling, she skipped into the cavernous terminal, as she searched for the perfect hiding place.

Her father argued with the flight agent. His Arabic was laced with a thick Assamese accent taxed the agent at the ticket counter who had not left his post for ten hours. All the while, Songee laughed, skipped and ran in long lazy serpentine curves through the empty terminal. She could stay here all day. She stopped dead in her tracks, as the sudden roar of a jet engine startled her. It sounded much different from the small Air India flight she had come in on. She darted over to the window to see what it could be.

The long sleek tube stretched as far as her tiny eyes could see. The plane had barely stopped and there were already people scurrying about it—lots of people. She watched fascinated, as men secured the giant wheels. Rolling stairs were moved to various hatches which popped open, while the plane was still moving. Workers scurried about with clipboards and tools. She watched, as men in black jumpsuits bubbled out of the plane like bugs from a rotten stump. They scurried about in all directions. They looked like they were trying to find something, but she couldn't imagine what. One of the men spied her in the terminal window. She smiled brightly and waved. He scowled and spoke to his hand. She wondered if his hand would talk back. She had never played that game. She held her wrist up. "Hello hand. This is Songee. How are you?" His eyes narrowed to slits, as he looked at her. She watched, as another hatch opened. She moved away from the talking hand to see of anyone else talked to their hand. Many strange looking people walked cautiously down the second stair. This time, they were all dressed differently. All of them were very pale, like prisoners that had been locked away in a tower. A pretty lady watched everything around her. The man behind her was pretty, too. He had yellow hair. She had never seen anyone with hair like that. The next man was the strangest of all. He was larger than the others, with odd hair. It was yellow mixed with red, making it look almost orange in color. For some reason, he seemed different from the others.

They walked down the stairs and to the ground. Square black trucks waited on them. There were more men with guns and black jumpsuits standing outside the trucks. Maybe these strange people are villains that had to be guarded? They didn't look like villains should look though. They looked quite nice. She waved again. This time, the man with the odd hair looked up at her in the window. She smiled brightly and waved harder. He smiled back. His hand raised in a return wave. Songee clapped and waved again. Giggling, she ducked behind the window frame, playing hide and seek.

When she came up, he was almost in the square truck. Oh well. She turned around to find a tall severe looking man in a gray uniform behind her. He said something she did not understand and pointed toward the door. She guessed he wanted her to leave. She breathed a long sigh and climbed off the chair. She walked toward the door, looking at as much as she could take in from her limited vantage point. She darted toward the exit to find her mother waiting. Her mother's face looked drained. She scolded her, as they walked back to the terminal. "Where have you been?" Songee was not listening. She was lost in thought about the tall man with strange hair.

The roar of the Humvees echoed hollowly against the red walls of the canyon. The sandstone walls were modestly cooler than the scorching heat of the mid-day sun. The small caravan lurched to and fro, as they drove swiftly through the canyon. Only the truck carrying the Ark drove carefully to avoid jostling their precious cargo. The jeeps accelerated through the city. There were no tourists today. The Jordanian Government had declared it a Holy day of atonement. No tourists were allowed. This confused the locals who knew of no such day. The promise of monetary compensation for the declaration eased their concerns. Everyone stayed home.

The closer the group got to the mountain, the darker the skies became. By the time they had reached the bottom of the mountain, fierce lightning danced across the blackened sky. The pressure against them was immense, like the mountain was trying to repel them.

At the base of the mountain, the Litter Bearer Team assembled. They carried no weapons and they dressed in handmade robes fashioned in the same manner as the ancients. The duke left nothing to chance. With clockwork efficiency, they embarked on the steep winding path up the mountain. The group worked like a well-oiled machine. They were almost out of sight before the others were allowed to exit the jeeps.

It was a difficult trek for those not carrying anything. Marty struggled with how these men would carry the Ark. Undaunted, the team moved unfalteringly up the treacherous path. The skies swirled angrily above them. Lightning traced like a spider web above their heads. Marty had never seen such a vicious storm. The air was oppressive and thick. While it was a refreshing treat compared to the blistering heat of the desert around them, it unnerved them as they struggled to climb the narrow path. Marty wondered if they would even survive the short journey to the top. The duke followed the Ark closely. His body guards surrounded him in a ring. A bolt of lightning struck the ground next to one of the front Litter Bearers. He lost his footing and stumbled forward. The Ark began to tip forward.

One of the men quickly moved into position to steady the relic. He reached up with a gloved hand and touched the side of the Ark. His face turned ashen and his eyes bulged. His lifeless body dropped where he stood. Another man in black stepped forward and dragged the body to the side, while the team kept moving. The litter bearer steadied himself and the Ark, and continued with the team. The team silently exchanged glances, each wondering what they had gotten themselves into. The wind buffeted them, as they crested the plateau. There were tall thin eddies of dust that swirled and danced about the open stone crest. They reached a plane of flagstones the size of a football field. The Litter Bearer Team moved the Ark to a short raised slab centered in the expanse. Immediately, the plinth began to glow, energized by some hidden energy.

The duke stood to the side and donned his ceremonial garb. In the center was the Star of David. Gem stones were embedded at each point of the Star and each intersection within the Star. Marty's diamond was at the very top.

A small wooden table was placed beside the duke. On it were a series of eleven wooden containers like Marty's. Each contained a Sappir. The duke began to remove the Sappirs, placing each one in a unique setting. The small evenly spaced settings were on all four sides of the Ark. He was seemingly untouched by the energy that was flowing through it. At the last setting, he stopped. He looked toward Marty. His eyes glowed with energy. "Mr. Wood, could I have your stone, please?"

Marty suddenly felt the hard steel of gunmetal under his chin. Carefully, he eased his eyes to his side and found McPherson standing there leering at him. In a decidedly Scottish accent, he began to goad Marty, "Come on, Lad. Let's give it up. His eminence 'as waited a long time for this. No need to disappoint 'im now."

His only chance would be to throw the box over the edge. Marty looked at Gillian. She knew what he was thinking. She was staring at the gun, with tears in her eyes. She shook her head. Slowly, he removed the wooden box from his pocket. He held it away from his body, handing it to no one in particular. Before McPherson could pull the trigger, Marty slapped the gun and rolled away from the Scot. He drew back to throw the box over the cliff and stopped. His strength left him. It was all he could do to breathe. The sudden paralyzing pain in his back made him look down. McPherson's other hand firmly held the long thin dagger of his family's namesake. The blade was as deep as it would go into his side. McPherson left the blade in, as he secured the pistol in his belt and carefully removed the small wooden box from Marty's hand. When the container was firmly in his hand, he pulled the blade free. Marty crumpled to his knees and pitched sideways. A scream lay frozen in Gillian's throat. She fell to his side, desperately clutching him. It wasn't supposed to happen like this.

McPherson leered, as he leveled the gun at her. He considered the term for this in baseball. A double play is what he believed they called it. He wanted her to look up, so she could take the round between her eyes. But she wouldn't take her eyes off of Marty. It was of no consequence. It was her time. It didn't matter if she saw it coming or not. McPherson savored the moment like a rare steak. He squeezed the trigger. The report seemed loud, even amidst the crashing thunder around them.

Gillian's head snapped up at the sound of the crack. Much to the surprise of both, Franz's body fell with a thud between them. The round ripped into his back, as he dove between them. He landed hard on the stone beneath them. For a moment, Gillian watched his eyes widen, as the bullet ripped through his heart.

There was no time for an exchange between them. There was an instant of eye contact before his eyes hazed over. She watched an ever-widening arc of blood encompass him, mingling with Marty's on the flagstones. She caught the glimpse of a tiny smile on Franz's lips before he died. Perhaps it was atonement that gave him peace? They would never know.

McPherson screamed, "Idiot!"

He shook his head and adjusted his aim at Gillian. Instinctively, she began to concentrate on McPherson's energy. She would help him understand the Frenchman's last thoughts, as the gun exploded in his hand. She never got the chance. McPherson stopped. His gun hand dropped to his side, uselessly. The automatic slipped from his fingers and clattered hollowly to the stone below.

Coco swallowed the raw emotion, as she watched Franz's lifeless twitch on the warm stone floor. As she drew back the long thin steel of the blade, she called on the strength of Kuan Yu to guide her hand.

McPherson's eyes widened, as he looked down. Gillian thought he almost looked surprised at the broadening crimson oval on his chest. The merest hint of the stainless steel throwing dart protruded from the epicenter of the spot. The little Scot dropped to his knees and slumped forward onto the waiting stone below. Franz's and McPherson's bodies lay almost head-to-head.

Gillian whirled to catch a glimpse of a fleeting black form melting into the shadows of the rock formations behind them. A volley of automatic weapon rounds followed her, but to no avail. Two men in black jumpsuits darted after her, only to be stopped in their tracks by their Squad Leader, Gunter. "Stay with the duke! Don't let him out of your sight."

Like foxes watching a rabbit run into the brush, they adjusted their eyes from the disappearing form and returned their attention to the man in the ceremonial gown before them.

Coco disappeared like smoke in the wind. She had fulfilled her promise to Franz; partly from loyalty, partly from love. He had never allowed their relationship to become intimate. She thought it odd, but she respected his wishes. She had never stopped desiring him, though. He was such a sweet, strange little man. She missed him already. Quickly, she returned to the present. Black forms were all around her, silently moving toward the Ark. Skillfully, she weaved in and out of the rocks, avoiding them. They were no longer her problem.

****

Gillian's face filled him and the world began to slow down. In flashes, he saw her lying beside him, fields of orange and purple flowers; the sunrise from that morning. He couldn't speak. He couldn't move. There was a horrible buzzing in his ears. Then it began to close in. He viewed his life as a spectator from above. A single tear slipped from her cheek toward him. It seemed to float weightlessly in the air above him. The tunnel began to close in, as the darkness overwhelmed the light. It closed toward the very center of his vision, so that all that was left was a single point of light. And through that tiny pinhole of perfect light, a small hand reached out for him. He smiled, or at least he thought he smiled. He assumed it was Gillian reaching for him. The small hand took his and pulled him gently forward into the light. A beautiful sapphire blue light pushed away the darkness. The child-like hand gently pulled him forward. The dark clouds receded and he saw Rachel smiling radiantly, bathed in light. She welcomed him with a long kiss on the cheek and a hug that she reserved for family. Marty felt warm in a way he had never experienced. Digger walked up beside her. Leaning over, he hugged Marty, as well. Marty looked at them, confused, "Where am I?"

She placed a gentle hand on his cheek. "The safest place in the universe."

****

Gillian barely knew that Digger was standing over her. She looked up through the tears and could see the small smile on Digger's lips. Amidst the grief, she misunderstood the look. "Why are you smiling?" she sobbed.

"I'm not afraid now. I know what I have to do."

She gave him a confused look. "What?"

He kneeled beside her and kissed her on the forehead. "Trust me. He'll be fine."

She simply stared at him. She wondered if they had all gone mad. Gillian looked into Digger's eyes. They crackled with some distant energy. He began walking toward the duke.

Gunter snapped at Digger. "Halt!"

Digger ignored the petty little man and continued forward. Gillian tried to focus on the entire team, but there were so many of them. There was a short burst from a MAC 10. Instead of falling, Digger disappeared before their eyes. Gillian sat stunned. Her world was unraveling before her eyes.

****

One of the Black Jumpsuits approached McPherson. Never taking his eyes off of Gillian, he retrieved the box from McPherson's lifeless fingers. He backed away from her, never taking his eyes off her. Gingerly, he placed the box on the small table within reach of the duke and quickly backed away. The duke carefully inserted the last stone. It glowed brighter than the rest. But nothing further happened. Something was wrong.

It was Gunter that noticed the blue glow emanating from Gillian's bosom. "Duke!"

The duke turned to see Gunter pointing at Gillian. She seemed confused until she looked down. She saw the blue glow from her brassiere. There was no sense in hiding the stone any longer. She stood, reached inside her top and retrieved the glowing blue orb. It felt warm to the touch, but not hot. She held it out for all to see in her open palm. "You want it? Fine! Choke on it." In a final act of defiance, she turned and tossed the glowing stone toward the open face of the cliff.

The duke scowled, but otherwise seemed unruffled. He raised his open hand. With a small guttural sound from his throat, a glowing orb appeared in his palm. He pointed at the stone and gave a command. It shot toward the falling stone like a tracer round. Like a dog chasing a Frisbee, it engulfed the Sappire in mid-air and raced back. An instant later, it dropped the Sappire in the duke's waiting hand and hovered there, expectantly. She shook her head in amazement

The duke turned toward the Ark. Almost with disdain, he plucked the dull stone from the Ark and tossed it to the ground. He pointed his finger at the Ark and the gem moved into position, drawn in by an unseen force Gillian dropped her head in despair. After all they had strived to do, there was nothing left. They had lost.

The duke turned toward Gunter. "We don't need her anymore. Please make sure she does not cause any further annoyance. Gunter nodded and turned toward Gillian, leveling his MAC 10 on her.

Marty watched the scene unfold from high above. "Rachel, can you protect Gillian?"

Her laugh was like the tinkling of a chandelier. "Well, of course."

It amused her at how easy it was to trick humans. She cupped her hands around Gillian and Marty's body and blew a bubble of ethereal energy that encompassed them. Gunter watched, as Gillian and Marty disappeared before his eyes. His head turned side-to-side to see if they had moved, or the light was playing tricks on his eyes.

She looked at Marty. "Sweetie, she will need to close her eyes. When the singularity opens, there will be too much light for her. It will destroy her eyes."

Marty nodded. Somehow, he was beside Rachel now. He closed his eyes and reached out to Gillian.

The Sappirs on all four sides began to flash faster now, in sequence. The dots of light cycled faster and faster until they were no longer dots of light, but a solid ring of blue. The broadening blue circle of light surrounded the relic like a planetary ring. A deep rumbling like an earthquake could be heard from the Ark.

Gillian began to hear a tiny voice deep within her. *Gillian, there is going to be a bright light. I need for you to protect your eyes.* It drew her attention back to Marty. She didn't understand, but she hugged his prone figure and began to rock back and forth. She closed her eyes and wept. Not only had she lost Marty, she was going mad.

That's it. Hold me close.

She hugged him tighter, trying to force some of her life force into him. The odor of ozone grew thick, while the air crackled with energy. Dust and debris began to eddy and boil around the rings of blue light in mini cyclones. The turbulence flowed over her, though she were in a protective bubble. The single ring began to divide into larger spheres broadening around the Ark. The duke's men began to back away from the Ark, as the energy increased and a hum became deeper and more resonate.

The voice inside Gillian continued. *Sing with me.*

Tears flowed from her clinched eyes. Thickly, she whispered. "I can't remember any songs."

The tiny voice coached her. *Sure you do. Row, row, row your boat...*

Softly, she began to sing. She continued to rock back and forth, as she sang. The voice in her head sang with her. "Row, row, row your boat" Row, row, row your boat... It seemed to block out the rumble of the Ark. She kept her eyes squeezed shut and kept singing.

The outer ring suddenly flared sending a wave of energy at them. It gently washed over Gillian. She heard the Security Team yelp in pain. She sang louder. Rachel, Digger and Marty watched the duke through a portal of blue energy Rachel looked worried. "His pronunciation is horrible, but I think he just said that my face is a purple dung heap."

Marty looked at her surprised. "But I thought he had an ancient script?"

She smiled, drolly, "He had half the script."

They could hear a growing clatter, like a chain about to come off a sprocket. Marty looked at Rachel. "What's that noise?"

"The Sappir. They're confused."

Digger looked at her. "Because of him?"

There was concern in her eyes. "Yes. He's giving them conflicting commands. They don't understand, so they're continuing to cycle up."

Marty looked at the duke. "What does that mean?"

She looked at him grimly. "I believe you call it the Big Bang. Because he is only giving them half the information they need, they continue to harness more and more power. Eventually, they will reach critical mass. This galaxy will be no more."

"You mean he can't open the portal?"

"Only partially. If he continues, the portal will become unstable."

Digger looked concerned. "So, what do we do now?"

"I can open the portal for him, but I have no directions on where to send him."

Marty could see Digger thinking. He looked behind them. Like peering through a telescope, a map of the solar system appeared behind them. Rachel smiled at him, impressed that he had adapted so easily. His brow furrowed. He pointed toward twin suns and twelve planets. "Where is that?"

"That's your solar system."

"That can't be. They're binary suns and twelve planets."

"Because you haven't seen them before now doesn't mean that they don't exist. The second sun and those planets are in another dimensional plane. You know it as dark matter. It is the Dark Universe. It is hidden from your view by dimensional barriers."

Digger seemed excited. "Are any of those planets inhabitable?"

She nodded. "Unlike your dimension, there are three to be exact."

He pointed to a planet in a color he didn't recognize. "What about that one?"

She nodded. "Oronas. It's very similar to earth. Do you want to send him there?"

Digger nodded. "Yes."

"Very well. This is what we're going to do…"

Foot high Cherubs facing each other on the top of the Ark began to glow. Each began to pulse lit from within. The duke watched, as they began to grow. Ever so slowly, they stood in unison from their kneeling positions and turned toward a very startled duke.

The duke chanted louder. The figures continued to grow. The Sappirs chattered in an ancient, deafening language. The figures grew until they were taller than the duke. Both stepped down from the golden chest and glided to the stone below them. Both glowed so brightly that the duke could barely look at them. He fell to his knees. In a voice like thunder, the angel on the left spoke. "I am Michael. What is it that you seek?"

The duke trembled before him, without speaking. In a soft voice like that of a waterfall, the angel on the right repeated the question, "I am Gabriel. What is it that you seek?

In a tiny voice, the duke managed to eke out, "Da'ath, I seek Da'ath."

The Security team shrank away in fear. Some fell to their knees, as blood dripped from their ears. Gillian continued to sing. "Merrily, merrily, merrily…"

The duke arose. With a modicum of composure, he squared his shoulders aristocratically at the angels spoke more confidently. "I command that you to take me to Da'ath."

Gabriel thundered, "So be it."

Michael and Gabriel turned, facing each other. They drew flaming swords that formed an arch between them. This time, it was Michael who spoke. "Go forth and be recognized, Priest."

Somewhat hesitantly, the duke stepped through the arch into the abyss. A great vortex opened and began to draw everything around it in. The Security team clawed desperately at the stones beneath them, but to no avail. One at a time, each disappeared into the giant sucking void. When the last man passed through, a crack of thunder sounded, as the portal closed behind them. The Ark sat silently, smoldering under the dark skies.

Marty watched as the duke and his men tumbled past him like tumbleweeds through the wormhole and out of sight. He could swear that the duke recognized him, as he rolled by. He smiled at him. The portal closed and it was silent again. Marty looked around to find himself in the library with Digger and Rachel. He looked around, curiously. "So, now what happens?"

Rachel smiled. For the first time, he saw her as Digger did. She was radiant. "It is your choice. You may stay here, or return to your world."

"What about Gillian?"

"She is on the other side of the plane. She must stay there."

Marty nodded and smiled. "I've just found her. I'm not ready to let her go."

Her eyes glowed, as she smiled. "I thought you might feel that way."

Marty turned and instinctively started for the door. Digger didn't move. Marty stopped and looked at him, quizzically. "Are you coming?"

Digger smiled and shook his head. "I can't."

Marty looked confused. "Why?"

"Your spirit passed over without your body. She can guide you back. I passed over completely, body and soul. I cannot leave until the doorway is re-opened."

"But what do we tell your parents, your friends, your loyal following?"

He smiled. "The truth... I disappeared."

Marty looked at them. He could see an almost tangible connection between them. "Are you sure about this?"

Digger reached over and hugged Rachel at the waist. "Yeah, I'm sure."

Marty nodded. He walked back toward them and hugged them both. "I'll miss you guys."

They returned the hug. Rachel responded, "We're only a dream away."

Marty turned back to the door and walked through,

without looking back.

****

The voice inside her head had stopped singing. There was silence. She opened her eyes to see him smiling at her. As her lips touched his, she could feel the crackle of thousand tiny electrical charges passing between them. She drew back and drank in his sapphire blue eyes. As gently as she could muster, she slapped him lightly on the cheek. "Don't do that again."

He smiled. It was good to be back. They sat with his back to her, her arms holding him tight. The weathered rock beneath them was swept clean. Not so much as a single strand of cloth belonging to the duke or his men was left behind. A single beam of sunshine broke through the clouds and bathed them in a white glow. Finally, she looked at him and uttered a single word, "How?"

He smiled. "We have plenty of time to talk about that later. Let's figure out how we're going to get out of here."

It was a while before she realized Digger was gone. Marty took her hand in his. Quietly, he explained. He wrapped his arms around her, as the tears flowed down her cheek. She shook her head in disbelief. "I don't understand. Why couldn't Digger return?"

"He passed over physically when the doorway was open. He is alive and well, but he's trapped there until the portal is re-opened."

She looked at him. "Can't we open it?"

Marty shook his head. "The stones in the duke's vest were the key. The Sappirs were the lock. The duke still has the key. Besides, I think Digger knew what he was doing. He's there because he wants to be." He smiled. "Besides, we can always visit him in our dreams."

They held each other. He winced, as she squeezed his knife wound. It was good to be back.

Chapter 41

They sat quietly for the longest time. The sky above them began to clear, enough so that they could see a waning sun on the horizon. Silver-lined clouds of orange and salmon seemed to reward them for surviving. Marty could feel his strength coming back. In fact, he was beginning to feel quite normal. They both stood before the Ark. He placed his arm around her shoulder and she leaned back with her arm around his waist. In a quiet voice, he said, what they both were thinking. "Now what do we do?"

She smiled and she looked up at him. "I guess we go see if we can get a good deal on a late modelused Hummer."

He smiled. "Sure hope they left the keys in it."

Suddenly, her arm dropped. He felt her body go rigid beside him. In less than a heartbeat, she was all business. In a voice barely above a whisper, he heard her say, "We have company."

His arm dropped. He could make out nothing against the onslaught of darkness. The torch looked odd, as it appeared from behind the monolith. Perhaps it was not the torch that looked odd, but the pair accompanying the torch? Even at the sight of the wizened old man and his companion, Gillian did not relax.

"We're surrounded," she hissed beneath her breath.

Marty didn't think he would ever get used to her ability to sniff out trouble. He hoped he would have a long time to consider that about her. The old man moved slowly but steadily to their position. He seemed completely unafraid of either of them. His voice rang of purpose. In a long-forgotten language, the old man called out. They looked at each other. It didn't sound remotely like anything either one of them had ever heard. In retrospect, it was not a language that been spoken in two millennia. They were close enough that Marty could see the old man's face. His eyes were quick, intelligent and purposeful. It was evident that his mind was sharp even though his body appeared frail. The companion spoke for his master. "My Master asks if you need help."

Marty gave him a bemused smile. "I think we probably do… thanks."

Gillian's eyes narrowed. She wasn't so sure they wanted their help.

The old man spoke again. "He would like to know where the other Golden Hair Warrior has gone."

Gillian spoke to Marty, without taking her eyes off the cliffs around them. "I think he means Digger."

Marty looked at the old man. "Our friend has gone to the other side." He didn't think it would make sense.

The companion relayed this. The old man nodded in understanding, which surprised Marty. Much to the companion's surprise, the old man spoke in English for himself. "You have performed a great deed. You have saved this world from the Shadow Man. You have brought the Sacred One back to the guardians. For this, we are grateful. We will help you find your way back to your world."

Marty gestured to the Ark. "How long have you guarded the *Sacred One*?"

He smiled a toothless grin. "Solomon's ambassadors brought Her to us to protect Her from the Romans. That was over forty generations ago."

Marty asked openly, "What will happen to Her now?"

The companion spoke. "We will return Her to the sanctuary, where we will care for Her until she is called for again."

Marty found it interesting that they referred to the Ark as *Her* versus *It*. He was sure this would all make sense someday, but he was too tired to think. From the darkness, several men dressed in ceremonial frocks approached the Ark. Several more appeared with torches to surround the Ark. A fabric cover was placed over the Ark, as they readied it for movement. Marty could feel Gillian gearing up for a fight. He gently placed his hand on her forearm and said softly, "It's okay. They're taking Her home."

She looked up at him, expectantly. "You mean— She belongs here with these people?"

He nodded. "This is where she was taken from."

The Litter Bearers gently raised the Ark and began carrying it in the opposite direction from where they had come up. The old man carefully supervised the team. As they all moved forward, he would give short direct commands to them, as they walked. The Ark bearers stepped carefully, and together. The Ark barely jostled, as they moved. It was most impressive. The companion walked with Marty and Gillian. He began to tell them some of their history with the Ark. "The Shadow Man took the Sacred Vessel from us many

In the Shadow of Men

years ago. He took it by force. Many of our priests were killed trying to defend Her."

Curiously, Marty asked, "Couldn't you use the power of the Ark to defend yourselves?"

The companion shook his head. "We are the Vessel's guardians, not the Chosen Ones. We are not allowed to use it. Only the Children of Moses may use the Ark."

"Why do you call him the *Shadow Man*?"

"When he came for the Ark, he always traveled in the shadow of men. That is how we know him."

The companion continued, "Millennia ago, the Children of Moses brought us the Holy Vessel to hide until the time of turmoil had passed. When the time of turmoil has passed, they will return for it."

"Turmoil?"

"The time of turmoil…that is when the soldiers of Rome occupied the great temple of Solomon."

Marty felt a little confused. "I thought Solomon's Temple was a myth?"

The companion laughed. "A myth? Oh, no. I can assure you that it is quite real. The Hebrews worship on the Sabbath there. Our tribe chose to live here at God's Mountain and worship. We are the Edomites."

Marty changed the subject. "Your English is remarkable. Where did you learn to speak it?"

"The strange little man who traveled among you taught us before the Shadow Man arrived. He told us many amazing tales about the outside world. It has been many years since we have seen him. We are sad that he is gone."

"Which strange little man?"

"He called himself *Franz*."

Gillian bristled slightly when she realized that they were talking about Franz. Marty placed a hand on her arm. She breathed deeply to relax.

Marty asked the companion, "Did you show Franz the Ark?"

The companion looked down, but said nothing. Marty suddenly understood how the duke knew where to find the Ark. He did not press the companion further.

The small group continued to walk for a while. Wide trails dwindled to narrow paths. Other trails crisscrossed over them. The barren terrain all looked the same.

Within minutes in the smothering darkness, neither Marty nor Gillian could distinguish where they were. Every so often they would pass the yawning mouth of a cave in the hillside. After a while, they all looked pretty much the same.

After ten minutes of walking with the aid of a meager glow of torchlight through ravines and short sandy tunnels, Marty was beginning to feel uneasy. There was no possible way for them to find their way out of the place without guidance. If this was a trap, they had no hope of escaping.

At last, they stood before a roughly hewn maw in the side of the mountain. It was like many of the rest, with the exception of an amber glow from torchlight inside. The brawny litter bearers ducked down to ensure that they did not strike the top of the Ark on the low entrance, while they barely squeezed into the opening on either side without scraping their arms.

While the opening was narrow, the interior was quite a different story. Inside, the amber glow came from a ring of one hundred torches spaced out on the walls, forming a large open oval with a pedestal in the center.

As they entered, hundreds of men, women and children silently bowed in revered silence. A weathered old stone pedestal waited patiently for them in the center. Each leg was intricately carved. The four columns with roses rode each column, forming a bed of leaves at the top. The Litter Bearer team carefully set the Ark in place. Marty watched in amazement as the cover was removed and the room transformed before him. The torchlight glittered against the gold of the Ark, reflecting off of the torchlight and leaving the room basking in a golden light. Painted figures on the wall aligned with the amber glow of the Ark. He nodded, realizing that this chamber had been designed for the Ark.

Not a single whisper was uttered. They silently filed out, each leaving a single flower at the pedestal. In a while, they were alone in the cavern with the companion and the old man. The fragrance of fresh flowers wafted from the mound of flowers, making Marty ponder which was more amazing; the utter reverence on the moment, or how so many flowers were gathered in the middle of the desert. Marty looked at the old man and asked, "Aren't you afraid that someone will find it here?"

The old man winked at him. He chuckled, as he responded, "You are connected to the Ark like few others. Could you find this place in broad daylight?"

Marty smiled, shaking his head. "I see your point."

He patted Marty on the hand, "Come with us. You can rest in our village and we will take you to your vehicles in the morning."

Marty put his arm over Gillian's shoulder. She smiled at him with dark, warm eyes. "Sounds like a plan."

Chapter 42

The brilliance of the bluish white light had blinded him. He stood still, feeling the breeze across his cheek and enjoyed the spicy sweetness of a nearby bloom. It was a few moments before he began to blink and make out images around him. He looked around the peaceful blue grass of the alien landscape. He couldn't help but smile. He had been right, all along. He looked up into the twilight and watched as clouds moved past quickly, high above his head. Yet, the hint of a breeze on the ground was light and pleasant. The big chunky clouds looked like every other cloud he had ever seen, with the exception of color. He couldn't put a finger on it. He didn't recognize the color at all. The ground was thick with swirling gray fog which eddied and rolled like the surf.

In the distance, he could make out the tall round spires of a city. Long, thin bases, with bulbous tops reminded him of the Space Needle. He carefully maneuvered through the layer of mist to a small hill that gave him a vantage point to survey his surroundings. At the top of the hill, he stood under a fragrant tree with dark blue bark, bearing a fruit that looked like a white plum. Frederick thought better of trying it. He had no intentions of being poisoned so early in the game. He stood under the tree, breathing in the alien air which was cleaner than the Alpine forest air he was used to.

He pondered on how he would approach the leaders of the city, all-the-while relishing the first experience of an alien world.

As light as a feather on the wind, a tiny blood red scorpion dropped to his shoulder. The duke stood lost in thought. The scorpion crisscrossed closer to his neck, its tiny eyes assessing where to strike. The tiny creature maneuvered toward the hair line at the base of his skull. The duke crossed his arms and mused about how long it would take to learn the alien's language—or if they even used language. The small creature balanced itself precariously on his collar at the closest vertebral notch. He considered the strategy—convince them he was here to warn them of an impending attack by foreign aggressors and offer himself selflessly as an ambassador of peace…

Like a bee sting, the duke slapped his neck too late. The tiny body was gone, swimming in his spinal fluid up toward his brain. The sudden ringing in his ears followed by numbness in half his body signaled the beginning of the living nightmare. He stood, wondering why he had a sudden feeling of dread. The spasm that coursed through his body threw him to his knees. His entire body writhed against the unseen invader, as he frothed at the mouth like a rabid dog. The fit passed. He rolled over on his back in the dewy grass and gasped for breath. A passing wave of nausea washed over him and was gone. His eyes were wide as he sat up, involuntarily, unclear as to why he had. He convulsed involuntarily. As he sat gulping in fresh air, his body stood somewhat awkwardly and began to lurch forth. A constant pain in the back of his skull made him feel weak and disoriented. Still, he continued to lurch and sway like a drunk.

A new sensation gripped him. He whirled around, expecting to find someone behind him. He was alone on the knoll. Paranoia gripped him. He scanned the tree line around him. He sensed someone or something was watching him. He could feel it intensely. From out of the blackness of his own mind, he heard the voice. It spoke without pretense or subtlety, "Greetings, Duke. We have been expecting you."

****

Rachel held out her hand and took his in hers. They kissed for what seemed like an eternity. She kissed his earlobe, as she whispered, "Hello, David. You're finally home."

His arm around her waist felt like it belonged there. He pulled back slightly to drink in her eyes. The deep blue crystals which danced in the light around them almost rendered him to tears. "You know my real name. Only my mother calls me David."

She smiled and her eyes shown brighter. "Of course, I know your name. I know more about you than any other creature on earth. I have watched you through many lives through the eons. Yours is a very old soul, indeed."

He blinked. He didn't really understand what she meant. She kissed him gently on the lips. "It's all right, my love. We have ages to understand this."

They walked slowly, hand-in-hand. The library lifted in a million pieces, leaving them in the salty tang of warm sea air. Digger lifted his face to the wind like a dog in a car window. He soaked in the moment, as the beach formed around them. Echoes of crashing waves filled his ears, as a light breeze ruffled his hair.

Giggling, squirmy children surrounded them with their small nut brown bodies. Sandcastles emerged in the light of a sparkling sun. A small boy rushed up to Digger and hugged his leg. His blonde curls shimmered in the sun. "Come play with us, Uncle Digger. Pleeease…"

Digger looked expectantly at Rachel. She smiled and kissed him gently on the lips. "Go ahead. Go play."

The tot scampered off, with Digger not far behind. Rachel looked to find Peter standing beside her. His white beard and hair was now neatly trimmed against a backdrop of a Hawaiian shirt of surfboards and orange flowers.

"Better?" she asked.

"Much. Thanks. That whole Peter thing was beginning to wear a little thin."

"And how is our guest on Oronas?"

"Adjusting. I don't think it was what he had planned on. I guess it's always a little easier to be born into aristocracy than forging it on your own."

She smiled. "I suppose. Our King was a shepard, as I recall."

"We each have our paths, Gatekeeper."

The surf licked at their heels, as they stood quietly for a moment. They watched, as Digger laughed and dug in the sand with an enclave of laughing, wiggling little bodies. Some were light, some were dark, but all relished the warm sand and cool ocean. Peter smiled, as he watched. "He really is the one, isn't he?"

"Yes, he is. Through it all, he never lost his innocence. He is quite remarkable, as mortals go."

Peter sighed deeply. "I've got to go. If I don't get back soon, they'll think the world is ending or some such nonsense."

She reached over and gave him a kiss on the cheek. "My best to the family."

"Always." He smiled and dissolved until there was nothing left but his smile, and then it was gone.

Chapter 43

Marty flipped through a pre-release copy of the Washingtonian. He stopped when he came to an article on the US Mint and the history of the pyramid on the One Dollar bill. He stared at the inscription beneath it: Novus Ordo Seclorum. It was the same inscription from the duke's crest. He was almost irritated when the secretary spoke to him. "Mr. Wood, the President will see you now."

He sighed and put the magazine down. She used a practiced mask of a smile that had been worn for heads of state and diplomats. Marty returned the smile with one of his own, one far more genuine. "Thank you."

His disarmed her, as did almost everything about the young man. The door opened to the Oval Office and a muscular man met Marty at eye level. The young Secret Service Agent checked him with a metal detector before patting him down. It was Marty's fourth such screening and he was getting used to them. The room was empty, except for another statue-like agent standing in the corner. The agent spoke. "Feel free to sit anywhere you would like, except behind the desk. The President will be out shortly."

"Thanks."

He nodded ever so slightly, never taking his eyes off him. Marty walked past him and settled onto a small comfortable settee facing the agent. He took in the series of photographs on the wall across from him. He was too far away to see much detail, other than there seemed to be a lot of pictures of handshaking. *Typical of a politician's office*, he supposed. Benedict Fawkes emerged from a hidden doorway. He moved as gracefully as a cat from across the room toward Marty. He smiled like an old friend at the sight of him. Without hesitation, he extended his hand, smiling. "Benedict Fawkes. Thanks for agreeing to meet with me, Mr. Wood."

Marty rose to greet him all-the-while thinking *Well you are the President*. Instead, he smiled warmly. "Thank you Mr. President. It's an honor to meet you, I assure you."

"You can lose the *Mr. President* if you like. Ben is fine, if you're okay with it."

He continued to smile. "Thank you, Sir. Please call me Marty, if you would."

"Swell, Marty, just swell." His capped teeth and tan made him look like an actor.

The young Secret Service Agent never smiled. He watched the two from a distance, never missing a single movement of Marty's hands.

"Marty, have you ever heard of our Rose Garden?"

"Well yes, Sir. I have."

"It's such a nice day. Let's walk in the Garden, if you don't mind."

"That would be very nice, Sir."

President Fawkes eased toward the door, putting his arm on Marty's shoulder. Marty could see why this guy won by a landslide during the last election. He'd never met a stranger. The President spoke to the Secret Service Agent, as they moved forward. "Bob, give us a little room, please?"

"Yes, Sir." His voice was tight. He didn't like stepping away from the President at all, especially with a stranger. But, he would do what he was told—to a point.

Marty and the President followed the paths through alternating beds of hyacinths and tulips. Just out of range of the clatter of sprinklers, they chatted like two old chums. It was an unusually warm morning for April in Washington, so they enjoyed the mixture of warm sun mixed with an occasional cool breeze from the north. It was quite exhilarating. Bob reluctantly lingered thirty feet or so behind them, careful to keep his distance, but not too far out of range of his charge.

The President wasted no time getting to the point once out of ear shot. "Marty, we understand that you may know something about the whereabouts of Duke Fredrick Lindenspear?"

Marty assumed the conversation would eventually steer in that direction. He had rehearsed the response in his mind a hundred times. Sometimes, it almost seemed like the truth. He measured his words, carefully. He looked at the president, earnestly. "Thank you, Ben. My friends and I had a terrible experience and we haven't really known what to do about it. You're the first person to provide us with a way to talk about the situation."

The President eyed him, curiously.

"We were invited to Syria on an expedition when things went horribly awry."

The President prodded, gently. "Go on…"

"We thought that we had found the resting place of a lost religious relic when there was a terrible explosion."

The President's eyes narrowed, slightly. "What kind of explosion was it? Were you attacked?"

"I can't really say. It seemed like it was more of some freak atmospheric disturbance."

The President knew there was more to this than the weather. He gave Marty a dazzling smile that was usually reserved for a Senate Sub-committee when they were asking a lot of pushy questions. He lied, skillfully. "Let me confide in you. Our intelligence in the area had detected a cell of political insurgents that were planning a coup of the Syrian government. Naturally, we were concerned since there has been such a history of political instability in the region. We were able to track their stronghold to a location close to where you were." Without a shred of dignity, he continued with the compelling lie. "The duke graciously agreed to step in as a liaison to negotiate a diplomatic solution to the issue that we could stabilize the situation. My resources in Langley were able to develop a profile of the extremists that attacked your group. We believe that it was an effort to sabotage the diplomatic process."

Marty could smell the manure that was being used to fertilize the hyacinths. His face filled with concern. "Well, I knew we had heavy security, but I didn't know what happened. Thank you, Sir. That certainly clears things up for me."

The President looked confused for a moment before returning to the pitch. "I'm sure you can appreciate how complicated matters of foreign affairs are. What we were really hoping was that you could provide us with information on the expedition that would help us find the duke."

Marty recognized the sacrificial pawn and moved around it. "I would really love to help you, but as you may be aware, we also lost a friend on that expedition. Whatever happened to the duke and his men also caused our friend to disappear."

"Oh, yes, that's right. It was a Mr. David Delgado, I believe?"

"Yes. We call him Digger."

"We are always gravely concerned about the welfare of our own citizens, first and foremost."

"Thank you, Ben. So, is there a plan to rescue them? That is what you're saying, right? That our colleagues were kidnapped?"

Fawkes stared at him for a moment. He had to hand it to kid. He was as slick as a District Rep hiding a pork barrel in a Bill for widows and orphans. They would have to watch him for a while and see where it led. "I would love to be able to confide about our actions, but unfortunately, in the interest of National Security, there are limits on what I can say. I'm sure you understand."

Marty smiled at the President. "I believe we're on the same page, Sir. I will be sure to let you know if I learn of any information that will be helpful."

Marty could see it in the eyes. Fawkes smile was more polite than genuine this time. "Thank you, Marty. We'll be in touch. Feel free to wait here. Someone will see you out." He motioned to a small comfortable-looking bench under a cherry tree.

Marty assumed it wouldn't be a long wait. With a quick handshake, he was gone. Bob happily began to converse with his wrist and fell in tow with the president back into the building. It was less than a minute before another man in a black suit instructed

Marty tersely, "This way, sir."

Marty found himself on a sidewalk from a side gate, without as much as a good day. He guessed that the President was disappointed with the fishing today.

Two meetings later Benjamin Fawkes sat in a squeaky wooden office chair dating—from the Eisenhower era—in a room free of electronic monitoring equipment. He loaded a data stick into his laptop and waited, as the file loaded. With no particular introduction, a crystal clear digital recording began with an occasional glitch from unseen electronic interference at the time of the recording. It was the only shred of evidence left from a lonely mountain top in Syria.

It was the fourth time the President had watched the recording, hoping for some insight on what had happened. He watched as McPherson mortally stabbed Wood. The camera's focus stayed on the group. He watched as McPherson shot the portly little Israeli, only to catch a throwing knife with his chest from somewhere outside of camera range. He watched the duke launch an orb of energy across the sky and loop back to him. Moments later, the Ark began to pulse and glow. In a sudden pulse of blue energy, the camera went static. Wood knew more than he was telling. He would assign a team to watch him—just in case there was a rendezvous with Delgado.

Chapter 44

Marty strode briskly, as he moved away from the White House. He found his way to a quiet bench in Potomac Park and plopped down. He stared out absently over the millions of cherry blossoms before him. The wind whispered his name. He closed his eyes and quietly drifted away. He opened his eyes in Bess's kitchen. Her portly form was swaying over a bubbling pot on the stove. She turned to face him smiling. "Rachel?"

A rather portly version of Rachel responded. "Yes, Dear?"

"For future reference, I never actually saw Bess cook. Irene did all that."

She sat down. "You know you're awfully picky, don't you?"

He grinned. "Sorry. How's Digger by the way?"

He swaggered into the room. His waistline was four times wider and he sported a pair of red suspenders. His straight brown hair had a pronounced widow's peak. "Hey, Guy, how's our girl?"

"A bit cranky right now. The baby's due in a month." He changed the subject, jabbing his finger at Digger's rotund midsection. "Dude, you might want to pace yourself on the paste. It's only been eight months. You're starting to look a lot like Gillian."

He chuckled. "Why? No need to worry about

cholesterol here." He snapped his red suspenders. "You like 'em?"

"Oh, sure. They look good on you."

They both laughed.

Marty watched, as Rachel stirred a cup of hot tea. He looked at her, seriously. "Did I fail in what I was supposed to do?"

She smiled and shook her head. "Sweetie, you're thinking in terms of absolutes. This is over for now."

"But the duke is still alive, isn't he?"

"Yes, but that is not our problem. He cannot return until he finds Jezz's reliquary on Oronas and all the jewels to activate the portal."

He blinked. "Who's Jezz?"

She sipped her tea. "She's my sister."

"You have a sister?"

She smiled. "Six to be exact, all on different planets. Gabriel, as it turns out, was quite the busy beaver in those days."

"So, will the duke try to control her next? What do we need to do?"

She stirred the cream in her tea with a crystal spoon. "There is nothing to do. This is out of our hands. He is trapped there, indefinitely."

Marty opened his hands wide. "Why did you let him live? You know how dangerous he is."

She removed the spoon and placed it in a saucer beside the cup. It made a musical chime, as it touched the saucer. She sat back and sighed deeply. It was like she was trying to explain to a child why they couldn't have dessert before dinner. "I am not the Judge here. I am governed by rules just like you. It is not my place to make those kinds of decisions. That is up to Him. I did what was called for within my power. He asked to be taken from this world to another, so I did. Ultimately, I didn't inform him of the consequences and, thereby, was able to separate him from his position of power."

"So, you sent him away."

"Technically, I did what he asked me to do. The caveat was that for every positive there must be a negative, which is why I had to keep Digger here. That is how I maintained the balance of the system."

"What about the duke's men? Where did they go?"

"That was tricky. They were all linked to him. I was able to separate them, so they didn't arrive together. It will take them time to regroup, if at all."

"So, we wait."

"Of course. That is the nature of things. We all wait. Sometimes, we wait for others. Sometimes, others wait for us. Existence means waiting for something. The key is what you do while you wait. So, go live your life. If something happens, deal with it then. Don't waste your time living for the happenstance of a maybe." She smiled, as she reached across the table and placed a hand on his cheek. "Bess and Barb wanted me to let you know that they are very proud of you. You did the right thing."

He felt a lump in his throat rise before returning her radiant smile. "I can live with that. Speaking of waiting, I have a farm and a wife waiting for me. It's time I got back to them."

Digger reached out and squeezed his shoulder. "It's good seeing you, Guy."

Rachel began to glow. "Dear child, we will always be here when you need us. Go in peace."

The light filled him. He opened his eyes just in

time to see a storm of cherry blooms fluttering in the breeze. He felt his cheek. It was still warm from her touch. It was time to go home to his wife. He missed her, desperately.

****

As always, Rachel was right. As he rose from the bench, someone was waiting on him. A lone dark figure watched him dispassionately from a distance. And he was waiting, as well. He would wait for as long as it took.

A word about the author…

As a career professional spanning the disciplines of corporate security, safety, and environmental management, Darren has spent 30 years in technical fields. Born and raised in North Carolina, he has experienced a diverse background as supervisor, police officer, husband, and father.

As an international traveler and marathon runner, he has experienced physical and mental challenges. His lifetime of experiences have seasoned his view of the world and provide a unique blend of cultural perspective with a thirst for understanding the human condition.

Thank you for purchasing
this publication of The Wild Rose Press, Inc.

If you enjoyed the story, we would appreciate your
letting others know by leaving a review.

For other wonderful stories,
please visit our on-line bookstore at
www.thewildrosepress.com.

For questions or more information
contact us at
info@thewildrosepress.com.

The Wild Rose Press, Inc.
www.thewildrosepress.com

Stay current with The Wild Rose Press, Inc.

Like us on Facebook

https://www.facebook.com/TheWildRosePress

And Follow us on Twitter
https://twitter.com/WildRosePress